The Undiscovered Island

DARRELL KASTIN

The Undiscovered Island

University of Massachusetts Dartmouth
Center for Portuguese Studies and Culture
North Dartmouth, Massachusetts
2009

PORTUGUESE IN THE AMERICAS SERIES 12

General Editor: Frank F. Sousa
Editorial Manager: Gina M. Reis
Manuscript Editor: Richard Larschan
Copyeditor: Christopher Larkosh
Graphic Designer: Spencer Ladd
Typesetter: Inês Sena

The Undiscovered Island / by Darrell Kastin

This publication was made possible in part by a grant from the Government of the Autonomous Region of the Azores.

For inquiries regarding the Series, please contact:
University of Massachusetts Dartmouth
Center for Portuguese Studies and Culture
285 Old Westport Road
North Dartmouth, MA 02747
Tel. 508-999-8255
Fax: 508-999-9272
Email: greis@umassd.edu
www.portstudies.umassd.edu (publications)

Printed by Signature Printing, East Providence, RI

Library of Congress Cataloging-in-Publication Data

Kastin, Darrell.
The undiscovered island / by Darrell Kastin.
    p. cm. -- (Portuguese in the Americas series ; 12)
ISBN 1-933227-23-0 (alk. paper)
1. Missing persons--Fiction. 2. Azores--Fiction. I. Title.
PS3611.A787U53 2008
813'.6--dc22
                                              2008004131

Dedicated to the memory of
Josefina Amarante Freitas do Canto e Castro
& Francisco do Canto e Castro

Acknowledgements

First and foremost, I would like to express my gratitude to Professor Frank Sousa, Professor Richard Larschan, Gina Reis and Judite Fernandes of the Center for Portuguese Studies & Culture at the University of Massachusetts Dartmouth, for all their devoted editorial and production work on the novel.

Many thanks also to the Casa da Saudade Library in New Bedford, MA, not only for access to reference materials but for the friends I made—Maria José Carvalho & family, Dineia Amaral Sylvia & family, and Anna Monteiro, who enriched my life more than they could ever realize. My thanks likewise to J. A. Freitas Library in San Leandro, CA.

To friends and family members who read the novel or parts of it along the way, thank you so much—particularly Sarah L. Wood and Jonah Bornstein. But special thanks to my wife, Elisabeth, for reading the manuscript more times than anyone can possibly imagine, as well as for her advice and help with background material. My daughter, Shawna, and Bernard Kastin also provided continual support and encouragement.

And finally, to Luís Vaz de Camões, Fernando Pessoa, Antero de Quental and Pedro Barroso for the inspiration—*obrigado!*

The University of Massachusetts Dartmouth gratefully acknowledges the following for permission to use previously published material:

A.M. Heath & Company, Ltd., for Ernle Dusgate Selby Bradford's *Ulysses Found,* 1964; Chambers Harrap Publishers, Ltd., for Claude Dervann's *The Azores,* 1956; Ecco/Harper Collins Publishers, for Edwin Honig and Susan Brown's *Poems of Fernando Pessoa,* 1986; The Hispanic Society of America, for Leonard Bacon's translation of *Os Lusíadas* by Luís de Camões, 1950; Oxford University Press, for Landeg White's translation of *Os Lusíadas* by Luís de Camões, 1997; Random House, Inc., for Charles Berlitz's *Mysteries of Forgotten Worlds,* 1972; Souvenir Press, Ltd., for Kenneth McIntrye's *The Secret Discovery of Australia,* 1977; University of Oklahoma Press, for Henry H. Hart's *Luís de Camoens and the Epic of* The Lusiads, 1962.

It was a time the people of the island would refer to as "the Year of Miracles," due to the number of extraordinary events that occurred: fish rained down on several villages; a drowned man's body was discovered halfway up the steep slopes of Pico; a ghost ship drifted in the waters off the isles; men who could always be found in the bars or working their fields disappeared without a trace; a mysterious, luminescent woman was said to wander the shores at night, or swim out beyond the waves, singing in a voice that would deprive a man of his senses. Some claimed the luminescent woman appeared only to certain individuals on whom she bestowed great powers, granting their every wish, every desire. Others, however, were just as convinced that it was only an early grave that she provided her hapless, unwitting followers.

In the Taberna Mendes, as in numerous other cafés and bars, men, young and old, gathered to drink and discuss these latest events.

"I was on my rounds just before dawn," Carlos Neves told his companions, "when I saw a glow moving on the water." Carlos, a refuse collector, had driven his truck up the hill towards the old cemetery, when he turned to see the trail of light upon the water. "It could only have been this siren, perhaps Venus herself, leaving a stream of fire in her wake."

"You were drunk again, eh Carlos," Manuel Mendonça said. "You're always imagining things. Like the time you told everyone you had made love to Maria Soares de Almeida and Luís threatened to gut you like a fish, until you admitted you had simply drunk too much and let your tongue run away."

"I remember, too," said Raimundo Pinto. "Luís said he would come for you if you so much as thought or dreamt of his wife again."

Carlos cringed and paled at the unpleasant memory. Luís was not a man who made idle threats. "I tell you I was sober," Carlos said. "I didn't drink anything the whole night."

"Well, that would be a first," Raimundo said, with a snort.

Carlos was always eager to share in the latest rumor, which led him to accept everything as fact, and to add his own touches to every story. Today or tomorrow or the following day, he was convinced, a miracle would greet him during his early morning refuse runs. For no one could say with any certainty that one day a man might not turn a corner and come face-to-face with a treasure, or a pretty woman waiting with open arms, or a sight that no one else had ever seen. Manuel, on the other hand, expected and found only the worst in everything and everyone.

The dingy, closed, smoke-filled atmosphere of the tavern mirrored Manuel's mood.

"They say she is the most beautiful of women," Carlos continued, inspired not merely by the first flush of intoxication, but also the melancholy of regret and longing. He hadn't actually seen the luminescent woman with his own eyes, only an eerie sheen that shimmered across a stretch of the otherwise dark water. But this was enough to waken his desire. "A goddess who could lure even the most happy and contented of men if he gazed at her beauty even for a moment."

"Anyone as beautiful as that is bound to be the source of endless sorrows," Manuel said. "You should count your lucky stars, Carlos, that you were spared the unhappiness that would have dogged your heels the rest of your life, if you had actually seen this beauty."

Raimundo and Carlos exchanged looks. "Manuel," Raimundo said. "If Our Lady Herself came down to bless you, you would be sure to find fault in it."

Manuel grunted. "That's because I know that what God gives with one hand He takes away with the other, and while blessings come one at a time—when they come at all—they are usually followed by misfortunes which always bring company."

Later that night an anguished voice was heard bellowing in the early morning hours: "Who is this woman who comes in the night, singing songs of the sea? Your sorrowful voice kills me . . . but I die happy . . ." The singing was accompanied by a cacophony of dogs, roosters, cows, sheep, and goats all squawking, barking, baying and bleating in discordant response. Villagers stirred in their sleep, roused by the plaintive cries; others, if awake, shook their heads, and proclaimed, "Ai, there goes another poor fool to his doom."

There were also earthquakes day and night, the terrifying sound of stone grinding against stone, of basalt slowly being worn to dust, a groaning and rumbling heard from deep beneath the ground—the world straining at its seams.

"Any moment," the islanders murmured anxiously, "the seas will boil, fire will fall from the heavens and the island will sink below the ocean." Some left their homes to spend days, even weeks, in the small sheds in the fields where their cows grazed, further up the mountain, believing the higher elevation might protect them from disaster, or at least delay the inevitable. Others gathered on the shore determined that if their time to die had come then resistance was futile. People searched the skies for a sign of Christ's impending return, apprehensive of any sudden movement or unexpected sound: the flight of a bird nearby, the honk of a horn, a baby crying.

The slightest tremors sent people scurrying in every direction, filling the air with the screams and cries of those who didn't know where to go, which way to turn. Nothing was secure, no place was safe. Although the threat from crumbling buildings was the more immediate danger, there was also the terrifying possibility of being burned alive by lava, smothered by ash, swallowed by gaping rifts in the earth, or drowned by tidal waves. Nothing but an inscrutable God prevented a complete catastrophe, such as the entire island sinking back beneath the sea. And if there was one thing the people of the islands had learned over the centuries, it was that if God was somewhat sparing in the production of bona fide miracles—the parting of the seas, or raising of the dead—He was generous, perhaps to a fault, when it came to displays of natural disasters.

Word spread quickly that a new island was rising from the depths of the ocean, igniting disputes as to whether this was an ordinary volcano, as people generally believed, or the Enchanted Island, as a number of devotees claimed. They whispered the old prophecy of a missing king who would return, while others spoke of a Messiah and the end of days. Some awaited the outcome with hope and expectation, while those who had the means abandoned their homes and fled the islands with their families, fearing utter devastation. Reports spread of entire villages swallowed by the gaping earth, the sea churning and boiling, set afire by bursts of lava and explosions. And when an impenetrable blanket of smoke and ash turned the daylight into night for three days, people naturally assumed the worst.

"The sun has been extinguished," they cried. *"O fim do mundo*—The end of the world!"

The passengers emerged from the twin-engine airplane on the tiny airstrip at Castelo Branco, on the island of Faial. Among them, travel-weary, yet anxious and expectant, Julia Castro paused before disembarking. She swept several strands of loose hair behind her ears—hair blacker than the cooled plumes of lava that marked the shore—then slowly stepped down the ramp, as if the presence of solid land might be conditional, and revoked at any moment.

A magical place, she had believed as a young girl, and was ready to reaffirm now. Touching the tarmac with a tentative step, she wondered if her foot would sink through the island and shatter the illusion. But it held firm.

She sampled the warm air, breathed in the scent of the sea and the rich, volcanic soil that she not only recognized at once, but which instantly transported her back thirteen years to her last visit. How the sunlight from the same sun that shone back home could be so different here, Julia didn't know. But it was, as was the smell and taste of the air. The light cut through the atmosphere in a unique slant, with a quality all its own, as if the sea had invisibly risen to the sky; a mysterious blend of light, air, and sea—like sea-shine.

Thirteen years. Too long, she thought, scanning the bright green hills that climbed toward the large crater at the center of the island. The island was so fertile, so lush. She had forgotten, and yet hadn't. It was just more vivid, more startling seeing it here and now, as opposed to what she remembered, or had seen in books or photographs. To the south the sea sparkled, undulating without interruption clear to the horizon. Pico was visible to the east, although amassing clouds appeared intent on concealing its beauty. The mountain was just as she remembered: perfectly formed, mythical, reaching nearly eight thousand feet above sea level, how one would imagine Mount Olympus.

She pictured the gods huddled together above Pico's crater observing the goings-on of the mortals down below, and devising all manner of trouble for their own amusement.

Julia entered the airport terminal, squeezing her way through haphazard groupings of passengers and crowds of family members and friends who greeted them with hugs, kisses, laughter and tears, none of whom were in any hurry to disperse.

The women who noticed her split into two camps: some looked at her with feelings of tenderness and maternal protectiveness. *"Ah, coitadinha,"* they mumbled to themselves. "Look at the poor thing! So thin." A few, however, eyed her up and down, appraising her in an instant, before turning away, grumbling about girls who made themselves up to look like Jezebels, although Julia wore no make-up and was dressed simply in black slacks, a red scoop neck top, and a gray sweater. Her appearance was deceptive, for her eyes were dark, not like obsidian or pools of ink, but like the deepest sea; those who looked too long into them felt a sudden loss of balance. Her lashes were long, and her eyebrows curved alluringly—all of which suggested that she had made herself up to enhance her looks, though these were all gifts she was born with; men gazed at her, as well, but were easily more forgiving of her looks.

"Excuse me," Julia said repeatedly, as she made her way through the crowds, *"Com licença."* People shouted and waved to one another, some crowded and pushed, while she searched for any sign of her father, Sebastião. Maria Josefa, who with her husband, João, owned the *residencial* where Julia's father had lived for the past several years, expected her. Julia knew that if Sebastião had suddenly shown up, Maria Josefa would have told him, and he certainly would have come to welcome her. But there was no sign of her father. With a sharp twinge of disappointment, Julia retrieved her bags and quickly stepped outside to find a taxi. Finding Sebastião might not be as easy as she'd hoped.

She approached a queue of green-and-black cabs, where a group of drivers was huddled, smoking and chatting. Before Julia reached the first taxi a short, stocky man with extremely dark features intercepted her. Grinning at her with a mouth full of large, white teeth he took her bags, while his companions eyed Julia with a combination of begruding appreciation and brooding wariness, as if a lone woman represented a provocation. She turned away shaking her head.

Things have changed. It wasn't quite the reception she had imagined, remembering the way people had fawned over her, Senhor Canto e Castro's little girl.

"Good afternoon," the driver said in English. His skin looked charred by long exposure to the sun. He wore a cap on his head, which he tipped in greeting, then opened the trunk and carefully placed Julia's luggage inside.

"Bom dia." Julia returned the greeting using the Portuguese she'd been taught as a child.

"Watch out for cab drivers," her Aunt Maria had warned before Julia left California. "They'll be all over you, telling you sad tales about loveless marriages, how their wives neglect them, dropping not so subtle hints that you might want to get together some evening, as if every foreign woman on her own is ripe for a fling."

Julia sat in the back seat, hoping she could avoid having to deal with amorous taxi drivers. "Horta, please. Residencial Neptuno," she said.

It was fitting that Sebastião would stay in a place with such a name. No Hotel Silva or Residencial Lopes, not for Sebastião, who had a fondness for the aptly named. "When on the islands," he would say, "it should be something out of the glorious past, Vasco da Gama or Infante Dom Henrique," (her father would never let Julia or her brother Antonio get away with referring to Dom Henrique as Prince Henry the Navigator) "or mythology. If not Atlantis or Venus and the Island of Lovers, then Neptune, the god of the sea."

The man nodded and slumped into the driver's seat. *"Sim,* senhora." He paused ever so slightly before saying, senhora, as if trying to decide between *menina,* which meant young lady, or opting for the safer, more respectful form of address. Although Julia was in her late twenties, she looked younger. Her skin was pale and smooth like her mother's Northern European ancestors, which contrasted sharply with the dark hair and eyes she had inherited from her father's more Mediterranean features, which again gave her a youthful appearance.

A moment later they sped down the narrow road toward the capital.

"You are a tourist?" the driver said, sounding hopeful.

"No, I've come to see my father. He lives here in Horta."

"Ah," the driver said. "You are from America, no?"

"Yes." Julia weighed her responses, not wishing to be too friendly, but at the same time not wanting to appear too reticent either. If Sebastião were here it wouldn't have been a problem. Her father could out-talk anyone, or end a conversation with one decisive word.

He grinned, evidently pleased with himself. "I have a brother in Massachusetts," he said, cheerfully, "and cousins in California. They have a dairy farm, in Turlock. Gil and Maria Furtado?"

Julia smiled, wondering if he thought she might know them. "There are a lot of Portuguese in California," she said.

"Yes, of course." The driver repeatedly turned to Julia when he spoke, which made her more than a little nervous since the road was narrow and people tended to drive fast on the islands. She opened her window and gazed at the scenery hoping that would stop him from turning around to face her.

"You have come at a crazy time," the driver said. "Usually, it's too quiet here, but now with everything that's been happening, there are many people. Scientists, reporters, doctors." He waved his hand. "Many people. Crazy!"

"You mean the earthquakes?" Julia asked, relieved that the driver seemed oblivious to her sex. She'd bet that he was friendly with everyone he met.

"Earthquakes and more," he said, raising his eyebrows and speaking with an air of mystery. "Much more."

During the long flight Julia couldn't help but wonder how serious a matter Sebastião's disappearance was, and if her grandmother, Isabel, the family matriarch, was worried about nothing, as most of Julia's aunts and uncles believed. No one had heard from Sebastião in several months. They had written, but received no response. Telegrams were sent, but went unanswered.

Dona Isabel finally telephoned the *residencial* and spoke to Maria Josefa.

"He left several weeks ago," Maria Josefa had explained.

"Did he say where he was going?"

"Not a word, Dona Isabel. Nothing. And we haven't heard anything from him since"—there was a slight pause—"except for some very strange stories."

"What stories?"

"First, a drowned man's body was discovered halfway up Pico," Maria

Josefa said, followed by an audible sigh. "Then, a ghost ship has been seen off the islands. And if that weren't enough, there have been other stories, too, even worse. Ridiculous things!"

Maria Josefa was easily excitable, but not someone given to flights of fancy. She was no-nonsense and clear-headed.

"It sounds as if everyone on the islands has gone *louco*," Isabel said. "What has happened there?"

"I can't tell you," Maria Josefa said. "But there is definitely trouble in the air."

Isabel shared the wild stories with the family, laughing away the rumors of strange goings-on, which no one in their right mind would take seriously. Still, she was troubled, and went out of her way to instruct Julia to be careful and to return home at the first sign of danger.

"I promise I'll leave at the first sight of a ghost ship," Julia said.

Julia stared at the back of the driver's head, wondering if she should show him a photo of her father, but decided to wait. For all she knew, Sebastião would be at the *residencial.* If not now, perhaps tomorrow. She also didn't want to have to answer people's questions about what might have happened to him, at least not until she'd had a chance to speak to the police.

"We've heard about the earthquakes, of course," Julia said. "And a few crazy tales."

The driver nodded. "People have been talking about *a mulher luminosa*—the luminescent woman." He turned toward her again and grinned. *"Uma sereia."*

"A siren?" Julia said, raising her eyebrows and smiling in amusement.

The driver's eyes grew wide and he spoke quickly, as if this were the topic of the moment. "Yes, yes," he said. *"Exactamente.* People say she has taken some of the men. That they have gone off with her. One or two have been seen going down to the water at night and begging her to take them." He laughed, shaking his head.

"Incredible," Julia said. "People actually claim to have seen this siren?"

He shrugged. "Everyone says that those who see such things are drunk. But there are others who say they know what they saw, drink or no drink."

"Fantastic," Julia said, pleased with the idea of a place where someone could claim to have seen a siren or a ghost ship. Not in California, she thought. Some places were conducive to supernatural events, while

19

other places weren't. "It's a mystery, then, no?"

"Yes," the driver said. "I think maybe I should have stayed in Madeira."

"Did you drive a taxi there?" she said, relieved that he had stopped turning round.

"No, I was a fisherman," he said. "Before that I hunted whales."

"Whales?" Julia said. "Why did you stop? Was it too dangerous?"

"No, well, dangerous, yes. But I loved the whales. I was never afraid of them. They closed the factory, so I tried fishing with my cousin, Paulo. Unfortunately, there weren't enough fish. Too many fishermen, big fishing boats. My wife wanted to move to Faial because she has family here. My mother was born here, too. They offered to help me start a business with cows, but I didn't trust them."

Julia only half-listened as she marveled at the small, dense woods and the profusion of shrubs and flowering vines that grew along the roadside. She gazed at the tiny village of Feteira, remembering its strange twisted lava formations and caves along the water's edge. Sebastião, she thought, would love the stories and rumors about what was taking place on the islands.

"The family?" she said.

"No, no, the cows. Big monstrous things that chew and stare at you with enormous sad eyes. What are they thinking? I always wonder. They made me nervous." He laughed. "I was scared to work with them. So I bought this car. I thought I'd make money off the tourists, only nobody told me there aren't very many tourists here." He shrugged. "Are you staying long?"

Julia hesitated before answering. "I'm not sure," she said. Ordinarily, it would have been a simple question requiring a simple response—a week, a month—but so much depended, really, on what she found or didn't find. Where *is* Sebastião? she wondered for the umpteenth time.

The taxi sped down the road as it approached the two hills, Monte Queimado and Monte da Guia, which stood like sentinels beside the city, balanced by the sheer bluff of Espalamaca at the other end of the city.

"Here's our big city," the driver said, as they reached the outskirts of Horta. "People say the best thing about Horta is Pico. But often the mountain is hiding."

Julia peered out the window at Pico. Only the lower part of the mountain was visible. They drove through Horta's narrow cobblestone streets, past rows of whitewashed buildings, and the harbor. Julia smiled at the old women who gazed out their windows, or stood in doorways, talking to their neighbors. Some things never change, she thought.

"Has it been a long time since you were here?" the driver asked.

Julia couldn't remember whether she had mentioned that she'd been on the islands before. "Yes," she said. "A long time."

"It has changed, then."

"A little," she said. "The airport's new, of course, and some of the buildings on the outskirts of the city. The harbor, too, looks bigger. More boats."

The driver pulled up in front of the *residencial.* He jumped out and unloaded the luggage, placing the bags just inside the entrance. Julia paid him, adding a large tip, which he refused. "No, no, senhora. Don't pay more than the fare." He handed her a business card, "Call me any time you need a ride. I'll give you the best rates. Just ask for Miguel Carneiro."

He shook her hand, gave a slight bow, and sighed, before jumping back into the car.

"Thank you," Julia said. The driver exuded a physicality, an earthiness—not unpleasant—that was of the islands, the animals, the sea itself, as though he were fashioned out of these very elements. She wondered if he returned to them each night, only to be reformed each morning. He glanced at her one last time, all smiles, and sped off down the *Avenida.*

Julia stood on the steps and looked around at the busy intersection, the rows of shops, the harbor to her left, the park of the *Infante,* and Pico across the narrow channel—sights she hadn't seen in many years. Life, she had explained to herself, had gotten in the way. But it seemed as if time too had slipped, or skipped, and now that she was here, it was as if no time at all had passed.

She turned toward the doorway of the Residencial Neptuno, took a deep breath, and stepped inside, still clinging to the hope that she would find Sebastião busy at work writing an article on the current strange goings-on.

The *residencial* is smaller, was her first thought, the stairway narrower, steeper.

Maria Josefa Correia peered from behind the counter. Julia recognized her instantly, although Maria Josefa appeared smaller, rounder, and grayer than she remembered.

Julia felt slightly disoriented, like Alice having grown abnormally large. "Good afternoon, Senhora Correia," she said, as Maria Josefa looked her up and down with a mix of inquisitiveness and suspicion, as if she weren't about to let anyone march in and put something over on her. "I'm Julia Castro." She had wondered if Senhora Correia would recognize her after thirteen years. "Sebastião do Canto e Castro's daughter," Julia added. "You don't remember me?"

"Ah, *minha querida,*" Senhora Correia said, rushing from behind the counter to embrace Julia, and kissing her several times. "My dear, child. Why didn't you say so? I didn't recognize you. What happened to the little girl with the big eyes who ran up and down the stairs singing like a bird?"

"She grew up, I'm afraid," Julia said. "But you haven't changed at all, senhora." Of course the woman wouldn't know her by Castro. Sebastião would have filled her head with stories concerning his famous ancestors: exaggerated tales of conquests and adventure, royal love affairs, bloody murders and wars between ancient kingdoms. Julia could only guess what Sebastião might have concocted to impress her: "The entire island was our very own, senhora. All of this was ours!"

"Has Sebastião returned?" Julia asked. "Have you heard from him?"

Senhora Correia shook her head and frowned. "No, *menina.* No word from your father. Not since he left." She threw her arms up as if to indicate that he had simply vanished without the good sense to let someone know beforehand of his plans. An unpardonable sin of omission.

Julia had clung to a small hope that there had been a gross misunderstanding: she'd arrive to find Sebastião and the two of them would have a good laugh over this excessive fuss and worry, Julia traveling thousands of miles to find Sebastião, who'd appear contrite but appreciative of all the commotion nonetheless. She at once began to feel the weight of the trip and the concerns over Sebastião, which she had tried to allay during her travels.

"Have you saved me a room, senhora?"

"Call me Josefa," Senhora Correia said. "Yes, of course we have a room for you. You are alone? No one is with you?"

"No. I'm here by myself."

"*É uma pena,*" Maria Josefa said. "What a shame!" She gazed at Julia the way one would look at an orphan or some other unfortunate, her down-turned mouth set in indignation.

"I chose to come alone," Julia said, hoping to soothe Maria Josefa, although it wasn't altogether true.

"Your father should be here. He shouldn't have disappeared, to have you come here alone, with no one to look after you. Where is Antonio? Why didn't your brother come with you?"

She couldn't very well tell Maria Josefa that Antonio swore he would never return to the island. "He couldn't get away," Julia said. "He's very busy, lots of work. Besides, I don't need looking after. I'm a big girl."

"So I see." Maria Josefa looked Julia up and down. "Pretty, but why aren't you married?"

"I'm afraid no prince charming has come to sweep me off my feet." Maria Josefa snorted as she scrutinized Julia, as if trying to find the flaw or defect that would have kept someone from marrying her.

"Who needs a prince," she said. "Find a man. That's enough."

Julia laughed, but thought it best to steer the conversation elsewhere. "And you have no idea where Sebastião might have gone?"

Maria Josefa shook her head. "No, we've only heard stories that one has to be crazy to believe. Your father is a gentleman, and your family, of course, is a fine one. I myself have tried to ignore all this talk of witches and pirates, and such things, though some of what I have heard has been scandalous!" She waved her hand. "A few earthquakes and perfectly sane people start losing their heads, suddenly talking about devils, ghosts, naked sirens, and curses. We must be careful. I can't afford to scare away customers."

Maria Josefa shook with emotion as she spoke. Julia half-expected the woman to start wagging a finger at her.

"People like to gossip and exaggerate," Julia said. "Especially where Sebastião is concerned. I'm sure there's a logical explanation. He's probably doing research or off exploring a remote part of the island."

"Perhaps." Maria Josefa appeared mollified, at least for the moment.

"Now then, about the room?" Julia said.

"You can take your father's apartment, until he returns, of course." Maria Josefa then added as an afterthought, "After all, there's no reason to take two rooms while he's not here."

"That would be fine," Julia said. "How much is the room?"

Maria waved the subject away. "Don't you worry about that, *menina.*" Sebastião had worked out an arrangement with Maria Josefa and João for his room in the *residencial.* He didn't pay a regular monthly rent. There were still people too proud to accept money. Over the years Sebastião had paid for and arranged repairs and remodeling on the building. Julia smiled at Maria Josefa's use of the term *menina* while the cab driver used *senhora*. Maria Josefa would probably always remember her as the young girl who followed her father all over the islands. Maria Josefa sighed. "He's always coming and going, that man, God only knows how, or where, showing up when you least expect him."

Julia pointed toward Pico. "Do you think he might have gotten lost or hurt climbing the mountain?"

Maria Josefa grunted. "That is just the sort of thing your father would do, as if a man belongs up there in the clouds," she said, rolling her eyes up to heaven. "If a man is foolish enough to climb the mountain, then no one should be surprised if he disappears."

Maria Josefa spoke in quickly changing tones, sweet one moment, and vinegary the next, while mumbling to herself and interjecting accompanying sounds to emphasize her opinions.

"He might have fallen," Julia said, "or sprained an ankle and hid in one of the caves, or perhaps made his way to some remote farm."

"The police have checked the mountain already, since they discovered the drowned man. Thank God it wasn't your father. None of the guides said they had seen your father for some time." She shook her head. "Goats climb mountains, men belong down here. If he had a wife to look after him, he wouldn't go off getting himself lost."

Julia knew Pico could be dangerous. She'd heard stories of people going up and losing their way. "Still, a lot of people climb the mountain and make it back down again," she said. "Sebastião has climbed it more than once."

"And many people have disappeared on the mountain, as well," Maria Josefa said, evidently unimpressed with the story of Sebastião's daring. "Some people are too smart to listen to the warnings. They go up and a sudden storm comes, or they lose their way in the clouds. There are fumaroles that people stumble into and fall to their deaths. Some, they say, have no end, but go down into the belly of the earth. No, it's best to leave the mountain alone."

"Yes, Dona Josefa." Of course there was no way Maria Josefa could possibly fathom why anyone would want to climb a mountain, even if that mountain was Pico. Sebastião would point out that for being the descendants of explorers the islanders were surprisingly staid, seldom knowing what was right under their feet, or just down the road. "Strangers come to the islands and discover marvels the people here don't know exist," Sebastião would say. "Like warmth-loving butterflies that live at the top of Pico and nowhere else, or caves, lava tubes and craters."

"You aren't thinking of climbing Pico, too?" Maria Josefa rested her fists on her hips, her expression stern and imposing.

"No, senhora."

Maria Josefa sighed. "Even a burro knows where he shouldn't go, but a man is too thick-skulled to avoid danger. He goes out of his way to look for it."

"I doubt Sebastião would climb Pico alone," Julia said, "especially with the earthquakes." Maria Josefa didn't look convinced; perhaps she knew Sebastião better than Julia thought. "But he might have gone on a boat that stopped off here, maybe doing undersea archeological work."

"Boats!" Maria Josefa said, as if that were something as distasteful as climbing a mountain. "Your father should have stayed here in Horta where he belonged. He should have bought himself some land and some cows and stayed put, instead of running around like a man with ants in his pants."

Julia was amused at the idea of Sebastião settling down as a gentleman farmer, raising cows. Maria Josefa may frown and sound gruff, she thought, but she laughs with her eyes. Although tough and bossy, Dona Josefa had a wicked sense of humor, which made her all the more endearing. Julia would have given anything to see how she dealt with Sebastião.

"I'm afraid Sebastião was never one to stay at home," she said.

"Well, if he did he wouldn't have disappeared, and caused all of us to worry about him," Maria Josefa said. "Now, first things first. Do you have your passport?" Julia took her passport from her purse and set it on the counter, then signed the registration book. Maria Josefa took a key down from a pegboard and opened a back door. "João," she called. A moment later, João entered the room. He wore rough work clothes, a cap on his head, and smiled broadly when he saw Julia. "This is Senhor Canto e Castro's daughter, Julia. Do you remember her, husband, or have you forgotten the little girl you always used to spoil with ice cream and sweets?"

"Just look at you," João said, kissing each side of her face. "You've grown into a beautiful young woman. The last time I saw you, you were only this tall." He put his hand out halfway up his chest.

"That was a long time ago, Senhor Correia," Julia said.

"Now, why, the men must throw themselves at your feet, eh?" His eyes sparkled mischievously.

"*Really,*" Julia said. "Don't you believe it. You're a terrible liar and a flatterer, but it's good to see you again, senhor." Though he had aged and had grown stooped and fragile since her last visit, João still possessed a warm smile, a sweet tone, and more affection than any of her own relatives. His face crinkled when she called him a flatterer. "People tell me my eyes are too big, I'm too skinny, and too pale," she said. "So much for being beautiful."

"Firstly, call me, João. No need to stand on ceremony with old friends. And secondly, I do not flatter unless it's true. I know a thing or two about beauty, and you *are* beautiful."

"Of course he knows about beauty," Maria Josefa said, "He's been married to me for forty years. Bring her bags up, João." Maria Josefa turned and started up the stairs, as Julia and João followed, laughing.

João set the luggage down in the room. "I'll see you later, young lady," he said. "I have more work to do."

"I'll see you soon, then," Julia said.

"If you need anything just let me or João know," Maria Josefa said.

Julia thanked Dona Josefa. "I only need some sleep, right now."

She examined the room after Maria Josefa left. It wasn't remotely luxurious as far as accommodations went, but was certainly clean and quiet and, located in the very heart of Horta, had obviously suited Sebastião.

The furnishings were sparse: a bureau, a desk, one chair, and a nightstand. There was a stack of books, some pens and papers. A manual typewriter, empty, sat on the desk, more books and papers on the nightstand, but surprisingly little else.

Julia peered out the window, and smiled to see it faced Pico. Sebastião would insist on that. The ever-changing face of the volcano wore a crown of mist or cirrus cloud one moment and was completely obscured the next; only rarely did the mountain show itself uncloaked, with no clouds in sight. At times you could almost forget Pico was there, until you looked to find the clouds were gone—there stood the peak, startling in its beauty, the unexpectedness of being.

"The mountain is naked," Sebastião would say, with the kind of awe normally reserved for events such as a comet or a total eclipse.

As Julia unpacked, she noticed her father's suitcases neatly arranged in the closet, as were his clothes, making it unlikely that he had taken an extensive trip anywhere. The room was too neat, too empty, to have served Sebastião properly. Not nearly enough books, for one thing, and none of the manuscripts, stories or poems, he would have been working on.

She rested on the bed, closed her eyes, and soon fell asleep. She dreamed a disquieting dream of a ship sailing in a storm, lashed by waves, wind and rain, and voices calling, disturbing the night, a strange sound like a banshee wailing.

Julia woke with a start still feeling the swaying of the sea beneath her. She glanced at the clock on the table beside the bed. It was eight-thirty, and already beginning to darken outside. She stepped into the bathroom and made a face at her reflection in the mirror.

27

"God, I look terrible!" Julia stuck out her tongue. "Beautiful my foot!" She shook her hair. It'd been cut short, but was growing out, and reached just past her shoulders. She looked down at her hips and frowned. They were too big. It wouldn't have been so bad except that her aunts and uncles liked to say she was built to produce babies, as though she were a cow.

She washed her face, brushed her teeth, thought about putting on some eyeliner and lipstick, but decided to skip it, then combed her hair, and went downstairs. She passed the front desk, but didn't see Maria Josefa or João.

Julia stepped outside, crossed the street and walked through the *Praça do Infante*—the Prince's Park, named after Infante Dom Henrique. She passed the Café Internacional and the ancient fort of Santa Cruz, as well as other places she remembered from long ago: Café Sport, which everyone called Peter's Café, popular with tourists and sailors; the harbor, the seawall—everything looked as she remembered it, if smaller, less imposing. Beyond the fortified gate at Porto Pim was the closeddown whaling factory. That was different. It had been operating when she was last here; the whales hauled out of the water with enormous chains and cut with long steel blades, while their blood flowed down the flensing platform and turned the ocean red.

She remembered the whalers—tough, sun-burnt men, weathered by the sea and the difficult life they lived, pursuing the cachalot, the sperm whales, with hand-held harpoons. She'd been torn between a romantic desire to accompany the men in their boats, to experience the chase and danger straight out of the pages of *Moby Dick,* which Sebastião had read to her when she was young, at the same time hating the fact that they killed the whales. If only they could be like the Portuguese bullfighters who, unlike their Spanish counterparts, never killed the bulls. But then Sebastião pointed out that the whales were often more than a match for the whalers, whose methods had changed little over the past hundred years.

Her father had gone along on the whaling boats once or twice, just for the experience of hunting a whale, and she had begged him to take her along. He had laughed with the whalers, telling them that Julia had wanted to go, too. "A girl hunting whales?" they'd said, surprised and amused.

"She's another Violante do Canto," Sebastião told them. "Violante would not only board her father's ships and inspect them before they patrolled the waters of the islands to guard against pirates, but sometimes sailed with her father."

Julia gazed across the channel between Faial and Pico, her eyes again seeking the mountain. If there had been an Atlantis here, as Sebastião liked to say, Pico might well have been its crowning glory.

She stopped at a restaurant. It was new and nearly empty. There were only two other tables with customers. She ordered a bowl of *caldo verde*—kale soup, bread, and a glass of red wine.

"Is that all?" the waiter said.

"Yes, thank you. *Nada mais.*" He nodded, and curtly turned away, as if disappointed. She had a quiet dinner, and as soon as she was finished returned to the *residencial* to sleep off the effects of jet lag, and the eight-hour difference in time. She hadn't slept at all the night before.

As she was preparing to turn in for the night, there was a tap on the door. Julia opened it to find Maria Josefa standing before her. "Do you have everything you need, *menina?* Did you eat something?"

"Yes, Dona Josefa. I ate."

"I can bring you some bread and cheese, or some fruit, if you're still hungry."

"No, thank you. I'm fine, really."

"Be careful where you eat," Maria Josefa said. "Ask me first and I'll tell you where the food is good and where it's not."

"Okay."

"And remember, breakfast is at seven o'clock."

"Yes, Dona Josefa, I know."

"Breakfast ends at nine o'clock. If you don't get up you'll have to find somewhere to eat. And if you go out at night, don't stay out late. Several people have disappeared already, and I don't want to be responsible for losing another member of your family. A young woman shouldn't be out alone, especially a pretty girl like you."

"I know, Dona Josefa," Julia said. "I know. And don't worry, I won't be staying out late." She wanted to ask what looks had to do with whether or not a woman should be out alone, whether good looks were a provocation, or mattered more than someone who was homely, but she bit her tongue.

"You seem to know everything already," Maria Josefa said, her hands on her hips. "Well, then, I'll say good night, *menina.*"

"Good night, senhora." Julia closed the door and settled into bed wondering how Sebastião could have managed to disappear while Maria Josefa stood guard so vigilantly.

She looked through the books, papers, and the notebook on the table beside the bed—her father's things. She picked up the nearest book, *Mensagem,* by Fernando Pessoa, and climbed into bed. Pessoa was one of her father's favorite poets. His heteronyms, each with a complete biography and a particular style, greatly appealed to Sebastião— the many men within the man; even the name Pessoa meant 'person,' a perfect name for a man obsessed with identity.

She thought of the Pessoa books Sebastião had given her as gifts over the years.

Slips of paper marked certain pages in the book, but she was too tired to read. As she put the book back on the table, however, a postcard fell out. It was a picture of Pico with nary a cloud in sight. On the back it was written out and addressed to Julia.

The card simply read: "Julia, Come immediately. Don't delay. Residencial Neptuno, Horta." Nothing more, no inquiries, no explanations. No, "Dear daughter," no, "How are things?" or "I miss you." Just a point-blank directive. This, after nearly four months of silence.

"Jesus," she said softly. It was as if icy cold fingers had reached up from under the bed and seized hold of her. She rose from the bed, checked the door and the window, and drew the curtains shut, for the first time feeling alone and a sense of vulnerability.

It wasn't all that surprising or extraordinary finding the card addressed so simply and directly. Sebastião had a definite flair for the dramatic. What *was* extraordinary was that Julia had sensed enough that she should come, without having received the card. And the words written there, she wondered, did they indicate some possible trouble or danger? Why the urgency and, more to the point, why hadn't Sebastião mailed the card?

The next morning, Julia showered and dressed, then went downstairs bringing the few papers she had found on the nightstand with her, as well as the discomfiture that had made its presence felt since stumbling upon her father's postcard. The dining room was empty except for an older couple seated in the corner who ate in complete silence. Maria Josefa brought Julia a tray filled with coffee, fresh rolls, butter and quince jam, which she placed on the table where Julia sat.

"Good morning, *menina.* I hope you slept the sleep of the just."

Julia returned the greeting and thanked Maria Josefa. "I slept wonderfully."

She poured sugar and cream into the coffee, before taking a sip, then buttered one of the rolls and bit into it, savoring the deliciousness of the simple breakfast.

Among the papers was a letter from her grandfather, Mateus. He'd had little contact with most of the family, since his abrupt departure from the United States for Brazil, when Julia was four years old. Unable to adapt to life in California, and dismissing the North American continent as a land "where they care nothing for the old ways, the old places, where the name Canto e Castro is unknown," Mateus had packed his things and left for Rio de Janeiro to live a self-imposed exile from the islands and his family. Sebastião alone kept in regular touch with Mateus, and had visited him on occasion.

Julia drank her coffee and read the letter:

Dear Sebastião,

I know nothing about what you mentioned in your last letter concerning

Dona Inês de Castro's ring, or any treasure. I've never heard of a secret cult of Dona Inês, and I'd forgotten her sister, Joana—both queens, as you said, robbed of their kingdoms. The murder of Inês is lost to the vicissitudes of time, so that the truth is impossible to determine.

I cannot tell you why she was murdered, except what we have all heard: advisors to the king feared her powerful influence upon the prince, thinking that her children could prove dangerous to the rightful heir to the throne.

Perhaps you have uncovered long-buried secrets, I don't know. I am old, and very tired. Perhaps it would be best to leave things as they are. Digging into these matters may only disturb sleeping ghosts.

Saudades,
Mateus

Julia put the letter aside and wondered if Sebastião had left the papers where he knew she would find them. The allusions to treasure, to Inês de Castro's ring, the cult of Inês, a sister named Joana, to say nothing of her grandfather's admonition not to disturb sleeping ghosts, were puzzling. She'd grown up listening to the stories Sebastião and her grandmother told about the famous love affair of Inês and Pedro, and its gruesome conclusion when Pedro's father, King Afonso, ordered Inês's murder. She'd always been conscious of her own connection with Inês de Castro. Sebastião had wanted to name her Inês, but Clara insisted that was out of the question: "I will not name my daughter after some-one who was decapitated," she had said. "Besides, with a name like that she'll be teased." They compromised, naming her, Julia Inês. Sebastião spoke as though he had won the battle, but Julia's mother had never once referred to her daughter by her full name.

Sebastião would tell her how brave, strong, and beautiful her name-sake was. "She refused to back down, so they killed her, just like Joan of Arc. Inês," he would add, "died for love."

But there's more, Julia thought. Sebastião had always claimed that when people found themselves lacking facts concerning a topic, they exhibited an irresistible tendency to project suppositions, to sketch with perhaps, what ifs and maybes, aligned with preconceived biases and prejudices. No one could adequately answer many of the questions that arose surrounding Inês de Castro's murder, the whys and wherefores; huge gaps existed in the historical record, which left many an investigator uneasy and dissatisfied. And her grandfather's closing words, about sleeping ghosts, she knew, would be just the thing to drive Sebastião to probe further, deeper; he'd love nothing more than to disturb sleeping ghosts. To say nothing of the living.

A whisper reverberated through the ages like a breeze blowing up leaves and dust; something's missing, it murmured, something left unfulfilled. Julia heard and felt it, the chill this breeze brought with it, as if Inês were only the first act of a play that had yet to conclude. And, of course, it was the possibility of this unforeseen conclusion that left Julia feeling unsettled, as if she'd stepped onstage at the beginning of the second act without having been given a script.

33

"She's like a ghost," Julia said aloud, "that's haunted our family since her death."

With a shudder she looked through the remaining papers. Some were written in ink, but a special kind of ink, metallic like mercury, and a script that was unfamiliar, definitely not Sebastião's; it was an ornate style, a specialized calligraphy, unlike anything she'd ever seen, and appeared to have been hastily written. The paper, or parchment, if that's what it was, was ragged, as if the sheets were torn out of some ancient book.

. . .

It was known as The Year of the Sea, and by others as The Year of the Flood. Never before had the waves reached such heights, never had it rained so furiously, so relentlessly. It was as if the islands were being washed back into the ocean by the combined forces of the waves and the skies.

Between the rising sea and the wind-lashed rains it was impossible to escape the wet or the cold. Water found its way into holes and crevices, trickled into the homes, no matter how securely windows and doors were fastened shut. The wind also found secret avenues through which to gain entry, providing a multitude of sounds that disturbed the people within: screeches, cries, howls and moans.

It was amidst all this that a man appeared as if summoned by the very fury of the storms, for no one knew from whence he had come.

"He crawled from the sea," one said. "No, he came from the sky," said another. "From the mountain, that crack in the earth," said a third.

He frightened the women and unnerved the men. He appeared when least expected, vanished just as suddenly, left people peering over their shoulders and jumping at unexpected noises.

"He's like a shadow, that man," they said. "A ghost."

"A Sorcerer," whispered one brave soul who dared to call a thing by what it appeared to be. The others shuddered and agreed. "Um Feiticeiro."

The waves climbed higher and higher, breaking over fields, streets, and houses; rain poured from the heavens and the wind lashed from every direction, threatening to drown everything.

The Sorcerer, who ventured out regardless of the cold of night or the fierceness of the storms, was seen in the village, on the roads, and by the shore—everywhere at one and the same time.

"Where is he now?" the villagers asked.

"I saw him go toward the mountain."

"No, to the sea."

Some who dared go out claimed they saw him calling out to the ocean, using his magic to conjure demons, or perhaps the waves themselves.

But it was soon seen exactly what the sorcerer had been up to, when old man Raposo pointed to the sea with a shout. "Look, there!"

Through the rain and the wind-tossed waves, a dark fearsome shape rose from the water.

"Dear Mother of God," the villagers cried.

It was a terrifying sight: an ancient nau or caravel, a ship of discovery, many of which had sunk in the waters off the islands several centuries earlier. Many of the men called out, "God help us," several women fainted, and the rest were struck dumb.

The terrible ship rose from its watery grave where it had lain for hundreds of years, its timbers and sails rotted, its cannons rusted.

The villagers watched helplessly as the sorcerer climbed aboard a small boat that carried him without the assistance of oars or sails, moving through the water as if propelled by his will alone, and which brought him to the ship.

The sorcerer boarded the ancient vessel, then sailed away from the island, leaving a pale incandescence in its wake. The horrified villagers stared in disbelief.

"There'll be hell to pay," old man Raposo said.

. . .

Julia put the pages aside. "Strange," she whispered, wondering whether this was a story fragment, an excerpt from one of Sebastião's books, perhaps. Or something he had discovered—a copy of an ancient legend, even a bizarre personal account from some obscure historical record. Of course, there was also the question of whose hand had written it out.

She finished her breakfast, and left the *residencial*. She walked down Rua Serpa Pinto toward the police station. Her grandmother Isabel had telephoned, demanding that they investigate Sebastião's disappearance, before Julia had come to the islands. If they hadn't yet located her father, perhaps they had at least ruled out some possibilities.

The building was drab, cold and sterile, little different from police stations everywhere. The room was poorly lit, sparsely furnished, and so quiet it unnerved her. She expected a flurry of activity, people coming and going, investigations being carried out, interrogations conducted, but there was none of that, at least as far as she could see.

The policeman behind the counter didn't deign to look up when she entered the front office, but flipped through some papers on his desk. Julia cleared her throat. "Excuse me," she said. The policeman raised his head with a pained expression, the irritated look of an official disturbed by a citizen with a problem, demanding work or information. As soon as he saw her, however, his expression softened, and a smile creased his features.

"Yes, senhora, how can I help you?" he said, in a voice unexpectedly soft and honeyed.

Julia's response to his sudden change in demeanor was cool. She mustered up the most fleeting smile she could offer, then settled on a neutral expression, as if to say, don't think I'm here on pleasure. "I need to speak to someone about Sebastião do Canto e Castro," she said, in as disinterested a tone as she could.

"And you are?" he said, raising his eyebrows, as well as the intonation of the last word.

"His daughter, Julia Castro. I've just arrived from the United States." She took out her identification, but the policeman waved it away.

His attitude changed again, and his smile vanished. "I'm sorry, but as you can see, I am alone at the moment." He looked her up and down.

35

"But if you'd like you can wait here. Someone should be here soon." He gestured to several chairs where she might sit.

"Isn't there anything you can tell me?" she asked. "I've heard nothing so far."

"We're still looking into it," the policeman explained. His tone, however, gave the impression that so far the matter hadn't exactly been relegated to a position of high priority.

"In other words, you have no idea where he is?" Julia asked. "There's no news?"

The policeman shook his head. "It's only a matter of time. Please, senhora, the best thing is to try to be patient."

She took a deep breath. "He's just disappeared, that's what you're saying?"

The policeman put down the papers, as if they were a tremendous burden, and sighed. "People do not disappear from these islands," he said. "Right now he is simply nowhere to be found, which, for all we know, is exactly where he wishes to be."

"You're suggesting that he might be hiding?" Julia said, sitting down at last on the chair in front of the policeman's desk.

He shrugged. "When people can't be found it is usually because they have decided to run off with a lover, or because they've broken the law."

"Sebastião is no longer married," Julia said. "He and my mother separated years ago. Since he has no wife to run away from, he has no need to hide anything. And he certainly isn't a criminal."

"Perhaps," the man said, again raising his eyebrows, as if to show he had no firm opinion one way or the other on the matter.

The man's insinuations, condescending manner, to say nothing of the difficulty in keeping his eyes above her neckline, needled her. If he hadn't been so obvious, it wouldn't have mattered, but it was done with a self-satisfied air, borne out of long-established habit. No doubt he thought it passed for charm with some women. Also, his words were cagey, as if he were more interested in obfuscating than informing.

"Why would he have sent me this note asking me to come?" Julia asked, taking the postcard from her purse. She waved it at the policeman, but, of course, didn't let him see that it hadn't been mailed.

The officer shrugged again. Who was he to try and guess why an *americano* would do such a thing? "We're looking into the matter," he repeated. "We will notify you as soon as we find anything. Everything possible is being done."

He resumed his work. Julia stood. "I'm staying at the Residencial Neptuno," she said. "I'll check back later."

The policeman nodded. "As you wish, senhora."

Julia left the building, determined that next time she'd be sure to speak with someone in authority. She walked to the waterfront to work off her frustration. Still, she reasoned, it's probably best to give the investigation a few more days to turn up something, to try to be patient.

The police, it turned out, had more pressing matters with which to concern themselves. The unsettling reports of a new island rising up from the sea had everyone's nerves on end, and perhaps explained the latest miracle people had been talking about: seventy-two hours of complete darkness, experienced a week earlier. Gigantic plumes of smoke and steam had erupted from the sea and spread for miles like a shroud, blocking out the clouds, the sky, and the sun, leaving people unable to distinguish night from day and filling the churches beyond capacity. As a result, there were a number of car crashes, and several boats collided or ran aground. Sailors returned to the docks, where shaken fishermen told stories of sailing through seas full of pumice, lava, and scores of dead fish—some the men had never seen before—and where streams of liquid fire set the nighttime sea aglow.

"Never name the islands," Sebastião always said, "not to anyone. If people find out they'll come in droves and spoil the place in no time, build fancy hotels and resorts, and turn it into another Puerto Rico or Hawaii. They'd strip it of all its magic."

"What if someone asks where we're from?" Julia would ask.

"Tell them we come from the Undiscovered Island."

When Julia and her brother Antonio were young, Sebastião sometimes entertained and amused their friends. He was nothing like the other fathers; he spoke with a strange accent and told wild stories.

"Where is he *from?*" Julia's friends often asked.

"We are the last of the Lusitanians," Sebastião invariably said, and if one of Julia's friends was bold enough to ask, "The *what?*" he'd answer, "The Lusitanians," pronouncing the word slowly, as if to emphasize its profound significance. "Long, long ago Lusus, the son of Bacchus, the god of wine, founded the kingdom of the Lusiads." Or he'd tell them of the Undiscovered, or Hidden Island. "Once a year it becomes visible, but only for a short while, before it disappears again, plunging back beneath the waves."

Julia's friends would stare incredulously, while Antonio would shake his head, sulking, "Why does *our* dad always have to be so weird?"

"The islands are our secret," Sebastião would say, with a wink.

Now there was another secret, one more mystery associated with the islands: where was Sebastião? What had happened to him?

Isabel had summoned a family council to discuss the matter of Sebastião's disappearance. They'd gathered at Isabel's modest home in San José, California.

"Something must be done," she said.

"We have jobs, families," various uncles, nephews, and grandsons, each said. "We can't leave. Besides, Sebastião can take care of himself." Isabel, they believed, was overreacting. Sebastião was a poet, folklorist, occasional fiction writer, something of an adventurer, and a pain in the neck. The cause of his silence, they reasoned, was likely due to thoughtlessness and irresponsibility. They had also heard about the earthquakes, however, and that was enough to convince them it was probably best to stay away. "It's impossible to go now."

"Something must be done." Isabel was adamant. She was in her mid-seventies, ever on the verge of death, and determined to have her way. Her family shielded her from every possible evil, thinking bad news would upset her, bring on a tantrum or fainting spell, or worse, even kill her, but Isabel was tougher than the lot of them put together. "Someone has to go."

"But who?" said Uncle Frank, whose name was Francisco, "Until America got hold of it," Sebastião liked to say.

"I'll go," Julia said.

Julia's independence and self-assurance worried her relatives. That she was unmarried and likely to remain so, and possessed her father's streak of eccentricity, unlike Antonio, who was practical and predictable, was a constant source of irritation.

"You?" Uncle Frank said. "But you're a girl."

"*What?*"

"A woman," he said, cringing. "Woman, girl." He waved his hand in the air as though to dispel his lapse. In his mind a girl was a girl until she married and had babies. That was the prescribed process whereby a girl became a woman, and until then she remained a girl.

"So what if I'm a woman," Julia said, rising to the challenge. "What does that matter?"

"Are you crazy?" Julia's mother Clara, interrupted. "You can't go *there.*" Clara had divorced Sebastião when Julia was fourteen, but still participated in family celebrations and important get-togethers, perhaps in part to make up for Sebastião's frequent absence during such occasions, but also because she liked to think of herself as indispensable.

"*There?*" Julia said. "Can't you even name the islands?"

"Of course I can," Clara said. But she didn't do so.

"Your mother's right, Julia," Isabel said. "It's too dangerous for you to go alone." Clara, Isabel, even Uncle Frank and Aunt Maria all turned to Antonio, who stood by as if none of this concerned him.

He cleared his throat. "Don't look at me," he said. "I'm not going anywhere. There's no way I can leave right now. I have too much at stake. I'm up to my neck in work."

"It's funny," Julia said. "But I seem to remember a certain woman who left the islands alone, at the end of World War II, and came to this country when there were still unexploded mines in the ocean and she didn't know a soul here."

"Things were different," Isabel said. Her voice lacked conviction. If Julia had bothered to glance at her grandmother at that moment she might have seen a smile working at the corner of her mouth. Julia may be reckless, but Isabel couldn't help but feel proud of the only one in the family who showed the same stubbornness and backbone she herself possessed.

"Maybe it would be better to wait until someone else can accompany you," Aunt Maria suggested.

"Yes, there's no need to rush off alone," Uncle Frank said.

"I'm going to find out what's happened now, not later. And that's all there is to it." Julia was soft-spoken, 'of little voice' Sebastião would say, but her family knew better than to argue with her. Once she'd made up her mind, she wouldn't back down, and if pushed, would display a calm determination that was far more startling and effective than any loud outburst. "These are the 1980s," she said. "It isn't like a hundred years ago when a woman traveling alone would raise eyebrows and start tongues wagging. I'm perfectly capable of taking care of myself."

"What about your job?" Clara said.

"I quit, gave notice."

Clara, shocked and wounded to the core, stared at Julia at a loss for words before finding her voice. "Why would you do that? What will you do?"

"I'm sure I'll be able to find another place to waitress, if I need to," Julia said. "I'm ready for a change. I even have some money saved up."

"A change I can understand," Clara said. "Doing something that makes sense, like getting a job with your brother, but *this?* This is, well, primitive."

Isabel's attitude, Julia understood, but the rest, she knew, were distressed not only by her single status and her lack of children, but her interest in music, which not only evoked images of a seedy lifestyle, but lacked any real solid future, and mostly by her independence.

"When will that girl marry," her aunts and uncles asked, as if it were inconceivable that a female could be happy on her own.

"It's her looks, you know," Aunt Manuela said. "They put people off."

"What are you talking about?" Uncle Frank said. "Her looks are fine. It's her attitude. She's too cold. People get close to her and end up with frostbite. Who the hell wants a woman who doesn't need anybody, who's so haughty?"

Aunt Manuela nodded. "Why should a girl live by herself? It's not right."

"She should learn to cook," Aunt Maria said. "To cook and to eat. She needs something on those bones. That'll help to thaw her out."

Julia was condemned to be forever compared with her father. Writers and musicians were lumped with artists of all kinds and equated with irresponsibility. It was convenient to condemn Sebastião through her— not that they would admit this, or were even conscious of the fact that they transferred their disapproval of Sebastião to Julia. They each knew Julia was capable of doing something for which they were unprepared, and that she wouldn't bother to consider the consequences. As with most dislikes—for it was nothing less, demonstrated by the fact they would never even think to ask about her music—it was a gnawing fear, which made them recoil and judge her harshly. That she didn't care what others thought was akin to blasphemy.

Later that evening, after an unusually subdued dinner, Clara took Julia aside. "I wish you wouldn't go," she said. "It's not safe. Since you've quit your job, why not get Antonio to help you find something better? You can't work menial jobs the rest of your life." This was her mother's favorite refrain. Pursuing music, instead of settling down sensibly like Antonio, struck her as mad and childish. "Bohemianism suits Sebastião," she would say. "But not *my* flesh and blood." She'd always regretted that Julia had quit school, and cherished a secret hope that her daughter would come to her senses and return to follow in her brother's footsteps. But Julia had known, as soon as she started the few classes she did take that school wasn't for her. She'd quietly withdrawn from school and pursued music on her own. That didn't stop her mother from mailing Julia brochures from business schools and pamphlets on MBA degrees.

"I guess I can't stop you," Clara said, finally relenting. There was certainly no chance that Antonio would go—not to search for his father, not to the islands.

Antonio was Sebastião's only son, and while it was true class distinctions were not what they had been in the past, certain things were still unavoidable, and of the utmost importance—especially when it came to familial responsibility, to being the eldest, *and* being a male. Isabel at least made a halfhearted appeal to Antonio: "Are you going to let your sister go alone? Shouldn't you accompany her?"

"No one's making her go," Antonio said. He had sided with their mother years earlier, both against the islands and against their father. "Let him come looking for us for a change," was Antonio's final comment concerning Sebastião's whereabouts.

Antonio kept tally of an impressive list of resentments, the way a miser might count his secret hoard of money. Instead of reciting prayers, he tallied slights. He possessed an uncanny memory, replaying each and every incident when his father had let him down, from earliest childhood: school functions he'd failed to make, baseball games he'd missed, moments when Antonio had felt his world was coming down around him, when he had needed a father's guidance and advice. Antonio, under Clara's careful tutelage, had studied business, and was already on his way to becoming moderately successful in real estate and the stock market—matters that didn't interest Sebastião in the slightest.

"He's an American," Sebastião said of Antonio. That word alone defined the gulf that couldn't be bridged between father and son. Illustrative of the fact, Antonio went by Tony in the U.S., allowing only Julia and Sebastião to use his given name. He cared nothing for the history of the family, nothing for poetry or music, and in particular nothing for the islands, although unlike Julia, he was born there. Clara, Sebastião, and Antonio had lived on Faial when Clara was pregnant with Julia, during the eruption of Capelinhos just off the coast, in 1957.

"I won't stay here to have all of us killed by a volcano," Clara had said. "I want to go home." And of course Antonio had faithfully echoed his mother's sentiments.

Sebastião had driven repeatedly to the southwestern side of the island to watch the eruptions. He'd go at dawn or the middle of the night, and photograph the volcano spewing lava, getting as close as possible.

"It's perfectly safe," he assured his jittery wife. "They'd evacuate if it weren't."

Clara, however, watched as hundreds of islanders abandoned their homes and fled for the United States. When she finally threatened to leave him there, Sebastião relented, heartbroken that the baby would not be born on the islands, but in an American hospital, on American soil.

"You have ash and lava in your blood," he would tell his daughter. "You were conceived at the same time as the volcano." Perhaps this explained why Julia felt a special connection with the islands, while Antonio had no desire to ever see them again.

Sebastião was disappointed by Antonio's denunciation of everything that he, Sebastião, cared for, but Julia was glad her father had never made her feel he wished she were a boy. "There's nothing you can't do," he'd say. He'd urged her to be fearless and independent, and to appreciate the arts, beauty, and imagination. "The things that are truly important."

Julia purchased a ticket and packed her bags, excited about returning to the islands for the first time since she'd gone back with Sebastião thirteen years earlier, when her father had begun spending more and more of his time on the islands, and looking forward to seeing him as well.

. . .

The sea exhaled and the sky sighed, filling the warm, clear air with a breeze and a touch of humidity, which reminded Julia that, after so many years, she really was here again, where she hadn't been since her adolescence. Having read and heard stories about it, in the interim made her feel as if she had stepped into a place of dreams, a place of legend.

Julia strolled around the harbor, the park, and walked to the hill of *Espalamaca,* hearing the words her grandmother used to tell her when she was a young girl, like a faint far-off echo:

"Long ago there was a tenth island. All men and women came from this island, and spread out to all corners of the world."

Julia wound her way to the bay of Porto Pim, and the sea-filled crater of Monte da Guia, called Caldeira do Inferno—Hell's Crater—landmarks that reminded her Horta was built upon the flanks of a volcano. The land rose precipitously, as if breaking through the surface of the sea it had eagerly stretched molten fingers up towards the heavens, where they froze in place.

"Everything came from this island," her grandmother said. "No one ever died there. It was paradise. The beauty of the island and its people were unsurpassed, and its inhabitants were known for their wisdom, living peacefully with one another and with the world around them."

In Julia's mind, Isabel's description was a blend of the Garden of Eden, Atlantis, and a fairyland, superimposed upon the nine islands of the archipelago. A quaint story, told for the amusement of youngsters. But the natural beauty of the islands was something she had carried with her throughout the years like a precious memento: the black lava, the deep green of the fields, the quaint villages, the rich soil and lush gardens, all surrounded by the mid-Atlantic ocean.

"This tenth island," her grandmother whispered, "far larger, and more magnificent than any of the others, sank in a violent cataclysm of fire and water many thousands of years ago."

45

Out here, alone on these islands, it wasn't difficult to see how a person might actually come to believe her grandmother's story. If Julia remained long enough, perhaps she too would begin to see such signs—hearing, smelling, tasting, all in remembrance of what once was, lingering like a half-forgotten dream. What visions would rise up from beneath the waves, or appear out of the mists?

Up the steep heights of Pico—the grueling climb had taken her and the others an entire night to reach the summit—one could well imagine such stories were true. Sebastião had pushed her to reach the top, unwilling to let her wait below with her brother, who had refused to climb the mountain. Reaching the peak at dawn, viewing all of Pico from above, overlooking the surrounding seas, and the islands of São Jorge, Faial, Graciosa—and because the weather was exceptionally clear, even Terceira in the distance—made the exhausting ordeal worthwhile; tiny green mounds of earth, seen from that height and distance, dwarfed by the expanse of both ocean and sky, and the remarkable vision of Pico's enormous shadow cast upon the surface of the morning sea were sights she had never forgotten.

Returning to the towns and villages down below, however, there was only the spectacle of the daily harsh reality of scratching out a living. Instead of fanciful visions there were houses with dirt floors, families with little in the way of clothes or shoes; widows dressed in their immutable black, like a flock of ravens; tales of fishermen and whalers lost at sea, of boats that sailed away never to return again.

"After the large island sank," her grandmother said, "people eventually came back to the islands, and brought death with them."

Although there was nothing to suggest Sebastião was dead, Julia was increasingly apprehensive. Thus, she conjured situations to explain Sebastião's disappearance. It wasn't unthinkable that he had met an irresistible woman and had gone off with her to Europe or South America. Caught up in the whirlwind of a new romance, Sebastião would hardly have time for such mundane matters as notifying friends and family. But then why would he have written the postcard, and why hadn't he mailed it? He might have seduced a woman who was married to a jealous, perhaps violent husband, someone wealthy and influential, with powerful, if questionable, friends. Then again, he could have gotten involved in some clandestine political operation, or smuggled aboard a ship that had sailed into Horta and mysteriously slipped away under the cloak of darkness. Ridiculous, in this day and age, but still. . . ?

Sebastião had a penchant for recklessness. People still brought up his ill-fated attempt, some five years earlier, to re-create the voyage a distant ancestor had made from the island of Terceira to São Miguel, around the turn of the century, in a boat constructed entirely of newspapers. Sebastião's boat sailed only a few kilometers before it sank. Pulled out of the water by friends who had followed in a fishing boat, her father was undaunted by the failure. His response was simply to comment: "They don't make newspapers like they used to."

The crowd had accompanied Sebastião to the nearest tavern for drinks, as if he were a modern Ulysses returning from a long journey filled with marvelous adventures. They didn't care that he hadn't succeeded—it was one more example of the islanders' intrepidness.

Julia gazed at the buildings—mostly basalt gray and whitewash, with terra cotta tiled roofs—squeezed together as if huddling for warmth or protection along the steep cobblestone streets. The buildings blended and melded as she walked past, becoming a line, like a maze. She kept thinking: didn't I already pass here, the same houses, the same faces? Could Sebastião be hidden behind any of these doors, these windows?

"The heart is a labyrinth; there are dark passages we avoid, exploring only in fragments, in dreams. Passages inscribed with messages, containing age-old secrets preserved from the remote past, wherein our ancestors left their mark. A hall of mirrors that reflects a thousand different pasts, that make up who and what we are: a familiar smile, a favorite view that tugs at our memory, a scent or taste one remembers without knowing from where or when, a name etched in memory. Why do we feel we belong in one place and not another? Why do we take a sudden liking to someone or something and despise another? Why do we fall madly in love with this person as opposed to any one of thousands of others? Perhaps ten or a hundred generations ago one of our ancestors loved one of theirs." They were her father's words, found scrawled on a slip of paper stuck in the book of Pessoa's poetry—again, haunting her every step.

Along the shore, past spires of black lava that rose in strange twisted shapes, Julia listened attentively to the incessant yet incomprehensible language of the waves as they crashed noisily, reminded of Sebastião's old claim that not only was the ocean made salty with the tears of the Portuguese, but that the blood of the islanders was half seawater.

"Some of the old people of Pico," he'd once told her, "still put a touch of seawater in their beloved Pico wine, which explains why so many people from the island can't bear to leave the sea behind."

What secrets were buried beneath all the ash and lava, the remains of countless eruptions over the centuries? There was certainly no sign that any great ancient civilizations had been here. No towers or minarets, no colossal structures that one would expect when envisioning the grandeur of Atlantis.

"All sin begins with forgetfulness." Her grandmother's voice blended with the wind and the waves. "Forgetting what was and what might be. The terrible sin of closing one's eyes to one's dreams, to know what could be, and never lift a finger to try, that is our greatest sin!"

Ah, but what if one's dreams were at odds, or somehow contradicted those of the rest of the world, what then, avó? Her grandmother didn't answer. Julia had to admit her own dreams had stagnated. Her hopes of writing music had led nowhere. Only the tiniest voice deep within her still whispered: *I have something inside me, something of beauty and passion that longs for attainment.* But how long could she believe in such a faint calling, that might only be a dream without hope, like so many people had felt, but which had never materialized? Perhaps her mother was right, maybe she was wasting her time and talent.

Something else her father had written came to mind: "In a place of such improbabilities and remote possibilities, who can say what lies hidden beneath the mid-Atlantic, lost in that vast sea of secrets? Not merely dreams, but hints of where we have come from, and possibly where we are going."

Yes, she thought, what lies buried here, beneath this fertile soil? Sweep away the sea, and what would lie in eternal repose but a graveyard of dreams lost and forgotten over the ages. Had Sebastião been trying to realize some lost dream, or unravel a mystery? Perhaps a swan song: one final unforgettable act, one last dangerous feat, like Ambrose Bierce going off to disappear in Mexico. But Sebastião was only fifty-seven and healthy, hardly the age when one considers taking a last bow.

Julia saw so much to remind her of the past: quaint buildings, pink and blue hydrangeas, narrow streets and iron balconies on upstairs windows where, Isabel would tell her, young women would be wooed by men who spoke to them from below, who whispered poetry or sang songs, while across the street their friends accompanied them with a Portuguese guitar and an accordion, or who tossed up a flower to be caught by their love. Julia breathed in the past with the scent of the islands, the lava and the land, fragrant roses in bloom, and the sea.

Down the narrow roads on the outskirts of Horta there were fewer buildings and more fields. Julia passed several people who stopped and stared at her. She greeted the older ones, "*Bom dia*," and they too responded, "Good day," before moving on; an American and an islander passing one another with a salutary greeting, a nod, a wave. The New World paying homage to the Old.

Back in Horta's busier, more crowded streets, Julia stopped first at a café, then a market, where she showed her father's picture to strangers—waiters, shopkeepers, taxi drivers—inquiring whether any had seen Sebastião, and if so when.

"No, I don't know him," some said with a shrug. "I don't remember seeing him." But a few of the older islanders exclaimed excitedly, "Ah, yes, yes, Senhor Sebastião do Canto e Castro, the writer!" Two or three with a wink referred to Sebastião as *o feiticeiro*—the wizard, as if a man who disappeared without a trace must be capable of anything.

A boisterous crowd of men was gathered in the plaza in front of City Hall. They spoke excitedly, shouting questions, each trying to get a look at something one of them held in their midst. Julia approached and tapped an elderly gentleman on the shoulder, "Excuse me, senhor. What's happened?"

"Uma ilha nova!" the man shouted. "A new island."

Julia listened as the report was read aloud. The rumors were true. All the seismic activity actually was the result of a new island rising from the ocean floor. They waved the newspaper, pointing out the article it contained, a pronouncement made by a group of scientists visiting the islands.

"A tenth island?" Julia said, bewildered, as the image of her grandmother's face, nodding her I-told-you-sos, rose before her.

CHAPTER 4

No one could agree on what a dead man was doing halfway up a seven
thousand-seven-hundred-and-eleven-foot mountain. Moreover, they asked one another, what is a drowned man doing so far from the water?

Already the islands were crawling with an unheard of number of strangers. Not tourists per se, but those attracted by the publicity surrounding the
new island. Scientists from Europe, Canada, and the United States arrived
to monitor the seismic activity, and conduct studies on Pico and several of
the other islands. There were photographers and journalists, even a number of paranormalists who had caught wind of reports of the drowned man,
the ghost ship and the luminescent woman. Each attempted to discern
what these inexplicable omens might portend for a troubled humanity.

Specialists were consulted to give their opinion about the drowned
man, since the ghost ship and the luminous woman were much more
difficult to track, but no new light was shed as a result. Yes, the man
had obviously drowned—the body gave every indication of having been
submerged for a considerable length of time—yet there was nothing to
indicate that he had been moved or transported in any way.

All that had been accomplished thus far were protracted and heated
arguments among the various factions: doctors, scientists and police
officials, each defending his own position and claiming the others were
bungling incompetents.

"We know a dead man didn't crawl up that mountain himself," Senhor Andrade, a gangly, easily excitable government official from Lisbon
announced, pounding his fist on the tabletop.

"No, and he certainly didn't fly up there either," said Dr. Falcão, from
the hospital on the island of Terceira, just as emphatically.

"So then, what are you suggesting?" added Vítor Coelho, a specially appointed governmental investigator. "That he climbed up, lay down, opened his mouth and drowned on tears, perspiration and a surfeit of dew?"

Such terrible gaps in our understanding, our knowledge—like a persistent bothersome itch—do not easily go away but need to be filled by an answer, or solution, a rationalization, anything, if for no other reason than peace of mind, to allow those involved to get some sleep at night. And Vítor Coelho was determined to sleep that night. All these plaguing questions without answers, he was sure, were building to an ulcer, if not something worse.

"We need to put something in this report, whether a homicide, an accident, or suicide," Senhor Andrade said.

"Yes, something," Dr. Falcão said, hopefully.

"Anything," added Neves, a policeman from Madalena, Pico, who had first seen the body of the dead man.

"We know dead men don't climb mountains, and men don't drown where there is no water," suggested Professor Ribeiro, the learned scientist from Brazil.

"An enigma, this much is certain," Senhor Andrade said.

"Perhaps, an act of God?" Neves said, with a fatalistic shrug.

There were intruders everywhere, outsiders trying to prescribe sense, order and reason to the facts they were handed, like cards dealt by an unseen dealer, of whom it might be asked, "Is he grinning, amused at our expense, laughing through his teeth at our predicament? Does he know our fate?"

These men and women were from places far removed from the islands. "What am I doing here?" many of the scientists, photographers and journalists asked themselves after several days or weeks. "Best to get it over with and return home. What do miracles or the supernatural have to do with me?" They were sent to these islands, which after all were part of the same world they inhabited, whether Lisbon or London, New York, Washington, Rio or Madrid. It didn't matter what part of the globe they were from, nature was consistent, there was no dodging or escaping the laws of physics. If Senhor *João-Ninguém,* or John Nobody is dead, he must have at some time been alive, just as if Senhor *João-Ninguém* is alive he will surely die, as do we all in our own good time, as God alone mandates.

"O homem põe, Deus dispõe"—"Man proposes, God disposes," one of the specialists said laconically, amid the tumult. "What do I care about

sirens, ghost ships, drowned men on dry land, isn't it enough that an island is rising from the depths of the ocean?"

And to prove that the laws of nature do apply everywhere, who would find it odd or surprising if among the crowds of professionals and the curious, an investigator should find himself or herself in the arms and in the bed of a fellow journalist, or a scientist, or even a spectator, who happened by chance to be in the right place at the right time? A woman from Lisbon who happened to be here on vacation; a man—some kind of specialist—flown in from Brazil. Chance meetings, or incidental scribblings in the margins of the Book of Destiny?

"We may never meet again," she says.

"Perhaps we'll sink with the island," he says. "Who knows what tomorrow will bring? Is it due to fate that we find ourselves here, now, two souls swept along in all the vast world?" And with that they cast aside inhibition and good sense, and lose themselves in each other's arms, for a few hours of mad lovemaking.

All the thousand-and-one natural impediments to two people finding one another, let alone finding love at one and the same moment; and yet people still insist upon seeing signs that miracles do occur, demanding all manner of conjuring tricks as proof.

· · ·

As Ilhas Afortunadas

Que voz vem no som das ondas
Que não é a voz do mar?
É a voz de alguém que nos fala,
Mas que, se escutamos, cala,
Por ter havido escutar.

E só se, meio dormindo,
Sem saber de ouvir ouvimos,
Que ela nos diz a esperança
A que, como uma criança
Dormente, a dormir sorrimos.

São ilhas afortunadas,
São terras sem ter lugar,
Onde o Rei mora esperando.
Mas, se vamos despertando,
Cala a voz, e há só o mar.

The Fortunate Islands

What voice comes in the sound of the waves
Which isn't the voice of the sea?
It is the voice of someone who speaks to us,
But which, if we listen, is silent,
For having been listened to.

And only if, half-sleeping,
We hear without knowing we hear,
Does it tell us the hope
At which, like a sleeping child,
We smile as we sleep.

They are fortunate islands,
Unmappable lands,
Where the king dwells, waiting.
But if we start to awake
The voice is silent, and there is only the sea.[1]

—Fernando Pessoa

· · ·

Julia arrived at Peter's Café at eight-thirty the next morning. Returning to the *residencial* the night before she had found a note slipped
beneath her door. José Manuel, an old friend of the family whom she
had telephoned earlier in the day, had written: "Dear Julia, I'm so glad
you are here. I must speak to you about your father. I'll be at Peter's
Café at nine o'clock tomorrow morning. Please meet me there." That

he wished to speak to her about Sebastião, she hoped, was an auspicious sign. Perhaps the fog was beginning to clear, and José Manuel would provide her the first promising lead as to Sebastião's whereabouts.

Although the café was crowded, Julia was the only woman. It was somewhat disconcerting when nearly all eyes turned toward her and followed her as she approached the counter. There were groups of men, a few pairs, and the odd solitary figure seated alone, drinking in silence. Several leered at her, while one man, whose gaze she avoided, stared with unconcealed hostility.

"A nice girl like you shouldn't go alone to a place like that," Maria Josefa, or her grandmother, Isabel, would say. But Julia had spent time in Peter's and other cafés when she was here with Sebastião. She didn't see any reason to stay away simply because she was an adult. Besides, José Manuel had asked her to meet him here. Some found it easier to accept the status quo, to go where they were expected to go and avoid the places they were expected to avoid. Julia had wasted an inordinate amount of breath over the years trying to explain, mostly to family members, that she didn't consciously seek to challenge the way things were because of some perverse joy in doing so—it was simply the way she was made, a manifestation of who she was; not that others were capable of appreciating such fine distinctions. It irritated her no end how easily people justified doing what was expected of them because of tradition. "Well, then," she would ask, "why don't we all just happily stay stuck in the Middle Ages?"

After ordering a cappuccino, Julia selected a table as far from the other customers as possible. She set down the Fernando Pessoa book she had taken from Sebastião's room, and stepped back up to the bar to pay.

After returning to the table with her drink, Julia read the poem, "The Fortunate Islands" for the third time. Her thoughts shifted from the book of poems to the un-mailed postcard, the letter from Mateus, and the strange story of the Sorcerer and the Ghost Ship. If Sebastião intentionally left these things for her to find, they must hold some significance, perhaps regarding his disappearance. Each was vaguely troubling or curious, but didn't really seem to add up to anything, just shadows, and questions. So little to go on.

She glanced at the door and the windows, aware of an odd sensation, a shift, something out of place or out of phase—as if she had left California and the United States far behind, but in much more than mere distance, as if more than ocean and miles separated the islands from the United States, and Julia from her life back home. "Your past is calling," she could hear Sebastião say. "The islands have pulled you here"—as if they were a particular focal or end point, and fate had arranged for her to be inescapably led to this precise place at this precise time. The thought was absurd, but in the back of her mind she heard Sebastião's deepest, best vocal imitation of Orson Welles or Lamont Cranston: "Who knows what subtle forces, what intricacies and undiscovered machinations occur in the invisible universe? Isn't it fate, after all, that determines who we are, and that everything that occurs does so out of a prescribed order, the basic premise of which is that you cannot escape yourself?"

The Shadow knows.

Sebastião had no patience for astrology, or psychics, the occult. His belief in magic had to do with the magic of words and music, art, the mysteries of love, beauty, the sensual as well as the sexual, the creative spark in all its forms, as well as the magic of place.

"We are each of us an island," he had written in *A Ilha Cantante— The Singing Island,* "surrounded by a sea which masks the whole of who we really are, what lies hidden below the surface. The islands are a place of innumerable impossibilities, just waiting to happen."

She thought about her grandfather, so far away in Rio. It had been thirty years since Mateus had seen the islands. What wouldn't he give to be back here, in Horta?

There was something slightly reassuring about making the rounds of the cafés that Mateus and Sebastião had once frequented: Peter's Café, Café Internacional, Café do Mar—places where Mateus had sat with his cronies and read the papers, where he wrote poetry and articles on this writer or that musician or intellectual, and discussed the latest news with his friends. Now and then Mateus would proffer criticisms of one or two kings of the Bragança line—those who had ruled after taking the throne back from Spain in 1640, until the assassination of King Carlos in 1910—insinuating that a Castro, if not a Canto e Castro, would have done better by far. Canto e Castro was a joining together of one branch of the Castro family with a branch of the Canto family, and while pointing out that the Braganças did have Castro blood in their veins, Mateus would have been happier if someone closer to the family had been king.

"It's a shame that Dom João, the Duke of Bragança, became King João IV," Mateus would say. "A hesitant, overly-cautious man, ineffectual when it came to winning Portugal's independence back from King Philip IV of Spain. Dom João do Canto e Castro, or Dom Pedro do Canto e Castro, Knights of the Order of Christ, men responsible for the Azorean fleet, on the other hand, would have repeated the glory of Aljubarrota!" This decisive battle, celebrated in poetry and song, in which the Portuguese defeated the much larger Castilian force, was ever-present in the minds and hearts of the Portuguese people, notwithstanding the fact that the battle had been fought in 1385. Spaniards still sought excuses for their defeat, and the Portuguese compared every subsequent victory, whether in battle or in sports, with that greatest of triumphs.

Mateus would shake his head, wipe his glasses, and exclaim, "The world, everything has changed. So much swept away. And yet is it any wonder, when the Braganças never had a right to the throne in the first place? The duke must have felt the same guilt which his great great-grandfather, João de Avis felt, for taking a crown that didn't belong to him. Dom João de Avis assumed a throne that rightfully belonged to his half-brother, Dom João, the son of Inês de Castro. The sad fact is that more than one Castro has been robbed of a throne."

The volume of noise rose and fell as people shuffled in and out of the café.

"I tell you, I saw her," a deep bass voice rumbled like thunder. It was Vasco Machado, who was known simply as *O Barbudo*—The Bearded One. Julia was now aware of a number of men who had seated themselves at a table near hers.

"Saw who?" Vasco's friend, Guilherme Reis said, bleary-eyed with drink.

"That woman," Vasco said. "Will you listen?"

"Her?" several of the men shouted in unison.

"The very one," Vasco said, in a conspiratorial whisper, dreamy-eyed, smiling like a man who has chanced to glimpse a sight normally reserved for madmen, saints or prophets.

"How do you know it was her?" said Miguel Torres, who had spent a great deal of time at sea, and whose piercing eyes, nearly black in color and intensity, peered through the thinnest of slits, which made it impossible for anyone else to know where they gazed.

"Who else could it be?" Vasco continued, "I tell you, a vision floating across the shore in the dead of night and wearing absolutely—"

"Nothing?" the others stammered.

Vasco nodded. "Clothed in a light more brilliant than the full moon."

"Was she as beautiful as they say?" Guilherme asked.

"The woman of every man's dreams," Vasco said with a sigh. *"Que curvas incríveis!*—Such incredible curves!"

These were men who worked on the docks and boats, in the fields, and as mechanics. They worked hard and had little to show for it. Their clothes, for the most part, were coarse, worn and soiled, their skin just as weathered, and yet they spoke and listened to Vasco's story of this woman the way a group of children might listen to tales of fairies and elves.

"Why didn't you go after her, then, and pluck this jewel of the sea?" said Eduardo Neves, commonly known as Dom Ruivo because of his regal bearing and red hair.

"She rose in the air like a cloud," Vasco said, gazing upward, his eyes wide with wonder, as if he still saw the woman. "Before I knew it she was out beyond the waves, gone." He snapped his fingers and finished his drink in one gulp. He handed the empty glass to the bartender who stood nearby taking in every word. The bartender was called Peter, like his father who owned the bar and his father's father before him—the bar and the name considered one and the same, handed down from one generation to the next, assuring that come what may some things were bound to remain unchanged. Sailors heard about Peter's Café by word-of-mouth. "If you stop off at Faial, go to Peter's Café," sailors in ports from New York to Sidney would tell one another. "Give Peter my regards." Sailing from one coast to another, or voyaging round the world, they dropped by, eager to have a drink and deliver greetings from every corner of the globe. "Where's Peter?" they shouted, eager to meet the man who had served drinks to countless mariners, never mind that neither the café nor the father nor son nor even grandfather was named Peter, or Pedro—somehow the name had stuck.

"Did she have wings?" Guilherme asked, scratching his head.

"No, not wings, except perhaps on her feet."

"Making her way to that devil of a ghost ship they've seen out there, I'm willing to bet," Miguel Torres said. The others nodded and grunted in agreement.

"I heard that anyone who sees her vanishes in a dazzling flash, becoming one with the very light she radiates," Eduardo said. "Her luminescence, they say, is the result of all the souls she has lured to madness."

There was a slight pause as each of the men weighed Eduardo's words.

"I tell you, if you had seen the woman I saw, you wouldn't have cared," Vasco strugged. "You would have risked anything."

"I'd risk nothing for any woman," Miguel Torres said.

"That's easy for you to say," Vasco said. "You didn't see her."

"I heard that if you got close enough to lay a hand on her," Guilherme said, his voice thick with alcohol, "that she carried you off never to be seen or heard from again, dragged you to the cold depths of the sea where she and others like her would gnaw your bones!"

A protracted silence followed. Guilherme had dared utter the unspeakable. With his few words fear was now a palpable presence in the room. The scent of the sea was everywhere; the muffled whisper of the waves could almost be heard inside the café. The sea was reflected in the pictures on the walls, the fittings from boats, the samples of scrimshaw on display, even the wood of the ceiling and walls resembled planks and beams salvaged from some ancient galleon. Too many men over the centuries had been lost to the ocean: men pulled from their whale boats, fishermen swept from their vessels or the shore; entire ships and their crews swallowed up by an unpredictable and often angry sea; women on occasion vanished too from the top of a cliff or a rock, "official accidents," which belied the winks and nods masking an unspoken explanation.

During the interminable regime of the dictator, Salazar, it was forbidden to report suicides, not merely because the taking of one's own life was such a terrible crime against God's handiwork, but because it was feared such an idea might become contagious. Unhappiness and discontent could easily spread and become an epidemic, and such an epidemic would prove disastrous, not only to the government, but to the country at large.

A rash of suicides would prove disturbing to Salazar, reflecting poorly on the stern father figure, the benevolent leader. If the citizens began killing themselves off, how would all the other nations of the world look upon Portugal, and Salazar, in particular? Therefore, under his regime, nearly fifty years of an iron-fisted stranglehold ending only with his death in 1970, suicides were attributed to the unfortunate outcome of accidents, due to unforeseen circumstances, or the inevitable act of God. Were his concern genuine it would have been understandable enough, though at the same time, what with the number of people he exiled or sent to Angola and São Tomé, or condemned to torture or die in prison, he was like the jealous lover who, instead of allowing his woman to leave, kills her so no other man can have what he can't possess.

When Isabel and Mateus had visited the islands in the 1950s, they were warned against saying anything to anybody. "You never know who's an informer, who will turn you in," a friend told them. "You can't trust anyone." Salazar had assumed office as a reformer, but over the years became more entrenched in power, ruthless, and determined to prevent dissent. Julia's grandparents were stunned to see that Salazar had done nothing he had promised: no new hospitals, no new schools. Nothing had been done to improve the lives of the people. They went back to the United States and published scathing reports that the government had lied. Because of this they were prevented from returning to the islands until after Salazar finally died.

Julia stifled a laugh, reminded of the two pigs her grandparents had owned when they lived on Faial, before moving to the United States, one named Hitler and the other Mussolini. That was what they thought of Fascists.

A land where there were no suicides, Julia thought. Accidents, her grandmother always insisted, never took place here. A place of tranquil timelessness.

Sounds. A chair scraped the floor. A cough. Voices. Peter's Café, again, the present, reality. Sirens, too, were to be feared and respected. After all, many an Azorean spent eternity on the ocean floor. And if some were lured to their deaths by the songs of sirens, well, then, who would risk taking such things lightly?

"Where did you hear that?" Miguel Torres said, finally dispelling the heavy silence.

"Maybe that's why not one man has come forth claiming to have bedded this siren of the night," Eduardo said. There was some laughter, but it was strained, forced.

"And maybe that is where those who are missing can be found," Vasco said slowly, knowingly.

The voices in the bar were a steady hum: the sound of insects, the sighing of the wind, the steady rise and falling breath of the ocean; voices too low and muffled for Julia to more than half-hear, especially since she was trying to ignore them. But her senses sharpened on hearing Vasco's last statement. Julia glanced over and saw that the men were hunched around their table, sniggering and whispering, looking in her direction. It didn't take much imagination to guess who they were talking about now. It wouldn't have taken long for word to spread of who she was and why she was here. *"Caramba!"* she said in disgust, loud enough for the others to hear. "Sirens! Ghost ships! *Que crianças!*—What children! Grown men talking of such things, acting like they've just discovered some dirty little secret about a neighbor and sitting here gossiping all day."

She turned away and her eyes met those of a young man seated at another table. He wrote in a small, black notebook; a stack of books and papers lay on the table. He smiled, apparently entertained by her outburst.

The group discussing the siren quieted down, having been properly reprimanded by Julia; like recalcitrant schoolchildren taken to task by an angry teacher, they looked contrite and humbled.

How much of Sebastião's reputation is his own fault, she wondered. What might he have said or done that these people had seen and heard? What personal conflict might he have had with these or other men?

The day before she had phoned the police again, but once again had been put off. "Call tomorrow," the man said. "The inspector who's been assigned the case will be here then."

She'd suggested the possibility that perhaps Sebastião had simply fallen off a cliff or was swept from the rocks by an unexpected wave, a victim of the sea.

"I suppose it's possible," the policeman had said, and Julia could almost detect the noncommittal shrug the suggestion had received, as if to say what would the *americano* have been doing out on the rocks, what would the sea want with him? Not to mention the fact that no body had been recovered.

Still, after she pressed the policeman, he admitted there were instances when a body failed to be retrieved. "A remote possibility," the policeman said, his voice fading into silence as if hoping to dispel the unwanted thought.

Julia imagined Sebastião, like Jonah, carried away in the belly of a whale. At least she knew he would keep busy taking frantic notes if that were the case. It was far better to imagine Sebastião in situations that were ludicrous, even impossible, rather than contemplate the alternative.

She'd read her father's story, *"O Homem Retalhado"*—"The Patchwork Man," in an issue of the literary journal, *O Sul,* found among the poems and papers in Sebastião's room. In the story, the protagonist, a man prone to numerous disasters and mishaps, disappears. After losing an eye here, a leg there, now in failing health, he spends his time in a graveyard, half in the living world, half in the world of the dead. There he falls in love with one of the inhabitants of the graveyard, the ghost of a young singer who died the previous century, and together they seek an escape to a new island rising from the depths of the sea, an enchanted island where they could live whole again, in a world they could both share.

It was difficult to shake the feeling that this character, was based on Sebastião, and if so, perhaps the woman too was someone real. And what about the island? Could Sebastião have known it was going to rise from the sea, and written a story that was published some six to eight months before his disappearance? Had it been purely a product of his imagination and only a coincidence that now an island was rising up, a remarkable instance of synchronicity?

Julia checked her watch, hoping José Manuel arrived on time. She pushed her cup aside and rose from the table. Stepping over to the bar, she ordered another cappuccino. The air in the café seemed thicker, as if it had become liquid. Returning to her table she passed by the man writing in the notebook. He looked up and nodded, again smiling. She resisted the urge to respond, inclining her head without smiling in return, and sat down again at her own table. The last thing I need is to encourage anyone, she thought. The slightest interest could easily be misconstrued. He appeared to be close to her age. She wondered if he were a teacher or a writer. Sebastião had always teased Julia for her habit of observing people. My little eavesdropper, he would call her.

Writers, Sebastião said, hide the truth among lies and half-truths, and often one doesn't really know where the lies end and the truth begins. Her father was expected to live an eccentric life, to cause scenes, stir up trouble, everything in excess—drink and women in particular—to constantly live up to his reputation. It was assumed that his fiction mirrored his life, was in fact an extension of it, and in that world there was little room for half-measures or the mundane. Sebastião often commented that people needed their geniuses to suffer terrible defeats, whether in love, or the battlefield, or fortune—all three if possible—as a countermeasure to their artistic gifts. "If writers like Camões and Cervantes hadn't been injured," he'd said, "if neither had suffered in love or in the arena of popularity, they wouldn't have been quite so fervently revered. Genius isn't enough. People don't want their artists happy and contented. Men and women need to know that their idols and heroes suffer misfortunes, and are flawed. To live in poverty, die young, suffer the anguish of unrequited love, such are the laurels due the poets."

Julia thought about her dreams, which for the last few nights had been strange and intensely vivid, all the more unusual because she normally didn't remember her dreams, or they were typically of a trivial, unimaginative sort. Lately, however, she'd been haunted by visions of people running, pursued by faceless tormentors, hazy scenes of sacred rites and ceremonies; a shadowy figure kept under house arrest in a remote part of the country—dreams oppressive in their sense of secrecy and impending doom.

In the previous night's dream her grandmother whispered something urgent, something secret, and Julia had begged her, "What does all of this mean, grandmother? What does it mean? Please tell me."

She had replied, "The denial of truth, the suppression of history. Lies, all lies!"

Julia was jarred out of her thoughts by a voice, "Hey, daydreamer, look who's here!" José Manuel waved his hand in front of Julia's eyes. His bright smile instantly chased away her bleak thoughts.

Julia rose quickly, nearly upsetting the small table. "José," she said. "It's so good to see you." He kissed both sides of her face and embraced her. But before she could ask why he'd wanted to meet her several men in the bar called out, "Zé!" José Manuel shook hands with some and waved to others. He turned for a moment to the table of the man with the notebook, and then motioned to Julia. "I've kept this young lady waiting long enough." This time Julia returned the young man's smile, since he was apparently a friend of José Manuel.

José Manuel sat down at Julia's table. He didn't say anything about who the young man was, but right now her mind was occupied solely with thoughts of José Manuel. He was one person who hadn't changed one iota. He looked exactly the same as she remembered, as if he hadn't aged a single day.

José was a minor celebrity round town, known by most of the locals, and quite notorious for his eccentricities. He had a habit of knowing things before they happened. It wasn't unusual for him to bring a baby gift to a woman before she knew she was pregnant, or tell someone they were going to be missed before they knew they were going away. He would sit down with a young man and explain how the young man's love for Maria de Fátima and her love for him was a blessed event deserving much rejoicing.

"Look," José would tell the man, "this is a cause for celebration, not gloominess and storm clouds. Go on, don't try to pretend. You can't fool me. Tell her."

The young man would be struck dumb. "The two of you will have a very happy life together," José would assure him. "With many beautiful children." The young man would leave in a daze before finally realizing that everything José had said was true. Why hadn't he realized before how he felt about the lovely Maria de Fátima, a girl in whose presence he had often found himself feeling nervous, or agitated, to be sure, to the point where he had avoided her like the plague? She left him unable to think, unable to speak. He could only stutter like a fool. Now it all seemed so obvious—of course, he loved her!

Around children in particular, José Manuel was a magician, a Pied Piper, who loved to play tricks on people, ringing the bells of the church at Praia do Almoxarife in the middle of the night and disappearing for days at a time, only to reappear with books, musical instruments, games, toys, or art supplies, things for the children which were, for anyone else, impossible to find on the islands. No one knew how he managed to acquire the things he did. Neither could anyone explain how someone who was unschooled managed to be conversant in three or four languages, and knowledgeable about so many far-flung corners and people of the world. He was full of mischief and, of course, the children universally adored him.

"I'm so glad you're here, José," Julia said. "It's been such a long time." She spoke in a rush, pleased to be in the company of someone as warm and effusive as José Manuel.

"It has been too long," José said. "And see, I'm ancient. But look at you, all grown up, and very talented, too, I hear." He moved his hands as though he were playing the piano.

She smiled. "Sebastião exaggerates and you haven't changed at all. You have more life in you than any three men. I'm the one who's different."

José was of undeterminable age. His hair had always been nearly white, but he was sprightly and agile, with a mischievous twinkle in his eye. It was impossible to feel sad or angry in his presence or think of him as being old. "You've heard from my father? What did you want to tell me?"

"I'll show you," José said. "This, you have to see this for yourself." He picked up the book that lay on the table. "You're reading Pessoa."

"Yes," Julia said. "It was in Sebastião's room. *As Ilhas Afortunadas.* He had it marked for some reason."

José nodded. "Some people," he said, "say these islands are the Fortunate Islands."

"I've heard Sebastião say as much."

"Come, then, let's go," José said, handing the book back to Julia.

She followed him out of the café. They hopped into a small truck and headed toward Praia do Almoxarife on the other side of the hill of Espalamaca. It was little more than a ten-minute drive from the center of Horta, especially since José drove fast and reckless. Like a young man, Julia thought. But it seemed a hundred or so miles removed.

José drove the truck up the steep hillside behind Praia do Almoxarife. The land belonged to José and his family, who made up a large portion of the town's inhabitants. Praia itself was little more than a restaurant, one café, a store, a church, a handful of homes, and a pretty stretch of beach.

José stopped at the farthest building up the hill.

Julia followed José. "Sebastião stayed here for some time," he said, opening the door to the building. "This is where he worked."

The sight that greeted Julia when she stepped inside made her head reel. Letters, notes, manuscripts, books, odd page lying upon page piled along the walls and in columns across the floor. Maps and parchments, sheaves of paper, journals, articles, were stacked everywhere. She struggled to breathe. Standing inside the small, dark and cramped room was like stepping through a doorway that took her back several hundred years in time.

"All this is Sebastião's?"

José nodded. "It was empty before he came."

It wasn't a room from the twentieth century, but more like a museum exhibit, a scene belonging to another time—the pages of a history that had long since been closed, hermetically sealed, refusing entry to the present. Julia had the eerie sensation of being swallowed by the past.

It was like uncovering a pristine archeological site, a room with everything intact, exactly as it had been used, where nothing had been disturbed. In its closeness it was like a scholarly monk's cell, where everything had been carefully preserved—not only the ancient artifacts she saw lying here and there, but the very air itself. Here Sebastião must have sat up late, night after night, poring over these books and writings, before he had disappeared.

There didn't appear to be any order to the piles of written materials; it was utter chaos—books without covers, portions of books, illustrations, sketches—all stacked haphazardly.

"Why did Sebastião need this room," Julia said, "when he already had the room at the *residencial.*"

José shrugged. "He liked to be alone. He wanted privacy." It did explain why the room at the *residencial* had been quite nearly empty, aside from Sebastião's clothes, when Julia had arrived.

"I told him to make use of what he needed," José said. "I thought he was using the building over there." José gestured to the other buildings on the property, closer to the main house. They were newer, larger, and in much better condition than the tiny two-room structure in which they stood. "I told him to come and go as he liked, to make himself at home, but he made me promise to tell no one, not a soul. He said he needed a place to store some things, where he wouldn't be disturbed. I'm often away in Pico and didn't realize that he had been staying here.

"He seems to have come and gone at night, and obviously spent many days here, though he was away a great deal, too, days or weeks at a time. I never asked what he needed the place for. What business was it of mine? I thought he was writing one of his books, so I left him alone.

"But since your grandmother wrote that you were on your way, and there was no word from Sebastião for so long, I had a look around. I peeked inside the other building, but it was undisturbed. I thought he had changed his mind. But then I decided to check here, although no one has used this building for many years. Perhaps that's why he liked it. It's at the end of the property, away from everything else. I unlocked the door and found the room just as you see it."

"What about the police?" Julia said. "Have you told them?"

José shook his head. "I've just discovered it, so I haven't told anyone. Besides, I don't think they would be very interested. They seem to have their own ideas about what happened to your father, though they won't talk. I thought it would be best to show it to you first."

"I'm glad you did," Julia said. "I'd certainly like to go through this before anyone else, if that's all right."

"Of course, that's why I brought you here."

"I appreciate it," Julia said.

"I have to warn you, there have been some, well, unpleasant rumors about Sebastião."

"I'm not surprised." She thought of the men she'd overheard at Peter's Café.

"Still, we don't know if any of what they say is true," José said.

The building was quite old, run down, and otherwise empty, Sebastião's room the only one in use. This corner of José's land had long been neglected and overgrown. No one had had any need to venture in quite some time among the hedges and vines that grew between the few tall pine trees and the stone walls.

There was a small, brass oil lamp by the bed—an old wooden cot with a thin shred of a mattress—and candles here and there, on the floor, on the table, by the single window. Beside the mattress lay an ornate dagger, perhaps Moorish, with a carved ivory handle. On a large table, which served as a desk, sat a human skull, amid more papers and books.

"Where could he have gotten that?" Julia said, pointing at the skull.

José shrugged and laughed. "Sebastião would return from Morocco, Portugal or Spain with collections of things he had found, in boxes, or wrapped up like treasures."

"I wonder where it's from, who it was?"

"Perhaps an ancient knight, one of your ancestors who fought in Africa," José said, picking up the skull. "Maybe your father found the head of another Sebastião," he said, with a wink, "our missing king."

"I wouldn't put anything past my father," Julia said, remembering the stories her father would tell her of the fanatical King Sebastião, who had disappeared on the sands of Morocco, while leading his army in battle against the Moors in 1578.

There were other strange, exotic implements, all extremely old: a sword, an armillary sphere, a quadrant, navigational charts, compasses; there were boots, rocks and pieces of metal; several large ancient keys on a metal ring, among a number of things Julia couldn't identify; three or four carved stone slabs, their features nearly worn smooth; and several large pieces of scrimshaw, finely worked, with a real artistic touch, upon which were etched the life-like faces of real whalers and fishermen, a young woman, her gaze fixed on some remote point on the sea.

There was nothing new, however, nothing modern in the entire room. No suitcase, or calendars, no diary, no wallet, no electric razor. Though long acquainted with Sebastião's affinity for the bizarre and his taste for the unusual, the room with its strange atmosphere and even stranger accouterments surprised Julia. Ten minutes or a hundred miles from Horta, this room was hundreds of years distance when measured by any means Julia would have used.

"You could drop Sebastião anywhere, in any century and he'd make himself at home," she said.

"Yes," José said. "Your father's a chameleon. I've got some things to take care of, so I'll leave you here."

"Thank you, José." José Manuel departed and Julia sat down on the cot. She picked up the dagger and turned it over in her hands. "Where could Sebastião have gone?" she said. The room remained silent and close, with merely the faintest whisper of time turning back a page or two, leaving her with a growing sense of apprehension.

CHAPTER 5

I seek a mirror that, held up to the distortions which are the present   *69*
and toward the as yet fantastical future, will reflect the veritable past,
to destroy that which blinds us, keeps us tethered at the end of time,
and exists for each generation from time immemorial, who look back,
see the past infinite, and believe time has no future.

—From the notebooks of Sebastião do Canto e Castro

. . .

Julia sat in Sebastião's room for several hours, poring over the numerous stacks of books: *The Knights Templars, The Order of Christ and the Discoveries, Inês de Castro and Dom Pedro, Queen After Death, The Life of Vasco da Gama, Chronicle of the Life of Dom João de Castro, The Secret History of Portugal, Lost Islands of the Atlantic.* She then began looking through the piles of notes and papers, stopping when she found several sheets of paper written in ink, in a script similar to the pages she had found in the *residencial:*

. . .

Portugal, 1362

The procession wound its way like an enormous serpent along the ancient Roman road beginning in Coimbra, that fair city nestled on the banks of the gentle Mondego, whose dark tranquil waters reflected the solemnity of the occasion.

The town's bells tolled incessantly for the woman whose butchered body rested on a bier drawn by white burros and covered in white roses, her favorite—perfect petals of luminous white, radiant and full of life, which would too soon fade and wither—as she was carried to her final resting place in Alcobaça, one hundred-and-two kilometers distance.

Nobles, clergymen, soldiers and townspeople filled the roadway. They wept grievously for the fallen princess, slain by order of Pedro's stern father, King Afonso—may God keep him in heaven!

Amid the sobs of men and women, and the sounds of the hooves of horses and burros, could be heard the drums, steady and constant, funereal in their stately beat.

King Pedro led the procession, riding in splendor for his lost love.

Through each village the church bells tolled the same mournful refrain. Past Arrifana, Venda Nova, Pombal, Leiria, the road littered with flowers and lined with rows of somber men holding torches—a dismally subdued lighting for such a radiant vanquished beauty.

Night and day they rode. Hour after agonizing hour, Pedro pushed them, intent on reaching Alcobaça, on finishing what he had begun, his mind absorbed with thoughts of Inês, slain like a common criminal.

The air grew heavy, and smelled of rain, as if the skies too would shed tears for Dona Inês de Castro.

The procession at last reached the town of Alcobaça, stopping at the monastery where, overcome by the strain of the ordeal, Pedro collapsed in exhaustion. Friends rushed to his side, and carried him inside where the friars revived him and tended to his needs.

Later that day, the monks carefully placed Inês, clothed in royal robes and a gold crown, to rest in the marble sarcophagus carved for her.

The finely-carved stone bore her likeness on its top, crowned by a sculpted canopy and tiny angels, the sides carved with scenes from the life of Christ. The tomb was borne on the backs of several marble dogs, each bearing the likeness of one of her murderers, and placed beside the matching tomb that Dom Pedro ordered the mason, Jerónimo Gonçalo, to make to await Pedro's own death, when he would be laid to rest beside Inês. The sides of Pedro's tomb depicted scenes of their brief life together, scenes showing the close friendship of Inês and Constanza, Pedro's wife, who had died, leaving him free to love Inês, and showing, too, how Pedro's father had been affectionate to the woman Pedro loved.

The words "Até ao Fim do Mundo"—"Until the End of the World," were carved into the stone.

When the trumpets of the Last Judgment sound, the two lovers shall rise and face one another again, at long last, to embrace in eternity.

A lifetime ago the two of them had been happy and carefree. No, never quite that, for Pedro's father had done his best to keep them apart.

Constanza, the woman Pedro's father had arranged for him to marry, arrived in Portugal, accompanied by her cousin and lady-in-waiting, Inês de Castro. As soon as Pedro saw the fair Inês, he began to live. He didn't love Constanza, daughter of the famous Don Manuel, of Castile, though he was indebted to her for bringing him Inês.

O Colo de Garça—The Heron's Neck, they called Inês, because of her fine, slender neck. It was mostly said in awe, though there were some who used the term contemptuously, jealous of her beauty and grace. She possessed bewitching eyes of emerald green, and flowing curls of golden hair. But more than that, her warm smile and her laughter could melt any but the most unfeeling beast's heart. She had wit and charm, and spirit in abundance. Spirit enough to stand up to powerful enemies, to a king, even, and to ignore the gossips and rumor mongers, the veiled threats.

When Constanza gave birth to her first son, Luís, she named Inês as the prince's godmother, natural enough since Inês was her cousin and friend. Some people claim she did this so that Inês and Pedro couldn't become lovers, since in the eyes of the Church the godmother to Pedro's son would make her a sister to Pedro. Unfortunately, soon after his birth, Luís died.

Hearing stories of Pedro's love for Inês—which neither one could disguise nor hide—King Afonso banished Inês to Castile. It was a miserable time. Messengers were frequently sent back and forth, carrying the impassioned letters Inês and Pedro wrote one another. When Constanza died giving birth to Fernando, Pedro immediately brought Inês back to live with him.

Now there was nothing to keep them apart. Inês and Pedro were free to love openly. Inês gave him four children. The first, Afonso, died soon after his birth, then João, Dinis, and finally their daughter, Beatriz. They enjoyed mad, joyous escapes to Serra d'El Rei, to Atouguia da Baleia, north to Vila Nova de Gaia and distant Bragança, and throughout everything, their passion, their love for one another never faltered or wavered.

When he brought her to live in the palace of Queen Isabel, Pedro's grandmother—who in the eyes of the people was already a saint—their enemies worked to turn the people against Inês, spreading cruel and malicious rumors: Had Inês murdered the infant prince, Luís, so that she could be with Pedro? Had she poisoned Constanza? Was she a witch?

They escaped into the serenity of the gardens there, what would later be called the Quinta das Lágrimas—The Garden of Tears.

Pedro was hounded and questioned constantly. "Do you plan to marry?" "Come back to court, see your father, talk to him. You will be king soon enough. Would you rule your kingdom without a queen?"

Pedro would demur, finding reasons why this one or that wasn't suitable. He wasn't ready to remarry. It was too soon after the death of Constanza. He knew that many of the nobles disliked Inês's brothers, Álvaro and Fernando, who were both good friends of his. He was informed of the whispers heard round the court, that the Castros had ambitions, that Inês was a sorceress who had put a spell on him.

Pedro laughed. "A spell, yes," he said. "But not evil or self-serving, like those whose petty jealousy and enmity fill the court with their plotting and intrigues."

How could he tell his father or his father's officers the truth—that Dom Gil Cabral, the Bishop of Guarda, had secretly married Pedro and Inês in Bragança, that he couldn't take another wife because he already had one?

At the time, Pedro knew such action would be far more dangerous. He, too, had his confidantes. He was aware of King Afonso's mistrust of the Castros. Inês's father had been a close friend of Afonso Sanches, the Portuguese king's half-brother, whom he banished, persecuted, and tried to kill as he had his other brother, João Afonso. Inês had considered Afonso Sanches's wife Teresa a second mother, since her own mother had died when she was young.

King Afonso was angry, too, that the Castros had revolted against Pedro's nephew, King Pedro of Castile, who was feared and despised for the murder of his father's lover, Leonor Gusman, Pedro's half-brother, Fradique, and the slaughter of a number of noblemen.

King Pedro of Castile had turned the Castro family against him. After meeting Inês de Castro's sister, Joana, he proclaimed his love, praising her unique charms and beauty, second only to Inês. Joana, however, was mistrustful of the capricious and volatile king, and refused to surrender to his amorous whims, unless he proved himself by first marrying her. The Castilian king pressured the clergy to annul his previous marriage, and then *quickly wed Joana de Castro. The next morning, having satisfied his desires, he abandoned Joana, leaving her with her wounded pride, and the castle of Dueñas, his wedding gift to her, none of which prevented her from giving birth nine months later to a son, whom she named Don Juan.*

King' Afonso's ministers claimed that Inês's brothers, who spent much of their time in Portugal in and around the court, exerted tremendous influence upon both Inês and Pedro, and that her family was involved in dangerous intrigues, plotting for their own interests and gains.

Pedro saw his chance to proclaim himself the rightful king of Castile. Once his nephew, the younger Pedro, was out of the way, he would rule with Inês at his side. And, of course, her brothers, Álvaro and Fernando, had offered their support.

It was better to lie, or feign indifference, to wait and see. How could he have known his father's spies would uncover so much of their plans? How could he have known the severe measures that his father would take? How could he have know that someone would betray him?

Even now, so long after her death, he sometimes saw Inês, heard the music of her voice, her crystal laughter. He would still reach out in the night for her body, as he had done so often before, as if she were still there beside him, until the horrible truth descended like a black cloud, engulfing him in its gloom. He would drown out the sound of those memories by going off with friends, drinking and dancing to music.

The King's closest advisors, Diogo Lopes Pacheco, Pedro Coelho, and Chief Justice Álvaro Gonçalves, plotted and planned Inês's destruction. The prince and his lover, they said to the king, are flaunting the memory of your revered mother, the holy Queen Isabel, buried in the very church of the castle where Pedro now keeps this brazen woman, who has already given birth to four children; four bastards to threaten the security and stability of Portugal, as your father did with his many bastards.

They whispered their poisonous insinuations in the ears of the king.

"Consider Fernando," they entreated the king, "the legitimate son of Dom Pedro and Constanza, who might be robbed of the throne by one of the children of Inês de Castro. Perhaps she or her brothers would plot to kill young Fernando? The country itself might end up, as a result, in the hands of Castile. Is it worth risking the peace you have fought for with Castile, or risk Portugal being swallowed by Castile?"

Waiting until Pedro had gone to Montemor-o-Novo to hunt, on Janu-

ary 7th, 1355, the king and his advisors left Montemor-o-Velho and rode to Coimbra to murder Inês.

Inês, instead of pleading and begging the king to spare her life, was defiant. "Will you leave these children bereft of a mother," she said. "Look at them. João, Dinis and Beatriz. My children, yes, but they are Pedro's children, and your grandchildren.

People say that moved by her pleas, the king finally turned and rode away, but almost instantly his men urged him to dispose of her now, once and for all. We are told that King Afonso the Brave, victorious warrior of the Battle of Salado, a man who had beheaded his own brother, Dom João Afonso, rode off leaving his counselors to return and murder Inês.

But in truth King Afonso's spies had informed him that Inês and Pedro had secretly married. He put the question to Inês, and when she did not deny the charge, he had his men quickly dispatch his daughter-in-law.

Pedro quickly learned of Inês's assassination. He and his troops stormed the countryside, destroying everything that lay in their path. They razed the lands and villages that belonged to the king's advisors, and Pedro sent messengers to Inês's brothers, who invaded from Galícia. Together they fought against King Afonso, and laid siege to the city of Porto.

Peace was established several months later, when Pedro's mother, Queen Beatriz, finally intervened, like his grandmother, Saint Isabel, who had made peace when Afonso had fought against his father, King Dinis and Afonso's half-brothers. As part of the reconciliations, Pedro was made chief of the administration of justice. In return, Pedro agreed not to persecute the men who had murdered Inês.

Instead he waited patiently, quietly planning his retribution.

I will punish those responsible, Pedro vowed to her brothers, to Inês, and to himself. His father had punished him by killing Inês, because they had dared to dream of what was possible: she, the descendant of Castilian and Portuguese kings, and Pedro would rule a combined Portugal and Castile.

If only he had not left her alone. If only he had stopped them somehow, anticipated their actions, and their cruelty. If only. If only his father had not learned of their secret marriage and the plans they had made.

When King Afonso died, Pedro became king, and immediately asked his nephew in Castile to hand over those men responsible for her murder. The Castilian king had something Pedro wanted and Pedro had something his nephew wanted: a number of Castilians who had fled the country under sentence of death for plotting against their king. Pedro had the men seized and sent to his nephew, a necessary evil, for Pedro would let nothing stand in the way of his vengeance. In turn, the Castilian king had Álvaro Gonçalves and Pedro Coelho tied onto an ox cart and delivered to Pedro at Santarém. Diogo Lopes Pacheco had escaped in the guise of a beggar.

The two men were tortured with a blacksmith's tong heated to a fiery white. Pedro asked them who else had been responsible for Inês's murder, the names of those who had betrayed him. As Pedro calmly ate his dinner, the screams of the two men filled the night. Still, the men refused to talk. One of the men cursed Pedro, saying he was to blame. When it was clear he would learn nothing from them, Pedro had one prisoner's heart cut from his chest, and the other's torn out from the back, and ordered their bodies burned.

75

People said Pedro was mad. He heard of the rumors whispered round the court, reports that he had eaten the hearts of the men he had tortured and burned. Let them say what they will. Let them fear his wrath. They had destroyed everything soft and kind and good in him. He would give as he had received, and show brutality for all he had been shown. He'd make a mockery of his father's sternness, his moral laws; he'd show the clergy, the nobles and the commoners alike the sting of justice, for having condemned Inês for the life they had lived.

Pedro publicly proclaimed that he and Inês had been secretly married. In all documents he referred to their children as Os Infantes—"The Princes," unlike João, the illegitimate son he had with Teresa Lourenço. Of course, there were murmurs and grumblings in the court. When, how, where, they asked? They mentioned his numerous lovers, as if that made any difference. As if, had he truly loved Inês, he would have had no need of other women. As if a mere memory could suffice. Solace and comfort might momentarily be found in the arms of a willing woman, in music, dance and drunkenness—all temporary measures, at best.

Should he sleep alone? He had desires, longings, a need for companionship—better to numb his pain with a few moments of fleeting pleasure. He took none for a wife.

He tried to do what he could to make sure his children were rightfully recognized, plans in the event of Prince Fernando's death, or in case Fernando had no children of his own, to assure that a son of Inês would then rule the country.

Before the funeral in Alcobaça, the wasted, broken body of Dona Inês de

Castro, once famous throughout the Iberian peninsula for her unsurpassed beauty and grace, was taken from the convent of Santa Clara where she had been buried in haste immediately after her assassination, and brought to the cathedral, where she was dressed in the finest gowns.

Those same nobles and clergymen whom Pedro would later force to participate in the funeral and the procession to Alcobaça, he now commanded to appear at the cathedral. The huge wooden doors were shut behind them and heavily guarded, while vassals, noblemen, priests and advisors all pressed forward, curious to know why they'd been summoned, none eager to upset their irascible king. They approached the platform where Pedro sat awaiting them. Beside him, in glorious robes, as befitted a queen, the mutilated, rotting corpse of Inês de Castro, was seated on the ornate royal throne, where, in the solemn ceremony ordered by Pedro, she was finally crowned Queen of all of Portugal and the Algarves. Queen after death.

Each nobleman, priest and advisor was forced to bow down and kiss the ring on her finger, while columns of smoke from several incense biers, incapable of overpowering the odor of decay, permeated the large room. Pedro watched on, as they stumbled, retched and paled, none daring, however, to refuse the order of their king.

The old bishop tottered and trembled, as if he would faint dead, while the ceremony was carried out, bestowing in death the power and prestige upon the woman who had been denied such honors in life.

There was another child of Pedro's, unnamed in the chronicles. Some believed it to be a boy, others a girl; regardless, the child, it is known, survived and was provided for, and in time also had children.

There were rumors too of secret travels into the dark Atlantic Ocean, of islands found and lost, and the bloodline of the unspoken name that continued in secret . . .

· · ·

The pages ended abruptly. The document was a far more detailed account of the story of Pedro and Inês than anything Julia had seen or heard before. The references to other children, to a mysterious bloodline and lost islands, as well as whose hand had written it left her with more questions than answers. If Julia were slightly more suspicious she might have thought she had found Sebastião's room not by accident, but by design. But then how could that be, since José Manuel explained that he had just chanced to look inside the building?

All the sights, sounds and smells of the islands, combined with the images of what she had read, left her feeling somewhat disoriented.

She returned to the *residencial* in Horta, thinking it best to keep the news of the room to herself. Others, she was afraid, would see Sebastião's need for privacy and secrecy as a further example of suspicious behavior. Julia didn't want the police snooping around, or anyone else knowing where she was spending her time, until she could examine everything in the room to her satisfaction.

The moment Julia entered the *residencial,* Maria Josefa appeared, as if from nowhere, her face full of hope and expectation, "Well?" she said, obviously eager to know if Julia had any information concerning Sebastião's fate. It was a look Julia had already come to anticipate.

"No news," Julia said, with a shrug.

Maria Josefa clucked her tongue and shook her head. "What a shame."

"I'm not worried yet, Dona Josefa," Julia said. "I'm sure he isn't in any real danger." This was what she repeatedly told herself, though she didn't know whether she actually believed it was true, or if it was merely a platitude, a hope, easily spoken, but without real import. There were times when she almost agreed with her brother Antonio, who when speaking of their father said, "Why couldn't we have a normal father, like everyone else? Why couldn't he work a nine-to-five job, come home and do all the things a normal father does? Instead, he cares more about his books, his ancestors and those damn islands than he cares about anyone living, anyone real!"

If nothing else, Julia simply wished Sebastião were more predictable.

CHAPTER 6

Julia wrote to Mateus, letting him know of her return to the islands, of her search for Sebastião, hoping that he had heard from Mateus since her uncle Frank had notified him that Mateus Sebastião was missing.

Dear Grandfather,

I'm sorry to report I have no news of Sebastião. There is nothing to do but wait and hope the authorities will turn up something. I keep thinking he'll show up with some wild story. At the same time, I'm glad to be here again. I only wish it were under different circumstances. I realize how much I've missed the islands. It feels strange being back here, especially with all that's taking place, strange talk of new islands, ghost ships, and sirens. The islands have changed and yet they are the same as when I was here last. I realize that I could say the same for myself. Like Sebastião, I feel jealously possessive of these islands, which I haven't seen in so many years. Perhaps you feel the same. Have you heard anything from Sebastião, a letter or postcard? I'm curious to know what he was working on, and about your letter about Inês and Dom Pedro, the mention of cults and treasures, as well as other writing I found here concerning them. I wonder whether all this had something to do with a book he was working on? Or are these historical facts? I'll let you know as soon as I hear something.

Love,
Julia

. . .

"Come have dinner with us tonight, *menina*," Maria Josefa said, in her most insistent tone of voice. "I'll make sure you eat well. I'd never forgive myself if you got sick." She quizzed Julia on where she had eaten, her expression showing these cafés and restaurants didn't meet with her approval.

"You mean to say you weren't poisoned?" João said. "Should we call a doctor?"

"No," Julia said. "The food wasn't bad, actually."

"Bad!" Maria Josefa answered, with a wave of her hand. "Why eat food that isn't bad, when you can eat food that's good?"

"No one's cooking is ever good enough to satisfy Dona Josefa," João said, solemnly.

"Hah!" was Maria Josefa response.

"I'd be happy to join you and João for dinner," Julia said, eager to maintain peace, and because she remembered that Josefa was a fabulous cook.

"Good," Maria Josefa said. "We'll keep an eye on you until your father returns, since I see with all your coming and going that you have taken after him." She crossed her arms over her ample chest and scowled fiercely, as if to drive home the point.

João welcomed Julia in when she knocked on their door later that evening. Julia handed him the bottle of red wine she'd bought. João thanked her. "You didn't need to bring anything," he said.

Maria Josefa bustled in and out through the kitchen doorway.

"Is there something I can help with?" Julia said. "Anything I can do?"

Maria Josefa waved João and Julia away. "No, sit down to eat, and stay out of my way." Julia breathed in the aroma of olive oil, garlic and spices as she watched Maria Josefa work.

"Will you have a drink?" João asked, as he deftly opened the bottle of wine.

"Just water, please," Julia said.

"*Water?*" João said, incredulous. "Water isn't to drink, water sinks ships. It's for washing, not for drinking."

Julia laughed. "Okay, wine, please." João smiled and filled a large glass with wine for Julia, as well as one for himself.

"Drink," João said, speaking English and grinning broadly.

"Thank you," Julia said. "To your health."

"*Saúde,*" João said, then in a more somber tone. "What about your father? Still no news?"

Julia shook her head. "Nothing so far."

"How can a man disappear like smoke?" Maria Josefa said, setting a plate of olives and a basket of bread on the table. "Is Sebastião a magician?"

"Not that I know," Julia said, uncertain how to respond to the odd question.

"Your father's a good man," João said.

"A good man, yes," Maria Josefa said, "but even good men are like children. I can't imagine what trouble your father could be in, but hopefully he will set it right, and get back here where he belongs. A man should be married, with a good wife to look after him, someone to keep him out of mischief."

81

João winked and Julia took another sip of wine. "Perhaps you're right," Julia said. "Maybe Sebastião should settle down. Although he'd say that a woman would be with him because he's a rebel, but would then try to change him and turn him into someone else."

"Humph! All men need wives to improve them," Maria Josefa said. "Does everyone in your family go without husbands or wives, a family of *solteiros*—bachelors?"

"Perhaps they are smarter than you think," João said.

"Be quiet, husband." Maria Josefa stood mystified, waiting for an explanation to this conundrum that defied belief.

"I don't have anything against getting married," Julia said. "I guess I'm waiting for someone right to come along. I don't want to marry just anyone."

"That shouldn't be a problem," Maria Josefa said. "There are many men to choose from."

"Let the young woman be, Maria," João said. "People shouldn't interfere when it comes to love."

"I'm not interfering. I'm only suggesting that she find a man who will make her happy and marry him."

Julia decided to change the subject. "First I must find Sebastião," she said.

"He will return, God willing," João said.

"If God would only be helpful for a change," Maria Josefa said. "I've had enough of troubles, earthquakes and volcanoes, our good friend disappearing right under our noses. What next?"

"It does seem I've come at a strange time," Julia said.

"A time of miracles," João said.

"Stop talking foolishness. Miracles indeed!" Maria Josefa said. "If people disappearing are God's idea of miracles—" She stormed back into the kitchen.

Julia marveled at how different they were. While Maria Josefa eternally struggled with everything—the elements, customers, neighbors, the government—João, on the other hand, was at peace with everyone and everything. Although Maria Josefa was critical of the Church and religion in general, she permitted the obligatory pictures of Christ, Our Lady, the Pope, and one of a smiling President Kennedy, so loved by the Portuguese—the Catholic President, to be hung on the walls in order to mollify João's sensibilities.

Maria Josefa never ceased her activities from morning to night. She woke before dawn and went to bed late, as if she were afraid to stop, even for a moment. If she wasn't busy cooking, she was cleaning rooms, the halls, working in the yard, or out shopping. She was plump, yet her arms and legs were strong and muscular from years of hard work. Every movement, every gesture, revealed a woman with little tolerance for anything less than what was practical and efficient. Tough, stubborn, outspoken and sharp-tongued, yet Julia knew Dona Josefa possessed a fine inner sentimentality, a tenderness, which had led her to marry João, a man so different from her.

João was calm and reticent. Stocky and broad-shouldered, with rugged pleasant looks, if not exactly handsome, he was strong, and yet was gentle and soft-spoken. He always wore a smile and never lost his good mood—a man of incredible patience and warmth.

João was a hard worker, too, but unlike his wife, he moved deliberately, slowly. He pondered everything, contemplating his surroundings and pausing to take note of everything around him. He enjoyed the dawns and the sunsets, the rain and flowers, the birds that sang in the trees, the children who played in the street. Julia doubted that Maria Josefa noticed any of these things. She would shoo the children away with a wave of her hand, as if they were flies.

Maria Josefa swept into the dining room as though she were taking charge and placed a large plate piled with *bacalhau,* the staple Portuguese cod dish, in front of Julia. The serving was enough to feed two, the cod layered with sliced potatoes, olives, onions, and steeped in olive oil.

"Eat, *menina,* before you disappear like your father," Maria Josefa said, brandishing a ladle. She tisk-tisked, as if Julia were a chicken someone was trying to sell her that was all skin and bones. "Do you have enough? Do you want more?"

"No, no, I'm fine," Julia said. "Thank you."

"You've got to eat to stay healthy. Women these days are too skinny." Maria Josefa scooped out a large portion of *bacalhau* for herself as if to illustrate her point.

"Do you know about *O Encoberto?*" João asked, refilling Julia's glass before she could stop him. He smiled. "It's good for you." Julia made a mental note to drink slower.

"The Hidden One?" Julia said.

João nodded. "King Dom Sebastião."

Julia shook her head. Again, King Sebastian, she thought, remembering what José Manuel had said the day before.

"Ah, this crazy husband of mine," Maria Josefa said. "Be quiet, already. Such foolishness."

João ignored his wife. He wore a look of deep concentration. Julia sat waiting, looking at the two of them. João lifted a finger in the air and began reciting:

Levando a bordo El-Rei D. Sebastião,
E erguendo, como um nome, alto o pendão
Do Império
Foi-se a última nau, ao sol aziago
Erma, e entre choros de ânsia e de pressago
Mistério.

With King Sebastião there on board,
And raising high the flag of Empire
As his name,
The last ship sailed into the sun,
Alone, ill-omened, to anguished cries, impending
Mystery.[2]

Maria Josefa mumbled about grown men believing in nonsense, but João only shrugged and said, "On a foggy morning, they say, King Sebastião will return, and he will lead his people again, and Portugal will regain her glory of old, a new empire, the Fifth Empire."

"Yes, and they have been saying that for four hundred years now," Maria Josefa said, raising her arm as if hoping for some validation.

"Is that Fernando Pessoa?" Julia asked.

"Yes, 'A Última Nau'" João said. 'The Last Ship.'

"I thought so," Julia said. "Sebastião adored Pessoa."

"Long ago a Jewish shoemaker in Portugal, named Gonçalo Bandarra," João said, "wrote ballads about The Desired One, who, like the Messiah, would appear to fulfill prophecies and bring about great changes in the world. One of your relatives, Dom João de Castro, wrote a book after King Dom Sebastião disappeared in Africa. He said that The Desired One was Dom Sebastião, who hadn't died, but was in hiding and would return."

"One of my ancestors?" Julia said.

João nodded. "The grandson of Dom João de Castro, the viceroy to India. He was captured by the Moors at the battle of Alcácer-Quibir, and held prisoner until his family ransomed him. He refused to return home while King Philip of Spain ruled Portugal. He later became convinced that Sebastião still lived, and that his return would be the salvation of Portugal. He wrote his great work, *The Discourse on the Life of the Appearance of the Long-Hoped-for King Dom Sebastian, Our Lord The Hidden One From his Birth to the Present.* He was the first apostle of the Sebastianistas, those who believe in the prophecies."

"What happened to him?" Julia asked.

"He settled in France and wrote other books. He was also a lawyer for one of the supposed Sebastiãos, who appeared years later, and was executed."

"How do you know all this?"

"The library. I read the chronicles and history books when I have time."

Julia gazed at João for a moment. My, my, she thought, shame on me. I should know better. She had underestimated João, who, though he looked like a laborer, had obviously read extensively, able to recite poetry by memory, and knew a thing or two about history.

"Enough talk. Let the girl eat, João," Maria Josefa said.

"This food is absolutely delicious, Maria Josefa. I haven't had *bacalhau* like this in ages."

"Have more, there's plenty," Maria Josefa said, obviously pleased. "This husband of mine is a dreamer. Here we are poor and old, and he thinks of poetry. *Incredible!*"

"Poetry keeps me young," João said, winking at Julia. "Don't pay any attention to her. We are not poor. We have a good house and food and friends. And don't all women love poetry?"

Julia smiled wistfully. "I'm afraid I don't know many men who can recite poetry," she shrugged. Most of the males she met were more boys than men, who might know an obscene limerick or two but not poetry.

She thought about Dom Sebastião and the coincidences of recent events that were like echoes: a new island rising from the sea, Sebastião's story about a new island, and the real possibility that he had also sailed to this very island. And then there were the legends of Dom Sebastião, who was said to reside on a mysterious island where he awaited the moment of his return.

"I'll bring some coffee," Maria Josefa said, returning to the kitchen.

Julia showed João a piece of paper she had put in her purse, a verse from another poem by Fernando Pessoa, she'd found in her father's room:

No imenso espaço seu de meditar,
Constelado de forma e de visão,
Surge, prenúncio claro do luar,
El-Rei Dom Sebastião.

In his boundless realm of thought,
Constellations of form and vision,
Rises, in prognosticated moonlight,
His Majesty, King Sebastian.[3]

"Yes," he said, "that is the legend," as if it were no surprise. Maria Josefa placed a tray of pastries on the table. Julia couldn't eat another bite, yet she knew that Maria Josefa would accept no excuses. João started to pour more wine, but Julia moved her glass away. "No more wine for me," she said. "I'm not used to it."

João smiled. "That's okay, Dona Senhora Canto e Castro. Wine helps the digestion."

"Call me Julia," she said, "not dona or senhora, and not Canto e Castro, please. I only use Castro."

"Why don't you use Canto e Castro?" Maria Josefa said.

Julia shrugged. "It's easier."

"Easier?" Maria Josefa said. "Listen, Canto e Castro is your name and you should use it," she said. "You have every reason to be proud, and not go around hiding from your own name."

"I'm not hiding, Dona Josefa," Julia said. "It's just that in America things are different."

Sebastião had always used the full name, but other members of the family, embarrassed by the pretentious sound of a name comprised of several words, of having to explain its unusual vowel sounds, what the words meant, its uncertain nationality, opted to use the simplified surname Castro.

Like Mateus, Sebastião was proud of the name, and spoke at length about America's fear of complicated names, what he sneeringly referred to as the land of homogenized masses, where everything was by necessity distilled to its simplest form, everybody fitting in nicely, neatly, "without blemishes, and without beauty marks," a country populated by people who had forgotten where they had come from, cut off from their past, and from themselves.

Sebastião fumed when he met people whose Portuguese names had been changed upon their arrival in the United States—Silva or Silveira to Sylvia, Castanho to Brown, Pereira to Perry, Mendonça to Mandly, Ferreira to Smith—all attempting to fit in with their neighbors, blending into American blandness.

"What are they trying to hide?" he would ask. "They anglicize their names the way the Jews changed their names, to blend in, when the Inquisition forced them to hide. Only these people want to be Americans."

Of course, Julia had nothing to hide from. It was only a matter of going along with the rest of the family, and avoiding complications. Canto e Castro, she felt, was a name that belonged to another time and another place.

Julia excused herself after dessert. "Thank you so much for everything," she said. "Including the poetry."

"Good night, *menina,*" Maria Josefa said.

"Good night," João said. "*Sonhos cor-de-rosa*"—pink dreams.

Julia laughed. "I haven't heard that since I was a little girl."

As she lay in bed that night she experienced a strange sensation, almost but not quite a fear, as she imagined that Sebastião had indeed sailed off into a dream of madness, going to sea in search of Pessoa's Enchanted Isle, and *O Encoberto*—"The Hidden One."

"But how, why?" she whispered to the night. "What would make him do such a thing?"

. . . when returning to Ireland, after an absence of seven years, he [St. Brendan] appears to have discovered and landed upon one of the Atlantic Islands. . . . This happy land was said to tantalize the faithful in search of it, by appearing like a Will-o'-the-Wisp, and as suddenly disappearing. Many were the vain endeavours made to find this supposed abode of the saints.

The Azores: or Western Islands
Walter Frederick Walker, London, 1886

· · ·

Julia stopped off at the police station the next morning. It was difficult to keep from suspecting the police of negligence. She doubted whether they ever had any serious investigations to conduct; furthermore, their equipment and methods, such as they were, were likely ten or twenty years out of date. Her father, grandmother, and other relatives had often complained about Portuguese officials and the bureaucracies they served, leaving her with the impression of things perpetually mired in paperwork and red tape, people with insurmountable prejudices and biases, and gastrointestinal matters on their mind, as opposed to trying their utmost to locate the whereabouts of a missing man, especially a man with Sebastião's reputation. Her earlier conversations with the police had done nothing to lessen these concerns.

Julia was ushered into an office as neat and sterile as a doctor's examining room. The man at the desk, Lieutenant Ferreira, had been assigned the case. He smiled pleasantly and shook Julia's hand as if he hadn't a care in the world.

"I would like to know why no one has located my father," Julia said.

"We are waiting for word to come from Lisbon," the lieutenant said, in somewhat hesitant, but precise English. "We are waiting for notification from the other islands, and from Madeira. We are checking with various European and American agencies. Awaiting verification, awaiting documentation."

"I haven't heard a word," Julia explained.

"Nothing has changed," the lieutenant said. "There are no new developments."

His tone remained level and calm. Julia wanted to goad him. "He's been missing for weeks, if not longer," she said. "Someone must have seen him leave. Someone must know something. There must be clues, a trail."

The man shook his head. "I'm sorry, senhora, but no one appears to have seen him leave. No one has come forward with any helpful information. I'm afraid—" He threw his hands up. There was nothing more he could do.

"Aren't there *any* facts to go on?" she said, unable to let the matter rest. "Did he leave the islands, and if so, when, and how might he have gone?"

"We aren't absolutely certain if or when he left," the policeman said. "He doesn't appear to have gone by plane, that much we're fairly sure of."

"By boat?" Julia asked.

"Well, presumably not by the island boats," Lieutenant Ferreira said.

"That leaves what?"

The man shrugged. "A private sailboat, perhaps a fishing boat. He may even have gone aboard a cargo ship." He sounded extremely doubtful. "We are currently checking on all ships which have stopped here. Until then, we must be patient." The lieutenant's tone suggested that Julia not bother them, but let them get on with their work.

Julia decided on a different tack. "Do you think it's possible Sebastião might have made some enemies," she said. "That someone may have wanted to hurt him?"

"You are speaking of murder?" the Lieutenant asked, incredulous.

Julia nodded. "Or kidnapping?"

"There's no reason to believe your father was the victim of any violence," the Lieutenant said, his voice rising a notch. "None at all. And

why would someone want to kidnap him? Your family no longer—"
again he didn't finish the sentence. Julia met his gaze, ignoring the
implied dig concerning the decline of the family's prestige, thinking she
must have struck a nerve. "Please, senhora, do not let your imagination
create solutions with no facts to support them."

"I just thought it might be worth looking into," Julia said.

"This is a very precise and difficult process of elimination," the Lieutenant said. "We look at the evidence and see where it leads, and there is
nothing that suggests violence." He stood, extending his hand, in effect
dismissing her. "Sometimes on the Azores things take more time than
we would like," he said with a sigh. "There are many small, isolated villages. We're not the United States. We cannot send the cavalry to find
your father."

Julia grimaced, unimpressed with Lieutenant Ferreira's feeble joke.
She wondered if the last comment was a suggestion that she return to
America. Furthermore, the Lieutenant's insistence on speaking English,
no matter that Julia spoke and understood Portuguese perfectly well,
was a snub carefully calculated to show that she didn't fit in, as if to say,
*You speak with an accent; You are a stranger here, I cannot be bothered with
you; I will not take you seriously.*

"Perhaps if a reward were offered," Julia suggested. She regretted it
almost as soon as she said it. Lieutenant Ferreira met her gaze with a flat,
slightly pained smile, a look designed to make clear that Julia was out of
her element, that her suggestion was rather vulgar and unnecessary, and
it would be wisest to leave police matters in the hands of those who were
accomplished professionals.

"We do not need to offer rewards," the Lieutenant said, sounding
offended. "Your father is only one man. We have been busy with many
disturbances and problems, due to the earthquakes and other matters.
After all, he isn't the only one we are looking for."

"You mean there are others who have disappeared?"

The lieutenant coughed, and quickly began rifling impatiently
through the papers on his desk. "I am not at liberty to discuss this case
any further," he said, obviously disconcerted by saying more than he
had intended. "You will hear from us when we know something more."

"I've heard that a body was found," Julia said. "A drowned man?"

"Yes, yes," he said, clearly irritated. "On Pico, but it doesn't fit your father's description at all. Trust me, we will let you know when we find something that concerns Senhor Canto e Castro."

"Thank you," Julia said. "I'll be waiting."

She left the building, perturbed by a feeling of helplessness. It was as if the more she pushed and tried to make things move faster, the slower everything proceeded. How might the lieutenant have treated her if she were a man? Would he have been so condescending, so dismissive? Things certain *had* changed, since her last visit. In the past, if something like this had occurred, the police would have rushed to solve the mystery at once.

She was perplexed as well by the lieutenant's inadvertent confession that there were a number of people missing, that Sebastião wasn't the only one who had disappeared.

Julia rushed to the taxi stand, and rode back to her father's room in Praia do Almoxarife.

· · ·

CHAPTER 8

It is currently reported that no one here ever dies . . .

Among the Azores, Lyman H. Weeks
James R. Osgood and Co., 1882

· · ·

"Remember who you are," Julia's grandmother had repeatedly said. "Never forget you are a Canto e Castro." Isabel had whispered these words in Julia's ears to convince her granddaughter that even if she had nothing else in all the world, she had her name. "No one can ever take that away from you."

Isabel do Canto e Castro had filled Julia's mind, and Sebastião's before that, with stories of who they were, and where they'd come from, making it perfectly clear that their name was worth far more than any worldly goods one might possess, as though the name held some special guarantee or entitlement, a benediction that God bestowed only upon the chosen few. Perhaps it would grant them a pass into the kingdom of heaven Julia had believed in when she was a young girl. So far the name had brought her family little benefit here on earth.

Julia thumbed through each of the books, each scrap of paper, in Sebastião's room. Although her father was no longer here, and Mateus and Isabel hadn't seen the islands in years, she sensed their presence as if they were nearby, or their impressions still lingered.

The familial connection meant little, she knew, if not augmented with the deeper, more tangible ties which neither time nor distance could destroy or diminish, the requisite blood imbued with seawater, the Azorean soil, and its products—*maracujá,* passion fruit; *amoras,* mulberries; wines of the Azores, like *angelica*—if not the spirit of the islands, for it was clear that everybody had family somewhere. It mattered little where a person's family was, or from where they had originated. After all, the islands were filled with people who shared the same last name, the same ancestors, the same history.

"Unfortunately, there are very few Canto e Castros left." Isabel spoke as if an awesome responsibility and burden, as well as a blessing, accompanied the name. That, coupled with her talk of paradise, the unmatched beauty of the islands (the two things inextricably linked, as if one couldn't possibly exist without the other) had filled Julia with a vague sense of foreboding about returning to the islands of her ancestors, a feeling that something awaited her.

It was more than just a name, of course, for with it came a past.

In the U.S. everyone assumed the family was Spanish or of Latin American descent, which was another reason why Sebastião refused to use the shortened form, and one more reason why Mateus had left the States for Brazil. There, the Azorean community embraced and honored the past the name represented, and there was no question as to where he was from. As Sebastião often said: "How the hell could Mateus—a man who carries a name steeped in history, a name that evokes the Azores and Portugal of old, legends and tragedies and great deeds, not merely a handful of forgotten islands and a long-neglected country—be expected to live in a place where he was just another nobody?"

If pressed by skeptics to name kings and kingdoms, Sebastião smiled, and recited, from memory: "The ancient kings of Asturias and Leon, King Ordonho, King Fruela, the earliest kings of Portugal, as well as the counts and Kings who ruled over Castile. Not to mention our English ancestors, dukes and lords, a member of the Order of the Garter."

Much of the family legend was unstated, denoted only in the vaguest terms, as if to speak openly of the subject were an act beneath someone of such a noble and distinguished lineage. It was the same way the islands were spoken of; no one had to say they were the last remaining vestige of Atlantis, or the Island of lovers, that anything was possible here, it was understood, just the same.

But there were also tales of tragedy, gruesome murders and betrayals, brother against brother, father against son, sister against brother;

of exiled kings and discarded lovers, treason and lost fortunes, which, while not mentioned as a present threat or possibility, were nevertheless referred to indirectly, like a secret shame: where and when would the shadow of misfortune appear next?

It was this very question that filled Julia's mind and increased her anxiety. She was aware, too, of a lingering suspicion that misfortunes rarely came singly, but typically in twos or threes, as she tried to concentrate on reading, looking over the contents of her father's room, while the wind, the waves, and the sound of murmuring voices intruded and disturbed her thoughts—a whisper that those who seek greatness often meet disaster.

· · ·

There exists a song in each of us. The song of the sea, a song of longing, every Azorean or Portuguese knows, whether or not they know the words; the tune is there, the instruments play the melody and the heart cannot fail to respond and the name of the song is saudade, a touch of sadness at what is lost, gone, but a gleam of hope as well for what may yet come again.

—Sebastião do Canto e Castro

· · ·

Julia read Sebastião's account of the legend of *Sete Cidades* or "The Seven Cities," which recalled an earlier visit to São Miguel when he had taken her to see the twin lakes of *Sete Cidades.* She remembered the breathtaking sight of the lakes on the bottom of the enormous crater, one blue and the other green, separated by a bridge. The edge of the crater rose sharply, ringing and protecting the two lakes from the outside world, the bustle of the roads and the sea far below, keeping them hidden with the clouds that often encircled the mountain.

"There's an old story about *Sete Cidades,*" Sebastião had told Julia. "A princess fell in love with a poor shepherd boy, but her father, the king, grew furious and forbade his daughter to see the shepherd. The tears the two shed filled the lakes, making one blue and the other green, matching the eyes of the two lovers. When I first saw the lakes, I knew I would marry a girl with eyes as blue as the lake of *Sete Cidades,* to match my own green eyes." And, of course, true to his word, he'd married Clara, whose eyes were indeed blue.

There was another, much older legend of *Sete Cidades* among Sebastião's notes, that told of seven Portuguese bishops who left the Iberian peninsula to escape the Moors, and discovered an island where they settled, a city for each of the bishops, thus called *A Ilha das Sete Cidades*— The Island of Seven Cities.

Julia cleared her mind by taking a break from the reading and exploring the area in and around Praia do Almoxarife. She was soothed and reassured by the insistent lowing of the cows, the squeals of pigs, and bleating of goats and sheep—those first inhabitants of the islands, perhaps descendants of the very animals Prince Henrique had ordered his men to load onto ships and bring to the newly discovered islands, where they were set free to wander and multiply, in order to feed the men and women who would settle there.

The green fields, crisscrossed with numerous walls of black volcanic rock, piled by the islanders to protect crops against the fierce winter winds, took her back.

She listened to the murmuring of the waves. *"Ama-me, acha-me. Lava-me, toma-me,"*—"Love me, find me. Wash me, take me," the sea whispered. She peered at the ocean that held captive the bones of countless Azoreans, countless Portuguese sailors, fishermen, explorers, whalers, soldiers; as if, were she to look long and hard enough, she might see the innumerable ships hidden in its depths; the ocean that had become salty through the tears shed by those lovers, mothers, sisters and daughters who had wept for those who had left, those who would never return; a sea that held many secrets—secrets it wouldn't easily relinquish.

"At night when the moon is full the ocean shows its bounty to those who come to see the faces of loved ones in the surf," José Manuel told the children of Praia do Almoxarife, who tagged after him like a troop of puppies, his face aglow with an eerie half-light, his eyes wide. "The waves become a roaring chorus of a thousand voices. There are proclamations, secrets told, amid the shrieking of the wind and the crashing of waves, announcing those treasures the sea has recently claimed. Drowned sailors and sunken ships appear in the white foam of the waves!"

The children stared, enraptured by his words, their mouths gaping with wonder.

"Ancient treasure ships and sea chests overflow with treasures of gold and silver," José would continue, "rubies and emeralds, ancient ruined cities, pirates, sea monsters and all the other creatures that live in the sea appear as far as the eye can see."

Julia stood at the water's edge feeling the tug and pull of the sea's power.

She supposed there was still a possibility that Sebastião had impulsively decided to explore Africa or a remote village in Asia—some forsaken place from where it might take months to receive a piece of mail. Or had Sebastião heard the call of this mysterious woman, the vision the men in Peter's Café talked about, and tried to follow her out across the waves?

What could she say about her father? What did anyone truly know of Sebastião do Canto e Castro? She tried to imagine what she might tell the children she didn't yet have, or her future grandchildren, about Sebastião. A coiled snake of ash unwound deep inside her and reared its head as if to strike, before seizing its own tail and swallowing itself.

"Children, let me tell you of your grandfather. This is who he was, what he did, this is what he handed down to me, to hand down to you, passing the cup from one to the next; do you wonder what is inside this cup for you?" What filled the cup? Julia knew there was something she had inherited from her father, something she did not receive from her mother. What was it? That voice inside her, that passion for something she hadn't yet found? It was something that kept her searching the way Sebastião had searched his entire life.

He wasn't simply the mad dreamer Antonio and Clara accused him of being, lost to his own musings, with no concept of reality or propriety. Sebastião believed in beauty, in myths and legends; he knew that we are what we are because we carry the universe within us, our connectedness to one another, past, present and future, and to the stars, the air, water—all the elements and all things. The magic of finding like minds, like bodies, like souls amidst the billions of our fellow travelers, and coming together to create something new.

Perhaps he was lost below the waves, and she would see him there, if not the ghost ship or the luminescent woman.

Frequently it isn't straight on but only by the most circuitous of routes that one arrives at the truth.

—Sebastião do Canto e Castro

. . .

During a break from her reading, Julia heard singing mingling with the sound of water; a clear blue note blown over or through a fissure in an outcropping of igneous rock, a cool breeze across the opening of a *fumarole*. Throwing her hands up, she gave in to the pull of strange forces, and left the room, an instrument in the hands of the gods, experiencing an incredible sense of calm. There was no other place she would have chosen to be.

Come what may, Julia thought. Islands, ghost ships, dead men, luminescent women, mysterious voices in the night, hidden monsters of the deep, legends and myths—when reason fails to deliver the goods, rely on instinct and imagination.

The irony of this wistful surrender wasn't lost on her. Less than a week earlier everything was cut and dry, black and white. She'd arrived with her perspective in order, satisfied that a rational explanation could be found for the mysterious events that had been plaguing the islands, in particular, Sebastião's disappearance. Now she was ready to put aside logic and skepticism and face the unknown, to accept at face value whatever she encountered.

As if lost in a pleasant dream, Julia made her way through the hazy half-light of a dense grove. She followed the path through shrubs, climbing vines and thin trees. Stepping into the clearing, from shadow to light, she discovered a woman standing in the midst of a yard. For a moment, Julia mistook her for a statue.

Several colorful birds perched on the woman's arms and shoulders, one rested on her head, which was wrapped in a bright yellow and blue scarf. Flowers at the ends of lengthy stalks leaned toward her, as if she were their source of sunshine and warmth. It was difficult to determine where the flowers ended, for her dress, surprisingly unlike the typical garb of grays, blacks and whites normally associated with older women, was instead a colorful print of vivid flowers of pinks, yellows, blues and greens. The entire garden, perfumed with the drowsy scent of flowers and filled with the sounds of bubbling water and the chirps and playful singsong of a rainbow of exotic birds, had a surreal otherworldly quality.

"Good afternoon," Julia said. Her uncertainty made it more a question than a declaration.

"Good afternoon," the woman said, gazing at Julia with a warm smile, as if she'd been expected, and extending her arm. "*Bem-vinda*—Welcome." As she stepped toward Julia, the birds didn't move, but stayed where they sat, even as the woman's hands clasped Julia's.

"I'm sorry, I thought I heard someone singing," Julia said, ready to explain that she hadn't meant to intrude, but the woman brushed it aside with a sweeping gesture.

"I'm sure it must be gas," she said, nodding her head vigorously.

"What?" Julia said.

"Gas." She gestured toward the water. "It started with the last earthquake. I think the world must have a terrible bellyache." She calmly coaxed the birds off her. With only the slightest flutter they settled onto the ground, trees and shrubs.

Julia saw the water bubbling and thought she understood. "Yes, I see," she said. "There was no water before, then? Perhaps a tremor opened a natural spring?"

The woman shook her head with a frown. "The water would lie still and quiet every full moon," she said. "A clear pool whose surface showed the future."

Julia stepped forward to get a closer look. The water gurgled out, but then flowed back through some nearby crevice, as if it had changed its mind and decided to return underground.

"The future?" she asked.

The woman nodded. "Now all that is gone."

Julia bent down over the spring. "Is it safe to drink?" She reached a hand out toward the water, but was stopped by the old woman.

"Never, never touch that water." The woman's sudden vehemence took Julia by surprise. "It was said long ago that anyone who drank from this spring would have eternal life, which is to say an eternity of sorrows."

Julia stood, her curiosity piqued. "Really? Has anyone drunk from it before?"

"There have been tales of those foolish enough," the woman said, with a dismissive wave of her hand. "But they have been forgotten."

Did I hear correctly, Julia thought. Eternal life, eternal sorrows, and did the woman say that eternity meant oblivion, forgetfulness? What had happened to those who had dared to drink from the spring, she wondered. "Who were they?" she said.

101

"Blind men," she said. "Men who didn't realize there were things more terrible than death, men who dared to try and cheat the fates." She turned away from the water, shaking her head. "No," she continued, "there are enough sorrows in this world without our adding to them."

Julia listened to the music of the woman's voice, which seemed far off and yet near, the voice of someone very old, and quite young. Why did it make her think of mermaids and sorceresses?

"Does the water have any uses?" Julia asked, determined to satisfy her curiosity.

The old woman leaned close. "A drop or two rubbed on a forehead can ease a child's bad dreams. It has healing properties, too, when used properly."

Julia recalled the strong mineral taste of the natural springs from which she had drunk years earlier on São Miguel. She hadn't realized there were any on Faial. "I wonder what it tastes like?" she said. "It must be very pure. Where do you think it comes from?"

"From beneath the root of this mountain," the woman answered.

"Faial?" Julia said.

"Faial and Pico, they are part of the same mountain, one of the tallest mountains on earth, only the very tops stand above the sea. From deep below the mountain, the water comes. But, forget about that now and follow me. It's only old men who try to find this place. Let them search for magic fountains and eternal life. You are far too young to be concerned with such things."

She led Julia away from the spring, to the clumps of fruit trees and the flocks of brilliant birds.

"All these are yours?" Julia asked.

"Nothing here is mine, my dear. These flowers, which grow here and nowhere else on the island, and these birds that come upon their own wings from goodness knows where, have made this their place. I belong to them; they are not mine." Her expression changed with each word she spoke, serious one moment, radiant the next, then quixotic or pixyish. "I am Maria dos Santos."

"I'm Julia Castro." She explained what she was doing on the islands, how she'd come from far away California.

"California," Maria dos Santos repeated, as if she weren't entirely sure of its existence. Julia might as well have said El Dorado or The Island of Saint Brendan. Once again, Maria dos Santos leaned closer, as if to make sure Julia was real, too, and not an apparition, a mischievous spirit, perhaps produced by the spring or the earthquakes.

"I'm here to find my father," Julia said. "Sebastião do Canto e Castro. He's disappeared. No one knows how or why, or where he's gone."

Maria dos Santos nodded. "Many strange things have occurred lately," she said. "It's a shame about the spring. If the water would be quiet it might show you where you can find your father."

The flock of birds suddenly rose and became one fluttering wave of wings, before coming down again, alighting on Julia's arms, shoulders and head, nearly covering her completely. At first she thought they were attacking her, but when their wings were still she found herself nearly enveloped by the countless soft-hued wings. She laughed softly. "This is amazing."

"Ah," said Maria dos Santos. "It's a good sign as well as a bad one."

"What does it mean?"

"That a tremendous gift will soon be yours, or that you are close to death; perhaps both."

Maria dos Santos gently brushed the birds off Julia. They fluttered to the ground, flew up into the trees, or sidled up her arms. Julia was relieved, but tried not to show it.

"Come inside, I'll make you some green tea," Maria dos Santos said. "And I have some fresh-baked cookies." Julia turned around in time to glimpse a face peering through the back window of the house. It was gone so quickly, she wondered if she'd really seen anyone.

Maria dos Santos led Julia inside. The old house was warm and homey. The rooms were full of large wooden furniture and rugs. Julia spied a piano in the living room, shelves of books, fine hand-painted ceramics, and a number of paintings, mostly scenes of village life, or ships in the harbor. One wouldn't have guessed from the outside that the house was filled with such things. It also looked as if the old woman wasn't the only one who lived there.

A large kettle of water was already steaming on the wood stove. Maria dos Santos busied herself with making tea.

"Do you live here alone, senhora?" Julia asked.

"No, my grandson Nicolau lives here. Sometimes his sister, Teresa, comes and brings my great-grandchildren from across the water, from Pico, to visit. But I am never alone."

She handed Julia a cup of tea, and placed a tray of sugar, milk, cookies and jam on the counter. Julia scooped a spoonful of sugar into her tea, took one of the biscuits, then Maria dos Santos ushered her into the dining room. On one wall were hung a number of photographs. Julia noticed several that were obviously a much younger Maria dos Santos and her husband.

"Senhor dos Santos?" Julia asked.

"Yes," she said. "My husband, Teodoro." There were pictures of children and several photographs of a young man and woman perhaps Julia's age.

"Nicolau?" Julia said, studying the photos, and pointing to the man. Julia recognized the person she had seen with the books in Peter's Café when she waited for José Manuel.

"Yes."

The pictures besides Nicolau's of a woman about the same age, olive-skinned, with dark hair, and large, round, dark eyes, struck Julia viscerally.

"This is Teresa?" Julia said.

"Yes, Nicolau's sister."

"She's stunning," Julia said, awed by the startling beauty of the woman in the photograph. Teresa hadn't smiled for the photo and didn't appear comfortable with posing for a photographer. Still, she was radiant. Her half-smile and dark eyes revealed a glimmer, a small fraction of the vastness they contained. "Is she here now?"

"No, no. Teresa lives mostly on Pico. *Nossa sereia,* Teodoro always called her. Our siren."

Julia was curious about Nicolau, too, but didn't say anything. Maria dos Santos seemed to anticipate her thoughts. "Nicolau spends much of his time in Pico, too, and in villages on the other side of Faial. But here, your tea is getting cold."

"And Senhor dos Santos?" Julia asked, before sipping her tea.

"He died six years ago. Not that he's really gone. He's still here with me." She rested her palm on her chest. "Nicolau is just like him. Teodoro used to say that Nicolau and Teresa held all the secrets of the sea. He was like that, too. Some people know animals, and some know people, but those three, they knew the sea, and the sea knew them. Nicolau and Teresa adored their grandfather. Teodoro told them stories about how the sea would call to them, even after Teodoro was gone, because they were the same, and they each heard the sea inside themselves."

Julia marveled at Maria's voice. It was extraordinary, something beyond the human, a voice capable of invoking so much, like the *feiticeiras,* the sorceresses of old.

"Teodoro used to say Nicolau and Teresa had half-blood and half-seawater flowing through their veins."

"Is the piano yours or does your grandson play it?"

"The piano is Nicolau's. He's a musician. You will see." She spoke as though their meeting were inevitable, a simple matter of destiny.

Julia drank the rest of her tea. "I look forward to meeting him."

"You must visit us soon," Maria dos Santos said.

"I'd like that, very much," Julia said. "I'd better go now. I have to see what I can do about finding my father. Thank you for the tea."

"It was nothing," Maria dos Santos said, showing her to the door. "You will find what you're looking for, I'm sure. And perhaps discover even more than you are hoping to find."

"I've already rediscovered these islands. That in itself was worth coming here."

Maria dos Santos peered at Julia, and raised her eyebrows knowingly. "Sometimes our eyes and hearts hold onto an object we desire," she said. "We see nothing else. Only much later do we sometimes realize we have gained not what we dreamed of having, but another desirable yet unexpected gift, while what we thought we wanted has lost its importance."

Julia nodded, thinking again, *feiticeira.* "Good day, senhora."

"The Azores are a microcosm of the world," Sebastião always said, "with many singular examples. Here, among the most ignorant and simple souls can be found the inventive, the brilliant, and the exceptional; the poetic, the philosophical, the whimsical."

"Good day," Maria dos Santos said. *"E boa sorte*—and good luck."

The great mystery of the ocean is that of its island legends. From Plato's Atlantis to the vanished island of St. Brendan, there has always been talk of mysterious islands, which are supposed to exist somewhere out in the western seas. Ships, riding storm-swept waters, have sighted them in a sudden ray of sunshine. Helmsmen, lulled by the trade winds, have caught glimpses of their blue ridges. And fabulous tales of this archipelago, and a yearning to discover it have been handed down through the ages.
After Homer's Hesperus, and Plytheas the explorer's Thule, came the islands of Celtic folklore which were the offspring of foam and evening twilight. They include Avalon, where King Arthur sleeps watched over by nine fairy sisters, the Isle of the Youthful Heart, seen at sundown in the pearl-tinted mirror of the waters, and the Isle of Seven Slumbers, where shipwrecked souls repose in the legends Breton fishing folk used to tell each other after dark.

Stories told by Arab geographers and explorers from Genoa sent Portuguese caravels oceanward in search of an enchanted isle which "was said to exist on the distant confines of the West and appear, every seven years or so, to seamen ploughing its waters. . . . Shores shrouded in mist, cradles rocked by the swell, a spellbound oasis reserved for those who could break the spells that encompassed it."

Of this dream the Azores were born, lost in the ocean wastes between Europe and America, found again like the enchanted isle, hidden at times by heavy clouds, at others bright and clear on a summer sea as smooth as a mirror.

The Azores, Claude Dervenn, Paris, 1955

• • •

Early the next morning, Julia was jarred awake by violent tremors that shook the island of Faial. Maria Josefa marched through the halls of the *residencial* shouting, "Everybody outside, quickly, before someone is killed," although she herself made no attempt to hurry, as if the earthquake and the procedures to escape without injury were beneath her dignity. She wasn't about to show concern for herself. Her husband, João, on the other hand, muttered a litany of prayers: "What a terrible punishment," he cried. "God is angry. Our Lady, please intercede for us, forgive our sins." He knocked on doors and urged people to flee.

Julia rushed to join the burgeoning crowds that congregated outside, seeking safety and solace from friends and neighbors who gathered at the nearest clearing to face the dangers out in the open. She struggled to remain calm amid the confusion. "Are we really safer here?" she asked one or two standing nearby, but receiving no answer, deferred to these people who had, after all, hundreds of years' experience in these matters.

Once things quieted down most people dispersed and went about carrying on with usual tasks of their day. Many, however, refused to return to their homes and businesses. Whole families camped out in the parks, the beaches, and in the nearest fields.

Julia returned to the *residencial.* "Everyone is okay," Maria Josefa assured her. "It wasn't too bad this time." Julia nodded, but wandered off on her own, convinced that she had good cause to be nervous. There were vast differences between the earthquakes she had grown up with in California and those on an island, out in the middle of nowhere, where many of the buildings were little more than simple stone slabs piled atop one another, cut from the very same volcanic rock which had been disturbing the islands on and off for the past month or so. And there was nothing to prevent these stones from tumbling to the ground when shaken violently.

An island didn't provide the reassuring illusion of terra firma. No one could say whether the cooled volcanic rock and the silent craters might not return to their former state, erupting in explosive streams of liquid fire, like those convulsions which had first formed these islands. The whole archipelago could self-destruct and vanish from the face of the earth without leaving any trace.

It was only then that Julia thought of Sebastião's room in Praia do Almoxarife. She rushed back to make sure the old building and its precious contents hadn't been damaged in the earthquake. She arrived to find the room unchanged. She settled in and resumed examining the books and notes Sebastião had left behind.

Julia imagined herself discovering Sebastião's location, unraveling the too-few clues like a sleuthhound, a woman of adventure and mystery, dangers and risks be damned. However, she heard a voice whisper, "Those who follow the path of misfortune or evil can expect nothing but the same fate"—likely a poorly translated Portuguese proverb she had heard from one or more relatives who had tried to talk her out of coming to the islands.

What lies secreted inside Sebastião, she wondered. Inside myself, as well? What makes us who we are, so different from mother, Antonio, my aunts and uncles, what essential element? Maybe it's been there all along, handed down generation after generation, from grandparent, to parent, down to me. A dissatisfaction with ordinary life, a desire for something more; feeling pitted against the fates; a sense of loss, inherited from Mateus and all who had preceded him? Could the first drink she had tasted on the islands, the first breath of air, have caused this kernel—this seed which had carried through the ages, from the time of Inês de Castro and Dom Pedro and the fathomless mysteries which lay before them—to germinate at last?

Maria dos Santos had said that her grandchildren, Nicolau and Teresa, had the sea in their blood, that the sea knew them, was a part of them—something they had inherited from their grandfather, Teodoro. Julia wondered, "What is my legacy, handed down from Sebastião and Mateus?"

It wouldn't occur to many of the women she knew to think about what they may have inherited from their fathers, with whom most had poor, troubled relationships, if any at all. People wondered how and why she could manage an ongoing relationship with Sebastião. He's so difficult, they'd say. He's erratic, unreliable, obsessed with his stories, his ideas, his islands. He's hardly ever present, even when he's here.

Julia could deny none of what they said. Sebastião had his passions. They filled his life and work; he believed in them with his entire being, and while he had high standards and expectations, he was harder on himself than anyone else. Maybe it was the fact that he was truer to himself than most people were. Julia had her music, such as it was, which mattered far more than anything. Without music, she thought, what would I have? She couldn't imagine being involved with someone and giving up music, not for any reason.

Julia didn't have a problem with men per se. While she hadn't seriously dated anyone recently, she did have a number of male friends, and often preferred their company over the females she knew. She enjoyed their energy, while too often the interests of women annoyed her with talk of shopping, clothes, and money; they were often catty and manipulative, while men were simpler, and easier to deal with, unless, of course, the subject of sex entered the picture. Then it was a whole different story. Too many women seemed content to gloam onto a man who had a profession, or who pursued a creative dream, as if the woman were an adornment and nothing more. How can they be satisfied with so little, she wondered. The only time she lost interest in men was when they were in groups, when the mob mentality took over, and rendered them anything but interesting. But one on one, they were for the most part fine.

Sebastião had never put the past behind him. Everything he wrote was steeped in his rich ancestry, his recollections of tastes, smells, sights, sounds, characters and places throughout the islands. All her life her grandmother, Isabel, had continued to write poems and paint pictures of the islands. And though Mateus was practically blind, the fields, harbors and sea of the Azores were ever-present in his poetry and music, his paintings, and his dreams.

"What about me," Julia said, looking at the stacks of Sebastião's notes. "Am I an American like my brother, or does the ash and lava, the essence of the islands that flows through my veins, as Sebastião used to say, make me different? Have I ignored that part of me?"

So far there was no trace of the islands in her music. Perhaps the volcano rising from the sea called to her, and that sensation she was aware of, which she couldn't even qualify, was the awakening of those notes and rhythms demanding to be heard.

She knew intuitively that there was a part of her she needed to rediscover, to awaken some slumbering element within her, to remember what she had long ago left behind. Each day was a step deeper inside herself, an exploration and rediscovery of all the things that took her back, further and deeper into the past: the eerie cries of the *cagarras* in their invisible flight paths, swooping low in the darkness overhead, the sounds of the wind, the waves, and the sea.

Julia read the words of Fernão Lopes, the fifteenth century chronicler of several of the Portuguese kings, who wrote: "a man must always fail . . . when it comes to judging the reality of our own land or people of our own nationality . . . this conformity stems from the seed at the moment of fecundation, which controls to such an extent that which is generated from it, that it leaves the imprint of country and ancestry upon it." What these lines meant to Julia, and seemed perfectly obvious under the circumstances, was that she was not, indeed, could not be the same person she was before coming to the islands, back in California, not when over four hundred years of her past lay here. The words had evidently meant something to Sebastião, too, for him to have copied them out and left behind; a message or clue to the daughter he knew would come.

111

There were too many unanswered questions, jarring notes which kept Julia tossing over the problems in her mind, references in her father's notes about the origins of the family, of things unspoken, kept hidden, and vague hints about a book Sebastião mentioned, of which she so far found no trace, *Crónica da Ilha Encoberta—Chronicle of the Hidden Island.*

Mystery, which Mediterranean lands now lack, bathes these Atlantic islands. Daughters of fire and water, their very strangeness attracts, and they never release those who fall under their spell.

The Azores, Claude Dervenn, Paris, 1955

• • •

Excerpt from the writings of Sebastião do Canto e Castro:

The evening was incredibly clear, the air tremulous, palpable, and so finely tuned, I was left thinking it was possible to send or receive desires and thoughts across hundreds, perhaps thousands of miles.

I stood on the stone steps outside my room and held my breath. I touched the rough, worn stone of the building, thinking of the times over the years I had spent here. My parents had breathed the fragrance of these hillsides, the thick gardens beyond the yard, gazed upon these same stars, as did their parents before them. Friendships endured, not merely between individuals but between families, just as animosities and hatreds continued from one generation to the next. And if my grandparents and great-grandparents had been here, who else before them? Dom Fernando de Castro, returning from his failed expedition to capture the Canary Islands in 1424? Columbus, Luís de Camões, Vasco da Gama, Bartolomeu Dias? Was it possible that time only visited the islands now and then, that, rigid laws of nature be damned, the islands eluded or bent time to its will?

I walked down the steps of the building, lured by some inexplicable pres-

ence in the air, a hum, or buzz, a fine current that pulled me through the night air, as if I were on a tether.

I skirted dense shrubs and flowering crocosmia, to where some crypto-meria trees grew beside a wall of piled stones. Hearing a trickle of running water and the sounds of birds, I made my way through the trees, until I came to a clearing. It was a garden, and at the far end I could see the side of a large stone house. I stepped toward the building and paused in the shade of a eucalyptus tree. Leaning unsteadily against the trunk of the tree, I heard the mellifluous, hypnotic voice of the old woman, Maria dos Santos, who lived in that house, and whose words, though she spoke barely above a whis-per, were incredibly clear, as if she stood right beside me: "Only here, my children, are we completely alone, and yet, somehow never alone."

The old woman's voice awoke in me the taste of something long-lost, for-gotten, yet hauntingly familiar, as if those rich tones held a secret knowledge, a music from another time and place. I tasted the salt spray from the waves that broke against the rocks, the air saturated with the smell of a fine rain, which had fallen less than an hour earlier. Clouds skimmed unimpeded over the sea, the land acting like magnets, drawing the clouds like covers, hiding the isles from sight, as so many mythological islands throughout the Atlantic had appeared and just as quickly disappeared over the centuries.

As night fell, stars and planets appeared, shimmering like waxy drop-lets of light that might be swept farther by the warm wind. The moon hung like a pale, swollen fruit, ripened, ready to burst, surrounded by clusters of starry leaves that looked close enough to touch. Locked in its eternal struggle to summon the tides, the moon trembled, drawing closer to the earth as the dark waves climbed higher upon the black sand and rocks of Praia do Almoxarife.

Drawn out of my thoughts by Maria dos Santos's words, and above all else, by her voice, I listened to the old woman:

"The universe has certainly gone mad here on this tiny strip of land we call Água Zangada, though why the water should be so angry I cannot say. Here, where tears fall from the skies, masquerading as rain, which the two of you caught in that glass there. Taste it. Go on. You, Manuel, that's it. Don't make a face. The skies are all cried out now. And you, Maria Ange-lina, don't look so sad.

"It's true, of course, that something isn't right. Perhaps it is only the cry of a cagarra out there, wandering, lost, for like the milhafres, those birds *might well contain the souls of those who have died at sea. But, no, I don't believe that's what it is. That sound, that cry—the saddest sound in the world. Is it not?*

"Everything is topsy-turvy. There's no need to get upset about it, for nothing can be done. Not when all the universe is out of sorts. So much so, in fact, I can't begin to tell you. How can I speak to you of the girl who comes to me at night, for instance, a mere child, out of nowhere, it seems, as cold as the sea, and trembling from head to foot? She nestles like a kitten looking for a little warmth, and in the morning is always gone again. What am I supposed to do? Leave her alone out in the cold?

"Perhaps she's lost, too, or is only some poor unfortunate soul who died too young and hasn't had time yet to accept her fate.

115

"If these eyes of mine weren't so weak I might tell you what she looks like. Sometimes I think she's a ghost, she's so pale. I don't know who she is, or why she's chosen to grace me with her appearance, but all of life is nothing more than learning to accept the things we cannot understand.

"We can sit here all day and all night, and say nothing exists beyond the horizon. But beyond sight, beyond memory, beyond the little we know, in the deepest, darkest corners and chambers of our hearts, who knows what we might find, if we took that solitary journey?

"I can tell you there are dreams out there bigger than anything you've ever seen; bigger than Pico even, which, after all, is nothing more or less than a mountain. Still, it's often impossible to be sure what is real or only something we have clung to as a hope and thus believed. We could disappear, as well as these islands, and these dreams. Just like the young girl.

"Don't worry your heads about it. Nothing can be done about it now. We are here, naked to the world. The worst is sure to come—you will see. It will seem like an unbearable eternity, then it will all be over with, and seem like no time at all. That's how time makes fools of each of us.

"You too will have such dreams. So many, you couldn't possibly count them all, and each so dear, so close, because your hopes are strong enough to make you see them before your eyes and want them so dearly. But then one day you will find your dreams have forgotten you, or you'll have no time for them, and it will be left to your children or your children's children to carry their dreams, which you will hope they are strong enough to bear.

"Ah, God, that sound! It's enough to stop my heart from beating. Little Maria Angelina crying out, her sleep disturbed by troubling dreams, which

may or may not be her soul attempting to escape from her body, as some people believe. I don't pretend to know.

"I'm sorry, Manuel, if I close your mouth to stop your snores. I'm not a superstitious woman, but I believe it is safer not to take chances with such things. Who knows what may happen if one is too careless?

"The skies are clearing now that the rain has ended, and through the window, I see a cloud move across the smiling face of the moon. Such changes occur from one moment to the next. As they say, here on the Azores we have all the seasons in one day!

"Do you remember, Maria Angelina, when you made up your mind that somebody made the clouds, and Manuel, you got upset with me because I couldn't tell you who made them? I finally said that they came out of the open mouths of snoring children as they slept. You said you didn't believe me, Manuel, but that was the night I came in and found you had put a piece of tape across your mouth, to see if it was true. And you woke early in the morning, rushing through the house as if you'd burst, because there were no clouds in the sky that morning.

"It reminds me of a time long ago when a star fell into the sea. The starlight transformed a number of fish, and the birds were created.

"Can you imagine a million or more wild birds flying off in all directions, trying to find their way back to the heavens, but still chained to the earth, such as we are. At least they can fly, though being half fish and half star they can only soar between the stars above and the sea below, reaching neither one nor the other, as if they were our dreams and hopes, fluttering towards the heavens. This is what will sustain you through the worst of times, the hope that, like the birds, you will leave the ground behind and soar freely upon the wings of your dreams.

"Little Maria, you insisted, of course, that the clouds were created to keep the birds from seeing the stars they missed and longed for, to help them forget.

"Yes, things were truly different in those days. Then the dead didn't sit still in a hole in the ground, nor did they wander sadly across the world, alone. They stayed right here with you to remind you of who and what you are. And you talked to them, told them your problems, and they listened, too, for what else could they do?

"Sometimes they would offer a word or two of advice. Well, not a word really, because as everybody knows dead people don't talk, at least not in a way we can usually hear; but they nearly always gave a sign to show you

what they thought. Yes, there were a lot more signs then, with the dead doing their best to interfere with the day-to-day affairs of each of us, as if once you're dead you suddenly have all the answers. Sometimes there would be such a fuss. Families erupting in a big argument about some such thing, and so much carrying on, disturbing everyone's sleep and peace of mind, until finally one half of the village would no longer speak to the rest. Family against family, brother against brother, neighbor against neighbor—and after it was all over and everybody settled down once again, someone would discover that the whole thing began with a dispute in the graveyard. Two dead souls disagreeing about one thing or another. Isn't it just like them to bother the living with their spats, too? As if we didn't already have enough to worry about. And it would take the kind patience of the good Father Alves, or Monsignor Pereira da Silva, that sainted man, to come and finally set things straight, so that two dead fools would stop their foolishness. Ah, to make peace between dead men. Perhaps this is what happens when there isn't even enough soil to bury our dead, and everyone has to be buried on top of fathers, mothers, grandparents. One would think that a justly-deserved eternity would be a bit more comfortable.

"*We always say things were better then. I'm not so sure. Sometimes when you think back upon what used to be, you say, yes, it was better; there was much more love in the world, then, or so it seemed, the skies were bluer, there were more fish, and more friends. Certainly more hope, because of course, you were younger and there was so much more to hope for.*

"*Other times you shake your head, and remember that there was more sadness, too, more death and misery, friends and family dropping dead; droughts, famines, disease. You never saw so many ways to die.*

"*Perhaps nothing has really changed, after all. Maybe everything remains as it always has, and there is only the illusion of change, which keeps us going.*

"*It's easy for you children to drift off to sleep while you listen to a foolish old woman who is too afraid to stop talking. But do you know what happens when you're asleep? Don't ask. How can I tell you anything you don't already know? Isn't it enough that you fill your heads with all sorts of foolishness all day long so that at night, overcrowded and confused, your minds can't make heads or tails of anything, and your tired bodies can't help but fall asleep?*

"*It is said, however, that when the world of men and women, of grown-ups and children, is asleep, then all the plants rise out of their deep slumber and dance like children. There is music, too, though from where we can only*

117

wonder. Joyous dancing and song fills the air of night, which everyone knows is the time when all true magic occurs, before the sun rises again and lulls them back to sleep. Just the way the ocean, which you can hear at this very moment, lulls each of you to sleep with the sound of its endless waves, which are the sighs for her lost children. For the ocean is, as you know, our true mother. These islands have risen from her deep womb, and each of us as well, for we still carry the sea in our tears, whenever we cry, which is often, longing to return to her breast. The sea is in our blood and in our sweat, too—each of us is a shell with the roar of the ocean echoing inside.

"I don't worry that you've fallen asleep and can't hear me; that I sit here and talk to myself, for I speak to your hearts, and your hearts can hear whether you are awake or asleep, or so Dona Maria Ana do Carvalho Freitas once told me.

"Who am I telling all this to, to you children now asleep to the world, to myself? Perhaps I speak to some great-great-grandchild not yet born. Or maybe each one of us carries everyone and everything that will be deep inside us when we are born, the way we carry our own death from our birth, until the moment when it is time for death to exist in the world outside ourselves, and we cease to exist for our own selves, but only in others.

"Then again, sometimes I'm ready to believe that the mute child, not yet a woman, who appears out of the night is who I might have been, had my life been different; maybe she's come to mock me. But then I tell myself to stop being such a superstitious and irreligious old woman, to think that my life could have possibly been different from this.

"I only wish I could give each of you something more than the world. Not that the world is so poor a gift, but I am afraid our human world too often is. It's sometimes such a disappointment, and if I had my way, I would certainly shake things up and change one thing or another around here. But I am old and weak, a poor woman, left a widow by a man who had the thoughtlessness—so typical of men—to die before me, leaving nothing but memories and the words to remember what I have lost. Such saudades, this aching and longing, to have so many words without the one person who could understand, who lived those words with me. Sometimes I speak aloud to him of those moments we shared a lifetime ago, and although it is terrible not to hear him laugh or speak, often enough I do hear him, just the same, a whisper from the past, so he is never truly gone.

"What can I do but continue to hope, if not for me then for you? And if not for you then the next to come along. And so on. What more can any of

us do? For surely there must be some point to all of this. Unless it is true that we who are alive are merely the dreams of those who are dead. Since the dead must sleep for an eternity, they must therefore have countless dreams, which only seem more real to us since we are here, and the dead are where they are.

"Don't ask me when these words of mine will cease. All things, they say, come to an end. I am ignorant about such matters. I don't know if there is any difference between ending a tale and reaching the end of one's life. It's all nonsense when you realize neither has an end. Perhaps we are only here because the first tale was told by Adam and Eve to end their miserable loneliness, and each one of us keeps the story going in our own way. Perhaps, as long as I am telling you these words, we shall continue our struggles. And when I'm gone, each of you can continue to tell the stories, too, for my words will lead you to your own.

"As long as this story continues, we will escape the shadows which come creeping quietly at the end of each day. Sleep, children. Keep snoring, Manuel, you can't expect that all those clouds will find their way back into your mouth. And you, Maria Angelina, dream to your heart's content, for why shouldn't your dreams soar like wild birds? Don't worry, I will sit here and talk away the night while you sleep, until dawn, if I must."

Maria dos Santos's voice grew softer until it faded completely. Only then could I move again. Her words and the sound of her voice had kept me entranced. I stepped carefully back to my room, and knew I would return to discover more about Maria dos Santos as soon as possible, if only to hear that mellifluous voice once more.

CHAPTER 12

Julia do Canto e Castro
Horta, Azores

My dear Julia,

Since I have not heard anything from Sebastião in several months, I fear the worst. I wish I could come and assist you in your search. I don't know what the authorities are doing. It would take a miracle for them to find anything. Men grown effective only in their inefficiency! What do they care that a Canto e Castro is missing? Perhaps glad to be rid of him. Our family has its enemies. In the past fate has wronged us, stepping in at every opportune moment to deprive us of what is rightfully ours. There is no reason to think enemies wouldn't try to do the same now, if they could. Perhaps Sebastião stepped on someone's toes. Maybe he discovered something they didn't wish found, secrets they might be willing to kill to keep. I don't know about the jewels, or the ring he mentioned that belonged to Inês. Perhaps he uncovered new facts. Perhaps these things were stolen. I cannot say. But please be careful!

Many hugs and kisses,
Mateus

• • •

Julia stopped at Café Mar early the next morning with the hope that the ordinariness of the café and the familiar surroundings of Horta would keep her rooted in the here and now. I'm losing my bearings, she thought. She struggled to keep track of the days, as if time alone kept a thousand loose ends from unraveling, kept her in the present. Lose time, and loss of perception, clarity, even reality, could follow. Perhaps it was only the effect of being on an island, which appeared to run on its own time and made the mainland and the rest of the world seem increasingly less real, more vague and uncertain with each passing day.

Reading Sebastião's story about Maria dos Santos hadn't helped matters, but only created the sensation that Julia had stepped into Sebastião's fictional world.

"There are still sixty seconds in a minute, sixty minutes in an hour, twenty-four hours in a day," she reminded herself. Ah, but how long has it been for Sebastião, since he disappeared? Even if there were a definite date, a block of time marked out, a month, say, that he'd been gone, what would that really mean? An eternity or an instant—time, like happiness, fortune, luck, love, being freely noted and regarded, but rarely equally experienced. Time could flow swiftly, or crawl interminably, depending on the circumstances of the experience.

Julia used this escape clause of time to explain that if her father were engrossed in a new and exciting venture, something novel, he might forget how much time he'd been gone, while to Julia each hour of each day seemed to stretch to an eternity.

She eavesdropped on the patrons of the café, who repeated the latest rumors. The police, Julia overheard, were busy investigating several boats that had been found with no one aboard, contributing to an unheard-of flurry of activity, and a fair amount of speculation among the islanders.

Word of Sebastião's mysterious disappearance was repeated by idlers and gossips, who also mentioned the ghost ship and the luminescent woman, as if he were somehow to blame for all of these strange events.

Julia tried to remain levelheaded as she braced herself for bad news, such as a summons by the police to come and identify a body. Nothing was quite so unsettling, or lent itself to the fantastic, even the absurd, as a missing person. The fact that no trace of Sebastião had been found fueled wild rumors, and enhanced his reputation until it attained the magnitude of a man gifted with occult powers and mystery—as if all along he'd been one of the hidden Jews practicing the Cabbala, or belonged to a secret order of alchemists probing the secrets of life and death.

"I say he's in league with *her*," said a man seated at the table in the Café Mar, where he and his cronies were holding court. "He's a devil and she's his witch, and they've gone off together to frighten sailors, or worse."

"Of course," said a second man. "When the root is bad, nothing good can grow of it."

"A bad time for mariners," said a third.

"A bad time for each of us," said the first man.

"*Eh Pá!*—Oh man, just listen to you babbling idiots," a man seated at another table interjected. He was evidently a man of some means. "You've let the alcohol go to your heads. You sound like a gaggle of old women with your talk of witches and devils. Senhor Canto e Castro is likely keeping company with all the drowned pirates and Spaniards in what the English call Davy Jones's locker."

"This is what comes of leaving," said yet another man. "These islands don't easily forgive those who leave."

"*Os americanos,*" one of the others added contemptuously.

Julia did her best to ignore the talk, though at the same time she was eager for news, any news, even the spurious, for when a man goes missing who can say what is real, what is false? The regulars in the cafés were firmly convinced that all *americanos* were mad and more bother than they were worth. Such troubles obviously came from having too much money, of living with people who cared nothing for the old ways, the old country. This opinion was reinforced by every Azorean, like Sebastião, who tired of America and came back to the islands.

"How many times have we seen these fools come back," said the first man, "waving their money around, all puffed up, full of themselves, flaunting their success, to show that they are as good, if not better, than those who never left."

"Zé is right. Look, I was poor as dirt, I owned nothing, and now I am a rich man, a somebody; money, they say, is the universal equalizer. How quickly fortune changes hands. Just because a man is born rich doesn't mean he won't end up poor, and because a man is born poor it doesn't mean he won't die rich. Love and Fate are equally fickle, no?"

"Bah, fancy talk," said the man named Zé. "A pig in a suit is still a pig. I couldn't count the number who have run off with their tails between their legs leaving half-built homes behind."

The emigrants who tired of Canada or the United States, and

returned home to Portugal or the Azores paid for the largest, fanciest homes, drove the best, most expensive cars and dressed unlike anyone else on the islands: loud colors and flashy shoes, gold watches, gaudy jewelry, and loud voices. Thus they made themselves the objects of much scorn and ridicule, as well as a fair amount of envy. Many came back after years of saving their hard-earned money, the words of their neighbors and relatives still ringing in their ears: "You'll never amount to anything." "Don't say I didn't tell you so, when you end up meeting disaster in some forsaken place, far from your friends and family." "You think the world out there will welcome you, will care for you, the way we at home have always done?" They returned with an overwhelming desire to prove the others wrong, to show everyone that they had made something of themselves.

Sebastião, as was fit and proper, was born on the Azores, emigrating to the U.S. when he was fifteen. But as far as the islanders were concerned, anyone who left to live in the United States and came back was an *americano*—or a *brasileiro,* if they had gone to Brazil—no matter how long they stayed. It was as if any foreign land left an indelible mark or odor, which the Azoreans—much like birds after their own young have been handled by humans—no longer recognized. Fascinated by Sebastião's sudden and mysterious disappearance, the islanders continued to refer to him as the *americano* whenever they mentioned the tale among themselves.

Julia's case was worse. She wasn't born on the islands, and therefore suspect; she was someone too far removed, too distant to be given proper consideration. After all, what connection could she claim? She hadn't drunk of the Azorean sea air, the sea salt. She hadn't grown from a babe on what the Azoreans reaped from the soil and the sea. What had she suffered? What could she know of the sunshine, the rain, or the storms, winds, the deprivations and the pervading separateness that the islands provided for their children?

Thus, she would be treated like anyone else, but for the fact that she was a young woman, and therefore subject to attentions, both welcome and unwelcome. As far as the Azoreans were concerned, she was an outsider, a stranger—certainly no *açoriana,* like those who, if they had nothing else, at least had the good sense to know where they belonged.

As her father might have said, Julia hadn't been suckled on the wine of life which Pico, that magnificent breast-shaped mountain of the Atlantic, proffered—"While I," Sebastião was always quick to boast, "cut my milk teeth on the black stones of the Azores." Even Julia's brother, Antonio, had the advantage of being able to say that he'd been born on the islands, not that it was anything but an embarrassment to him. He hated explaining what the Azores were, where they were located, what his heritage was.

Living on the islands left indelible traces of Azorean soil in the marrow of one's bones. A person could taste the Azorean air and water by merely putting his mouth upon his arm. Sucking on a cut finger and tasting the drop of blood would instantly transport you back. Your eyes would roll heavenward, and you'd exclaim: Ah, my Azores!

Sebastião possessed an insatiable zeal for anything and everything grown or made on the islands—cheeses, wines and breads, fruits and vegetables—all made sweeter and more flavorful by the proximity of the sea and the rich volcanic soil, as well as some indefinable quality of place.

He would go to ridiculous lengths to procure a special bottle of Pico wine, like Lajido, and he would drink it as if it were the rarest of ambrosias. "Taste this nectar," he would say, "You are drinking the lava of the Azores. Can you taste it? The essence of Pico is in that glass, the mountain itself. The favorite wine of the czars of Russia."

Sebastião's home in California had been filled with artifacts from the islands. He'd brought souvenirs of the Azores and Portugal with him whenever he traveled. He couldn't bear to be far from these reminders of home: maps, books, flags, scrimshawed ivory, pieces of basalt, a jar of black sand, another filled with reddish clay, tapes of Azorean music and songs. A rock or shell from the Azores was no ordinary rock or shell, but by virtue of where it was found was imbued with some ineffable quality by which its possessor could feel himself, if not transported, then at the very least closer to home. Sebastião had sold the house when he returned to the island, but it had been a way for him to retain some part of the Azores when he had lived in the United States.

"If Sebastião could sling the Azores over his shoulders, he'd carry them wherever he goes," Julia's mother, Clara, often said. She couldn't understand this *saudade*—a word that Sebastião believed captured and defined the Portuguese soul, which not only conveyed a sense of intense longing and yearning, but which also implied a feeling of incompleteness; what you miss is over there, and you are over here, but a part of you is there, too, leaving you partially in exile or separate from yourself—this feeling for a group of islands, which, as far as she was concerned, anyone in their right mind should be happy to have gotten away from, but which Sebastião never truly left.

"Your father and his *saudades*. What a burden!" she would say. "How can someone be so enamored of what is only a forgotten archipelago, some isolated rocks in the middle of the ocean? What makes a place important is family, the friends one has there. He can have his islands if he thinks they are paradise."

It was something Sebastião never forgave her, a fault in her character, which failed to recognize the magic of the islands. "To miss the beauty of such a place," he had said, "is like listening to Mozart or Beethoven, or seeing the work of any great artist, and failing to be moved. It's being closed to life, a lack of understanding."

Julia understood Sebastião's reaction. She knew people for whom music meant nothing, just sounds, background noise. She had met people who had left the Azores, who, like her brother, never wanted to return, to whom the islands were nothing but distant rocks; the sea, nothing but salty water; the Azores just a place. They had gone to Canada, the United States, or Portugal, and never looked back. She had never understood how someone could have no desire to return, to experience the assault on the senses yet again. But then how often have we seen that which is beautiful, or brilliant go unappreciated and neglected, until it is gone, and then its loss is bemoaned? The call would be heard and answered perhaps by one of their children, or their grandchildren, or even a great-grandchild who would come to the islands to rediscover them, to find that part they carried within, that missing piece of a puzzle.

"The Azorean people possess a fierce tenacity," Sebastião would say, "a stubbornness and fatalism that are the result of many generations of experience, where everything has been distilled to the barest essentials. Hundreds of years of weathering plagues and famines, droughts, storms and pirates have strengthened and augmented those particular traits necessary for survival." The same characteristics Sebastião would find both infuriating and intriguing.

"The Azoreans," Sebastião would say, "are much like the *lapas*—the limpets they so love to eat, clinging tenaciously to their rocks."

Julia left the café and walked to another, while people pointed or gestured, whispering, "Look, that one there, the daughter of Sebastião do Canto e Castro, the *americano, o desventuroso*—the unlucky." Each proceeded to relate the story of his unexplained disappearance, how each of them foresaw, in his demeanor, his attitude, the telltale signs so easily discernible in his voice and eyes, the inevitability of his tragic end.

"I always said that one would come to no good, eh, Manuel?" Rui Gomes, standing in the doorway of his near-empty cheese shop said, with the tone of one declaring an official edict. "I said he was looking for trouble."

"Sure," Manuel replied. "Another big-shot *americano* coming over here like he owns the place."

"He had the look of a marked man," said Rui.

Each person devised his own favorite theory of what had happened to Sebastião, where he was and with whom, none of it good, most of it improbable, though there were one or two in the cafés who waved the matter away impatiently, as if to say he wasn't worth their time or bother. They seemed to compete with one another, dreaming up the most outlandish explanations: he'd been murdered, or he'd been in a brawl and killed someone and fled; he'd been swallowed by a crevice that had promptly closed up again, during one of the earthquakes; he had changed into some creature, or had vanished with the use of some unspecified "magical arts."

The one thing they were all certain of, however, was that Sebastião had met with some terrible misfortune. It was easier to envision disaster or a mysterious event, as opposed to a far more likely case of simple thoughtlessness, or a case of amnesia. There was something Julia couldn't quite remember, something Sebastião had once said, perhaps, or something of his she had once read, how a mystery loves a vacuum, that with a dearth of facts supposition often suffices and stated frequently enough readily becomes accepted as proof, especially when the theory centers on the bleakest viewpoint.

Sebastião obviously had it coming, was deserving of his fate, as was anyone who thought too highly of himself. And people were quick to point out that the Azores—like jealous gods—were easily offended and swift to punish.

127

The seeker will act without understanding, will hear without listening, and know without comprehending. He will see without believing, and arrive before knowing he has left. He will feel himself on the trajectory, and look to see where he is headed, without pausing to see from where he began.

—Sebastião do Canto e Castro

. . .

Julia returned to Maria dos Santos's garden, drawn by a lingering uncertainty: had she overlooked something important? Perhaps the gurgling water of the spring, or the melodic voice of Maria dos Santos, the photographs of Nicolau and Teresa, or the fleeting glimpse of a face seen through the window, called to her, until she needed to go back and see for herself, if only to confirm what she thought she had only imagined—a natural enough reaction of someone exposed to the unexpected or the supernatural—*Did I really see that? Was that what I heard? Do my senses deceive me?* We often distrust our ability to judge what is, what isn't, while at the same time put such unrealistic demands and expectations on these same senses, relying on them to judge our fellow man, to fathom the mysteries of life, love, and death. In the end, these very senses play a determining role in our lives: a scent triggers certain forgotten memories, a face or a few words transport us back to another time and place. Our senses, after all, being the instruments by which the phenomenon of déjà-vu occurs, the catalyst whereby love is roused and ignited, that which motivates us to follow some and shun others.

As if this strange urge to retrace her steps were a ruse wrought by the fates, a conspiracy designed to confirm her suspicions that subtle forces were afoot, Julia entered the garden and met Maria dos Santos's grandson, Nicolau.

"Ah, here you are," Maria dos Santos said, as if she'd been waiting all morning for Julia. "You are in time to meet Nicolau, who has just returned." Maria dos Santos's smile was as bright as the garden that surrounded her. There was a ring of singsong, of merriment in her voice, too, as if with these words, she were the happiest, youngest, most joyful soul in the world. And though Julia knew better, she couldn't shake the thought that Nicolau's grandmother was somehow responsible for her presence, as if she'd put Julia under a spell to return at this moment.

Nicolau greeted her warmly, as if she were an old friend. They clasped hands and he leaned in to kiss both sides of her face. "So we finally meet," Nicolau said. He wore sandals, a t-shirt and jeans. He was of medium build, and struck Julia as being comfortable in his own skin. His smile was warm, and his gaze pensive. His eyes were a luminous green, and seemed to take in everything, as though capable of seeing beneath the surface of things. There was an undercurrent of the raw, the natural about him, too, by which one could see he could no sooner be controlled than could the sea or the winds.

"Don't mind me," said Maria dos Santos, turning away and busying herself in the garden. "I have much to do. I'll leave you two to get acquainted."

An awkward pause followed. A moment of hesitation as Julia's and Nicolau's eyes met, looked away, and met again, as if neither was sure where to rest their gaze while they struggled with what to say or do next, on what subject they might meet as equals and share an interest, what words would lead to a profusion, and which—to avoid at all costs— would lead to silence.

"It's so nice here," Julia said. "I've never seen a garden like your grandmother's."

"Maria dos Santos has a special way with everything she touches," Nicolau said. "Flowers and plants, animals, birds, and children—everything and everyone." He looked Julia in the eye, and she wondered if he meant himself, or her, or something else altogether by his last comment.

Julia nodded, then said, "I guess I should have said I've never met anyone like *her.*"

"No, there's certainly no one like my grandmother."

They watched Maria dos Santos bustle here and there, one moment holding some flowers, the next gathering a few twigs in her arms, wrapping a scarf around her shoulders. She bent down and dug at one spot, then moved to another, speaking now to the birds, and then to the flowers, encouraging and commending them for their beauty: "Each day your beauty grows."

"She's a marvel to watch," Julia said. "I don't think I could keep up with her."

Nicolau shook his head. "She's incredibly strong, not physically, really, but more to do with her spirit, the wisdom of her years, knowing herself and the world around her. The way she coaxes the flowers and plants to grow so much brighter and fuller than they normally do."

Maria dos Santos poured water from a metal pitcher into the stone birdbath that stood in the center of the garden. The birds in the bath didn't fly away, Julia noticed.

They watched as she moved through the garden, so lightly, so nimbly, as if at any moment she might suddenly take flight, like the birds that followed wherever she went.

"I could show you pictures of her when she was perhaps the most beautiful woman in the Azores," he said.

"I don't doubt it." She turned toward Nicolau. "I'd like to see them sometime." She didn't admit to having seen some of the photos already.

Julia had never seen eyes so intense. She could feel them probing when Nicolau looked at her, and was bemused to find there was something vaguely disturbing about him. She thought for a moment that perhaps she should leave, but after all she'd come of her own accord, and he was nice enough. It would seem silly to run off so soon. What was she, a young schoolgirl? She put on what her father called her 'cold face.' It was a way of deterring interest, of becoming *fechada,* closing herself off. She'd be polite, friendly even, but not warm, not inviting—distant.

They both looked up and realized Maria dos Santos had left the garden. Again, an awkward silence followed. Julia stole glances at Nicolau as he looked to see where his grandmother had gone. Why is she leaving us alone, Julia thought. I hope she isn't trying to be a matchmaker. This is no time for romance. Sebastião would have corrected her: the time is always ripe for romance. She shook her head clear of the thought. Island of Lovers or not, this was the last thing she needed.

He turned to Julia with an expression of embarrassment and shrugged. "She can also be full of mischief," he said. His words broke the tension. "Let me show you the rest of the garden."

They rose and walked deeper into the garden where the scent of the flowers grew immediately stronger; the blend of jasmine, wallflower, honeysuckle, roses, and others she couldn't identify made her light-headed. With each step she encountered new scents that blended with others. Subtle changes occurred, as if the shape, scent and texture of the garden transformed and adapted to their presence. Birds cooed and flitted between the branches of the trees and in the birdbath, the colors of the plants sharpened, the flowers opened wider, exuding their fragrance, bestowing their charms, as the trees, bushes and shrubs unfolded. Julia realized the garden was much larger than it appeared. There was also an order and sense to it that wasn't apparent at first sight.

"It's a labyrinth," Julia said.

"Yes," Nicolau said.

"How wonderful."

"You are here to look for your father?" he said.

She nodded. "He has disappeared. Did you ever see him?"

"Sometimes at the cafés, or talking to José. I saw him several times on Pico." Did she detect a slight hesitancy to his response?

"Pico?"

"He would go to Quebrado do Caminho now and then, spend a few days there," Nicolau said. "I hope you find him soon."

"Thank you," Julia said. "It's a mystery. But then these islands seem to be full of mysteries."

"Really?"

"The strangeness of this garden, for instance," she said. "Unusual birds and plants, to say nothing of mysterious water that bubbles out from the ground and disappears again—a secret world where nothing appears to follow the normal way of things."

Nicolau smiled and shrugged as if to say this was really not so unusual.

"More and more these islands seem like icebergs," Julia said.

"Icebergs? Here?"

"Well, like icebergs, most of what's there you never see, but lies hidden below the water."

"What do you think is hidden here," he said, with an intriguing smile.

"I'm not sure," Julia said. "But I don't think my father's disappearance is the only mystery."

"No," Nicolau said. "People, too, are mysteries. Your father is mysterious, no?"

"Yes, well, his disappearance is certainly a mystery so far," Julia said.

"And perhaps there are other reasons why you are here?"

Julia stared at him at a loss for words. What could he possibly know of why she was here? He had a way of gently urging the conversation with his tone, a question, a suggestion.

"What do you mean?" she said.

"Maria dos Santos would say that we often don't see all the reasons why we do something. We see one cause, when in truth there may be many, or a cause different from what we imagine, just the way many effects can bring about one result." He was silent as they wound their way around the trees, before speaking again. "Might you have come here, even if your father had not disappeared?"

"You mean as if I were meant to be here?" Julia said. Was he mocking her?

He shrugged. "In a sense. Perhaps you would have come, even if your father hadn't disappeared. The time was right, the place was right, and you were right."

Julia didn't answer. How strange, she thought. It *had* been in the back of her mind to return to the islands for some time. She quit her job before she knew her father was missing, plus she'd been saving her money for just such an event. Over the past day or two she'd concluded Sebastião wasn't on Faial, and yet she stayed, waiting—for what? Was there something more that kept her here, something else she hoped to discover?

They sat down again on another bench, strategically placed beside a flowering loquat tree. They thought their own thoughts, felt their own feelings, in silence, as several birds trilled sweetly in the branches above their heads. The minutes ticked away, as the afternoon waned, and the garden grew softer, quieter. There was a quote she'd found among her father's papers: "A person acts without understanding, hears without listening, and arrives before knowing he has left." It could very well have been written about her.

He's so quiet. Please speak. After a few moments he broke the silence, and asked where she was staying. They exchanged bits of information, perhaps unremarkable to anyone else, but for the subtext occurring behind and between the words.

"What sort of work do you do?" Julia said.

"I teach, mostly, but I also write and play music."

"Here?"

"In Horta, sometimes Madalena, and other places, too."

"The piano?"

"Yes—and you," he said, "you're from California, a singer?"

"Yes. I sing, and play piano," she said, trying to remember if she had mentioned anything to Maria dos Santos about being a musician. "I'm hoping to write music."

"Perhaps I could hear you sing sometime?"

Julia smiled. "Sure. If I get to hear you play the piano."

He looked pleased. "You could hear the group I play with."

"I'd like that." She rose. "I should go now. It's getting late."

Julia returned to her father's room, surprised by the relief she felt, as if the room somehow represented safety, or perhaps she only felt closer to Sebastião there, less vulnerable to the whims and fancies she associated with Maria dos Santos, her garden, and now her grandson.

. . .

Fragment from the notebooks of Sebastião do Canto e Castro:

The visions came to Abílio Fula in his dreams. He rode on horseback, following his grandfather who rode just ahead of Abílio. They plodded slowly up the slopes of soft earth that rose sharply from the ocean below.

"We must find the water," vovô was saying.

His grandfather invited Abílio to help search for the elusive stream that bubbled from a crack in the earth, which grandfather's grandfather had told him about when he was a boy.

"The water does not flow," his grandfather said, "but seeps back into the ground and disappears."

"Do you think we will find it this time, vovô?" Abílio asked.

"Of course we will, and if not this time, then the next time, for certain."

"What then, when we find it?"

"Then, we'll know all that we have forgotten, Abílio."

The boy hoped they would find the brook of special water. He was tired of looking and finding nothing, and his grandfather wanted so badly to find it.

Once, when his grandfather's horse kicked loose some clods of dirt, there was a tinkling sound of metal against the hoof.

"What is that, vovô?" Abílio asked. His grandfather got off his horse and investigated. *"Ah!"* he said. *"Silver coins, that's all."* He picked up the coins and put them in his pocket. His grandfather was so upset that they hadn't found his beloved fountain, Abílio was afraid to say anything, though he was very curious about the coins.

A week later, Abílio finally asked about the silver. His grandfather mumbled that he had placed the coins outside on a bench, and moments later, when he had turned back, they were gone, swallowed by one of the geese or a goat.

Of course, there were often mysterious causes which prevented vovô from finding the spring, perhaps a result of the magical properties of the water itself: strange mists and clouds appeared, clinging to the land and making it difficult to see where one was going; sometimes the shrubs and vines grew such that it led one to search in circles.

His grandfather was old and easily forgot things. But the one thing that never left his mind was the water, which would change everything: make the family rich, allow them to live forever, and turn the island into the paradise it had once been, if used properly.

"He's just a crazy old man," people said about Abílio's grandfather. *"He's lost his wits, just like his father, and his father's father before him. River of life, lakes of fire,* louco!"

"What do they know?" his grandfather said. *"Doubters. All they have to believe in are the sorrows they would not leave behind even if they could. That's what they cling to. They wring sadness from life and drink down every last drop. They have forgotten how to dream."* He didn't speak angrily, but as though he felt sorry for them. Anyone, he believed, with any spirit or imagination, left the island to go find dreams in other places, while those who remained had forgotten how to dream. He shook his gray head sadly. *"So much has changed."*

Abílio looked at the hills, the mounds of thick earth, covered with rich blankets of grass and shrubs, flowers and trees—plants that grew so thick in places you could hardly walk or even crawl through. He wondered what was inside, hidden beneath, below those hills.

135

"The fountain," his grandfather said, "comes from the very center of the world, where the vast lake of everlasting fires is to be found—the lake of eternal life."

Abílio tried to imagine the spring traveling all that way, bubbling up through miles of rock. And the lake, what did it look like? Would they really live forever? It did sound crazy, but his grandfather seemed so certain, so sure of what he would find.

Abílio remembered the fire that had come out of the sea when he was very young. It had shaken the island and turned the skies black, then formed a new part of the island. Was that part of the lake of fire? These islands of rock and dirt were born of fire and water. The salty ocean surrounded them, and yet there were fresh water springs that came from deep in the earth.

"All things come from the lake," his grandfather said. "And perhaps, if you are lucky enough to find it, you could return to its source. One thing is for certain, it would be impossible to drown in that water."

Abílio often dreamed of swimming down through the stream, down to the lake, to the center of the world, from where all life had come.

Grandfather dismounted from his horse and put his ear to the ground.

"Do you hear something, vovô?" Abílio asked.

"Shh." He put a finger to his lips to silence Abílio.

Grandfather pushed aside the grass. There was a smooth rock just below the dirt, which he brushed off, then touched his ear to the smooth surface. He closed his eyes, and then leaped to his feet.

"We're close, Abílio. Come, get down from the pony."

Abílio, excited by his grandfather's certainty, jumped down from his horse.

"Right here. Put your ear to the rock." Grandfather sat back down again and put his ear to the ground. "Do you hear it, Abílio?"

"I think so!" Abílio wasn't sure. Was it the water, or his heart beating in his chest, the wind rustling through the grasses, his breath escaping through clenched teeth, or all these things together?

"Yes! Yes, the sound of water running, Abílio. Our river is right here, under this ground." Grandfather danced a few steps and clapped his hands.

They explored the entire area, poking under rocks and shrubs, trying to follow the river's path and locate where it might be closest to the surface, but in the end the elusive river once more changed its course. Putting their ears to the ground, they heard only the sound of their failing hope and disappointment.

Abílio loved his grandfather more than anything, but he was also embarrassed by the sarcastic comments he heard when people poked fun at him.

"You can't believe a word he says," Abílio's friends taunted, repeating what they had heard their parents say. "His head is full of nonsense."

Abílio fought back. "My grandfather knows more than anyone," he said, but his defenses were weakening, and lacked the conviction they once had.

Maybe they were right. Abílio had to admit his grandfather was certainly different from any of his friends' grandfathers, who never spoke about rivers of life, or lakes of fire, or searched for things no one else could see.

Abílio fished with his grandfather, and wondered if what people said about him was true. He wanted so much to believe the things his grandfather told him, as they sat on the rocks, casting their lines into the sea.

137

"Sometimes," his grandfather said. "You sit here and learn the secret of things." He leaned over, resting his ear against the fishing pole and closed his eyes. Abílio watched in silence, and smiled when his grandfather sat up again. "Yes, Abílio, this island has seen more than a hundred thousand million waves come and go, perhaps the same wave traveling around the earth again and again." He laughed. "We don't need to go anywhere, or leave the island—eventually the wave will bring everything to us."

"Hey, old man! Catch anything?" It was Miguel Alves, a young man, sailing his boat out in search of richer fishing waters.

"Not yet." The old man waved at the fisherman and laughed. "You watch, he'll go out farther and stay out longer than anyone, and even then, he'll be lucky to come back with enough to feed his family. I don't know how our people will survive. Before, when the river flowed, there was always more than enough fish."

After they had fished for half-a-day, Abílio peered into his grandfather's bucket full of fish. Abílio's was still empty.

"Vovô," he said. "I don't understand. We're both in the same place, using the same bait, and your bucket is full, while mine is empty."

"It takes patience, Abílio, that and learning to feel the line, the fish. You have to listen and call them, learn to talk to the fish."

Abílio looked at him, full of doubt.

"I'll show you." Again, his grandfather leaned his ear against the pole, put his finger to his lips, his eyes shut tightly, and jiggled the pole slightly, very lightly tapping it with his thumb, then ran his thumb down the side of the

pole, back and forth, whispering softly, his mouth against the pole—pausing a moment, then rubbing, whispering.

A moment later, he pulled the line in with the biggest fish of the day.

Later, they looked up and watched a boat pass in the distance.

"Vovô, why do none of the boats ever stop here?"

"They used to, once, long ago. When the first people came and brought the mountains up from under the sea, and the water flowed and they lived forever. But after many years they forgot, the people misplaced their dreams and hopes, the water disappeared, and before they knew it, people everywhere else forgot about them, and the boats stopped coming."

And in the evening, gazing up at the star-filled heavens. "Look, Abílio, a shooting star—another child has come into the world."

It was during these rare moments that Abílio felt very close to seeing, hearing, or knowing something very special. If he stuck his head out his open window, he experienced a sensation that the stars, which seemed so very close, were unscrambling some hidden meaning, for his eyes only. When he heard the voices of the wind sweeping down the sides of Pico, roaring and rumbling and whistling in the darkness, he swore he could distinguish, among its many voices one that called out to him.

He could almost reach out and touch something—a calling like that of the rising moon, the waves, the pull of the stars themselves . . .

•

Abílio awoke and his visions scattered, fleeing into the dark corners of the room.

"Vovô!" His heart beat rapidly and a sudden sadness squeezed his throat.

Grandfather was dead. He had been gone for years now. But the dreams, and the things he said made him so alive. The Lake of Everlasting Life! Abílio smiled. Oh, how they had looked for that imaginary river of water that would let them live forever. He had not searched in so many years, not since grandfather had died.

Why had the old man clung so tightly to that absurd dream, passed down generation after generation? Was that where his own father had disappeared to now and again, never speaking of where he was going, but silently getting on his horse and wandering over the island? Until he was too old to go riding as well?

There was no point to it. It was like chasing the past.

Abílio got dressed and ate. The islands had changed since he was a boy, and were still changing. Progress, though slow, came unavoidably, though in some ways things were no different from when his grandfather was a boy.

Was there ever a river of water that sprang from the earth, giving eternal life, or was his grandfather the mad old fool everyone said he was?

Abílio went out and took care of the animals. He did some work around the yard, yet couldn't rid his mind of the lake of fires and the river of life, or his grandfather. He fetched the saddle for his horse, and took the animal out into the fields. He mounted, guiding the horse up toward the hills. Both horse and rider knew the invisible paths. Abílio sniffed the air. He realized for the first time that grandfather's searching had been for Abílio's sake, not for himself. Soon his own grandson would be old enough to go riding with him. He had forgotten just how important it was to search, to always keep searching.

139

He listened. Did he hear the sound of water in the distance?

"Get going," he said to the animal. "We have a river to find."

. . . they [the Portuguese] began where the Arabs left off, by setting sail into the 'Green Sea of Darkness,' that vast uncharted ocean which classical and medieval fancy had filled with monsters and marvels. Greek myth, Norse, Arab and Celtic legend died hard among the seafaring folk of Western Europe, whose frail craft rarely ventured far from the friendly shore, and so rarely enabled the crews to test their superstitions by experience. It was well established that too arrogant a trust in the winds and waves meant the risk of an encounter with the sirens, whose beauty and sweet singing lured mariners to their doom. The dreadful Bishop of the seas, with his phosphorescent mitre, had been decried in mid-Atlantic, vast and menacing. Those who eluded his grip might still fall victims to the sea-unicorn, whose horn could transfix three caravels at a blow. . . . Such phantoms haunted the seas on the way to that ideal commonwealth, set in an enchanted island, of which men dreamed in the middle ages, until they so far mistook the island in their maps.

Vasco da Gama and His Successors, K. G. Jayne, London, 1910

• • •

The next morning Nicolau showed up on the doorstep to Sebastião's room in Praia do Almoxarife. *"Bom dia,"* he said, with a wide grin, looking every bit like a country boy in his straw hat, plaid shirt, rough work pants, and sandals.

Julia couldn't help but laugh. "Good day," she said. "My, what a sight."

"Would you like to take a drive around Faial?" he asked, bowing slightly.

Julia hesitated. There was so much to read if she were going to make any progress. On the other hand, she'd already put in a couple of hours trying to make sense of the thousand-and-one scraps and loose ends of Sebastião's notes, and felt she could use a break. She looked at her watch. It was noon. I probably look like hell, she thought. She had washed in the bathroom and changed into tan slacks and a red sleeveless top. Julia touched her hair. "I don't know," she said. "Am I dressed all right for an outing?"

"Don't be silly, you look wonderful," Nicolau said. "And I'm a very good guide. I know all the best spots."

"Sure," she said. "It'd be good to get out of here and see some of the island."

They drove first up to the caldera, the large crater of *Pico Gordo* in the center of the island. Although it wasn't nearly as tall as Pico the crater was quite impressive. They got out of the car and walked around. The rim of the caldera jutted downward in a precipitous slope, ending in a wide, flat recess that looked all but inaccessible, though Nicolau pointed to a narrow winding trail that led down. The floor of the crater wasn't a stark unearthly landscape, but quite the opposite, covered in lush meadows, green grasses, shrubs, small trees, and pools of water that in the winter formed a lake—though now it had dried to little more than several ponds. It had been a very long while since this particular volcano in the heart of Faial had spewed lava.

"More recently, Capelinhos erupted on the southwestern side of the island," Nicolau explained.

"My mother, father and brother were here at the time," Julia said. "They got to see it themselves, but they returned to the States before I was born. My mother was afraid of the volcano. She insisted they leave. My father likes to say I was conceived with the ash and lava from Capelinhos."

Nicolau smiled. "You have the fire inside you?"

"Perhaps. Maybe that's why I came so easily. I didn't have to think twice."

"It's interesting that you are here now when another volcano is coming from the sea, don't you think?"

"You're right," Julia said. "I hadn't really thought about it. Do you think it's happening in my honor?"

He laughed. "Perhaps so. A welcome home."

"Strange welcome," she said. "I wonder if there will end up being a tenth island? What would they call it, I wonder?"

"Well, since there's already a *Sete Cidades,* perhaps, *Antília?"* he said.

"Yes, why not," she said. "After the old legends."

Julia was struck by how much she trusted Nicolau, how at ease she felt, though at the same time she felt anxious, fearing she would speak too freely, perhaps say something he might misinterpret. *Don't show your hand, not until you know what the other is holding.* Strange, the things one thinks at times, as if we are not who we are in the here and now, but a reflection of another time, another place, other lives. As if so much hangs in the balance. For a moment she didn't see herself and Nicolau as two people in the present, with the only possible risk being hurt pride and rejection, where you can turn and walk away with no great consequence—at least not that one can foresee, the future being remote and obscure—instead, she saw a fleeting glimpse of two others: vaguely representational, remote shadows of themselves, far off, where and when such moves were fraught with dangers, where advances and declarations of one's feelings for another could bring death or ruin, where one's role was ordained, and freedom to pick and choose in short supply.

"It's beautiful up here, Nicolau," she said, hoping to dispel the disturbing thoughts.

He nodded. "You can call me Nick," he said. "Or Nico. Everyone else does."

"Nick," she said, "Nico," trying out the words. "I like Nicolau better." No nicknames, she thought. That's too familiar. Better to keep things at a level of awkward unfamiliarity.

"Me, too," he said. "Let's go. There's more to see."

They returned to his car and drove down the road, away from the *caldeira,* south toward the shore. After a short time they turned onto the main road and drove along the coast, past several ruined villages as they approached Capelinhos.

"There's the old lighthouse." Julia said, pointing at the ruined structure in the distance. In front of the lighthouse was an eerie sight, stark and bleak—the remains of the volcano that had appeared off the coast, spewing a gigantic plume of smoke and ash.

Nicolau explained how the new volcano had sunk after the first

143

eruption, but rose again a few months later. It sank again, then rose and connected to the island of Faial, burying the village of Capelinhos and destroying the lighthouse. The earthquakes and ash destroyed the villages of Praia do Norte and Ribeira Funda, and a large crack appeared in the *caldeira*. "Many people thought it, too, would erupt," he said. "They packed their belongings and left the island."

"But your grandmother stayed," Julia said.

"Maria dos Santos is not afraid of anything," Nicolau said, matter-of-factly. "She could never leave here. I don't think she'd survive anywhere else. This is her place."

"No, I couldn't imagine her anywhere else," Julia said.

"She lives for her little corner of the island. The house and garden are part of her, and she's a part of them. Like her, it's special, like nowhere else on the island."

"I believe that," Julia said. "Just what I saw of the colors, sounds and smells in the garden, is like stepping into another world—a dream world."

"My grandmother has not only learned to charm the birds from the sky, the flowers from the earth, and the winds," he said, "but more, Julia, much more than that. As long as I've known it my grandmother has been the heart of that garden. It too is full of life. I don't think it could survive without her."

He spoke passionately, his voice, rich, deep and sonorous.

Julia felt his gaze on her face, and with a flash of self-consciousness flushed slightly.

"And the spring?" she said.

He smiled. "Ah, yes, the spring, too."

Nicolau parked the car, then took out a basket and a bottle of red wine, hidden beneath a blanket in the back seat.

"A picnic," he said, grinning at Julia's look of surprise.

"Splendid," she said. "We can sit here and watch for whales and new islands."

They climbed to a rocky point that plummeted to the sea below. The water was a striking blue below where the waves smashed incessantly, as if intent on reclaiming the lava that had so impetuously sought the air and the sunlight, and left the ocean depths behind.

Nicolau offered his hand as they made their way over the rocks. They found a comfortable spot to have their picnic. Julia spread out the blanket, while Nicolau took a corkscrew from the basket, and opened the bottle of wine. He poured two glasses.

"To the new island," he said, as they touched their glasses together.

They peered at the vast ocean. "Nothing but waves as far as the eye can see," Julia said. They ate cheese and bread, drank wine, and listened to the waves, and the screeching sea birds.

"It's good to see all this again," Julia said. "I just wish my father were here."

Nicolau nodded. "I hope everything turns out well, that Sebastião is okay."

"Thank you," she said. "You certainly ordered a perfect day for us."

"Do you remember your first visit here?" he asked.

"No, not really. When I think of the past it seems I was always here, even though I grew up elsewhere. My dreams were so often of this place. I always heard stories, saw pictures, books—that must seem strange to you."

"No, not at all," Nicolau said. "The islands obviously made an impression on you."

"That they did," Julia said. "Tell me about your grandfather, Teodoro dos Santos."

He lay back and faced the sky.

"Teodoro used to tell us the most wonderful stories," Nicolau said. "His grandmother, he would tell us, came from the sea. *Uma menina do mar*—A child of the sea, he called her, a siren or mermaid. 'She was very beautiful,' he'd say. 'With the voice of the sea.'" He laughed. "He told us we were the descendants of the lost people of Atlantis, although he often called it *Antília,* and some day, he would say, Atlantis will rise again. He would take Teresa and me out on his boat. We loved to go and watch the dolphins and whales, to feel the sea breeze. He would teach us to read the sea, to listen to its language, the waves, the colors, and we would feel so much a part of it, Teodoro, Teresa and I.

"'You grow up, and listen,' he said. 'Always listen, and if you do you will hear me, and others like us, those who come from the sea.' And, of course, I have always done what he asked me to do. I've always loved the sea."

"Well, then, you could teach me a thing or two," Julia said. "The ocean always makes me nervous, even though I grew up near the sea."

"Really?"

145

"Its vastness, and depths, its unpredictable power. All the things you can't see."

"Hmm," Nicolau said. "You mean its beauty."

"That, too," Julia said. "Seductive and deadly, beautiful and terrible. We're so close in many ways to the ocean, and yet, we are separate from it. Speaking of beauty," she said, "your sister is extremely beautiful. Stunning, really."

He sat up and turned to her with a startled look. "Teresa?"

He sounded genuinely shocked. "I saw her picture."

"Ah," he lay back down. "Yes, she is very pretty."

"I hope to meet her."

"I'm sure you will, though when and where—?"

"She spends her time in Pico?"

He nodded. "In Quebrado, an old village on Pico."

"She's not kept there, is she?" Julia said. "I mean, she isn't some sort of black sheep you have to keep hidden from the rest of the world? Because I know a thing or two about that."

"No, it's just that, well, she is different." He sighed. "She belongs in another time. And Teodoro's death was especially hard on her. In some ways, she's never really recovered."

"Does she ever stay with your grandmother?"

"Sometimes. Teresa takes care of some people in Quebrado. She doesn't like to leave them, but now and then she brings one or two of the children to visit Maria dos Santos. Teresa's very shy. She doesn't go out, or speak often. But my God she sings like a siren."

"I thought I might have seen her at your grandmother's," Julia said. "Peering from a window."

"Perhaps," he said, raising his eyebrows and smiling.

"*Senhor Mistério,*" Julia said. "Your grandfather sounds a bit like José Manuel."

"Didn't you know?" he said. "They were cousins."

"Oh." Something clicked in Julia's mind, the strange synchronicity, the connections, as if certain things had to be, were ordained. Astounding, she thought, nothing could surprise me now.

"Have you read any Portuguese or Azorean writers?" he asked. "Poets like Camões, Pessoa, Quental, the Three Marias?"

"Some, but not nearly enough," Julia said.

"Camões was the greatest Portuguese poet. He wrote *Os Lusíadas*—*The Lusiads*, a poem about the history of Portugal and the discoveries of its explorers. But he also wrote beautiful sonnets and lyric poems."

"I've read what he wrote about Inês de Castro," Julia said. "And what he wrote about *A Ilha dos Amores*—The Isle of Love, do you think he meant the Azores?"

"I like to think so," Nicolau said. "The route for the return from India brought the ships past here, following the circle of the Gulf Stream. And of course Camões did sail to India and China."

Julia lay on her side gazing out at the sea. "Sebastião always said the Azores were those islands which Camões wrote about."

"Where do you think your father is," he asked, "what happened to him?"

"I don't know. I only wish I knew where he might have gone, and why he left."

Julia felt the warmth of the sunlight, the wine and the scent of the island beneath them, as Nicolau recited:

Ó mar salgado, quanto do teu sal
São lágrimas de Portugal!
Por te cruzarmos, quantas mães choraram,
Quantos filhos em vão rezaram!
Quantas noivas ficaram por casar
Para que fosses nosso, ó mar!

Valeu a pena? Tudo vale a pena
Se a alma não é pequena.
Quem quer passar além do Bojador
Tem que passar além da dor.
Deus ao mar o perigo e o abismo deu,
Mas nele é que espelhou o céu.

Oh salty sea, how much of your salt
Are the tears of Portugal?
To cross you, how many mothers wept?
How many sons prayed in vain!
How many brides remained unwed
To make you our own, oh sea!

Was it worth it? Everything is worth it
If the soul is not small
He who would sail beyond Cape Bojador
Must go beyond all pain.
God gave the sea its abyss, and its dangers
But in the sea, is the mirror of the heavens.[4]

The hairs rose on the back of Julia's neck. The poem was splendid in its own right, but made more so as a result of the voice that made it mesmerizing. The warm familiarity of one of Fernando Pessoa's most beloved poems. How many times over the years had she heard her father or her grandmother say, *"Tudo vale a pena, se a alma não é pequena."*

Again, Julia felt as though she were thrown back to another place, another time, that she was someone else, part of another story. How strange life is, she thought, how unpredictable. She remembered something Sebastião had written: "We are not merely living our own lives, but the lives of all who know us, and those who have preceded us."

"I love that poem," Julia said. "'Mar Português.' It's fantastic."

"Ah, so you know Pessoa. He too visited these islands. His mother's family was from Terceira. He's my favorite poet."

Julia nodded, speechless.

It wasn't only Nicolau's voice reading the poem that caused the chill she felt. It was also that she had gone so long without an awareness of mystery, and now, here, there were connections emerging between Sebastião and Nicolau, Pessoa and King Sebastião, herself and the past, that left her wondering where else this mystery would lead her.

CHAPTER 15

The heart is a lodestone, pulling, heeding the call. In the end everything is a   *149*
search for love, wanting to belong, wanting to fuse with another.

—Sebastião do Canto e Castro.

· · ·

After spending two days and most of two evenings in Praia do Almoxarife, concentrating on Sebastião's notes, trying to avoid any and all dis-
ruptions, no matter how enjoyable or enticing, Julia returned to Horta
to face interrogation by Maria Josefa.

"I see you've been busy," Maria Josefa said. "Or did you lose your way? I
hope at least someone is feeding you, or are you trying to starve yourself?"

"Yes, senhora, someone fed me," Julia said, struggling to keep from gig-
gling at Maria Josefa's theatrics.

"Julia is young," João said. "Young people don't think about food.
Only babies and old people think about food."

"Who will look out for you and keep me from worrying?" Maria
Josefa said. "I have enough to worry about with this husband of mine."

"You needn't worry," Julia said. "I'm under the protection of an old friend
of the family, José Manuel, and his neighbor, Maria dos Santos, in Praia do
Almoxarife, so don't go renting my room to anyone else while I'm gone."

"*Haja paciência,*" Maria Josefa said, shaking her head. Grant me
patience! She brought Julia her mail, and invited her to a lunch of
roasted chicken, potatoes and freshly baked bread.

There was a note from Julia's family. Her aunts and uncles had signed
their names to the letter. "Come back home," they said. "It's clear some-

thing unfortunate has happened, an accident or who knows what. Let the police handle it. They may never find Sebastião if he's lost at sea. You may be wasting your time waiting and risking your life with the earthquakes and volcanoes."

Julia penned a quick letter to Mateus, explaining that so far there was no news of Sebastião. "I don't know what else I can do, except wait. I'm afraid if I leave to look elsewhere, Sebastião might show up here. I don't even know where to search, so I'm leaving that to the police, who don't seem all that interested in helping. Things are very unsettled here. There are wild rumors. I don't know what to believe. It's hard to imagine anything sinister or evil happening here at all, the only danger being the earthquakes and volcanoes." She mentioned the room in Praia do Almoxarife: "I'm going through father's writings, and notes. Of course, as soon as I learn anything, I'll let you know."

It was one thing for Julia to confide in Mateus, to talk of her doubts and concerns, but the last thing she wanted was to upset her grandmother any further with rumors and allegations concerning Sebastião. Therefore, she sent telegrams informing her family that everything was fine, that she expected Sebastião to show up at any moment. She even addressed one to her brother, Antonio, blandishing him for his misconceptions of the islands. "You don't know what you're missing. It's beautiful here. You'd love it, should you change your mind."

Antonio, being of few words, had already anticipated her telegram by writing, "Don't bother to ask me to join you there. Enjoy your stay in the Middle Ages."

As Julia, João and Maria Josefa ate lunch at a small table in the kitchen, it began to rain.

"My cousin, Vitorino," João said, as they listened to the steady percussion of the rain beating against the awning, "sailed from Pico to Horta yesterday. There are people in Lajes, he told me, who say your father sailed on a boat with several men from Lajes, one or two from Ribeiras, and others from Faial, São Jorge, Graciosa, even."

"But wouldn't everyone know if they took a boat?" Julia said.

"Vitorino says they slipped away very early in the morning, before daybreak, to keep the voyage secret."

"I wouldn't listen to anything those friends of Vitorino had to say," Maria Josefa said. "A bunch of good-for-nothings who sit around drinking all day until they believe they are the greatest whalers, sailors and fishermen who ever went to sea."

"Perhaps you are right," João said, with a shrug. "I don't know."

"Of course, I'm right. If you asked each of them they would tell you that one time or another they have seen the Island of Sete Cidades themselves, not to mention sirens with breasts like ripe peaches."

Julia and João laughed. "Sirens, ghost ships," Maria Josefa said. "It's people like that who have nothing better to do than to convince others they have seen something or someone that no one else has seen."

João shrugged. "I just thought Julia might like to know what they are saying," João said. "I'm not saying any of it is true, but then I'm not saying it's not true either. They call Sebastião *O Desventuroso.*"

"The Unlucky One," Julia said. "Yes, I've heard." She knew of the Portuguese fondness for nicknames. Every king had a sobriquet: The Brave, The Just, The Fair, The Fat. The pages of the genealogies that she read in Sebastião's room were full of nicknames, some obvious, others puzzling: Big Tooth, The Old, The Blind, The Negligent, The Bull, The Lizard, The Seven Goats. Nicknames often replaced surnames, which were forgotten with time, signifying that if you call a rose by any other name often enough, it would eventually stick. Inês de Castro's father, Pedro Fernandes de Castro was called *da Guerra,* the Warrior, and a branch of the family retained that nickname, which in time supplanted their own name.

The islanders seldom referred to one another by their last names. A friend or neighbor of many years might be called Pedro Mendes or Manuel Lurdes, without anyone ever knowing that their family name was Sousa or Ávila. Sometimes someone could be distinguished by where he or she came from—Mário da Graciosa—another island, or José da Vila—a different town.

Julia had been amused to hear someone referred to as João Torto, *torto* meaning crooked, and another as Maria Azelha, *azelha* insinuating the woman wasn't all there, wasn't quite right in the head. Or Manuel Lobo, wolf, indicating someone who chased after women.

Maria Josefa gathered up the dishes and carried them into the kitchen. João looked to make sure she couldn't hear. "They say it is because of that woman," he whispered.

"A woman?"

"Yes, the siren," João said. "Perhaps he saw her and could not forget, but followed her."

Julia's eyes widened. "You mean the stories are true, then?"

"I don't know. It's possible that some of it is true."

Is it really so preposterous, Julia thought, especially given Sebastião's notes, and everything else that was occurring?

After lunch she said good afternoon to João and Maria Josefa, and decided to go for a walk in spite of the rain. She stepped up to the door with a cloak and an umbrella.

Maria Josefa stood in the doorway. "You are going out in that downpour?"

"Yes, senhora."

"But you will drown."

"It's all right," she said. "I can swim." Maria Josefa threw her hands up as Julia stepped outside. The rain fell in a deluge that made the umbrella useless. She folded it up and, pelted by the rain, hurried to find a taxi to take her back to Praia do Almoxarife.

. . .

Some phantom islands may be accounted for by the numerous offshore banks and seamounts that extend from the Faroe Islands to Spain. Possibly, at one time portions of these subaqueous grounds surfaced as islands; temporary uprisings and subsidences of the ocean floor provide support for this speculation.

Other phantom islands are not so easy to explain, or explain away. In spite of new discoveries and advances in cartography, belief in islands now known to have been phantoms persisted for centuries or even millennia. The search for fragments of historical truth reveals a strong underpinning of verity beneath the legends; myth and reality are not as disparate as one might think.

Phantom Islands of the Atlantic, Donald S. Johnson, New York

. . .

Julia had never forgotten the way she and her family were treated by the people of the Azores when she was younger: their names in the newspapers, in articles and poems; the friendliness and helpfulness of clerks and shopkeepers; people who spoke of her grandparents with reverence.

Sebastião and Mateus could rattle off the names and titles of one ancestor after another, proudly recounting the stories for anyone who cared to listen: "Listen, one thing before you go. Have you heard of Baltasar de Castro—one of our ancestors, of course?" In 1520 he and Manuel Pacheco were sent to explore Central Africa by our King Manuel I, known to all the Portuguese as the Fortunate King because he reaped all the riches of India, the Spice Islands, and Brazil—though sarcastically and enviously referred to as the Grocer King by King Frances I of France.

"Baltasar de Castro was the very first European to explore the Congo. I, myself, have not seen the report they made to their king upon their return—no longer King Manuel, who had died, but King João III—but just imagine the incredible things they saw and experienced, in such a remote and hostile place, where no European had ever been. They spent six unhappy years there, roaming the heart of Africa, clawing their way through the jungle, seeing beasts no white man had ever seen, all for their king. If they also found beautiful wives there, perhaps that was one reason why they stayed so long, for the Portuguese were not only great soldiers, but great lovers, as well. Still, who remembers Baltasar or Manuel? No, instead people remember the English, who waited a good three hundred years before venturing where we had gone before."

Julia felt a hundred lifetimes removed from the strange names and legends of her ancestors, but for Mateus and Sebastião there was no distance, no gulf of time separating them from the past; the names and people they invoked were no less real or alive than they were. They spoke of heirs and followed the intricate meanderings of those who determined entitlements, next in line, primogeniture, the inheritance of fame and fortune. As far as Julia was concerned, the family line had ended with her grandfather's generation. Who, in this day and age, was concerned with the rights and privileges of being the first-born son of the eldest son? Antonio never considered himself anything but the heir of Nothing.

Julia's aunts, uncles and cousins back home weren't interested in learning the history of the family or the country. Like so many modern

Portuguese and Azoreans, they asked instead, what have we got now? Where are we now? What does the past matter?

While Sebastião boasted of the Portuguese and Azorean exploits, and the accomplishments of his ancestors, others responded by counting off all the losses. Sure, the Portuguese had colonized Brazil and Africa, parts of India, islands in Indonesia; yes, they were the first Europeans to land in Japan, Australia, and among the first to land on the Northern American continent, establishing a base in Newfoundland before anyone else had settled on the continent. But that was then. As far as the present was concerned, their sphere of influence had nearly ceased to exist, their fame limited to events of the distant past.

"Who cares about the Azores?" Antonio had once asked their father. "No one knows anything about Portugal, except that's where Port wine comes from."

"The Portuguese," Sebastião replied, "are poor self-promoters, but we know the truth. Let the other countries spread lies or exaggerate, let them brag about their accomplishments. It was the Portuguese who led the way. We have our history, our poetry, our music."

The fate of the family was closely tied to that of the country. Where, after all, were the magnificent castles, the huge tracts of land the family had once owned, the exalted positions, the illustrious military orders to which they had belonged? Where were the great deeds that rivaled those of its most accomplished soldiers, scientists, admirals, and explorers?

In Julia's world the Azores were as remote and unknown as Atlantis. Portugal was like a number of various little kingdoms of Europe that had flourished for a short time and quickly disappeared, swallowed by the ravenous senior members of the continent, always hungry for conquests, as in the case of Spain—a conglomeration of many ancient kingdoms. Even today, some people referred to the northern region of Portugal as Galicia, which was swallowed up by the kingdom of Leon in 914, which itself was absorbed by Castile in 1230.

Reading her father's notes, page after page of genealogical trails, it was nearly impossible to keep straight the many names repeated with each successive generation, with the daughters of the Spanish kings marrying Portuguese princes, and the daughters of Portuguese kings marrying Spanish, or Castilian princes, not to mention an impressive list of bastard offspring of noble mothers from either kingdom.

Julia's head spun with the wondrous prodigiousness of it all, names like drone chords, repeated often in the same generation. If a king liked a particular name—Afonso, for example—he might name two or three of his children by that name, with slight variations, as did King Dinis: Afonso, Afonso Sanches, João Afonso, Pedro Afonso; including two daughters both named Maria Afonso. This was especially true if a couple were prolific enough to have twelve, thirteen, or more children, which was often the case. And if a nobleman married several times, each wife might have a child named João or Beatriz, Álvaro, Isabel or Afonso.

Julia found interesting patterns in the names, which she wrote down in order to draw the connections, or recited as she reclined in bed, trying to memorize them, trying to keep their chronology straight in her mind, father and son, mother and daughter, generation after another.

She mouthed the names of wives, sisters and daughters, and tried to envision what they looked like, what their lives were like: Urraca, Sancha, Esfania, Melia. Were they strong or weak, happy or sad, hated or loved?

She repeated the names of each generation softly, like a chant, an invocation: "Lain Calvo, Fernão Lains, Lain Fernandes, Nuno Lains, Lain Nunes, Fernão Lains"—the repetition, the similarity of names, soothing, almost hypnotic, like the incessant murmuring of the waves, "Rodrigo Fernandes, Guterre Rodrigues, Fernando Guterres, Estevão Fernandes, Fernando Rodrigues, Pedro Fernandes, Fernando Peres . . ."

CHAPTER 16

Who can resist the lure of an abyss, the desire to crawl to the brink and peer down the precipice, into the unknown depths below? Clinging to the safety of the edge, yet tempted by the very mystery of doom promised by the fall? Nor can we know, beforehand, what will speak to us. What hidden doors within our being will open suddenly, to reveal the unknown, which we carry with us: our latency of being, seeds, and germs of our pasts. What might cause each seed to germinate, to flower? What child's face, peering out from a window, what view of a street, or alley, stumbled upon by accident, what piece of art in a museum, or strain of music—it could be anything that sparks an awareness, that opens a particular door and brings the past rushing forth like a fountain.

—Sebastião do Canto e Castro

. . .

The next evening Nicolau brought Julia to a small, rustic house in the heart of Horta. Nicolau introduced Julia to more than a dozen men and women, an odd mixture of laborers, clerks, a secretary or two, mostly in their twenties and thirties, one or two in their forties, and several small children. They exchanged kisses and welcomed Julia.

The house was crowded with instruments and people. A table was set with codfish cakes, sweets, and a variety of drinks, but they wasted little time before sitting down to play.

Nearly everyone there was a musician. They played a variety of traditional instruments: the accordion, the *tambor*—a hand-held drum, flutes and violas, guitars and bagpipe. The music was enchanting, whether the song was joyful, humorous, or mournful, and of a quality Julia hadn't heard before. There was spontaneity at times, as if they were improvising; yet everything flowed and blended so well, as though each knew what the other would play next.

They sang traditional songs like "Olhos Negros," "Tirana," and "Pézinho," which Julia found both new and hauntingly familiar at the same time.

"What do you think?" Nicolau asked.

"I love it," she said. "It's grand." It was difficult to contain her excitement, as the music swept her from one emotion to another. There was a mix of voices in the room, some light and sweet, others rough, deep and gravelly, which blended and complimented one another.

They performed instrumental pieces, too. One of the members, Joaquim, played the Portuguese *guitarra,* a twelve-string instrument quite different from a standard guitar or mandolin; he played a moving, haunting melody that visibly transported the entire group of players and listeners. Nicolau played a beat-up old electric piano.

Julia couldn't keep her fingers or her feet still. The music was infectious, and then, without a pause, it changed. She recognized the tune. "Lágrima," one of Amália Rodrigues's songs; a song Julia's father had played a thousand times. She also knew the words, and joined in singing with the others:

Cheia de penas
Cheia de penas me deito
E com mais penas
Com mais penas me levanto
No meu peito, este jeito
O jeito de te querer tanto
Desespero
Tenho por meu desespero
Dentro de mim
Dentro de mim o castigo
Eu não te quero
Eu digo que não te quero
E de noite

De noite sonho contigo
Full of sorrows
I sleep full of sorrows
And still more sorrows
With more sorrows I rise
In my heart, this way
This way of wanting you so much
Anguish
I have for my anguish
Inside of me
Inside of me this punishment
I don't want you
I say that I don't want you
But at night
At night I dream of you[5]

159

The words of the song filled the room like a warm sea, carried each of the listeners away like so much driftwood. The others sang softer, allowing Julia's voice to be heard above the rest. Nicolau stared at Julia as someone would who had just discovered the ordinary girl who lived next door was in truth capable of performing miracles.

"You really *can* sing," he said, when the song was over.

"A beautiful voice," the others said.

"Another Teresa," a woman named Maria Aurelia said, winking at Nicolau, who nodded.

They played a number of traditional folk tunes of Portugal, some Celtic and others with a Moorish influence. And Nicolau asked Julia to play the piano on a few songs.

"I'm amazed," Nicolau said, when he dropped her off at the *residencial* later that evening. "I still can't believe it."

"What?" Julia said.

"It seems you aren't who I thought you were."

"No?"

She couldn't tell if he was being coy, playful, or neither.

"You're like a different person when you sing. *Tal paixão*—such passion. Teodoro always spoke about *feiticeiras* of the islands. Perhaps you are one?"

She laughed. "Me, a sorceress? Perhaps you too aren't what you appear to be. Good night, Senhor dos Santos."

"Good night, *Senhora Feiticeira.*"

They stood on the steps of the *residencial.* Nicolau kissed Julia's cheek, then turned, climbed into his car, and drove away. She stood for a moment, then entered the *residencial.*

Maria Josefa was at her station. "Ah, *menina,* I was just beginning to wonder if you were coming home tonight," she said.

"I made it before my coach turned into a pumpkin and my horses into mice," Julia said. "Good night, senhora fairy godmother."

"Good night," Maria Josefa said, shaking her head and looking at Julia as though she'd lost her mind. She muttered, "What's to come of this family?"

Lying in bed, Julia thought about what she'd seen and heard that evening. The sound of the *fados,* those melancholy folk songs so Portuguese in essence, in which one could also hear a mixture of Semitic, Arabic and Gypsy influences, stirred her, touched some remote genetic connection. "I have loved, I have lost, cruel fate, this life, this destiny." They evoked the breath of the deserts of Morocco, images like far-off mirages, fading in and out, striking chords long-silent, deep inside her: songs of longing, songs of *saudades,* melodies of loss and lament. She saw men heading out to sea, to distant ports of call, and the young women who remained behind shedding tears of longing, of regret, as they leaned from their open windows, their eyes gazing as if trying to traverse the incredible distances which separated them in time, space, life and death.

Many never returned. Yet there were those who waited, five, ten years. Such love, she thought. Was there still a possibility in this day and age? The absence of such devotion broke upon her like a wave, impossible to deny. People she'd known and met back home were different from her. At times she felt like an aberration. Why wasn't she content to go to clubs, drink in bars, attend parties, flit from one affair to another? Because she chased an illusion, an ideal? Because she felt there was more to life than amusing and entertaining oneself. That there were other pleasures more desirable.

None of her friends or acquaintances, even the musicians, artists or writers among them, strove to do anything of importance. "How presumptuous," they would say, with a laugh. *"Art?"* As if it were passé. They joked, they played, they dabbled, but none were truly serious. None put their whole being into what they did. She herself had so far taken only tentative steps in the shallows. She hadn't immersed herself, as she wished to do, in her art. And while she felt different from the typical American, she was different from the people here on the Azores, too. How could it be otherwise, when they had sensibilities and surroundings so far removed from hers, and vice versa? When, in fact, she felt as though she lived in some separate realm that lay somewhere between the islands and the United States, like one of the lost mythological islands.

"Enough, already," she said, turning her thoughts toward Nicolau. She smiled, happy that he had told her how much he enjoyed her singing. He too was different, passionate about everything creative and life-affirming. She thought about his sister, Teresa, to whom Nicolau's friends had compared her voice. "I hope I meet her soon," she whispered. She added as an afterthought, "If I don't I'll start believing she doesn't really exist."

. . .

Dear Julia,

Like some terrible curse, or fateful assignation wrought by the hands of the gods themselves, misfortune has plagued our family again and again, down through the centuries, to this very day. With Sebastião's recent disappearance, despair has once again darkened our lives. We can only hope and pray that he will be found safe.

I cannot say whether the things you mentioned are true or not, if Sebastião had some proof or if he had only heard rumors. God only knows what he discovered, or what it all means. Above all, be careful.

Saudades,
Mateus

. . .

Julia studied the multi-layered labyrinth in which, both figuratively and literally, she felt her way: Maria dos Santos and her bubbling fountain or spring, so similar to the river or stream found in Sebastião's story or legend about Abílio and his grandfather, which resurfaced again, slightly altered, in her father's notes on Ponce de León and the search for islands, the Fountain of Youth, as well as the story of Inês de Castro.

"The Ponce family," Sebastião had written, "which later became Ponce de León, rose to greatness from somewhat shadowy origins. In the mid-thirteenth century, Pedro Ponce married Dona Aldonça Alfonso, the daughter of Alfonso, King of León. Two of the children born to Pedro Ponce's grandson, also called Pedro Ponce, were Isabel Ponce, who married Pedro Fernandez de Castro, the father of Inês de Castro, and Joana Ponce, who married João Afonso, one of the illegitimate sons of King Dinis of Portugal. João Afonso was decapitated in 1325 by order of King Alfonso IV of Portugal, his half-brother. Pedro Ponce's brother, Fernão Ponce, was known as Senhor de Marchena. His son, Pedro Ponce, inherited the title, Senhor de Marchena, and fought against Portugal. This same Pedro Ponce's daughter, Maria married Álvaro de Castro, the brother of Inês de Castro. Afonso IV, if he disliked the Castros did so in large part because of their connection to the Ponce family, and their closeness to his banished brother, Afonso Sanches.

"Pedro Ponce was succeeded by his son, Pedro Ponce, who also had a son named Pedro Ponce de León. From this last Pedro Ponce de León, came the heroes by that name of Spain's wars against the Moors of Granada, the same Lords of Marchena who welcomed and aided Columbus when he came to Spain, and the Luís Ponce de León who sailed with Columbus on his second voyage; the same Luís who legend tells us, after being named governor of Puerto Rico, sailed in search of a mysterious island where he might find the famed fountain of youth."

Julia found connections between Columbus and Fernando de Castro, the Count of Lemos, between Ponce de Leon and Álvaro de Castro, António Peres do Canto and the Corte-Real brothers; the New World and The Old; secret voyages and Hidden Islands; both the Cantos and Castros, and their connection with the Albuquerques, the Dukes of Bragança, and the da Gamas.

There were long corridors Julia traveled, some brightly lit, others dim, and sudden turns and twists such as are found in any maze. As to what lay in the heart of this particular labyrinth, whether there was any way out or whether it merely wound on and on and on, ad infinitum, she couldn't say.

She made her way like a blind woman, following the pathways of successive generations, turning this way, then that, on occasion backtracking when someone married a cousin or an uncle, or some other relative, a retro motion. She wondered about the dimensions of the puzzle, obviously of staggering proportions, and far more complicated than any she had ever seen. There were occasional dead-ends: when a name was erased, or omitted, a question mark, an unknown—we know he or she was married, but we don't know to whom, or who, if any, their offspring were. Frequently, one trail opened into a whole other labyrinth when a Castro married a Coelho, or a Cunha, or one of several dozen others, and she would pore through the long, convoluted avenues of that surname, until it disappeared or merged into yet another, or simply returned from whence it came, making a satisfying, if not tidy, circle.

Many of these men and women married several times, and produced a number of bastards who sometimes outnumbered their legitimate half brothers and sisters. Many married at a young age, and while life expectancy was short there were always some who defied the conventions and lived to a ripe old age of eighty or ninety years. Then, too, many men went off to fight against the Moors or the Castilians, or sailed off to India or the Spice Islands. If these men died, their wives were free to remarry, often starting a new family.

163

Julia struggled to unravel the convoluted trails of family lines through name changes, multiple marriages and numerous offspring. Connections, oftentimes elusive and unsuspected, ran through the same families, reappearing with altered names, as Castros became Guerra, Deza or Eça, or when one family joined with another, as in Canto e Castro. Was it merely coincidence that these families were so intertwined with the family of Christopher Columbus? So many Colons and Castros.

How dangerous could it be, she wondered, if Sebastião had been tracking down some secret of Columbus and his heirs, another deeper connection? Perhaps, he had decided to follow the admiral's trail. But to where: Spain, Portugal, Africa, or out to sea?

Now and again Julia nodded off as she read the notes, dreaming of voyages and battles. She'd awaken with a start, hearing her grandmother's voice, "Remember who you are," as it echoed her father's words: "The past is not dead, it lives in you." For a moment Julia wouldn't know where she was or what had awakened her: the ground trembling, or the words of her ancestors reminding her of who she was, the voice of a woman calling from the distant past.

CHAPTER 17

The first king of Atlantis was Poseidon, who begat ten children; he divided the island into ten portions, giving to each of his sons a tenth part; to Atlas, the eldest, fell the largest and fairest portion, and he was made king over his brothers, who ranked as princes.

From him, the whole island and surrounding ocean received the name of Atlantis.

The Azores, or Western Islands
Walter Frederick Walker, London, 1886

. . .

Nicolau and Julia. A walk along the beach, a drive to the bakery, lunch in Horta, a brief conversation on Maria dos Santos's porch—their encounters for the most part quiet, tentative, and subdued, as if these were extremely delicate negotiations, and one wrong move could undo everything. Their eyes may be open wide to knowledge, possibilities, choices and decisions, but the path ahead is uncertain, as cloudy as Maria dos Santos's mysterious pool of water.

On occasion the subject they discuss creates a mood, and an intensity that surprises them both, and leaves them slightly short of breath: "What do you know about the Enchanted Island?" Julia asks.

"Which one?" Nicolau says. "There have been a number of islands over the centuries, one seen from São Miguel, one north of Terceira, another from Santa Maria, others seen from ships. Some people think they are a joke. They have a good laugh about explorers sailing around in ships to find these islands, many of them never returning."

"So maybe one of them *is* real?" she says. "Perhaps like Capelinhos, it rose and sank again."

"Maybe it's best to keep an open mind. After all, without the rumors of islands in the North Atlantic, and some found on ancient maps, the Azores might never have been discovered."

Julia is careful, showing an interest in the history, legends and music—or so she tells herself—though she enjoys getting to know Nicolau, as she is getting to know the islands, Maria dos Santos, José Manuel, Maria Josefa and João. It isn't only that they are close in age—she's twenty-seven, he's twenty-nine—there's also a familiarity Julia and Nicolau feel in one another's company, something they have in common that might not seem apparent at first glance.

Nicolau appears cautious, as though protective of her reputation, unwilling to take advantage of her possible naiveté. He's gallant, she thinks, as well as a considerate host. Still, she wonders if he were pushed would he show another side. After all, men are men. Can he really be so different? There's a nervousness she feels in his presence, a sense that she is seeing only part of him, that there is much more beneath the surface.

"Would you like to go out to dinner," Nicolau asks. And accompanying the words, the warmest of smiles. Their eyes meet, and that in and of itself can be just as palpable as a touch of skin against skin.

"Yes, that would be nice."

"Yes?" he asks, as if he's misheard. Why should he be surprised? Does the dreamer think the dream is too good to be true? Pleasant news always comes as a surprise in a world in which we constantly expect that things will turn out for the worst.

"Yes," she repeats. Later on, the flood of doubts, questions. Oh my, is it too much, too soon? No, no, of course not. But a quiet dinner is not the same as a stroll together in the park, a snack in a café. A dinner is, well, more intimate, riskier, suggestive. Again, there might be expectations. Everything could change as result. There's always the possibility of miscues, misunderstandings. What next? Another dinner, another night? Or, perhaps, nothing more, no afterwards. One sweet over-too-soon moment followed by a hasty retreat.

It's one thing to be brave about earthquakes and volcanoes, she thinks, while other matters, those between one soul and another, can leave you immobilized with fear.

But the dinner commences. There is wine—red, dry, room temperature. A table upstairs in the back corner of the restaurant, away from others, though there are but few customers this particular night, in this out-of-the-way spot. Two people occupying one small table, sharing a meal. As far as they're concerned there are only the two of them, the rest of the world is excluded. And, of course, how could Nicolau have predicted the dress Julia would wear, black as the sea this night, and just as alluring, clinging to every curve of her body? His eyes follow the contours of her shoulders, breasts, her narrow waist, all of which the dress enhances as if she were illuminated by soft, sensual lighting. The dress contrasts nicely with her skin, the smooth hollow just below her neck and the graceful arc of her clavicle. He averts his eyes, as if there is too much to see, and stumbles over his words, as if unused to speaking. *Caramba*, he thinks.

"It's a beautiful night," he manages to say, as if it's the night he's speaking of, and, as if in collusion, the night is warm, with just the slightest cool whisper of a breeze to tantalize the skin.

"Yes," Julia says, enjoying Nicolau's discomfort. Touché, she thinks. Why should she be the only one to suffer nerves?

He's quick with a smile, and then finally a compliment. "You look lovely." But he seems unsure of himself, at a loss for words, even as he makes the effort. It almost sounds begrudging.

Julia, determined to remain cool, looks him straight in the eye, unwilling to demur, hoping to plumb beyond the superficialities, to find out who he really is. To her chagrin, however, it unsettles her to look into those eyes for more than a brief moment. Thus his nervousness becomes hers.

They discuss music. She's surprised to find he's familiar with a large number of American and British musicians. He enjoys rock, folk and blues, especially, he says. "And you?"

"All kinds," she says. "Classical, of course." He nods.

"Have you heard Pedro Barroso, José Medeiros, Luís Bettencourt, Fausto?"

"No." She shakes her head. "Should I have?"

"Absolutely, especially if you're interested in music that's a blend of the old and the new. Brigada Victor Jara, too. They capture all that is Portugal." He speaks softly, quietly, then suddenly, quickly and louder, at first one-or-two-word responses, followed by many words rushing to make his point. Julia listens, finding his passion contagious.

He recites the first few lines from "Grândola Vila Morena"—the song that started the 1974 bloodless coup in Portugal, called the Revolution of Carnations.

"I remember that song," she said. "Sebastião used to play it."

"Zeca Afonso is definitely someone whose music you should know."

"I'd like to try to capture the islands with music," she says, "the way Sebastião and my grandparents did with painting, stories, and poetry."

"Maybe I could help," Nicolau says. Their conversation wanes and waxes with the appearance and departure of the waiter who brings a dish of olives, soup, bread, water.

"It was great hearing you and your friends the other night," she says. "That's just the kind of music I was hoping to hear. If only I could write something like that."

"We were glad to hear you, too," he says. "And I'm sure you can."

There is something far off in the depths of his eyes, a distant glimmer she can't quite make out.

"Perhaps I'll be able to write music . . . songs, while I'm here," Julia says. An idea thrown out, unplanned. A simple declarative statement that contains not only the information conveyed but that which is unstated, implicit: a song requires words as well as music, an instrument upon which to play. A look, an expression. "What?" she says.

"I was just thinking. You could use our piano, if you'd like. It's very old but it still works. It would be great to hear you play it."

There is a sudden dizziness, a strangeness, when realizing that, after you've had to fight tooth and claw for something to work out the way you want, now and then something will happen—when and where you least expect it—that couldn't have gone better if you had meticulously planned out every moment. One object finding its proper and fit companion, just as one person finds his or her mate, a piano and someone to compose and play music on it, another to sing, everything in its rightful time and place, the realization that timing is indeed everything.

. . .

Dear *Avô*,

I, too, know what it is to hear the call of these islands. The way they've appeared in my dreams. It's only since coming here that I realize how much I have missed them and how they have always, in a sense, been with me. Don't worry about me. I feel very safe here. The earthquakes haven't been too bad. I can't believe anyone had any reason to harm Sebastião, not here. I don't see how anything like that could happen in a place like this. No matter where he has gone, I don't think he can stay away too long. I'm sure he'll be back.

Saudades,
Julia

169

. . .

At the resumption of tremors, Julia rushed to the shore where she watched the coming and going of boats and people. With each new series of rumbles, she studied the surface of the sea, hoping to catch a glimpse of the new volcano that was expected to rise from the turgid water. She had no idea where to look. There were conflicting reports as to the location of the island, and confusion within many of the reports themselves. The island itself would likely be impossible to see from Horta, or anywhere on Faial, yet the smoke, ash and fires would perhaps be visible for many miles. She glanced warily at Pico, thinking of the incredible view from its summit. Many feared that Pico would also erupt, and were now wary of its potential threat.

"The mountain is asleep," they said. "But with all these earthquakes it might wake up."

Julia felt the increasingly forceful pull of the sea, and the call of an unnamable voice out of the most distant past—a voice that sang of blood, of love and passion, and a name spoken repeatedly down through the centuries—sounds she heard, but could not yet identify, and could no longer ignore. It was as yet a whisper, though it threatened, at any moment, to rise to a shout.

Would the ocean divulge its closely-guarded secrets, she wondered. Perhaps, if only her eyes would focus properly. But what occurred when she stared at the sea for too long, tried to capture all that immensity, all the ceaseless shifting movement, was that she saw shadows, vague dark shapes, glimmers here and there, the flash of light reflected off the water; it was difficult, if not impossible, to focus, or to be certain of what she saw. It was easy to become entranced. No wonder people had always claimed to see elusive islands or mythological creatures out there.

She sought distraction, if only to dispel the effects of the atmosphere, the air grown heavy with the taste of impending doom: a wave of unnatural warmth as one stood on the docks in the pre-dawn chill; a brief burst of hail the size of doves' eggs at midday; a ripple of inexplicable sensation, sudden crying or laughter, for no good reason; a smell that drifted through the streets, stopping people in their tracks, causing them to sniff the air, search their memories for some forgotten source of that mysterious scent. It was as if the skies were saturated, laden with potential disturbances, not merely thunder and lightning, but something else—vague but no less unsettling—as if at any moment the whole world might turn upside down.

It was as though each of the components, the players in this larger-than-life theater (herself included), were shifting into position, and once the right wave touched the precise stream of air, and both touched land (the island, her island), touched her, standing where she was meant to stand, once the proper words were given voice (the cues, like some magic charm or spell uttered), and whatever the trigger was, once it was pulled, then all hell would break loose.

Julia walked to the beach at Porto Pim, breathed the salt air and swept an arc of sand with her foot. She made her way toward the old whale factory, with no definite purpose in mind, roaming the hill where the whaler's church stood. When it began raining, Julia quickly descended and returned to Horta. Looking out to sea, she saw that another squall was coming up suddenly on the island, as if summoned by some conjurer.

Instead of running for cover, she went out onto the quay. There, she watched the waves arriving like row after row of mounted soldiers riding in formation, smashing into the rocks and stones of the harbor, the spray whipped into the air by the wind.

Julia stood staring at the onslaught of sea, rain and wind, when she too saw a dark, huge, foreboding presence lurking on the water. Is that the ghost ship, she wondered, or only a bizarre black cloud, perfectly shaped, in the form of an old ship?

"Like the angel of death," she heard. She turned around. An old fisherman stood beside her.

"You see it, too?" Julia asked.

The man nodded. "The past is returning."

CHAPTER 18

How to describe the indescribable, comprehend the incomprehensible? Mere
words cannot suffice, words only tarnish the image. Only the heart is capa-
ble of knowing. I don't ask is it possible? I imagine what might be, and grasp
hold of the idea as fiercely as I cling to life itself. I am not content to play
or pretend; I set myself up as ruler of the Empire of Dreams, and settle for
nothing less than this as my kingdom.

—Sebastião do Canto e Castro

. . .

Mysterious lights were seen out on the water at night. Animals were observed behaving in a strange manner: fish leapt ashore and aboard boats, whales gave birth in prodigious numbers and swam where they weren't usually seen, in the shallow waters between the islands; birds flew in puzzling patterns, following God only knows what design.

These events transformed the atmosphere of Horta. A presence loomed over the city, like a pervasive mist clinging to everything it touched. People asked whether the sighting of one thing would portend another; would these strange occurrences foretell even greater disasters to come?

The islanders watched the skies, the ocean, the faces of men who returned from the sea. There was expectation in their faces: What news do you bring us? What have you seen?

The islands were rocked repeatedly by earthquakes, the air filled with expectancy and fear, as penitents tore at their hair, flailed themselves, and joined others who made their way, inch by agonizing inch, on their knees to the churches, to give penance.

There were frequent cries to God, imploring forgiveness, begging to be spared any further torments. Some, convinced they'd been forsaken, wailed hysterically and threw themselves on the ground in violent spasms, tearing their clothes, their faces streaked with blood, dirt and tears. Some sat hugging themselves and sobbed, while others made promises and vows, pleas for intervention—heartfelt lamentations by people who expected the end of the world.

Julia's family telephoned and again pleaded with her to return to the States. Her mother was especially insistent. "Your father," Clara said, "was reckless enough to swim with whales, sail a boat alone, explore a dangerous sea cave, or go to the top of Pico in the midst of a snow storm." She didn't trust the islands—a place where disaster was just waiting to happen, as if they clung to a precipice at the very edge of the world. Julia remembered hearing how people had responded when her grandfather's brother had left the islands to study in Coimbra, on the mainland, and people there discovered he was from the Azores.

"My God, you're from the island?"—referring to the Azores in the singular—"Why, then, what do you do when the storms come?" Julia's great uncle, Miguel do Canto e Castro, had answered dryly, "We simply hitch up our pants and wait it out until the water subsides."

Julia's mother, of course, was no different. She regarded the Azores, at best, as extremely isolated, untamed, wild, where practically anything could happen. She couldn't be convinced that civilization and security could exist in such a remote place.

"Come back home," she wrote. "There's nothing for you there. Let well enough alone."

How could Julia explain that she was beginning to feel there was nothing for her back home, that there was something here, even if she didn't know what or where, and that it was something she heard and felt more and more with each passing day?

. . .

One of the singular beliefs of the Sebastianists is that Atlantis still exists enchanted at the bottom of the sea, and that El Rei D. Sebastião resides on it. Some day, they think, the spell will be removed, when it will rise again above the waters, and restore this adventurous prince to his country and long expectant followers. . . . A reflection of the Sebastianist belief still lingers amongst the inhabitants of St. Michael, for they firmly assert the existence of enchanted islands on its N.E. side, where they are said to occasionally appear in white, shadowy form. In Santa Maria, this tradition pictures a knight in armour appearing in ghostly shape, apparently sent to watch for all "female" islands which have once been disenchanted, and the nebulous apparitions to the north-east of St. Michael's are waiting for the disenchanted islands to become once more enchanted, that they may themselves break the chains which spell-bind them.

The Azores: or Western Islands
Walter Frederick Walker, London, 1886

. . .

Julia left Sebastião's room to escape the noise, which often seemed louder inside than it did out in the open. Murmuring voices, sometimes building to a screeching howl, filled the air, and appeared to come from everywhere at once, but at the same time, from nowhere. Though she had no meteorological tools to gauge, a pressure was building in the air, an electric current, she could feel, as though instruments were being strummed deep inside her.

Walking through Praia do Almoxarife, or drifting along the streets and the park, in Horta, Julia heard gossip, whispers, questions, fears— "Did you hear Senhora Mendes is missing?" "What do you think will happen now?" "I love you more than life itself!" "Is this the end?" "Is it true the sea was boiling?"

The release of emotion was instantaneous and complete; no half-measures, no holding back, no restraint. It was overwhelming, convulsive. At times it seemed the entire world would drown in the outpouring.

"Have you heard, Joaninha, what happened to Dona Maria da Conceição?"

"Dona Maria?"

"Yes, you know, the one who speaks with a lisp, the cousin of Dona Nélia Fagundes. She's cried so many tears, the servants are afraid they will drown. Her tears, they say, are forming pools, puddles, tiny rivulets, which, if it doesn't stop, will soon flood the house."

"Beware the coming calamities!" a shrill voice shouted. *"O fim do mundo!"*—The end of the world!

People wasted no time at all, but prepared themselves for the inevitable: lovers met for one long-awaited night of passion. "I've wasted all these years waiting, and for what, for nothing; now there is no point, I'm yours, even if it is only for one night." They threw all caution to the wind: "Look, I cheated you out of that land. You know it and I know it. All these years it's weighed on my conscience." They put aside their differences: "I never did like you, yet now that the end has come, I'm sorry that you too will die." People met to say goodbye and wish good luck to one another. Women prayed, clutching rosaries at the feet of their figurine saints, men steeled themselves with alcohol and silent companionship, a last drink among old friends.

Julia busied herself searching for ghost notes in the narrow cobbled streets, through the fields, down the steep terrain of dry riverbeds: the articulated rhythms of water slapping against the shore, boats rocking in the harbor, the song of sea birds, the intensity of the storms, the pulse of the sea. *Am I hearing what I hear?* As sweet whispered tones pulled her along by the thinnest thread of memory. A frisson of remembrance. The voice of the islands awakening in her. It was a sound both new and yet familiar.

She breathed the island scent, exuded by the porous rock, the life-breeding soil, the ocean. She moved through air that crackled with electric currents, sparks, questions, desperation and uncertainty, amid the feeblest flickers of hope, as if the seismic disturbances of earthquakes and eruptions, the new island rising from the sea, had their counterpart in atmospheric disturbances.

Looking up from the black, moon-like terrain of cooled lava, beyond darkly rich mounds of dirt that burst in prodigious clumps from the ground, like earth-tone versions of the hydrangeas growing along many of the roads, she half-expected to see a fleet of galleys off the coast, could almost hear the shouts of mariners, mixed with the sounds of gulls, wind and waves, the footsteps of explorers still resounding down the convoluted twists and turns of time.

It was as if she rode the turtle-shaped island of Faial—itself like an enormous ship—that swam so slowly it was still partially entrenched in the Middle Ages, taking her a moment or two for her eyes to readjust to the shift back to the present, the here and now.

Returning to her room at the *residencial,* Julia opened the door and discovered her brother, Antonio, waiting for her.

He stood to greet her. "Hey, sis." The sight of her brother in this room, in Horta, was completely incongruous. He looked out of place, and knew it; he hid his embarrassment.

"I don't believe it," Julia said, staring at him in disbelief. "What are you doing here?"

"That's what I keep asking myself," he said, with a grin.

She hugged him, then stood back and gazed inquisitively. "Seriously," Julia said.

"They insisted, bribed me, threatened me." Antonio threw his hands up. "What could I do but come and save my little sister from herself."

"*Save* me?" Julia said. "You'd better give up now and go back home."

"Gladly," Antonio said. "But not without you."

"I can't believe you're here," Julia said, simultaneously annoyed by his condescension and the assumption that she needed saving, yet at the same time touched that her brother could put aside his prejudices and actually come to the islands for her.

"I can't believe it myself. You owe me, big time."

"Yeah, I guess," she said.

Antonio looked around the room. He laughed and scratched the back of his head. "Everything is smaller than I remember: the island, Horta, this *residencial,* these rooms." He touched the books on the nightstand. "So this is where Sebastião lived?" She nodded. "Why are you staying?" he asked. "Don't you want to come home?"

"Not yet," Julia said. "I still don't know where he is. I can't leave without knowing."

"I'll tell you where he is," Antonio said. "He's either at the bottom of the ocean, or he fell into a volcano. This is just like him. He couldn't possibly have a heart attack or a stroke. That would be too ordinary. No, he has to disappear. Always the big spectacle."

"You sound just like mother," Julia said. They sat on the bed, and didn't speak for a moment.

"Enough squabbling," he said. "I'm beat. I'm going to my room. It's just down the hall, number six. We'll talk in the morning, okay?"

"Fair enough," Julia said. "Go get some sleep. I'll see you tomorrow."

"Good night," Antonio said.

Before he closed her door behind him Julia said, "I'm glad you're here, Antonio."

"Wish I could say the same. I'll see you in the morning."

He leaned over and embraced her, patting her back, before leaving. It was at moments like this that Julia was reminded how little she and Antonio had in common; she was petite, much shorter than Antonio, while he was broad and big-boned, taking after their mother's Nordic side of the family. She'd always felt she had to prove herself, to show that she was tough and undeserving of his condescension and protectiveness.

CHAPTER 19

Is it any wonder so many are restless, seemingly lost, searching for something
of which they have only a vague idea; a persistent hunger or longing—like a
buried memory of a forgotten god, ancient rituals, a lost paradise, a missing
island or a Golden Age—when so many of us have forgotten or otherwise lost
our pasts: who we are, where we came from. At best all we have are fragments.

—Sebastião do Canto e Castro

. . .

The next morning Julia knocked on Antonio's door. She'd had a restless night's sleep, excited by Antonio's arrival, convinced that the two of
them would likely get more accomplished than she could on her own.

Antonio greeted her with a kiss on the cheek. "Let's eat," he said. "I'm
starved." They went downstairs for breakfast. Over coffee he explained
everyone's concern back home, how the family had persuaded him that
she was in immediate danger and needed him to come and convince her
to leave before tragedy struck. They left unstated that it was Clara, their
mother, who was the primary instigator.

"That can only mean they nagged you to death," Julia said.

He nodded, grinning. "More or less."

Maria Josefa and João were overjoyed that Antonio was there.

"It's time you came back," Maria Josefa said. "Now Julia won't have
to wander out alone all the time. Keep your eye on her. I'm afraid she's
too much like your father."

"Don't worry, senhora," Antonio said. "I'll keep her out of trouble."

Julia smiled, watching him squirm. Poor deluded boy, to think he could show up, take charge, turn around without delay, and go straight home with her in tow.

"I've discovered a room where Sebastião worked," Julia said, after Maria Josefa and João left. She was going to relish convincing him to put aside his plans. "It's filled with books, papers, notes that I've been reading to find out what he was up to. I'll take you to see it."

"Great," Antonio said. He wouldn't put up any resistance just yet, but she'd have to show him what she was up against, and do it quickly, if she was going to convince him to help.

After breakfast, Julia and Antonio took a cab to Praia do Almoxarife.

"I've been combing through all of this," she said, as they examined Sebastião's room, "looking for clues."

"Better you than me," Antonio said. "So now you're a detective?"

She smiled. "Sort of."

Antonio looked the stacks of books and papers over as if they would best be fed to a fire, and rolled his eyes at the skull and nautical instruments. "Looks like something out of a B-movie set."

They stopped by to see José Manuel, who had just gotten back from Pico. "You have finally returned," José said. "I didn't think we would ever see you again."

"Well, you probably wouldn't have if it weren't for Julia," Antonio said. "The things a man has to do for his family."

José nodded. "I see. Well I hope you manage to enjoy your stay."

"Thanks," Antonio said doubtfully. Julia then took him to meet Maria dos Santos and Nicolau.

"I spend a bit of time here," Julia said, "when I'm not reading. Maria dos Santos and Nicolau have been letting me use their piano."

"We love to have Julia play and sing for us," Maria dos Santos said. "Are you a musician, too?"

"I'm afraid not, senhora," Antonio said. "I play with numbers, figures, money."

"I see," Maria dos Santos said, shaking her head as if she were really saying too bad.

"Julia has a beautiful voice," Nicolau said. "She's quite a good musician."

Antonio looked at Nicolau and then at Julia and raised his eyebrows. "Yes, I've heard," he said.

Julia blushed and whispered to Antonio, in English, "Wipe that smirk off your face."

They returned to Sebastião's room. "How long are you planning on breathing all this dust and ruining your eyes on this stuff?" Antonio said.

"As long as it takes." Julia wondered for the thousandth time how two people with the same parents could be so different from one another.

Julia tried involving Antonio in her search. She showed him a few pages, but he shook his head, "No thanks. Look, I'll take a walk, or go back to town and see what I can find, okay?"

"You sure?" Julia said.

"Positive. I'll see what I can dredge up on my own. I supposed you've talked with the police?" She nodded. "I'll check back with you later. I don't know what you expect to get out of all this." He swept his hand at the stacks.

"Okay, but let me know if you find out anything." She knew better than to expect Antonio would feel as she did, but it was a disappointment nonetheless.

Antonio left and Julia felt more alone than before. She wished she had a ready answer as to what she expected to find in the room. Examining the stories, legends and folk tales, the fantastical notes on the family, and genealogical records that splintered like a great river branching into several, then tens, then hundreds of tributaries, each going a different direction, meandering, rejoining, splitting anew, she felt renewed by the persistent feeling that she was ever on the verge of discovery. Stumbling blindly, haphazardly, she was sure she was about to unfold the elusive truths woven into and hidden between layers of illusion. It was like traveling toward a distant glimmering castle surrounded by hills, and feeling, with each summit gained, that the goal would be just over the next hill, only to always find yet one more ridge in the way. There was a recurring sense of déjà-vu, of believing there was something in front of her face, something she half-knew, should recognize, if only she could read the signs correctly.

Knowledge over the long numerous centuries was like a light that sometimes burned bright and sometimes dim. Discoveries were made, then later lost, forgotten. Some things came to light, while others disappeared, certain beliefs becoming accepted as fact, some as legend.

"The shoal Dom João de Castro," she read, "which formed an island in 1720 has recently become active again, rising from the sea floor.

There's no telling how many times this island has risen and sunk over the centuries. Is this the *Ilha Encoberta*—the Hidden Isle? Perhaps this island will rise up and the prophecies will come true. The Fifth Empire. *O Rei Esperando*—The Waiting King."

Julia had never heard of the island of Dom João de Castro. Not many people had. After all, for the time being, it wasn't yet an island, just a bar beneath the surface of the ocean. Occasionally, it broke through the sea to make another bid at remaining an island. Could it have been this same island that the explorers caught sight of again and again, and which inspired men to leave their homes behind and sail across the sea?

Sebastião's notes mentioned the island of Sabrina, on which the crew of a British ship by the same name had landed, claiming it for England, before it too sank, and the Baixo das Caravelas, also called A Balena or The Whale, that appeared off the northern coast of the island of San Miguel.

On still another page Sebastião wrote: "The Church, as it suppressed the celebrations of the Holy Ghost, attempted also to eliminate the smaller, secret cult of Santa Inês through fairly draconian measures, though vestiges of the secret society have persevered and continued, even if it has not flowered and spread.

"It operated in the utmost secrecy. Occasionally pamphlets and articles were printed, but always exceptionally few in number, passed among members of the order and not made available really to the outside world, except when a member now and again wrote and published a poem about Dona Inês and Dom Pedro.

"If on occasion a bishop received a letter suggesting Inês de Castro be beatified or canonized, it was always sent anonymously or signed with an assumed name. Of course, the Church had its own unspoken reasons for wishing to do away with a cult perhaps too closely aligned with various pagan deities—the goddess of fertility, for example—not to mention suspicions of much worse, hints of an association with the cult of Mary Magdalene. There were those who feared that if the Cult of Santa Inês spread it would proliferate a perverse doctrine of easy virtue, of free love, love of the corporeal as opposed to the love of God, love of earthly pleasure, love of the flesh, instead of spiritual love.

"Luís Camões—as well as many other poets, soldiers, nobles, princes, including Gil Vicente, Lope de Vega and Cervantes—was a member of this cult, writing his sonnets about other members, friends, including several Castros, and especially in his writing about the Island of Lovers."

When Antonio returned, several hours later, Julia showed him what she'd been reading.

He nodded. "Look, Julia, don't you think this might be a colossal waste of time? I mean, what have you found in all this nonsense?"

"More than you think," Julia said. "If you'd just take a look." She handed several pages to him, but he shrank away as if the pages contained some deadly contagion.

"Did you find out anything?" she asked.

"No." He stepped toward the door.

"Where are you going?"

"I can't stay here," Antonio said. "It's too quiet, too cramped. Gives me the creeps. I have an appointment in an hour with the police. Meet me at the *residencial?*"

"Okay," Julia said. "Maybe you'll have better luck with the police than I had."

CHAPTER 20

How can one determine the truth when confronted with huge gaps, lies, and half-truths in the factual record, when there are so many conflicting stories, each point of view at variance with the next, when even dates and names and lineage become changeable and vary with each version of the same story? What incredible assumptions we take for granted.

One must read between the lines, pick out the few facts which are solid, and weed out one by one the conjecture, the fancies, the supposition. Some people have reason to cover the truth, things to hide. Who is telling the story, and why? History loves nothing more than a repeat: generations play out the same sagas, the same goals, the same names. And the chroniclers and historians repeat the lies and falsehoods and mistakes that their predecessors spread, one lie built upon another; a house of cards, one glimmer of truth can bring crashing down.

—Sebastião do Canto e Castro

. . .

Julia and Nicolau walked together on the beach then sat and took turns playing the piano. She sang while Nicolau accompanied her. He showed her the scores of *fados* and Portuguese folk songs. He played chords, and she picked out the melody.

"That's beautiful," he said. She watched his fingers on the keyboard as he played a counterpoint to her vocal.

Nicolau kept his thoughts and feelings to himself, and Julia did the same. "The Azorean is *fechado*," Sebastião always said. Closed, sealed off. On occasion, Julia wondered, "Is he just being nice, or is he hoping for something more?" She struggled with whether to say something that could be interpreted as presumptuous, or to say nothing. "I don't need this," she told herself again and again, before reminding herself that perhaps Nicolau had nothing romantic in mind.

They faced one another across a small wooden table, placed strategically between them in the café. They rarely spoke, but gazed deep into their respective coffee cups, like paragons of self-restraint. Now and then their eyes met briefly, before looking away. An outsider would see them as brooding, almost surly, defiant; he might tisk-tisk about yet another troubled relationship.

They left the café and walked in the night air to the shore, where they watched the waves break on the rocks, the clouds parting to show the moon over Pico. These moments with Nicolau were dreamlike and vague, while the night shimmered with vibrancy, the air stretched taut, vibrating with sounds and colors, her senses sharp, keen, drinking it all in.

Sebastião's words played through her mind, "Memory is a tricky thing, like love, which, when pursued, is ever out of reach. No matter how hard you try it will always outdistance you. But then when you least expect it—indeed, when you've nearly given up and forgotten the object of your desires—it opens before your unsuspecting eyes like a budding flower revealing its presence, the secrets of its delicious scent."

"Look there," Nicolau said. Julia followed his gaze, pointing out some sight in the distance. During all this there was only occasionally a slight touch of two shoulders, a hand brushing against an arm, two figures surrounded by so much space and yet instinctively drawing near, externally appearing tranquil and still, while a storm of feelings raged just below the surface.

Again, as if to have the last word, Julia heard Sebastião's voice echo, "While we struggle to define truth or freedom we speak of love as a surrender, as a step toward danger, much as the ancient Greek tragic protagonists could not escape what the oracles ordained."

"It's the music and the island, and nothing more," she declared defiantly to the stars that winked so innocently above.

· · ·

Dear Julia,

I am afraid you may unknowingly put yourself in danger, not only from the earthquakes and volcanoes. We don't know if Sebastião's disappearance is a result of some sinister act. Perhaps someone had a reason for wanting him out of the way. Who knows what he might have uncovered? Please be careful and write soon.

Saudades,
Mateus

. . .

Julia had no idea how to respond to her grandfather's talk of enemies and sinister plots against the family. After all, this was the twentieth century, not fifteenth century Portugal. She knew better than to mention it to Antonio, who'd simply make some derogatory comment about "family lunacy." She did attempt to speak to Antonio, to show him what to her eyes was evidence of where Sebastião had gone, and, more importantly, why. "Mythological islands," Antonio said, in disgust, "missing kings, ghost ships and sirens. If he did go off the deep end on some suicide mission, Christ, we're not lemmings. We don't have to follow."

Julia stayed in the room reading until late, reading by candlelight, eating poorly, if at all, and finding more questions than she did answers. Some inexplicable impulse kept her from introducing into the room anything her father hadn't. As if the addition of the ordinary, the mundane, and in particular the modern, might cause clues and meaning to vanish like Sebastião.

She read through a number of the books in Sebastião's room that featured her ancestors: *O Castelo de Monsanto*—*The Castle of Monsanto*, whose hero was Rodrigo de Castro, considered by his king to be the ideal noble knight; *The Life of the Black Prince*, by the Herald of Sir John Chandos; *The White Company*, by Sir Arthur Conan Doyle, which featured Sir John Chandos as a character; various chronicles of the lives of the Portuguese kings. She worried that these books had gone to Sebastião's head. Had he pored over each of them until, like Don Quixote, he couldn't tell the fantasies from the truth? Sebastião, a man of the twentieth century, losing himself in his writings, his reading, and dreaming of the past.

She gazed at the ancient charts and maps Sebastião had collected: *Antilia,* the Isle of *Brasil,* the Island of Demons, the Island of Seven Cities; she saw them not as flat, guessed at, hoped for depictions on paper, but as living manifestations of hopes and dreams.

. . .

Spend a little time on the islands and you begin to feel that some kind of game—cat-and-mouse, hide and go seek—is being played. Something is hidden; you are not seeing all there is to see. The islands themselves appear to do the hiding, revealing only a glimpse here, then there, as if to keep certain secrets safe from the eyes of those who are peering too closely; an ability to camouflage what it deems necessary to hide. Then, when something is revealed, you are startled, unprepared for its discovery.

—Sebastião do Canto e Castro

. . .

"I'll be gone for a few days," Nicolau said.

"Where are you going?" Julia asked.

"To Pico. There are some things I need to take care of there." She nodded. His eyes beckoned, but she felt herself go cold. "I'll see you when I return?"

"Yes, of course," she said. "I'm not going anywhere." What to say, what not to say? "Have a good time." Wrong, wrong, wrong.

"I'm not going for pleasure. I'll be back soon." He leaned forward and lightly kissed one side of her face then the other, and with one hand—as if to steady himself—squeezed her arm before leaving.

He hadn't asked her to accompany him—that was clear enough. But there might be good reasons for that, especially now that Antonio was here. After all, Nicolau and she were friends and nothing more, with no claims, holds or expectations, why this sense of self-preservation?

Julia scanned the ceiling as she lay in bed that night. "My God," she said. "I'm acting like a complete idiot." She had always prided herself on never acting typical, yet here she was. "What's happening to me?"

The next morning she woke early, quickly dressed and walked down to the dock where Nicolau would catch the 7:00 am boat to Pico. There were a few people already gathered, waiting.

She spotted Nicolau standing beside a number of boxes and cases neatly stacked by the quay. He rushed over to her. "Julia!"

"Thought I'd come to see you off."

He greeted her with a hug. "I am glad you came. The boat will be here soon."

"What is all this?" Julia asked.

"For the people of old Quebrado," Nicolau said, "I bring them things they need. Food, books, clothing and blankets, basic supplies."

"What do you do there?"

"Whatever I can. I help build what they need, repair things. I teach the young ones, and make sure they are taken care of, that no one goes hungry or is sick."

"You'll see Teresa?"

"Yes, I assist her and the others."

They walked away from the gathering crowd of passengers, along the waterfront.

"You'll be back soon?"

"Three or four days."

She nodded.

Nicolau began humming as they stood side by side overlooking the water, then he sang:

"Tu és a brisa doce que sopra na minha pele. Tu és o mar sem fim que me rodeia. Tu és a canção que a noite canta. Tu és a ilha encantada que eu nunca deixei. Tu és o barco e as velas cheias que me levam lá."

You are the sweet breeze that blows against my skin. You are the sea without end that encircles me. You are the song that the night sings. You are the enchanted island that I'll never leave. You are the boat, with its full sails, that carries me there.

"What song is that?" Julia said.

"I wrote it last night," he said. "The melody is yours. You played it a few days ago."

"I like it. It's pretty."

"That's what I thought," Nicolau said. The boat docked at the quay. "It's time."

Julia nodded. They stood watching as the boat was being loaded. "I'd better go."

"I'll see you soon." She started to turn away, when without any fore-thought, without any warning, or provocation, he leaned over and kissed her.

Even as it occurred, Julia had no thought that it would be anything more than the simple return of a kiss. But momentum transformed it from a quick meeting of lips, an act of affection, to a sudden embrace, and an intensely passionate response, an affirmation and demonstration of desire and longing, which having finally achieved its objective, completely swept away all her objections about not being the proper time or place. Like certain words, unspoken at this moment, that could suggest or imply meaning, their kiss conveyed much more than would have been apparent to anyone who chanced to witness the event. But no one saw. Luck and happenstance favored this particular moment at this particular place, away from the eyes of strangers who, had they seen, would have noticed no more than a kiss and an embrace between a man and a woman—an ordinary enough occurrence. But to these two, entwined for that instant, there was an unspoken promise, and an assurance, a question and an answer, a conflux of two pasts, not to mention hints implicit of a possible future, appropriately accompanied by a sudden case of vertigo.

Although Nicolau meant to break off the kiss as soon as their lips touched, keeping it brief, without lust or passion, this intention was undermined by the unexpectedness of Julia's response, followed by Nicolau giving in completely, as feelings immediately seized control and were not about to be swept back under the façade of restraint and decorum.

Indeed, the passion of their embrace—her arms about his neck, his left hand pressing the small of her back, his right hand moving up the side of her waist, past her ribs, with a glancing brush against her breast—well, perhaps it was the timely introduction of language preceded by a gasp for air, that finally broke the spell. Nicolau could only utter a few disjointed syllables, "Oh, God, Julia," his tone of voice sounding like an apology.

But that was enough for them to separate, and a good thing too, because other passengers were beginning to congregate, preparing to board the boat.

"I'll see you soon," he said, squeezing her hand. Julia nodded and Nicolau turned and quickly boarded, then made his way to the stern.

Julia waited until the boat cleared Horta's jetty before turning away. She felt unsteady, as if she were the one on the boat, and she remembered the old saying, *Se há baleias no canal, terás temporal,* which translates, more or less, "If there are whales in the canal, bad weather will follow." Even if no storm could be seen on the horizon, the sighting of whales in the shallow straits between the two islands was a portent of perhaps a different type of storm, an outbreak of panic, confusion. It might refer to a storm of feelings, such as what just occurred, an outbreak of passion, typically recognized as between a man and a woman, but necessarily between individuals, intense sensations which afflict like a storm in the quickening heartbeats, the struggle to breathe, the loss of concentration, feelings of giddiness, even nausea, what some might dismiss as insanity, but is commonly regarded as love.

Perhaps it would be foolish to say that Julia was changed because of one kiss, yet everything *was* changed, subtly perhaps, but there it was, a detectable shift, an alteration, she perceived within and without her. She expected the unexpected, the unknown. She envisioned continents colliding, strands of time—the past and the present—overlapping, the inescapable product of their two worlds meshing.

CHAPTER 21

Dear *Avô,*

Antonio is here to help. I keep attempting to peer into the past, between the pages of this closed book. I open the covers, slowly, with difficulty, finding that some pages are torn out; others are so blurred by time, faded and worn. There are many mistakes, some legible, some not. It makes for very slow going, and never being certain of anything, for each time I believe I have finally cleared up a bit of confusion it leads me into a whole new mystery, yet another maze, leaving me just as confused if not more so than before. Did Sebastião know where he was going? Am I following the correct path he left behind, or am I completely off track, heading into quicksand? I wish I knew. Perhaps we'll find an answer soon.

Saudades,
Julia

• • •

A coarse, weather-beaten sailor of indeterminate age and nationality accosted Antonio, just as he left the *residencial* to meet Julia.

"I must talk to you," the sailor said, grabbing hold of Antonio's arm.

"What do you want?" Antonio said, as surly as he could, pulling his arm free. He looked the man up and down. The sailor clutched a cigarette and a tobacco pouch as if they were his salvation. He had a wild look about him, his hair matted and his skin burnt and chafed by long exposure to the sun and weather. He looked depraved, or drunk.

Antonio crossed the *avenida* toward the park and stood waiting for
the man to speak, not wanting the sailor to follow him to Peter's Café,
where Julia had arranged to meet him.

"I am Johan," the sailor said.

Antonio didn't offer his own name. Johan grinned like a man who
holds a royal flush and is about to sweep the winning stakes into his
pocket. His teeth were a sorry sight, and Antonio turned away in disgust. "You've heard about the troubles your Americans have caused here
lately?" Johan spoke English fairly well, but his voice was difficult to
understand, slurred with drink and a thick accent. Antonio, wondering why Johan referred to the Americans as his, assumed he was talking
about Sebastião, and as a result was guarded in his response.

"What Americans might those be?" he said.

"Two of your sailors got drunk in one of the taverns," Johan said,
holding up two fingers. "They argued with some French sailors about
who had reached the port of Horta by chance, and so far had not been
able to leave, afraid to sail. Many sailors who never sail before, by some
miracle, reach an island, but never leave. They beach themselves, and
haunt the docks and the cafés like ghosts, who cannot cross water. Did
you know that about ghosts?"

Antonio shook his head.

Johan hiccupped. "Hah, hah!" He slapped his thigh.

"Why wouldn't they leave?" Antonio asked. He didn't take his eyes off
the sailor, whose movements were erratic, like someone who suffered from
palsy or the shakes. His arms and legs were extremely thin, sinewy and
tough, the skin salted and dried by too much sun, sea and alcohol. He
fumbled constantly with a hand-rolled cigarette, his fingers stained brown
from tobacco. A bad eye left him with a peculiar leer, and a smoldering
intensity in his one good eye, like a fire underwater, for at the same time it
brimmed with liquid, as though it had sprung a leak. He laughed between
words, then stopped himself with a choked-off sound that was punctuated
with a coughing fit. He leaned close as he spoke, pressing his point forc-
ibly, needling Antonio. There was also a joyous tone of malice in the way
he spoke as though he enjoyed recounting the misfortunes of others, while
at the same time he seemed strangely unaware of the irony that he himself,
like those he spoke disparagingly about, also hadn't sailed out of port. He
was a seasoned sailor, unlike the others whom he referred to as amateurs.

"Isolation," Johan said with a wink, as if that one word said it all. Antonio expected to hear Johan say, 'aye,' like a pirate. "Isolation, fear of facing the ocean, mountainous waves, ruthless winds, desolation. A solitude that can lead anyone to take hold of a bottle and not let go." Johan relit his cigarette and took a few deep drags before continuing. Antonio waved away the smoke. "They talk of sailing tomorrow or the next day, but lose their sea legs instead. Better to drown slowly, sip by sip, on dry, solid land, rather than all at once, without even the pleasure of being drunk, in the middle of the ocean, completely alone."

"Sure," Antonio said, edging away from Johan and moving toward the edge of the park, nearer the water. He decided that Johan had clearly spent too much time alone.

"Ja, ja," Johan insisted. "Sailors are very superstitious, everything is a bad omen, a sign of doom. Friday is always a bad day to leave port. Tomorrow is no good because tonight there is an evil-shaped cloud in the sky. The only time they manage to leave is when they are good and drunk, when sitting still on land has made them so keyed-up they can't remain any longer."

Johan himself had sailed into port five years earlier. While he repeatedly spoke of leaving, of going back to sea, he'd been saying that since his arrival that first day. Every day he stepped outside, studied the sea, peered at the skies, shook his head and said, "No, not today. Maybe tomorrow." He lived aboard his boat, managed a shower only on rare occasions, and let his hair grow wild. He stank of sweat, sour beer and cigarettes, did odd jobs when he could find them, working on the boats of tourists or deep-sea fishermen, and regularly wired his family for money.

"Your Americans have caused the most trouble," Johan said. "It's as if your country breeds anger, people who go out into the world carrying their problems with them."

These weren't Azoreans Johan was speaking of, those who had emigrated to America, like Sebastião or Antonio, nor Luso-Americans—second or third generation Portuguese descendants, curious to see the land of their ancestors—nor those who had been exiled for some years and were now returning. These were people who had no connection whatsoever to the islands other than that it was a convenient stopover when crossing the Atlantic by boat. Some sought adventure, others attempted to escape from a wretched past or present, a marriage or love affair gone

195

sour, and still others chased a death wish. One or two found the islands only by accident. They sailed on impulse, often without having made any preparations, without even the rudimentary instruments necessary for assuring safety, into what they thought was a future with no tomorrow. How could they have known there were ports, safe harbors, a refuge, located in this oblivion through which they had navigated with the explicit purpose of losing themselves? They had neglected even the most basic of tasks, such as consulting nautical charts to see what lay beyond the familiar shores of the eastern seaboard. These islands, the harbor, and the islanders they saw and heard might merely be figments of a dream or hallucination conjured up by senses that, unused to such rigors and extremes, had fallen prey to the delusions of a debilitated mind.

"So, what happened to the two Americans?" Antonio asked, anxious to finish the conversation and get away.

"Listen," Johan said, waving his hand erratically. "Those two *americanos*, who had no more business being out on the ocean than I have being in kindergarten, started hurling insults and challenges, and as things sometimes go from bad to worse, especially where your countrymen are concerned, they soon hurtled fists, too—nothing too serious, a bloody lip, a blackened eye and a few bruises, but enough to land them in the comfort of the small jail up the hill." He laughed again, which was even less pleasant than the first time. "What some people won't do to make sure they stay put, even if it's only a lonely cell in the middle of the ocean. Even jail is better than battling a fierce Atlantic gale on your own, I can tell you, for I rode the back of the biggest gale in ten years when I came here. In jail, at least, they were able to enjoy home-cooked meals brought to them by the jailer's wife, and a warm bed. They were even given excursions to town now and then, which, of course, caused grumblings from those who say foreigners, even those who have broken the law, receive better treatment than do the Azoreans. But the Americans were released after a few days and quickly left the island, perhaps cured of their desire to be sailors."

Antonio was instinctively close-mouthed, convinced that Johan could not be trusted. His instincts, it turns out, were better than he could have guessed. The islanders would have warned him away from Johan, had they been less inclined to judge Antonio guilty by association. People watched him with a fair amount of suspicion, as if in being his father's son they only expected the worst from him. He attempted to negotiate this minefield, picking his way though the intricacies of culture and manners, the polite forms of addressing this person or that, proper responses, and those subtleties he couldn't overcome, which made him stand out as an outsider—his inability to master the European usage of a knife and fork, for example—all of which he failed at miserably.

"Those who lie down with dogs," the islanders muttered, "rise with fleas." Johan was known to gravitate toward the less savory elements, and was generally shunned.

Antonio took his cue to leave before Johan began discussing Sebastião, or questioning Antonio's reasons for being there.

"Well, thanks for the warning. I've got to run now," he said, rushing off before John could say another word.

· · ·

The surface of the nighttime sea is lit with an eerie glow. Jets of steam shoot a hundred meters high. At times the ocean churns and boils, and loud rumblings are heard miles away. The sea burns bright red, orange and yellow, and hundreds if not thousands of steaming chunks of lava float in the choppy water and spread in every direction, making navigation treacherous for many miles around.

Far below the surface of the sea there are fissures and cracks in the earth's crust. It is here where fresh water, fire, and new earth are born, spewed forth from the depths. Here the new island stirs, rising from the ocean floor, disturbing the so-called eternal sleep of shipwrecks, of drowned men and women, and sunken treasures littering the deeps. As the island reaches the surface it creates a new world above the waves, new impediments for the clouds and waves, for the currents that circle the globe, for travelers.

Imagine the surprise of someone who observes the span of ocean one moment and who turns and sees, in the next instant, an island, capable of destroying any boat or ship that may have been in its immediate path. Imagine, too, the contented repose of many a drowned mariner—those who had found a haven from the life of the living, there on the sea floor, the multitudes who had gone down with their ships over the centuries—their eternal slumber suddenly and violently shattered by the uplifting of the island.

· · ·

Julia stopped by Peter's Café to wait for Antonio. She ordered a coffee, sat down at one of the small tables, and tried not to think of Nicolau but what she should do next.

"The mountain is showing itself," she heard, without knowing who the speaker was, or to whom he was speaking. She didn't turn to see, but instead stared out at the channel. The mountain was clear of clouds. It looked so close, a fantastic monument. To what, she wondered.

"Have you just come from there?" There was no mistake this time. The question was addressed to her. "Or are you going to Pico?"

She shook her head.

"Pico is not like here," another voice said. The man explained, "Faial can be sad," he said, "but there is no place sadder than Pico."

"It is the saddest place in the world," said the first man. The other mumbled, agreeing.

She turned to see there were two men seated at the next table. She hadn't noticed them when she sat down. They were of that age when men achieve a state of invisibility, beyond threat or consideration. They wore ancient tweed suits and caps on their heads. A couple of characters, she thought.

"A friend went to Pico," she said. "Not me."

Julia remembered her grandmother explaining that babies came from *a ponta do Pico,* the peak of the mountain. How many Azorean children grew up believing that they were born of the volcano? The mountain had stood for so long, had seen so much come and go. She wished she could see what the first mariners had seen when they'd discovered the islands. She'd heard there were dense forests that were burned to clear the land, as in the case of Madeira. There had been a man left on Pico before any settlers came, a hermit, who roamed the island for several years alone. Had the old man climbed to the top of Pico? Did he have visions, dreams of ancient peoples? Did ghosts rise from the mountain to relive their lost history?

Antonio entered the café. Julia waved him over.

"Ungodly hour," he said, sitting down beside her. "What's new?"

"I just saw Nicolau off. He's gone to Pico for a few days," she said, trying to sound as neutral as possible. "Look at the mountain, isn't it glorious?"

Antonio turned to look. "Looks gloomy," he said, "the way I feel. Just had a narrow escape. Resident lunatic, a harbor rat."

"Do you want a coffee?" she said.

"No, let's go."

They rose from the table and walked toward the door.

"Boa viagem," said one of the men who had spoken to her. "May God go with you."

She waved goodbye to the men, who sat grim-faced, as if they watched a friend about to sail into the unknown. Maybe they were hard of hearing, she thought. Why did they insist she was going somewhere?

"So, are you and Nick, you know. . . ?" Antonio said, raising his eyebrows suggestively.

"Don't go reading more into this than there is," Julia said. "He's nice. We're good friends, that's all."

Antonio nodded knowingly. "Hm, I've heard that before."

She felt only slightly dishonest, for kiss or no kiss, how was she to know where things really stood? When she found Sebastião she would return home and things here would return to normal; Nicolau would remain here with Maria dos Santos and his sister Teresa. End of story.

They strolled through the park of the Infante when they met João Correia and a friend.

"Julia, Antonio, this is Vitorino," João said. "An old sea dog, one of the best fishermen on Faial. He gets sick if he stays too long on land. He's about to go to sea again."

They shook hands. Vitorino nodded. "Yes, I'm anxious to fish," he said.

"Is your boat here in the harbor?" Julia said.

"Would you like to see her?"

"Sure," Julia said, turning to check with Antonio.

"Why not?" he said, shrugging.

"Come along, then."

"I have to get back to the *residencial,*" João said. "You go, and I'll see you later."

Julia and Antonio followed Vitorino to where the fishing boats were moored. They walked in silence, until Julia broke the ice. "When do you sail?" she asked.

"Tomorrow morning, but not for fish." He winked conspiratorially. She assumed that being a friend of João's he was harmless, but he did look menacing. He was short and stocky with a thick neck and heavily tattooed arms. "Here she is."

Julia and Antonio followed Vitorino aboard. "You fish for something else?" Julia said. Vitorino nodded, but said nothing.

"This is my boat, *Fantasma do Mar*"—*The Sea Ghost*, Vitorino said proudly. "What do you think?" Antonio and Julia looked the boat over. It was old, painted blue and white and weathered by years of hard use.

"It's very nice," Julia said. "That's an interesting name."

"Yes, only unlike all the stories of ghost ships we've been hearing," Vitorino said, "my *Fantasma do Mar* is very much real."

"I'd like to see a ghost ship," Julia said.

"People see strange things when they look to the sea," Vitorino said. "But she is named *Fantasma do Mar* because in her day she was fast. She roamed far and wide on the sea like a cloud, like a ghost. And there is protection in the name of a boat or ship."

"I've heard a ghost can't cross water," Antonio said, remembering what the sailor Johan had said. Julia looked at Antonio as if he'd suddenly recited poetry or spoke French.

"People say that," Vitorino said, nodding.

"How is there protection in a name?" Julia said.

"Instead of naming it for a saint or a captain's daughter, which might perhaps invite misfortune, naming it a ghost or giving it a name that is not so innocent keeps away misfortunes."

"João says you were quite a fisherman in your day," Julia said.

"I was and still am," Vitorino said. "Only now, instead of fish, my nets catch other treasures."

"Treasure?" Antonio said.

"Careful," Julia said, "You might find yourself with my brother as a partner."

Antonio shot her a look, but Vitorino laughed. "He likes treasure, eh?" He opened the hatch and spoke in a rough and clipped Portuguese to someone down below. A young man came up on deck, holding out a delicate brown limb that fanned out in ever-finer branches, like filigree made of wood. He handed it to Vitorino.

"This is what I will fish for tomorrow," Vitorino said, handing the branch to Antonio.

"What is it?" Antonio said, turning the fragile limb over in his hands.

"Madeira do mar," he said, as though he were saying 'spun gold.'

"Wood of the sea?" Julia said. Antonio passed her the branch, clearly disappointed.

"Coral," the young man said. "The fishermen bring it up in their nets and toss it back to the sea, but here, look at this piece which has been cleaned." It was smaller, but much finer, with a polished glassy surface, as black as obsidian. "Hold it up to the light."

Julia lifted the branch and saw it wasn't black after all, but was a deep dark purple. "It's beautiful," she said. "I've never seen coral like this."

"It has to come from very deep to get this color. Which makes it difficult to find."

"My nephew, Manuel," Vitorino said, "he's the expert. If I can't fish for fish, I will fish for this, instead. Who knows, perhaps it is valuable. Manuel thinks so."

"People actually pay money for this?" Antonio said, his interest piqued.

"It is very rare," Manuel said. "And what is rare is expensive."

"That makes sense," Julia said. "They probably use it for jewelry."

"Perhaps," Vitorino said.

"Are you going, too, Manuel?" Julia said.

"Yes, I help Vitorino."

Vitorino explained that they went far, to the deeper waters. "Four or five days out, and we return with a hold full of this."

"What about the new island?" Julia asked. "Have you seen it?"

"No, it's dangerous," Vitorino said. "The boats stay away from it."

"My father, Sebastião," she said, "He may have gone there."

"Yes?" Vitorino scratched his head. "Why?"

"I'm not sure . . . a tenth Azorean island . . . perhaps be the first to land on it." She shrugged. "I don't know."

"You want to see the island," Manuel said.

"I'd go, if someone would take us," Julia said.

"If you want to go to the new island," Vitorino said, "you take them on your boat, Manuel, not mine."

"Will you pay?" Manuel asked.

"Sure, I'll rent your boat, or charter it, whatever they call it," Julia said.

"Will you go, too?" Manuel said to Antonio.

"I don't think so," Antonio said. "When boats travel over dry land, then I'll take one, but not before."

Manuel laughed. "When I get back we'll take my boat and find the new island."

. . .

The act of writing is a desperate and hopeless attempt to recapture lost knowledge, forgotten sensation, a vanquished sensate language—to remember all that is irretrievably lost.

—Sebastião do Canto e Castro

. . .

Julia returned to Sebastião's room in Praia do Almoxarife. She moved cautiously, examining everything with a critical eye, hoping against hope that she might open the door and come face to face with Sebastião, seated, writing out his latest chapter, smoking a pipe, a glass of *aguardente* at his side. Perhaps it was that very hope, this expectation, which explained the strange presence she felt whenever she returned. It was the act of inspecting the contents of the room that invariably caused her to reflect: Wasn't there an even twenty stacks of paper against that wall where there are now only eighteen? Or, weren't there more books on that table? The things the imagination is capable of conjuring and convincing even the most skeptical into believing, under the right conditions. To make matters worse, the possibility she was left with was that if there were things that had been there, which were no longer, then there could just as well be things which weren't there before, but which were there now.

She stepped outside and stood on the shore, faced the dark sea and breathed the breeze the ocean carried. She could feel waves inside her crash against the shell of her body, the urge to break free and join the sea that called to that part of her.

The faint luminescent glow she thought she saw out beyond the waves, she told herself, was likely only the faint glow of a boat's lantern in the distance, or perhaps the gleam of a new island rising from the ocean, its fires of molten rock setting the water aglow. Or was it the unnatural glow of a ghost ship adrift in the distance?

CHAPTER 22

Julia used all her powers of persuasion to convince Antonio to accompany her to Pico the next morning. "It'll just be a few hours," she said. "The boat trip's only half an hour, if that's what's worrying you."

"I'm not worried," he said, followed by a heavy sigh. "I'll go, if it'll make you happy."

"Good." Julia didn't tell him that she would have gone alone if he hadn't agreed to accompany her. Without Nicolau's diverting presence, she felt agitated. She needed to do something, go somewhere, if only to reacquaint herself with places connected to the family, though she kept that to herself as well. She didn't share her grandfather's letter with him, either, though she did mention that Mateus had sent his love.

"Poor Mateus" was all Antonio had to say. It was all he ever said of Mateus.

The sea was calm. From the prow of the boat Julia watched the town of Madalena materialize as they approached the island. She smiled, realizing that the old men in Peter's Café had been right after all about her going to Pico. A disgruntled Antonio sat scowling at the water.

Madalena was much smaller and quieter than Horta. Few people were out and about, as Julia and Antonio walked along the main street. They caught a bus to Cais do Pico, which had been a whaling village, then walked the short distance to São Roque, where many years earlier their grandparents had lived, and where Sebastião was born.

The weather was warm and the air dryer than Faial. Pico was sparsely populated with miles of sharp cliffs, inaccessible by road or trail. Numerous gardens and vineyards, surrounded by walls of black volcanic rock lay within, and beyond, emerald fields, where cows and sheep grazed.

There were no sandy beaches, only dangerous rocks and steep mountainsides with numerous ravines, where there was no telling how long a body could lie unseen.

Julia dragged an unusually quiet Antonio through several cemeteries. He rolled his eyes as she searched for the graves of relatives. "Only two?" she said. "Where are the others?" Had their graves faded away, covered or replaced by those of the more recent dead? Touching the silent stones, she marked the names and dates, as if some faint message or revelation might be transmitted or transferred across the generations, across time—the boundaries of life and death.

Julia had spent a night on the island of Terceira before taking the plane to Faial, and had walked the perimeter of the manor house her great-grandfather, Raimundo, had been forced to sell—the family crest still visible in the stone above the heavy wooden doorway. The house contained its own chapel where so many of the Canto e Castros over the centuries had been baptized, married, and entombed. The manor, which Sebastião always called "our castle," was a splendid building, or rather a number of buildings surrounded by thick walls, certainly much grander than most of the other structures on the island. But when Julia was young and heard Sebastião or Mateus speak of it, she had always imagined a true castle, one with towering turrets and bastions, like those that guarded so many of the towns in Portugal. Still, Julia had admired the manor, seeing it the way her father had seen it, as theirs—a five-hundred-year-old memorial to the family.

As they walked through Cais do Pico and São Roque, Julia recognized certain views, a building or landscape her grandfather had painted. "Look," she said, pointing, "Remember that one?" Antonio grunted. Once a year, even as he lost his eyesight, Mateus would send his grandchildren postcard-sized paintings of a scene from the islands. Antonio would quietly place them in a drawer. To be here and see these same places, for Julia was an odd experience, as if she had stepped into Mateus's art, just as she had earlier felt she had walked into Sebastião's stories.

They stopped at a small store. The sign on the storefront read Mercado Rodrigues. A tall man in his late fifties stood behind the counter.

"Bom dia," he said, when Julia entered the shop. Antonio waited outside.

Julia returned the greeting and looked the store over. There were only a few shelves of tinned goods, bottled juices and sodas, jars of fruit, cigarettes, candies, and a number of kitchen items in the store. Behind the counter were jugs of wine and bottles of beer.

She stepped outside. "Let's have lunch, Antonio."

"Here?" he said.

"Sure." She sat at one of the small tables in front of the market. Antonio joined her, looking dubious, as he sat in one of the plastic chairs that ringed the table.

A skinny, sullen girl, sixteen or seventeen, with stooped shoulders, who looked half-asleep, brought them a hand-written paper menu. Julia ordered a cheese sandwich and an orange drink. Antonio ordered a coffee and a ham sandwich. The girl turned away without a word.

"I think it would hurt her to smile," Antonio said.

When the girl returned with the drinks, Julia asked if she knew where the Solar Azul was. "No, I'm not from here."

"Are you the owner's daughter?" Julia asked.

"Yes."

"Did you grow up in America?"

"Canada. My father wanted to come home, so he dragged us here," she said, as though she couldn't think of a worse punishment.

"I know just how you feel," Antonio said. "I'm here against my will, too." She still didn't manage a smile, but her features softened somewhat.

"It's very different from Canada," Julia said. The girl nodded. "My name's Julia. This is my brother Antonio."

"I'm Joana. My father might know where you can find the place you're looking for."

"That's Senhor Rodrigues inside?" Julia said. Joana nodded, and finally smiled. "You have a pretty smile."

Joana blushed. "Thank you," she said. A moment later Joana brought their sandwiches.

"Why do you want to see that old relic?" Antonio asked.

"Just curious. It's been a long time."

"Not long enough, if you ask me. Place always gave me the creeps. Can't imagine it's any better now. In fact, I'll be surprised if it's still standing."

"I just want a quick look," she said. "I spent a lot of time there." Sebastião had had a falling out with the owners some ten years before and had had no contact with them since. But Julia had fond memories of the house and its enormous gardens and was curious about the people who, after all, were cousins. "They are family, you know?"

"Family," Antonio said, with a snort.

After they ate, Julia went inside to pay the bill. "I'm looking for the Solar Azul," she said to Senhor Rodrigues. "It's a very large old house near Quebrado do Caminho. Do you know it?"

Senhor Rodrigues scratched his head. "I don't seem to remember. But Paulo should know the place. He knows all the old families."

He stepped outside and went to the next building, which was a shoe repair. Julia and Antonio followed. Senhor Rodrigues spoke to a wiry old man who, as he grinned, showed a mouth nearly devoid of teeth. A hand-rolled cigarette stuck miraculously to his lower lip. One look at Julia and Antonio and he said, "Canto e Castro?"

Julia was surprised and nodded. "Yes," she said. Antonio rolled his eyes and said, "Uh oh." He'd always been embarrassed when as a young boy people had fussed over the family.

"I recognize you. I knew your family," he said, nodding his head as if there'd been no doubt whatsoever. Paulo asked Julia to give his regards to Isabel and Mateus, and assured her that he hadn't seen Sebastião in many months. Julia repeated what she'd asked Senhor Rodrigues. Paulo muttered something rapidly and crossed himself.

"You know the house?" Julia asked.

The two men spoke back and forth rapidly. Paulo kept nodding and Julia was bemused to see how frightened he appeared.

"Yes," Senhor Rodrigues said. "He says they call it *a casa mal assombrada.*"

"The badly shadowed house?" Julia said, confused. "You mean it's poorly lit?"

"No, it's how you say," Senhor Rodrigues said with a laugh, "with ghosts."

"Haunted?" Julia said. She noticed that Joana had approached and stood nearby.

"Yes, haunted," Senhor Rodrigues said.

"Great," Antonio said. "Why am I not surprised?"

Paulo spoke in a thick accent Julia found difficult to understand. From what she could see he had only a single front tooth, that caused his cheeks to cave inward, and yet at the same time he chewed something, perhaps tabacco. She stopped him several times, saying, "Could you repeat that?" Finally, Senhor Rodrigues began translating for her.

"He says that after the old people died some years ago, the others in the family fought over the will. One brother got most of the property near the house, another got the money, one sister got the house and another got a smaller house on São Jorge. Everything was divided up and much of it sold off. They fought over everything, even the furniture, the silver, and the rugs. It was very bitter. When it was all over nobody was speaking to anyone else.

"Often the house sat empty. The sister who lived there would go to the continent for long periods of time, but even then people say they heard noises and saw lights in the windows at night. The woman who lived in the house had nothing to do with anyone. She was never seen by anybody, not neighbors, not old friends of the family, no one. She lived there all alone."

"Does she still live there?" Julia asked.

Paulo shrugged before continuing. "Some say she's still there," Senhor Rodrigues explained, "but no one knows for sure. There are rumors. Some say she died in America, others say she is alive. It's always dark, no one comes or goes. But there are strange sounds, and strange things have happened there. People stay away from it. They're afraid. Even dogs shy away from that place." As if to sum up the general feeling about the house, Paulo added, *"Ghosts."*

"Is it very far?" Julia asked.

"No," Paulo said, pointing the direction they should go and telling them where they should turn. "But be careful."

"I will," Julia said, smiling at the old man's concern. "Thank you."

"Can I go with her," Joana asked, suddenly, *"please?"*

"I don't mind," Julia was quick to add. "It'd be nice to have her along."

Senhor Rodrigues shrugged, apparently at a loss as to what to do with his unhappy daughter. "Come back as soon as you're done," he said.

"Thanks," Julia said. "We won't be long." Joana's face beamed with joy.

They began walking towards Quebrado do Caminho and the Solar Azul. After a few minutes of silence, Joana asked in a hopeful tone, "Is the house really haunted?"

"I don't think so," Julia said, though she didn't sound convinced.

"If any house on Pico is haunted, that one is," said Antonio, walk-

207

ing ahead of of Júlia and Joana. "Whenever we stayed here when I was a kid I could never get to sleep in this house. I'd lie in bed awake the whole night hearing noises. It was spooky. I don't believe in ghosts, but I wouldn't spend another night in there."

"Good," Joana said. "A ghost would at least be exciting."

"You miss your friends, huh?" Julia said, looking at her brother curiously. He had never said anything to her about hearing strange sounds in the house.

Joana nodded. "Thanks for letting me come with you."

"My pleasure. You can keep us from getting lost." They continued a good twenty minutes or so and turned where Paulo had instructed them to turn before reaching the village. The house—one of the oldest on the island—was built on the outskirts of old Quebrado, where the village had originally stood before a severe earthquake had destroyed most of the structures. Instead of rebuilding, the villagers rebuilt the village farther down the road, leaving the old buildings where they stood. The Solar Azul was situated between the old village and the new one that had replaced it.

Julia thought of Nicolau, aware that he was somewhere close by. She might have tried to find him, but not with Antonio here. It was better to wait until Nicolau returned to Faial.

"Why do you want to see the house?" Joana said.

"I stayed there when I was young," Julia said. "I remember the plaster walls as thick as the pine trees that grew in the yard, ceilings higher than any I'd ever seen, and a massive cast-iron wood-burning stove that ran the entire length of a kitchen wall. The halls seemed to go on forever and the rooms were too numerous to count; there was a large attic upstairs and cellar below, both filled with innumerable trunks and pieces of furniture. I used to roam through the house, so different from any home I'd ever seen, full of shadows and silent corners."

"Sounds creepy."

Julia nodded. "It was kind of spooky. If there were secret rooms or hidden passageways, I never found them. But I did discover initials etched into the windowpanes of one of the rooms upstairs. My Aunt Josefina told me stories about the strange woman who had once lived there."

They reached a dirt road and turned. The ground was rust-colored, and crunched beneath their feet. The air was filled with the fragrance of azaleas, lemon verbena and hydrangeas growing along the roadside; away from the shore, *a terra*—the rich soil, the earth—piled ever higher toward the cloud-ringed summit of Pico.

"Who was she?" Joana said.

"Aunt Josefina said it was her great aunt who had spent her entire life in that room.

"She never left the room?" Joana asked.

"No. Aunt Josefina said the woman was afraid. She saw things no one else saw, heard things no one else heard. The family didn't want people to know. They would say she was crazy, or worse, that she was a witch.

"I asked what her name was, thinking perhaps the woman still haunted the room, trapped in the glass, where I had traced her initials with my fingertips.

"'Amélia,' my aunt said.

"'What did she look like, *tia?*'

"'She was very thin, and very pale,' my aunt said. 'She hardly ever spoke and when she did it was always in a whisper. I never heard her say more than a word or two. She always dressed in her nicest clothes, as if she were going out, no matter what the weather, and no matter that she never left the house. Even when she was old and frail, she was still child-like, impossible to think of as a grown woman. I often heard her roaming around her room late at night.'

"I thought Amélia must have been exquisitely beautiful. I imagined a woman with a haunted and melancholy demeanor, who would allow no photographs of her, but would sit by the window and stare out at the island or perhaps the sea. I sat in Amélia's room wondering what had driven her to stay inside all those years. Had a lover left her with a promise to return? Was she waiting for him? Perhaps he had married someone else or had died. A sailor lost at sea.

"What kind of things did she see, I wanted to know. What did she hear? My aunt said she didn't know, that Amélia would never say. Gazing through her window, I realized that certain pains and sorrows never healed or faded, but lasted beyond all recall, becoming distilled like ambergris—a thing of sacred beauty and awe. Some women knit shawls and sweaters, but Amélia sat alone in the old rocking chair upstairs, humming strange melodies and weaving a tapestry of age-old sorrows and regrets.

209

"Perhaps Amélia was buried beneath the floorboards or in a nearby family tomb. Each night she might wake to wander the halls, searching for her lost lover—forever chained to the mysterious tragedy that shrouded her life."

"A sad story," Joana said.

Julia nodded.

"Ah, the old family skeletons," Antonio said, dodging as Julia reached out to hit him.

They reached the old manor house. "This is it," said Julia, excitedly. "What do you think, Antonio? You think it's haunted, like they say?"

"What do I think? I think it looks like the House of Usher. I wouldn't trust it for a minute. I'll wait here," he said. "Don't blame me if it falls." He found a large stone to sit on.

The house hadn't weathered the years well, and did look as if it were on the verge of collapse. Julia walked from one end of the property to the other, transfixed by what was left of the old Solar Azul, pointing up at the window where Amélia had scratched her initials. The once proud walls were streaked and cracked, the roof in disrepair. Many of the tiles were broken or missing and while most of the windows had been shuttered, some shutters were missing. The house was little more than a ruin, and didn't look as if anyone had lived there for many years. The massive wall surrounding the yard kept Julia from seeing what the gardens looked like, but the trees that were visible were thick with vines. What little she could see had a wild look about it, overgrown and ravaged by time, like the house itself.

Julia knocked at the enormous wooden gate. There was no answer, no sound from the house. She walked from one end to the other, repeatedly glancing at the dark windows and wondering if that uneasy feeling she had was a result of someone watching, peering at her from within the ruined building. The house had been so full of life when she had last visited, bustling with family and friends coming and going, parties and celebrations. Before then musicians, writers, politicians and others would visit. Now it stood a mute testament to the family's decline.

She knocked a second time at the gate.

Antonio approached. "Looks like hell," he said. "It should be razed to the ground."

"I don't think anyone lives here," Joana said.

"No," Julia said. "I guess not."

"Let's go," Antonio said.

"I wish there was some way to get inside," Julia said. "I do so want to see the house."

"Why me?" Antonio said, rolling his eyes. He shoved hard at the gate, then pushed again, harder than before. It opened partially. "Let's make this quick. I don't want to spend more time here than I have to. And I sure as hell don't want to be arrested for breaking into this dump."

Julia rushed inside the gate, followed by Joana who stepped tentatively into the property, looking about as if she expected to be grabbed or attacked at any moment. Antonio entered, glancing back at the road to make sure no one had seen them.

They stood and surveyed the house and yard. "Ah, yes, the great, proud family estate," Antonio said.

"It's a crime," Julia said. She felt a lump in her throat, and her eyes watered. "It should be saved. This is an historical building, if nothing else."

She walked up to the porch, went up the few steps to the house. She tried the door, but it was locked. There was a window near the door. Julia peered inside. Joana and Antonio pressed their faces to the glass on either side of her.

"It looks bad," she said. "But not as bad as one would think."

"No?" Antonio said.

"No. It almost looks as if someone still comes in and cares for the place. At least on the inside."

Antonio shrugged. "So some neighbor stops by now and then and sweeps it out."

"It's creepy," Joana said. "How could anyone stay here?"

"I don't know," Julia said. "I certainly wouldn't stay here alone." The yard was just as overgrown and wild as she imagined from outside the walls. As they stood on the porch a few scrawny chickens came out of the shrubs and wandered through in the yard, pecking at the ground. "Would there be chickens if the place was completely abandoned?"

"They might slip in and out through a chink in the gate somewhere around the property," Antonio said. "Well, sister, dear, have you seen enough?"

"Let's just walk around the house first," Julia said. Antonio pulled a face but didn't argue. Julia walked to the right, toward the front of the building.

"I'll go this way," Antonio said, going in the opposite direction. "Let's meet on the other side." He was older, bigger and stronger, but since she was a child Julia had known how to get her way with him. She could appeal to his perceived superiority and let him think he was the one in charge, that he'd made the decision, or when all else failed, she would threaten to make a scene, which he would avoid at all costs.

Joana hesitated only a second, then followed Julia.

When they reached the corner of the house Julia turned around. Antonio had disappeared on the other side. She smiled. "Poor Antonio," she said.

"Why?" Joana asked.

"Oh, he's humoring me, letting me drag him to places he wouldn't go in a million years, hoping I'll go back to California with him."

Joana shook her head. "I wish I could go back to Canada."

The first floor had only a couple of small windows caked with grime. It wasn't a place in which people lived, but a storage space, with work areas constructed in sections. The main entrance was bolted shut, but on the other side, they found a small door, slightly ajar.

"Well, well, look at this," Julia said, as she pushed the door open and stepped inside.

"Are you sure we should go inside?" Joana said, looking around for an irate owner.

"For a moment, that's all," Julia said. "We'll just have a quick look."

It was dark. Julia wished Antonio had stayed with them. She moved slowly. Joana followed behind with one hand on Julia's arm. They shuffled their way across the floor, which was stone, not dirt, as it had appeared to be. There were a number of tools and machines, some farming equipment, as well as old lamps, furniture, and boxes and crates of old clothes and household items.

"Hey, look at this," Julia said. They reached a part of the building much older than the rest where a stone archway stood exposed. They stepped inside and stopped.

A stone slab on the ground had been moved, revealing an opening. Julia leaned forward. Though she could barely see, it was clear there was a heap of bones jutting out of the dirt.

"Let's go," Joana said. "I'm scared. Maybe that's who the ghost was."

"Don't be afraid," Julia said. "We won't stay." First, however, she bent down to the stone and felt the rough surface. There was something etched into the stone, but practically worn smooth. "Damn, it's too faded. If I only had a flashlight or something."

"Please," Joana said, shifting nervously from foot to foot.

Julia turned around. Joana was visibly shaken. "Come on, let's go."

They backed out of the archway. "They must have built the house on the ruins of a far older building," she said. "It looks like part of a chapel."

As they stepped forward, Julia found that her eyes had adjusted to the darkness. What she hadn't seen when they had entered was a large painting. "What's this?" she said. It had looked to be part of the wall, because the painting itself was nearly as dark as the building. It was at least four by six feet in length. Julia shifted the wooden frame and squinted at the painting. It depicted a rough ocean, a stormy night sky, and in the center an island as beautiful as one could imagine. In the foreground was a small boat being rowed by what looked to be a decrepit old man, and in the background a large ancient sailing ship.

"What is it?" Joana's voice quivered.

"The Enchanted Island," Julia softly. "Hold on." She bent down. There was a faint signature along the bottom right hand side. She could just barely make out the letters Am – l – a. "Amélia?" she whispered. "Could this be hers? Come on, let's find Antonio."

Antonio, after leaving Julia and Joana, had made his way around the other side of the house. With his hands in his pockets and kicking pebbles distractedly as he walked around the perimeter of the building, he was suddenly aware that he was not alone.

"Jules?" he said. It was one of his pet names for her. But even as he spoke it he knew it wasn't her he sensed. There was a shadow, a flitter of movement off to his left, and he looked up to see what was without a doubt the most remarkable face he had ever seen.

She had dark, shoulder-length hair, large, round eyes, faintly aquatic, luminous skin, and a mouth that was all sensuality. Everything else was a blur: how old she was, whether short or tall, what he read in her expression and in her eyes (volumes!), for in an instant she was gone.

He took a few steps forward but realized he had no idea where she'd gone. Shaken, and rubbing his eyes, Antonio continued his way around the house.

A few minutes later he met up with Julia and Joana. "Find anything?"

Julia asked.

"No, nothing," he said, a bit too defensively. He looked even more out of sorts, but Julia figured it was due to spending too much time near the house.

They left, and began walking back to São Roque. Julia decided to wait to tell Antonio about what she'd found. Antonio had no intention of saying anything about what he'd seen.

They walked back to the market a quiet somber threesome.

"Are you okay," Joana asked, at last.

"Sorry," Julia said. "Just thinking." She couldn't help but feel sad about leaving and going back to Faial. She sensed that Joana was experiencing a similar emotion.

"I know it's hard right now," Julia told Joana when they reached the market. "But you'll make friends. You'll see. It'll get easier."

Joana nodded. "Goodbye," she said. "And thanks."

"Don't mention it." She smiled as Antonio said goodbye to Joana, awkwardly shaking her hand, while the girl blushed.

Julia and Antonio walked back to the main road and caught the bus to Madalena. "I pity that poor girl," Antonio said after some silence. "It's a cruel thing to do to a kid."

"I don't know," Julia said. "She might adjust."

"Yeah, maybe." They took the next boat back to Faial.

CHAPTER 23

Reports reached Horta that the new island had risen above the surface of the ocean. Clouds of hot ash and steam, eruptions of lava and bellowing plumes of smoke filled the skies, and spread to the other islands. These reports were quickly followed by more news—the island had grown larger. Lava spilled into the sea, adding to the island. There were more earthquakes. Jets of smoke and ash darkened the skies, while the sea surrounding the new island boiled.

The newspapers were filled with the news, and people everywhere discussed the fact that there were now ten islands in the Azores archipelago.

"Will the new island sink?" people asked. "Or will it remain?"

"How big is this island?" others wanted to know.

People gathered to discuss the event, what the island looked like, and if and when it could possibly be settled.

"I hear it is an island of fire, burning day and night," someone said.

"An inferno," said another.

"Perhaps not," said yet a third. "I heard it was a green paradise—like Eden!"

Julia found a note of her father's that referred to the island.

"I see no reason why we should not, after all these years, have an island to call our own," he'd written. "Since it is the Banco do Dom João de Castro, it only makes sense to call the new island, Ilha do Dom João de Castro, though of course people will call it Ilha do Dom João for short."

Julia rushed to Maria dos Santos's house.

"Nicolau isn't back from Pico," Maria dos Santos said, before Julia said anything.

"I wanted to tell him about the new island," Julia said. "It's broken through the surface of the sea. Will Nicolau be back today?"

"Not for another day or two, I think," Maria said.

"I wonder if he's heard, there are now ten Azores," Julia said.

"It was bound to happen. These are the times we are in. Everything comes full circle, the past, the future, and the present. You are surprised?"

Julia shook her head. "Nothing surprises me anymore, senhora."

She returned to Sebastião's room, wondering why Maria dos Santos was so sure the new island was bound to happen. Her mind spun with the number of reflections and refractions, of the images that filled her head. It was as if there were mirrors everywhere, casting off shadow-images, and shadows of shadows: Antonio and Julia, Nicolau and Teresa, her father Sebastião and King Sebastião. She grappled with what was real, the concrete. Maria dos Santos and José Manuel. But what about the story of Maria dos Santos, the fountain of youth, and Ponce de León, which led to Inês de Castro and her brother Álvaro de Castro.

Julia shook her head clear. She couldn't pass up the opportunity, perhaps the necessity, of visiting the new island as soon as possible. She'd contact Manuel as soon as Vitorino's boat returned to Horta. In the meantime she would return to the *residencial*. Since visiting the old family estate on Pico, finding the old painting of the island and the tomb, it was as though she were hearing for the first time. Or to be precise, since she was a young girl. When she had spent so much time in that house, filled with all its untold secrets, its venerable past, sleeping in the massive mahogany bed where so many of her ancestors had slept and where she first heard the sounds she would always associate with the islands. Night after night, furtive rustlings and creakings disturbed the otherwise complete silence, the lack of the all-too-familiar background noise of televisions, radios, cars, jet planes—all the myriad ever-present sounds of Los Angeles. She had never known such stillness or such silence.

But there were other sounds, too. Haunting melodies had kept her awake and thrilled her, and at the same time filled her with uncertainty and apprehension. Would she too go mad and have to be locked in a room like Amélia? Were these the same noises Amélia had heard— strange voices and melodies, like medieval dirges or chants?

Julia had strained to understand the murmurings that teased her ears with the faintest whispers, at times thinking she could almost make out meanings if not words among the tantalizing bits of melody that wove in and out of her consciousness. With her heart nearly drowning out the sounds, she'd tiptoe down the halls, chasing its source. Was it from this room or that one there, someone mouthing prayers, or giving voice to their most secret desires, their most cherished dreams. At times she tried to convince herself that what she heard was nothing more than the wind and the distant rumble of the sea, enhanced by her wild imaginings.

She exhausted herself during the day exploring the lands the family owned. There were banana groves and honey bees, chickens, pigs and rabbits, vine-trellises and fruit trees she had climbed and sat beneath, while she read her father's stories about the islands, and where she momentarily succeeded in outrunning those sounds that haunted her nights and seemed to seek her out, as if they were for her alone.

She had mentioned the noises to Sebastião, but he hadn't appeared the least concerned. "It's your past you hear," he would say. Or, "That's the sound of the islands. They only call to those who are special."

Julia hadn't felt special, she felt different—even as a young child. It was only after she had spent time on the islands that she came to realize this is why I am different, because I come from this beautiful, mysterious place, because I'm a part of these islands.

Julia had heard the music again when she was twelve and accompanied Sebastião to the islands, and again when she was thirteen. By then she had more or less made peace with the sounds, pretending she didn't hear anything, deciding to become a musician, to sing and learn the piano, to manage if not govern notes and rhythms.

Now that Antonio had mentioned being disturbed by sounds when staying in the old family mansion, she wondered if she were alone in hearing those mysterious melodies; had her brother also heard what she had heard?

Before leaving California, Julia had wondered if she would hear that wondrous music again, those sounds that had come so unexpectedly like a strange recurring dream. Perhaps simply wanting to hear it again wasn't enough, especially since in the past she had wished it would stop and let her be. She hadn't wanted to be different. She'd never really fit in at school. Having a father who so obviously wasn't American made her self-conscious. It always seemed to her as if she had one foot in the States and the other on the islands, one in the present and one in the past, that she was split between two worlds. She couldn't shut out the one as Antonio could. And now she heard the sounds again, faint, but growing stronger with each passing day.

All her worries and concerns over the sounds she had heard when she was young were coming to the fore. She was afraid the dim, musty room where Sebastião had worked was affecting her. Resolved to spend time away from the room and go to the new island as soon as possible, she returned to the *residencial,* where she found that Antonio, had other plans.

218

"We're getting out of here," he said. "Now."

"No, Antonio."

"Look, it's dangerous. We're going to get ourselves killed. And for what?"

Julia's face was set, determined. He knew what her look meant.

"I'm going, Ju"—he only called her Ju when he wanted something from her, when he was angry, or trying to make her feel guilty. "I can't stay. I've had enough. Sebastião's gone. There's no reason to stay here. Look at the skies, the ground shaking all the time."

"I'm going to see the new island," Julia said. "I've got to at least see if he is there."

"I thought that was a joke. It's a damn volcano. It's dangerous."

"You don't have to go. I'm not scared," she said, though it wasn't true.

"You're crazy," he said. "Why go? There's nothing there."

"I didn't tell you but when Joana and I were at the house we saw something."

"Saw what?" He felt a tingle on the back of his neck. Had she seen the woman, too? He hadn't been able to rid his mind of that vision, that remarkable face, which had haunted him ever since.

"Under the house the floor is stone. It used to be a chapel. I'm certain of it."

"So?" She explained the archway they discovered, and the tomb with the bones.

"Again, so what?"

"There was no skull. The stone had some word or words carved into it. I couldn't read what it said. But that's not all. We found a painting of the Enchanted Island. It's huge."

"Listen to yourself, Ju. It's crazy. Sebastião was crazy. The whole thing, why it's—" His tone was sharp, not merely because he disagreed with her, but because he felt guilty for not mentioning the woman, and because he was beginning to think maybe, just maybe, Julia was right.

"When are you leaving?" Julia said.

Antonio turned and stormed off without a word.

CHAPTER 24

A small wooden boat in the most wretched condition—waterlogged, weather-beaten, and worm-infested—is tossed about on the open sea. There is only a single mast and a small triangular sail, threadbare, tattered in spots, used only when there is a sufficient wind, though it is of little use. An island in and of itself, it floats, covered with bits of seaweed, barnacles and driftwood, with soil blown by a thousand different winds and seeds that sprout in the accumulated detritus, the whole enveloped by clinging wisps of fog.

A lone man rows on and on, day after day, through storm and calm—it seems an eternity. He is old and haggard, worn down by his unending task, a brother to Sisyphus, sailing a boat to nowhere. Relentlessly, he rows over the waves, through the blue horizon, speaks to ghosts, vows to reach his goal, to escape his past, to find his fate, so long denied him. He rows, a man pursued, a man pursuing—secrets, truths, the past, illusions, whispers.

An Enchanted Island also rises from the depths of the deep, dark sea of green—O Mar Tenebroso—The Sea of Darkness—as the Arabs called it.

A boat or an island, either, or both, washed by the waves, bathed in the fresh spume, foam and strands of seaweed. Kissed by the winds from the four corners of the world. The seeker and goal one and the same. Waiting to be discerned. Awaiting discovery, disclosing itself in the light of morning. The fog lifts, the vision appears, revealing secrets long held close in mute reserve, in strained silence.

One vision begets others; visages appear: a face upon whose chin, head and chest clings strands of seaweed in place of hair. Is that you, Nereus? Father of the water nymphs, you old prophet. Selacia, too, wife of Neptune, naughty goddess of the deep. And there, in the foam, Venus rises, goddess of love, resplendent with legions of attendants, only to sink back down below the water, disappearing from view.

Furiously, blindly, the man rows his waterlogged boat, rows, chasing a chimera, an illusion, a mad hope. He has no fear of the future, and gives no thought to what will come, no thought of reaching safety or security, for he has glimpsed, however vaguely, not the future, but the land of myth, the half-formed mirage of that which all men desire.

He stares into the distance as he wanders over the surface of the sea. Like Ahasuerus, the Wandering Jew of old, he too is condemned to an undying living death.

He peers at the sea. Sometimes clouds or birds are reflected below, the gleam of the stars and moon; then, from the murky depths, the images of beautiful women, women he has keenly desired. Impossible though it may seem, there are not only women, but also fine, richly adorned animals, similar to horses, silvery unicorns, and proud ornate edifices, colorful banners unfurled. Perhaps, he thinks, they are Neptune's children, many of whom were said to be demigods and goddesses in the guise of horses. He stretches his arm down into the water, tries to touch them.

"Come unto me," he pleads.

The alluring visages below are a cruel mockery of his own image above: one beckoning, the other enticing, one tempting, the other imploring, the old and the young, the withered and the beautiful.

Might he swim down to where they are? But he is unable to hurl himself overboard, to abandon the boat. Neither the sight nor the proximity of unsurpassed beauty can break the spell he is under.

He calls to Selacia: "Fair goddess, pray, do not torment me. Don't play tricks upon an old fool."

Sometimes he sees islands in the distance. He paddles, determined to reach them. In the end, however, they are never reached, swallowed by the sea or fog, as lost as he and the boat, swept along by a strong current that runs away from the island. He can only wonder which is the worst madness, the islands above or the visions below.

His only companions are birds, two ravens that have traveled with him and the boat, though he doesn't know why. They have been there all along, accompanying him like those ravens that never left Saint Vicente's side, even after his death. Sometimes the birds flutter off and leave him behind, and he thinks he must have imagined them as well. It's never too long, however, before they return, bringing some small token of where they'd been: a branch from a tree with a few grapes or some berries, which he eats voraciously, so eager is he for anything of the earth, something sweet, warm, something more than the eternal sea and sky.

Even dolphins, those friends of ships and boats, have long since abandoned him, knowing a cursed man for what he is.

There is no longer time, though he feels an oppressive heaviness weighing upon his soul. He is keenly aware of the terrible gulf between him and the world, those for whom the legends and myths were merely stories. He wasn't like those men who went off to conquer the world, who heard the tales of King Arthur, of knights searching for the Holy Grail, of the magician Merlin, or those who read the reports of travelers to distant lands and the incredible things they saw in India or China, or heard of the fabulous Eastern kingdom of Prester John, and the riches and wonders of his far-reaching realm. Those who heard whispers about islands of gold, rivers of jewels, and had been quick to join crews sailing for the unknown.

These men had also heard of strange islands where miracles were everyday events, but they had no faith in such tales; they wanted to taste the riches of life here and now. Gold and silver, rubies and emeralds, that's what they desired. Glory, titles and conquest. Worldly wealth, not visions or dreams, not vague promises or ideals. Power, and the ability to crush one's enemies. They rejected those remote and elusive beauties recounted in tales of the Isle of Lovers, the sirens, as nothing more than fantasies.

Let others talk of holy acts and live lives of poverty and sacrifice. Let others talk about a future kingdom, an eternal life after death—it was this life on earth that concerned these men.

Each of us in the end believes in his own chosen chimeras, in something which once attained will make us happy; whether dreams of wealth, fame, and power, or those of eternal peace and love, of salvation and joy, the Promised Land.

Call it St. Brendan's Isle or The Island of Seven Cities, Antília or the Fortunate Islands, Atlantis, or any other name dreamt up over the ages for Paradise Regained, Paradise Found, staked and claimed! It was a tiny fair-weather haven of dreams to countermand the Continent of Lies, the world of vice and suffering, a world where Justice does not, in fact, exist. It was the last vestige of the Golden Age, moored beyond reach, a reward for those fortunate few who had long-traveled and travailed through the sorry realities of a life from which they longed to escape, and found by miracle, or

223

the blessing of a kindly god, their way to that enchanted place, where one's dreams become more real, more solid and true than the so-called world of reality on the other side of the ocean.

Wind, sea, clouds, fire and steam—a convergence of time and place. How else to explain the strange hulking black ship which approaches at the same instant the island appears, like a paradise imagined but never glimpsed, or glimpsed but never reached.

He mutters to himself, to the boat, the sea, the sky, to that which he has left behind, and towards which he sails: "I have seen her. I have seen her."

The sea is too vast for his words to resound, even in his own ears. The breezes snatch away every word almost before they are spoken, gone, scattered to the four corners of the globe.

Still the man rows for that place where not only one can dream—but such fantastic dreams! He catches a scent now and then, a waft of paradise on the winds. He hears melodious voices, and knows he is close, painfully close. The Enchanted Island lies nearby.

Somewhere in the remote distance a woman sings, perhaps, on the rocks of the island. We can only wonder to whom she sings—what strange words, what language—if indeed it is a language at all. Something tells us it is immaterial, for as one boat comes, another, larger sails closer, drawn by a voice, which transcends time and distance.

. . .

Julia listened to what Antonio said, but the words didn't register.

"Say that again," she said.

As Antonio spoke she kept interrupting, "Are you sure? Did he really say that?"

"The policeman was obviously uncomfortable," Antonio said. "He spoke strictly off the record. Sebastião wasn't the only man who disappeared, he said. Some fifteen to twenty-five men from all over the islands, all gone, and there's evidence he took a boat along with these other men, and sailed away."

"When?" Julia asked. "And sailed where?"

"He claimed there's only an approximation as to when, between the tenth and the fifteenth of the month before you arrived, but as far as where, he couldn't say." Antonio paused. "He said they believe the ship sank with all hands. There were storms, and they didn't believe any of those men were sailors, so—?"

"What happens now?" Julia said.

"They've decided to close the case for now. If any new evidence surfaces at some point in the future, he assured me the case would be reopened."

"In other words, officially speaking, Sebastião is presumed dead?"

Antonio nodded. "He told me this in confidence. His superiors, he said, have so far been reluctant to make a statement, a full report, but this is where things stand."

It's preposterous, she thought. Sebastião unofficially presumed dead. What could she do now? What would she tell her family, especially Mateus? Or Isabel? Did this mean she should leave? She thought of what Mateus might say under the circumstances: This was merely a ploy to get Julia out of the way, the authorities must want her to leave the islands.

225

It was a shock to hear that the police were throwing up their hands and assuming the very worst. Julia was unable to do the same, no matter what they supposed. So Sebastião *had* taken a boat, gone with a group of people (who? why?). It was a big ocean, a wide world, full of holes, nooks and crannies. And, besides, if that was what they honestly believed, why were the police so reluctant to come out and state it?

"I thought you were leaving," Julia said.

"I decided to check one last time with the police, to get them to tell me something," he said. "This one came forward at last."

"Boy's club," Julia said.

"What?" She was bothered by the fact that they had told her nothing, but Antonio had come along, and had been able to learn something from them.

"Nothing."

"Well, what now?" Antonio said. "I hope this changes your mind about going off in some boat. Are you willing to leave, to go back home?"

She thought about it, but, if Sebastião was dead, it was too convenient, too easy to say the boat had sunk, that there was no evidence. He wouldn't have disappeared without leaving some indication or proof of where he'd been, what he'd been doing. Perhaps there was something more the police hadn't said, something they didn't want Antonio or her to know.

• • •

Dear Julia,

Strange reports have reached me. News of fantastic events on the islands. Have you heard nothing concerning Sebastião? Is it true there is a new island? Friends assure me it is so. People here have received word from the Azores that a number of men have disappeared, perhaps sailed a boat to find this island. This is extraordinary. I don't know what to believe. Everything comes to me as if from a dream. I can only hope that Sebastião returns safe and sound. Please let me know what you have seen and heard. And be careful! Give my love to Antonio.

With many *saudades,*
Mateus

• • •

Again fate intervened. Antonio had thought he was going to leave. He had said as much to Julia, but something made him stop at Peter's Café to sort through his jumbled thoughts, where, of all people, it was Johan who caused him to change his mind.

A voice called out to him just as he entered the bar. He turned to see Johan lurking in the shadows.

"Come here," Johan said in a hoarse whisper, gesturing with a gnarled finger and glancing suspiciously around the room.

"Christ, there's no getting away from him," Antonio grumbled. Johan seemed to have difficulty focusing on Antonio. Once again he grasped at Antonio's arm, but Antonio moved out of reach.

Johan's eyes—once blue, but bleached by time and an excess of alcohol to a pale, washed-out color like slate—were wide with excitement.

"Do you know what I think?" Johan said, slurring his words. It was early in the day, yet already he reeked of the familiar sour combination of tobacco and alcohol.

"About what?" Antonio said, keeping his distance.

Johan made sure no one was within earshot before resuming. "The *americano,* the one they say is missing, Sebastião do Canto e Castro."

Thank God, Antonio thought, he didn't say *your father.* He must not know.

"I saw him," Johan said.

"So?"

"I followed him. He was up to something. He is either devil or saint, or crazy, a lunatic." Antonio smiled. Look who's talking, he thought. "I wanted to know what he was doing."

"Did you speak to him?" Antonio said. He wouldn't put it past Johan to know something about Sebastião's disappearance.

"I tried, but he looked right through me, as if I weren't there. If I spoke, he acted as if he couldn't hear me, couldn't see me. I asked what he was going to do—he was planning something, that one—but he disappeared just like that." He snapped his fingers."

"Aren't the police are looking for him," Antonio ventured to say.

"Bah, they're afraid of him." Antonio stared, as Johan nodded knowingly.

"Afraid?" Antonio said. "Why the hell would the police be afraid of *him?*"

"Perhaps he knows something they don't want people to know." Johan shrugged. "To them he is dangerous, but I couldn't get near him. One moment he was right there in front of my eyes, and the next he was gone!"

Whenever Johan became excited, a strong accent crept into his voice, occasional words in Portuguese, and several that sounded like German or Dutch, amid the English he usually spoke.

"Sometimes I saw him just up the street, go into or leave a building. But when I ran to see, he'd be gone, as if he'd grown wings and flown away."

Antonio wished he could do the same. Leave it to Sebastião to know how to successfully elude Johan. Of course, he would have enjoyed it, and done it with a flair, which had obviously driven Johan a bit nuts, causing him to concoct this story as if Sebastião could vanish at will, or fly away, leaving Johan in awe of Sebastião, and perhaps scared of him as well.

Johan muttered and shook his head. "I only wanted to know what he knew, to know what he was going to do. He had secrets, that one, many secrets." Antonio wondered if the police did know more than they were saying.

"There is a time to run," Johan said. "And there is a time to stay and fight." He waved his fist.

"Sure," Antonio said.

"Sebastião wouldn't take me with him when he left." Johan sounded hurt, as well as angry. "When all I wanted was to go, too."

"Go where?"

"He had information about treasure." Johan looked steadily at Antonio, and paused as if to let his words sink in. "Incredible treasures! He didn't fool me. I knew. It was only because he sneaked away, at night, while I was asleep. He tricked me. He should have taken me."

"Well," Antonio said, wondering what to say. "Perhaps he didn't know, or maybe he forgot."

"No!" Johan slammed his hand down on the table, nearly upsetting his beer and the ashtray overflowing with cigarette butts.

"Calm down," Antonio said, edging away from Johan, who appeared to shrink into himself, and now spoke in a whisper.

"No, he didn't want me to know. He didn't want me to see the treasure. He wanted it all for himself. You know these people. You're one of them. You could help me."

"I know nothing about any treasure," Antonio said.

"You'll find out," Johan said. "You'll see I was right. I'll share with you."

There was the sound of a dog howling in the distance, and Johan appeared to listen to the sound. "You know what the old ladies say . . . ?" Johan said, chuckling.

Antonio shook his head.

"You must turn a shoe upside down when a dog howls like that," he said, growling with a hoarse laugh. "It means someone is going to die."

CHAPTER 25

The power of wish and the power of words are chief gods in the world of fable.

The Coasts of Illusion: A Study of Travel Tales
Clark B. Firestone, New York, Harper, 1924

• • •

Antonio couldn't say what finally convinced him to explore Sebastião's room in Praia do Almoxarife. It was partially his concern for Julia, as well as everything he had heard since he'd arrived on the islands, from Julia, the police, Johan, and strangers concerning his father's disappearance. It was his growing belief that Johan, at least in part, was telling the truth: There was something precious Sebastião was after. And, if not, he told himself, then he'd show Julia how ridiculous her whole idea was.

It was also a curiosity that awoke in him. Antonio had learned long ago that matters concerning Sebastião were usually not what they appeared. It was best to assume most everything was exaggerated, subject to hyperbole, enhanced by Sebastião's imagination. Dislikes became hatreds, transitory affairs became burning passions, and ordinary deeds became outlandish or heroic. Antonio didn't know whether Sebastião got into as many fights or escaped as many close calls as he claimed—he doubted Sebastião was certain where the demarcation between truth and fiction lay.

Much the way an overeager method actor might become obsessed with a particularly riveting role, Sebastião lived as though in competition with the books he wrote. He frequently acted out the roles of his various characters, as if trying them on for size. He'd spend a few days as a drifter, then as an aristocrat, a criminal or a sleuth. He spoke of characters in books—his own and others—as though they were more substantial, more real, than their counterparts of flesh and blood.

His books, published in Portugal and Brazil—a collection of stories, *The Conjuror & Other Tales of the Azorean Nights,* several volumes of poetry, essays, and travel articles—had been translated into French, German, Italian and one or two other languages, but very little had been published in English. He had written for newspapers, helped to publish a couple of short-lived magazines devoted to the arts, and reviewed music and film.

"I am incidental," he liked to say of himself. "My stories and characters, including whatever talent I may possess, come down to me as a bequest. They are not mine, but belong to the past. I just happen to be the convenient receptacle," but this was a pose that belied the work he strove to perfect. He had strong feelings and opinions about almost everything, and would also go to absurd lengths to prove a point, or to win a bet from which he would never back down.

Sebastião spoke as if his stories about the Azores came from the islands themselves, that they were writing through him. In *"A Rapsódia Açoreana"*—The Azorean Rhapsody, he had referred to writers as conjurers, shamans who wove spells with words, invoking pasts and alternate worlds, embroidered realities—a hazy borderland where the supposed falsities of fiction and the half-truths and distortions of history blurred and blended, became one.

"The old books on Portuguese nobility refer to the Castros as Castilian," Sebastião wrote, "but they were firmly established in the region *'entre Douro e Minho,'* between those two rivers that were the very heart of Portugal, which at the time was part of the kingdom of Leon, where the oldest, most powerful families were from, before Portugal was yet an independent country.

"It's impossible to completely untangle the web of the genealogists, to follow the thread of our ancestors, sometimes referred to as "Crasto," or "Crastino." An early family stronghold, Castro Xeres, near Burgos, may have been predated by an ancient tower and castle, simply called Castro, near the River Cávado, in northern Portugal, where there are now only ruins.

"What does it mean to have the blood of our ancestors flow in our veins? Is there an inescapable fate, a personal legacy we inherit with the blood of El Cid, or the Castilian counts, the ancient kings of Navarre, León, Aragon, of Inês de Castro and Dom Pedro? What message is carried in their blood through the generations? How is this story encoded in us? Does it lie dormant, linked with our desires and ambitions, waiting for the right opportunity to resurface, or is it always present, guiding our actions, like whispered voices urging us on? Why does the man left alone turn the volume on the radio up so loud? Or busy himself until he's exhausted? Is he attempting to drown out these voices, the multitudes which exist within him?"

Antonio felt a twinge of something close to guilt or remorse. He'd been obsessed with success, with money. And had he not done so, at least in part, to avoid acknowledging some aspect of who he was and where he'd come from? It had never occurred to him that Sebastião was *related* to these people, that in some sense they had an impact on who or what he was. What they had lived through, and who they were had a direct bearing on who Sebastião was. And if that were true, then didn't it follow that by the same token there were forces they brought to bear upon Julia and Antonio? Was it possible that he too was a living representation of the loves and hates, the desires, passions and dreams of his past, and that the failings and struggles, instead of dying out, had, from so long ago, been passed on directly to him? And did that describe the sensations he felt, that sense of floating backwards in time, and the past rushing forward, rearing its head?

Sebastião also enjoyed nothing more than cultivating an aura of mystery around the family. "Every other generation has its *bruxa*—its witch and its *feiticeiro*—sorcerer," he'd say with a wink. He'd allude to various family members who were never spoken of, the details of their lives hushed up by their survivors. It was talk like this that drove Antonio crazy and embarrassed him.

Sebastião was quick to perform feats worthy of earning him a bit of notoriety, and enjoyed hearing reports—however false or exaggerated—concerning his behavior, his character, not necessarily because he thought he was above the laws of decency, or privileged to get away with more than the next fellow, but as if his reputation were more real than he himself was, as if he doubted his own existence. His persona could live a life wholly removed from the man himself, while he observed from the sidelines, testing himself as if to determine what the author within him was capable of, what his limitations were.

Sebastião sought out those who defied death as a way of life. He befriended men in their seventies who had spent their lives harpooning whales from the prow of a thirty-eight foot *canoa,* who had survived the destruction of their boats by the whales' flukes, or had lost friends to the jaws of a sperm whale, or had themselves been injured.

"My heroes are people who swallowed their fears and set out, putting all they had on the line," Sebastião would say. "Like my grandfather, Domingos, who at seventeen swam out from the island of Corvo and was picked up by an American whaler, on which he spent three years sailing the world, before coming to the United States. Or my mother, Isabel, who left Mateus and her children on the Azores in 1945, and came to America on her own, to make a new life for herself and her family, armed with nothing but a fierce determination. People who spoke out against the government during Salazar's regime, who had fought against the years of oppression, people who had been exiled, sent to prison, or shipped off to Angola."

He chose characters who had lost touch with reality in the face of a profound solitude, dragged down by phantoms—not monsters from out there, but from within; characters who surrounded themselves with the mad, maddening company of others, strangers, noise, things, in order to distract themselves, to remain constantly preoccupied, while descending into the maelstrom of their own fears, where there was nowhere to run or hide. Certainly more than one solo sailor had gone mad, forced to face those demons that are likely to be conjured by sailing the ocean on one's own, aside from the *de rigueur* sightings of mermaids, sirens, and a variety of creatures referred to generically as 'monsters of the Deep.'

"Those who sail long sea voyages well know that each member has to be carefully evaluated," he'd written. "Someone unsuited to the rigors, a novice or unstable candidate, can not only endanger himself but the entire crew. And that's with companionship, sailing with others who could naturally assert your existence, test your reality, the way a mother or father comes in the night to prove to the crying infant, *Yes, you really do exist, my child. You are real, I am real. We are our only reality.* For each of us now and again needs to be reassured. What better reassurance, how best to test the slippery waters of reality than to have another's perspective handy to use as a barometer? You see that there? Are we seeing and hearing the same thing? As long as you both witness an event equally—even if it is in actuality nothing more than a mirage or delusion—there is a comfort in numbers that's difficult to resist, an impulse for one to concur with his neighbor's view.

"How much worse for someone sailing solo, with no crew for companionship; where the only confirmation might be the sight or sound of his deepest, darkest fears, his own inescapable ghosts, where there's no escaping himself; where hallucinations are commonplace and the sound of his own voice seems that of a stranger—dull, flat, foreign; where there's not so much as an echo for company, and where reality might be tempered by these same qualities, while limited only by his imagination? Devil take the dreamer, the sailor with a flair for the imaginative."

These were the circumstances that interested Sebastião, conditions that could easily make or break someone, ennoble them or send them over the edge.

"Perhaps Sebastião attempted to test his theory," Antonio spoke aloud in the muffled atmosphere of his father's room. "If only to test his breaking point." The policeman had told him that Sebastião had taken a boat and set out for an unknown destination with a rag-tag but armed group of confederates, that they had sailed off in a large vessel, like an expeditionary force, or conquistadors seeking conquest. While some thought this boat sank, others believed the men had gone to sea as pirates and looked for boats to prey upon. And there were those who said they had sailed to find one of the *Ilhas Perdidas*—The Lost Islands.

There among Sebastião's charts and maps, Antonio thought it likely his father had found one that referred to a shipwreck, and that he had gone to salvage a galleon filled with gold.

Sometimes Antonio fell asleep, though his sleep was disturbed by the sounds of voices muttering, strains of verse, or song. Time and again, he woke and opened the door, peering outside, looking through the window, thinking it was Julia, even calling out her name, but there was no one out there, only the night. In the dead of night, he stared at the skull, too, as if it were perhaps capable of issuing sounds from its grinning jaws.

Returning to bed, Antonio tried to convince himself that he was dreaming bad dreams, as did all troubled souls. He'd awaken and remember the young woman he had seen in Pico. If he were completely honest, he would have to admit that he couldn't stop thinking about her, that his eyes were now open as never before. *Who is she?* he thought again and again.

"There are distinct differences between reality and fantasy, between fact and delusion," he reminded himself. He sought the truth, and truths were obtainable—obscured, perhaps, but discernible nonetheless—attempting to convince himself that things weren't as they appeared.

· · ·

The Ghost Ship appeared out of the mists, now far off in the distance, now in the swells just off the coast. It moved with what appeared to be supernatural speed, bearing down as if it were about to sail into the rocky coast of the islands, then sailing out of sight again as if swallowed by the sea, disappearing back within the impenetrable cloak of mists, which followed in its wake.

"Look, there!" people shouted, pointing.

If there were young children or women nearby they were invariably hushed away. "Don't look, stay away from the window," or "Go back inside, quickly!"

"What is it?"

"Why do you ask? Any fool can see what it is!"

But then, another, "It's nothing, just a strange shape, a reflection, that's all." Others murmured in agreement, but without conviction.

Either way the ship disappeared just as quickly as it had appeared, leaving the stunned spectators shaking their heads, and wasting no time in returning to their homes, their families.

· · ·

Against his better judgment, Antonio remained in the cramped room, immersed in Sebastião's notes. He no longer stopped to ask himself, "What am I doing?" Neither could he explain how his perceptions and perspective had altered. But here he was in no rush to leave the island, reading Portuguese, suddenly aware of his connection to the writings, his surroundings and his past, to his father—never suspecting the true cause of his miraculous transformation.

An otherworldly voice rose from the depth of the ocean, the distant past, ringing through the night, calling, he was certain, for him, to him, as if he were on a tether, pulling him to the shore. It was whispered in the waves, carried by the wind.

Was it human, an exotic bird? Or something else, something supernatural?

"All love is supernatural," his father's voice murmured.

Antonio's heart flip-flopped. It was a woman's voice: a sweet melancholy tune that filled his ears and ravaged his heart. He followed without resistance a music he had waited all his life to hear, followed it farther up the hill only to find himself, moments later, standing in Maria dos Santos's garden face to face with Teresa dos Santos.

. . .

235

From the notebooks of Sebastião do Canto e Castro:

We have forgotten who we are: Warriors, sons of warriors. The first Cantos, sons of Sir John Chandos, Knight of the Garter and the Constable of the Black Prince. Castros too numerous to list, many of whom took the appellation da Guerra—*the Warrior—for a name. Knights of the Order of Christ, which supplanted the Knights Templars in Portugal, captains and admirals operating covertly, with secrets and treasures to protect.*

Does our ability to fight, to plow the seas, to explore lie latent? Have we lost our true identities by remaining in our homes, on land, leaving the sea behind?

To recapture our lost selves, perhaps all we need is only to be in the right place at the right time, under the right circumstances.

. . .

"You!" He stepped out of the room into the cool night air and knew she was there even before he saw her, for her voice and the words she sang stirred him, roused him from his sleep. Of course it was her—as if he had read the story long ago, and now found it becoming reality. There was no mistaking the face he had seen on the grounds of the Casa Azul on Pico.

He gazed at the liquid night of her hair, her bare shoulders, her breasts, shadowed yet somehow radiant. He drank in the darkness of her eyes, as deep as space. Her expression was serious, yet a smile, or the beginnings of one flitted at the corner of her mouth.

Her voice changed him. He felt it internally, as though the image of who and what he was, which he had constructed himself, over the years, crumbled in an instant. Time itself shifted and changed. Nothing was the same.

He reached out to touch her. She came closer, pressed flesh against flesh. He breathed in her scent, kissed her skin, imprinting as he spoke: "*Minha querida*—my dear. I wish to remember your taste, your scent, your eyes that take me away from all this to another place, another time."

What had happened, how had this change come about? "*Impossível,*" he heard himself say, and yet he hadn't spoken. *Impossible.*

Fire burned between them. She opened her mouth and each word was a song, a spell, with an impact that was physical: her voice and her words pierced him, words he had rejected long ago, but no longer. *Fado*—Fate, *Coração*—Heart, *Tu e eu*—You and I, *Meu Amor*—My Love. And the fire burned brighter. There was no turning back, no alternate course, there was only destiny—forceful, determined, charging forward.

She was silent again.

They leaned toward one another and kissed, both spiraling down, down through the gaping *furnas*, the vents opening on the side of Pico, bottomless, through which one could hear the voice of the earth howl, down through the ocean, to the bowels of the earth. He called her name but heard another, heard many, echoes and reverberations: Maria, Inês, Joana, Amélia, Teresa—each a tune, an ancient memory, a sweet whisper in the night.

He peered outward and inward at the same time, thinking yet not thinking, dreaming, stirring. It's all a dream, he thought over and over. Let the dream go on and on.

In the morning he woke to find lingering traces of sea salt on his lips.

. . .

Se queres aprender a rezar, vai p'ro mar.
If you wish to learn to pray, go to sea.
—Portuguese proverb

. . .

"We must weigh anchor!" A harsh, shrill whisper regaled Antonio and jarred him out of his slumber. There was panic, an insistence, and although the voice was faint, that somehow made it worse. He resisted, tried to ignore the sounds, but they persisted. "Awaken from your slumber, recognize your past, the sea road awaits!"

"Skulls do not talk," Antonio said, putting his hands to his ears, trying to drown out the noise. "The wind and the sea do not speak, there are no ghosts and no ghost ships, no luminescent women." He recited this mantra, instead of counting sheep, hoping to silence the voice and soothe what were already badly shaken nerves.

"Navigate those dark waters, cast ourselves into the unknown, sail through the fog, follow the call, the song of the sea where the forgotten shores of the Enchanted Islands lie."

"What?" Antonio said.

"*O Encoberto*—The Hidden One," the voice answered. "*O Desejado*—The Desired One. Find the island where the Fates dwell. We must sail!"

"Sail?" Antonio said, rubbing his eyes and shaking his head clear. "A boat?"

It's the pressures of being on the islands, he told himself. That and the struggle to get Julia to leave, the writings he'd been reading. Still, the voices and sounds intensified and spurred powerful longings, which led him to believe in the words he heard and the visions he now saw: a distant lush island, a ship sailing, weathering storms and waves to reach that haven. And, though the fog came quickly, obscuring his view of these things, he could hear, through the veil of mists, and the waves crashing, a song that drifted across the seas.

"I need time to think," Antonio said, meaning he wasn't yet ready to leave behind his dreams. He clung to the desperate hope that his dreams were real, and his reality an illusion. During the day he pored over his father's writings; during the night he both lost himself and found himself in the waiting arms of Teresa—although she always managed to slip away before dawn. "What do you change back into?" he asked. "*Uma fadinha?*"—a fairy?

When he awoke, he'd remember their lovemaking and ask: Was she really here? Though he continued to taste her, to breathe her scent, and feel her touch.

He'd be besieged by countless other questions: Who is she? Where did she come from? Where does she go? What has happened to me?

For the first time in many years he wished he could talk to his father. There was no way on this earth his mother would understand what he was going through. She had clearly never known real passion. A need, a desire, a want, yes, but nothing like this. Sebastião would have known all about it.

When Teresa was by his side he murmured idiotic things in her ear: "I've never truly made love before this; not till now could I say I have ever loved. You're an angel, you're incredible."

She would smile enigmatic smiles, laugh, or murmur strange unknown words of her own. There was something so childlike about her, and yet she was by far the most intensely passionate and sensual woman he had ever known, both in giving and receiving. Both real, flesh and blood, of the earth, and at the same time, so otherworldly, as if of some ancient race, a siren or mermaid.

He drank repeatedly from her eager lips. He couldn't get enough of her. They made love in the tiny room at Praia do Almoxarife, in the garden of Maria dos Santos, on the sands of the beach—anywhere and everywhere, as if only the two of them existed, and their existence had waited centuries to be. He clasped her hands, kissed her breasts, and lost himself in her arms, listening to the restless rumbles of her heart.

"Your sister is preparing to leave," she said, snapping him out of the fog.

"What?"

"She leaves, on a boat, from Horta."

"My God, I have to go," he said. "I must go with her."

Teresa nodded. "Yes," she said, as if there were no other choice.

CHAPTER 26

In islands men placed their ideal states . . . to reach felicity one must cross water.

—C. B. Firestone

. . .

People stopped to stare as a strange, shrouded figure slipped silently down the street. They stood transfixed by his eyes, which blazed with an unnatural intensity. A long, black cape lay draped over one shoulder, and he carried a weathered leather satchel that was stuffed full. He wore black heavy boots and held something that stuck up from under the cloak, level with his shoulders.

The islanders shook their heads, convinced that here was another *americano louco* headed straight for jail, or worse.

A man standing outside the bar nudged his friend and gestured. "Take a look at that."

"Who is it?" the friend asked.

"*Outro maluco*"—another crackpot, the first replied. "The son of Senhor do Canto e Castro, the unlucky. He goes chasing after ghosts."

"You know what they say. *Tal pai, tal filho*—like father, like son, eh?"

They exchanged whispers, glances and knowing looks, for as much as it is human nature to mock our neighbors, we tend also to invent and believe the worst stories about strangers in our midst. They followed after the figure, curious to see what would happen next.

Manuel readied the boat for the voyage and Julia inspected the supplies when Antonio appeared. She stopped to stare, along with Manuel, and a number of people on shore.

"Tónio?" she said, calling him by his nickname, which she hadn't used in years, as he approached the boat. "What are you doing?"

"I'll be damned if I'm letting you go alone," he said. "I'd never hear the end of it if anything happened to you." He climbed aboard.

"Are you serious?"

"Do I look like I'm joking?" He turned, as if concealing something.

"Where have you been," she said, "I thought you had left. You'd checked out of the *residencial.* Where are your bags? And what are you doing in that ridiculous outfit?"

He shrugged. "I didn't want people to know who I was. I've spent the last few nights in Sebastião's room. I left my suitcase there."

"In Praia do Almoxarife?" He nodded, as her eyes widened in disbelief. He set the satchel down, and in doing so the walking stick and the skull were revealed.

Julia was too shocked to laugh. "And *that?"* She pointed to the skull.

"Maybe it'll ward off disaster. It looks like we'll need it." He glanced round at the boat. "This thing actually floats?" he said. The boat did appear to be in serious need of repair.

"Manuel swears it's safe," Julia said.

Antonio grunted. He took the skull and fastened it to the wooden mast, ignoring the mutterings and whispers of the crowd on the wharf.

It was early morning. The sea had turned silver, the sky looked threatening, yet a large number of people were now gathered as the boat, which no one present thought would sail anywhere but straight down to the ocean floor, was made ready to cast off.

"Damn," Julia said, under her breath. She had wanted to slip away early, quietly, with no one watching, and now, it seemed, the entire island had learned of her plans.

The sight of the skull made Julia especially nervous, since it represented part of what troubled her, the strange brooding atmosphere from which she wished to escape. And now that it was time to leave, Antonio of all people had seen fit to bring it along.

The skull beamed, or so it appeared, fuller, broader, if that were possible—as if grinning its approval.

Julia observed Antonio nervously. He was so different from the brother she knew. What had happened to him? She kept looking the crowd over, hoping to catch sight of Nicolau. She wished she could say goodbye, to see him once more before she sailed, but knew he would likely try to talk her out of her plan. And she knew it would be difficult for her to resist.

As if things couldn't help but get worse, they heard shouts and everyone turned to see Johan running toward the boat, a gray duffle bag in his hand.

"Stop," he cried. "Wait for me."

"What are you doing here?" Julia said, as Johan reached the boat.

"I must come with you," Johan said. "I'll help. You can't sail without me, as Sebastião did."

People in the crowd laughed, others muttered, "They're crazy, the lot of them!"

"We can't take you," Julia said. "Let's get out of here, Manuel. Quickly."

"I'll keep out of the way," Johan said, turning to Antonio. "Please, talk to her."

"Oh, let him come," Antonio said. "He may be helpful."

"He'll get in the way," Julia said. "We don't need trouble."

Antonio couldn't help but think that Johan knew more than he'd let on, that he might help in some way to solve the mystery. "He'll be all right. I'll watch him. Let's just get on with this."

Julia thought for a moment. "Hurry up then, and get aboard," Julia said, wondering how everything had gotten so out of hand.

Manuel shrugged, then raised the tattered sail and grabbed the tiller. Several young men pushed the boat away from the dock, and the four sailors sailed into the dark waters. The crowd stood and watched, pointing, laughing, expecting the sea to swallow the boat and its unlikely mariners, as they slowly sailed from sight.

For the next two days, the boat was observed from various points. Fishermen claimed to have passed within earshot of the small boat, some stating they saw no one aboard, others reporting they heard strange shouts and sounds coming from the craft, but no one dared approach too close to see for themselves, afraid of bad luck.

Word passed quickly around the island and to Pico about the vessel and its strange crew. For one day and night nothing was heard. It was accepted that the boat had sunk. However, the next day reports circulated that they'd been spotted off Lages, in Pico, and at the same time off Topo, at the far end of the island of São Jorge.

Again and again, the tiny boat was seen, and repeatedly disappeared. Julia and Antonio were compared with their father—talk spreading across the islands of a family curse.

BOOK TWO

Horizonte

Ó mar anterior de nós, teus medos
Tinham coral e praias e arvoredos.
Desvendadas a noite e a cerração,
As tormentas passadas e o mistério,
Abria em flor o Longe, e o Sul sidério,
'Splendia sobre as naus da iniciação.

Linha severa da longínqua costa—
Quando a nau se aproxima, ergue-se a encosta
Em árvores onde o Longe nada tinha;
Mais perto, abre-se a terra em sons e cores;
E, no desembarcar, há aves, flores,
Onde era só, de longe a astracta linha.

O sonho é ver as formas invisiveis
Da distância imprecisa, e, com sensiveis
Movimentos da esp'rança e da vontade,
Buscar na linha fria do horizonte
A árvore, a praia, a flor, a ave, a fonte—
Os beijos merecidos da Verdade.

Horizon

Your fearfulness preceding us, O sea,
Was lodged in coral, shores, and masts.
Once of night and fog, of bygone
Tempests and the mystery, unveiled,
Distance flowered, and the sidereal South
Sparkled on initiated galleons.

That far-off rigid coastline—
When the ship approaches, the shore now rises

With the trees, where the distance offered nothing;
Closer, land breaks into sounds and colors;
As we disembark, come birds and flowers,
Where before was but a far-off abstract line.

To dream is to see from some vague distance
Shapes invisible, then with the quickened
Motion of one's hope and will, to seek upon
The cold horizon, tree and beach, flower, bird,
And fountain—Those kisses truth awards.[6]

—Fernando Pessoa

In the beginning the sea rolls and flows in every direction—a living liquid carpet, its face inscrutable, its mysteries impenetrable. Still, there
is a face, though like its secrets, revealed momentarily, and only to the
lucky few. One sees a bearded Neptune, dark and angry, whose powerful
arm, in one sweeping gesture, uncovers tragic vistas of the death-strewn
sea floor far below, while another sees the lovely, radiant visage of Venus,
the Goddess of Love, sprung from the sea-foam, imploring, offering a
safe haven, a refuge of tranquil and luxuriant shores; or perhaps one of
the many demi-gods and goddesses said to inhabit the world's oceans.

With the sea comes a voice, distant and alluring. It entreats, plaintive, and forlorn; irresistible in its beauty and charm—sounds woven to
ensnare, to hold the listener fast, to lead him across vast chasms, across
depths, across time and space.

Histories are written and forgotten; civilizations come and go; myths
and legends rise from shadowy depths to tug at the edges of our consciousness. When there is nothing else there is still the sea revolving in
its timeless spiral-like clockwork.

. . .

Manuel's boat rocked and swayed as it sailed away from the island
toward the deep ocean. The day was fine, the sea calm. A brisk breeze
and a fine salt spray lashed Julia's face, invigorating her, and enhancing her excitement, for though she had no idea what lay ahead, she had
taken action, and was ready to come face to face with the uncertain consequences that would follow. Antonio grumbled and swore. "This damn

ridiculous boat . . . If I get seasick—" He left the sentence unfinished, and frowned at the ocean as if it were his sworn enemy.

Manuel stood at the helm, steering the boat, as one could readily see he had done countless times before. This was nothing new to him, although acting as a charter boat captain in search of a new island for two Americans and a drunk like Johan was certainly something out of the ordinary. Still, Manuel was completely at ease, indifferent to the venture they were embarking upon. He'd been paid well for his trouble. He had his eye on a certain Maria Lourdes, a beauty-and-a-half, whose father, however, would respond favorably only to the sound of money. Thus Manuel was willing to take considerable risks in order to procure what it would take to make Maria Lourdes his own.

Johan, on the other hand, was visibly shaken. He peered nervously every which way, offering a conspiratorial wink at Julia and watching Antonio's every move, mumbling and muttering constantly under his breath. Chuckling to himself one moment, snarling the next.

"We must find them," Johan said. "We can't let them get away."

"I hope we haven't made a mistake allowing him to accompany us," Julia whispered.

"If he starts anything," Antonio said. "I'll toss him overboard."

Johan opened his duffle bag, exposing a stash of several bottles of *aguardente*. Enough to last a long voyage, Julia thought—one far longer than she intended to make. With luck Johan would get drunk and quickly pass out.

"We too will have a share of the treasure. A father will share with his own children," Johan said, as if it were a challenge as a question.

So, Johan had learned that Sebastião was their father. Or had he known all along?

"If we find treasure, Johan, you'll get a share," Antonio said, deciding to distract Johan.

"There's treasure." Johan's eyes gleamed. "Gold and more!"

"*Treasure?*" Julia said.

"Just ignore him," Antonio said. "The poor fellow's lost his mind."

"He looks like a pirate," she said. "Just what we need."

Julia familiarized herself with the boat, the unfamiliar sensation of being on the water. She gazed back at Faial, behind them. There were other boats in the distance and sea birds flew nearby, calling in their incomprehensible language, not unlike laughter, as though they were jeering at these inexperienced mariners below.

Julia felt it was important to keep an observant eye on her surroundings. Peering through the old ship's telescope that Antonio had taken from Sebastião's room, she was on the lookout for new islands marring the horizon, or strange ships, ghostly or otherwise.

· · ·

Native-American folklore tells us that when the world was all water a raven flew over the sea searching for a place to land. Finding none, the raven dropped pebbles and made the first islands. In ancient times islands were believed to be enchanted. They could vanish or appear out of mists. Some islands float, like Aeolia, the island of the winds, whose god was Aeolis, god of the winds, father of Sisyphus. Some islands lie just below the surface; some exist deep beneath the sea, rising up only at night, or once in seven years, like the fabled Isle of Hy-Brasil, or once every year on a specific date, like the Enchanted Island, seen from Santa Maria in the Azores, but visible only under specific conditions.

249

· · ·

The boat sailed farther from Faial, following the coastline of Pico, and then beyond. "You all right, Tónio?"

Antonio nodded. "Sure," he said. "Just great." He looked miserable, unable to get comfortable in the cramped confines of the boat. He leaned on the gunwale near the prow, his cloak wrapped round snug for protection against the wind and spray.

Julia kept a vigilant lookout for any sign of unusual phenomena, and asked Antonio to do the same. "All I see is water," he said. "What the hell else is there?" She wished she or her brother had the capabilities and finesse of their ancestor, Dom João de Castro, who had observed the strange fires in the masts of his ships, the famous Saint Elmo's Fire. Dom João had possessed a burning curiosity: What is that strange occurrence upon the water there? What makes the Red Sea red? Dom João traced the paths of comets, chronicled and examined everything in his voyages along the shores and the seas beyond Africa, to India, over four hundred years before. Unlike Dom João, however, Julia wasn't sure what to do, what to look for, or even what was important. Having never been on the open sea, only between the islands, everything appeared unusual to her. Still, she kept careful watch on the water and the skies, a landscape of light and shadows, the islands in the distance, the sea rippling like a living beast.

Perhaps Antonio possessed a latent trace of their famous ancestor's gifts, or others who had been the captains of ships and armadas. Experience and environment might awaken what had been passed down genetically, but had lain dormant until now. After all, the brother who sailed beside her bore little relation to the one who had sworn he'd never return to the islands, and who had, just days before, insisted she leave. Antonio appeared unable to decide which was less trustworthy, the ocean or Johan, who settled down to drinking and murmuring, occasionally gesturing with a finger at the air, as though he were conversing with a phantom. Julia allowed herself to be lulled by the motions of the boat, her father's charts of the Banco Dom João de Castro, and the rhythm of the sea.

Manuel, for the most part, was silent, a cigarette stuck in his mouth, his eyes focused on the sea ahead, or perhaps he saw Maria Lourdes's visage in the distance. He brought out a jug of Pico wine, offering it to Julia and Antonio, who shook their heads, before he drank.

Occasionally, Johan sang what sounded like an old German or Dutch drinking song. Julia couldn't be sure since the words weren't in English and were slurred beyond recognition. Then he would yell a word or a phrase, as if some momentous thought suddenly occurred to him, or someone had whispered in his ear to remind him of the treasures he sought: "Gold . . . hordes of precious jewels . . . murder, destruction," followed by a few words in his own language.

Manuel caught Antonio's attention and gestured at Johan.

"What's the matter with him?"

Antonio shrugged. "He thinks we're going to find treasure."

"*Louco!*" Manuel laughed. "There's a lot of treasure down on the sea floor."

Antonio nodded. "I'm beginning to think he's not the only one who's crazy." He glared nervously at the water; one rogue wave and it would all be over.

Julia concentrated on the maps and charts depicting *As Ilhas Perdidas*—The Lost Islands.

When she looked up Johan was staring at her.

"What's the matter?" Julia said.

"What's that?" Johan said, his face contorted with suspicion. "What are you hiding?"

"I'm not hiding anything," Julia said.

"That's a treasure map you have," Johan leaned forward threateningly. "Let me see."

"I said it was nothing. Now back off," Julia said, harsher than she had intended, holding the map close to her to protect it from his clutching hands.

"Hey, keep still and let her alone," Antonio said. "Or you'll be swimming back to Horta."

Johan sat back down and was silent. He resumed nursing his bottle, smiled as if he were at peace with the world, and kept nodding his head like a beneficent holy man.

$\cdot$ $\cdot$ $\cdot$

God is everywhere—but the Portuguese were there first.
—Portuguese saying

$\cdot$ $\cdot$ $\cdot$

Julia stared at the line of the horizon as it blurred and grew indistinct; the infinite turning back upon itself, reflecting the past, like an endless number of reflections between panels of mirrors. She watched the waves, the cresting whitecaps. There's nothing so vast, or immense as the ocean, she thought. Except, of course, the sky. The ocean at least has an end, a limit, the sea floor, however deep. The sky on the other hand, is endless. As incomprehensible as infinity, or eternity, around which our consciousness can only skirt, fumbling as it struggles to explain by constructing earth-bound, life-bound metaphors. Unable to grasp the infinite, we put up limits: there must be an end to the skies, the heavens, the universe. After all, everything comes to an end. And until we can conceive of eternity and the infinite, how can we hope to attain immortality? But these limits then create new problems; for if there is an end, what then exists on the other side? Nothingness. And again the mind scrambles to envision a wall where nothing exists on the other side. Does the wall, then, itself go on and on, ad infinitum?

There was no evident danger Julia perceived of falling into the sky, however, of being devoured by its depths, nor any danger from creatures that could easily consume or disable a helpless, unwary victim. On the other hand, the sea floor was strewn from one shore to the other, from continent to continent, with the carcasses of men, women and ships. Man, her father would remind her, is never so defenseless as when he is at the mercy of the sea.

Julia tried to remember something she'd read or heard, claiming every myth and legend had its kernel of truth. Waves broke on the prow of the boat, in bursts of white spume, and farther, the swells rolled on in their continuous currents. What does that wave bring? She thought of José's comment to the children of Praia do Almoxarife. And that one there—does it carry a message from some far-off place, or does it per-haps bring death, the capacity to capsize this boat? Who knows until the last moment? Even a tidal wave is indistinguishable from other waves, until it reaches shallow waters. The ocean was a vast stream, like time itself, flowing in more than one direction, leading to more than one place. And the islands? What was their part in all this?

Julia kept an eye on her brother and hoped he didn't get sick.

There were questions she tried to avoid thinking about: Why she felt as if she were caught in the machinations of something—a story, a plot, a history—that careened toward an inevitable conclusion? Had she become so affected by her surroundings, by her father's writings, and her feelings for Nicolau that she had somehow become caught in acting out her father's stories, the legends and myths? Had she in essence become merely a character in Sebastião's book?

Nicolau. Once more, she gave herself up to fate. Before, in Praia do Almoxarife, when she had followed the sounds, the voices, and discovered Maria dos Santos's garden, that was merely a taste of far grander things to come, a weak precursor, if not a necessary first step. This now was a complete surrender, a shift from trying to control herself, her environ-ment, and the events surrounding her, to make all the pieces fit into an orderly, prescribed uniformity, a rational, logical model. She could no longer formulate a definite, accurate account of reality. Instead, she kept her eyes focused on the advent of an uncharted island, which could at any moment appear on the horizon, or rise from some spot below the waves.

"What's happening to me?" she asked, marveling at just how far she had come. She'd always found it a strange idiosyncrasy, especially of the older people of the Azores, who always sailed if and when the boats did, no matter how bad the weather, or the tossing of the boat. They prayed and crossed themselves, resigned to fate, as though it never occurred to them to simply wait it out until the weather cleared, to go another day. What will come will come. I will be there tomorrow, at three o'clock sharp, *se Deus quiser*—if God wishes, that is, or, *Oxalá*—if Allah wills it. Whatever the fates or gods decide, let us hope they are in a favorable mood.

But it was more than that. Julia had always prided herself on her skepticism. She'd never wavered in her belief in a universe that excluded the possibility of things inexplicable, things that the superstitious and irrational believed. And yet here she was roaming the seas in search of enchanted islands.

253

· · ·

Here, as on Santa Maria, we find the legend of an Enchanted Isle said to be visible on the northern horizon. The story is that it was ruled by a fairy Princess of wondrous beauty and wisdom who refused to marry for the love of her people. Angered at her refusal to wed him, a princely suitor came to São Miguel and entreated the help of a witch. The isle and all its inhabitants disappeared into the water. Every seven years, they say, it comes into view again, on August 15. To break the witch's spell a priest in full vestments would have to bless it at that very moment and agree to die immediately. Unfortunately, no priest has been ready to accept this act of self-sacrifice. And so when the torrent roars the old folks at Nordeste say that the voices of the Princess and her subjects are appealing to the world of the living.

The Azores, Claude Dervenn, Paris

· · ·

"Hey, that's enough drinking already," Manuel shouted to Johan. "I'll need you to steer soon, so I can get a few hours of sleep."

Johan grumbled and spat, but put down his bottle without an argument. He smoked incessantly, surreptitiously sneaking a drink whenever

Manuel had his back turned, and mumbled replies to an invisible partner in conversation.

"I think we need to steer to the northeast," Julia said. "Somewhere
between Terceira and São Miguel. That's where the new island should be."

"Are you sure?" Antonio said.

"As sure as I can be of anything."

Manuel nodded and steered the boat to the north.

Julia hadn't bothered to ask Manuel how old his boat was, or when
the last time it had been repaired. It was likely a boat his father or grandfather had handed down to him.

"Have you ever sailed a boat?" she asked Antonio.

"Are you kidding?" he said. "I hate the sea. And everything in it." Julia
grinned, remember how as a boy Antonio would refuse to eat fish or sea-
food of any kind, much to Sebastião's chagrin. "Ugh, it's fishy," Antonio
would say. "What's wrong with fishy?" Sebastião would answer. "Seawater
flows through your veins, boy." But Antonio wouldn't eat it, not under
any circumstance.

Julia prayed, invoking the name of St. Christopher, patron saint of sailors, but also Saint Peter and Saint Nicholas, saints long favored by sailors
and fishermen throughout the world, because in moments like these you
can never be too sure, or overly cautious. She prayed not only for safety
from the waves and wind, but for the guidance of her ancestors, Admiral
Rodrigo de Castro, Dom João de Castro, Violante do Canto.

Julia sniffed the air, and licked the salt from her lips. Although it was
humid, her face and hands were chaffed by the wind and salt air. She
felt uneasy, surprised by the darkness of the water, its green murkiness.
She couldn't see what lay hidden beneath the surface, any more than
she could see the minutes, hours, or days that lay ahead. "Can one read
the sea?" she wondered, testing her voice, which was snatched away by
the wind as soon as she spoke. "People read tea leaves, or the lines of a
person's hand, why not the sea?"

To the un-indoctrinated, the uninitiated—to a twentieth-century
woman like Julia, raised among the concrete and steel, the glass, fluores-
cent lighting, asphalt, as well as all the pervasive electronic gadgetry of
the United States—the observation of a fisherman 'reading' the sea, the
weather, the fish, or a farmer capable of foretelling an advancing storm
when there is not even a cloud in the sky, would seem a miraculous per-

formance, an act of magic and uncanny arts. In reality, of course, they are due to no less than a practiced eye, many years of keen observation and study, experience; no different, really, from the mysterious undertakings of a writer who can sit down and put words together to form a compelling story, or a musician who arranges notes into a mesmerizing piece of music: the evocation of minor over major, the impending resolution of suspended or diminished chords, the natural progression of the cycle of fifths—perfectly natural to a musician, trained or untrained, but a mystery to someone who is not.

Julia, however, could no more explain the source of inspiration and ideas, or how random, disjointed thoughts can take on a life of their own, flowering into poetry or prose, or the font of music, and indeed all art, any more than she could successfully explain a villager's ability to read impending death in the eyes of one person, or the reversal of fortune in another.

255

Sebastião's words came to her then: "If one wants a truly universal mystery, explain how or why a woman will fall madly in love with one person out of a hundred or thousands, shunning all others. What is it that singles out the one from all the others?" What would Sebastião say of her and Nicolau, she wondered. Would he approve? How could she explain her feelings to herself? Why him? Because it was impossible, that they were of two worlds?

It had to do with Nicolau's strength, as she saw it, coupled with the passion that lay just beneath the surface, belying his outer calm, the intensity that made her uneasy when she peered into his eyes. It was also the suspicion he knew what lived inside her better than she was able to admit to, or see. Though they came from worlds five or six thousand miles apart, she sensed they shared this secret realm, that she belonged more to his world than the world she had known.

If the Azorean woman continues to burn *alecrim, arruda, folhas de louro, salva*—rosemary, rue, bay leaves, and sage—or hangs a piece of a deer antler or an upside down horseshoe on the door, perhaps she thinks the first are merely to purify the air as protection against disease, as they were once thought beneficial against the plague, or simply to provide a pleasant, soothing, aroma; perhaps she no longer remembers that in her mother's or grandmother's time these herbs were also used to ward off the evil eye and other witchcraft, that the antler or horseshoe was to ensure good luck. As we lose touch with where we came from, leave behind our roots, our pasts, breaking all connection to the familiar ways of our ancestors, our connection to place, to the land, these sadly become lost arts.

This awareness and realization is nothing short of the sacred knowledge gleaned over many years of acquired wisdom and experience, generally passed down from father to son, mother to daughter, knowledge which teaches men and women to read omens and signs, both favorable and unfavorable, the difference which could mean life or death. Make no mistake about it—the fisherman, the whaler, the sailor, no less the lover, all learn to read the sea, the skies, the prey they hunt, the boat they handle with expertise, or the person they seduce or woo. Some people thus learn to read the clouds, the wind, the sea, the deeper mysteries which lie in a stranger's eyes, meanings hidden in a smile.

Diogo de Teive, a squire of Prince Henry. Born on the island of Madeira. On January 1, 1451, he disembarked on the island of Terceira and was one of the first colonizers. He made two expeditions to American waters near Newfoundland, the existence of which he had been convinced, and during the first of these, in 1452, he discovered the islands of Flores and Corvo.

Grande Enciclopédia Portuguesa e Brasileira, Lisboa, 1945

• • •

As if she hadn't enough to be concerned about, Julia fretted over Antonio, who surprised her by producing a satchel of Sebastião's papers. He sat reading them, sometimes to himself, sometimes aloud, then passing the pages on to Julia with a sober, "Here, take a look at this." It was out of character for him to come to the islands in the first place, but then to stay in Sebastião's room, to show up at the boat with her father's writings and the skull was beyond her understanding. Of course, she knew nothing about Teresa's and Antonio's meeting; she only saw the effects of what had occurred, not their cause.

Then there was Nicolau. She wished she hadn't left him, before she corrected herself. He had left first. "Oh, don't be such an idiot," she said, under her breath. "It was my decision to go. Nicolau had nothing to do with it." She clung to the hope that she had done the right thing going after Sebastião. Perhaps they were all somehow critically linked: father, daughter, Nicolau, Antonio, her father's writings, like intricate and beautifully worked tapestries—all roads leading to the Hidden Island.

Interspersed with Johan's intermittent vocalizations, shouting or singing one moment, swearing the next, then snoring loudly, Julia listened as Antonio quoted from Sebastião's notes:

"There are many esoteric and occult references found in Pessoa's *Mensagem*—'*Excalibur, a ungida, / Que o Rei Artur te deu*—Excalibur, the anointed, / that good King Arthur gave you.' '*Revele o Santo Gral!*—Reveal the Holy Grail!' '*A Rosa do Encoberto*—The Rose of the Hidden One.'"

"Secrets," Johan blurted out. "Secrets and lies. You can't fool me."

"There is no time on the ocean," Antonio mumbled.

Amidst this relentless cacophony, Julia heard another sound, one that reverberated as it traveled from somewhere in the distance, while at the same time, as if it welled up from deep within her.

She rummaged through the supplies she had brought aboard the boat: sacks containing water and tins of sardines, and rolls—already as hard and dry as the sea tack of old. There were sheets of notation paper and pens, as if placed there by some stranger who foresaw their necessity, for she had no recollection of taking them from the *residencial*.

Quickly, thoughtlessly, she jotted down the notes she heard, attempting with flourishes of her black pen, to capture the subtleties of timing and rhythm, the various melody lines, one playing off the other, repeated and evolving anew; never mind the key signature, there were shifts and changes, flats and sharps, incidentals, quite relevant, quite essential.

Each musical phrase in that wondrously evocative quality music uniquely possesses made a statement, asserted facts, then questioned and debated, searched for truth, searched for answers—this must be, this is so, probing deeper and deeper for the whys, hows and wherefores. She'd considered her skills rusty of late—it had been too long since she had attempted to compose, but she felt no hesitation or doubt now—a trill here, a triplet there, four beats to the measure, up a half-tone, a quarter note rest; the voices blending, developing one melody line after another, the bass line strong and pronounced, contrasting with the higher voices, delicate, playful, then those in the middle coming into play, seductive, alluring and taunting; a fugue.

And throughout, her notation was punctuated by Antonio continuing to recite, "Inês de Castro, the Magdalene, The Rose, The Cathars, The Knights Templar, Saint Isabel, Dom Dinis."

It was music too beautiful to miss a single blessed note. Julia only hoped she could capture each sweet nuance she heard.

. . .

What meaning is there in an island? Is it merely a result of geological forces at work, tectonic plates in collision? Or is there perhaps something more, something other than molten magma, lava erupting from cracks and fissures in the crust and cooling, becoming land mass, more than its changes upon the atmosphere, the sea? What might it mean to one who comes from the mainland, or to the person who leaves the island for whatever reason, finding himself lost on a vast continent, as vast as the sea which swims round the island he left behind. How does one measure its effects?

What does an island represent, what can it conjure? To a person on a boat, whether alone or in the company of others, an island can hold all hopes and dreams, no matter how fantastical.

—Sebastião do Canto e Castro

. . .

Manuel remained at the helm, while Johan continued to drink and grew ever louder, more belligerent and exaggerated in his gestures, flailing wildly as if he had no control over his limbs.

"Why are we headed in this direction?" he said. "Where are we going? You aren't trying to cheat me, are you? Don't keep anything from me. Don't fool me, like your father did." He laughed as though he were joking, and slapped his thigh, but the tone of his voice and the glint in his eyes made it evident that a threat lay behind the words.

Julia tried to appease him, to keep him calm. "Have you finished that bottle," she'd say, reminding Johan of his precious *aguardente*, figuring that so long as he was drinking he wouldn't get in the way, and would eventually pass out. Johan fumbled for the bottle and took a long swig from the brandy. He began lamenting his experiences with Americans and in particular the government of the United States.

"Did I tell you what they did to me?" he said. "They threw me in jail. Why? Because I had no money. Is that a crime? Isn't being poor punish ment enough? I wouldn't return to your country if it was the last place on earth." His tone was plaintive and hurt, like that of a young man severely wronged by society.

"Do you need a break?" Julia asked Manuel. His eyes looked crossed, and he kept veering off course.

He rubbed his eyes. "I'm all right."

Antonio pored over Sebastião's writing as if some precious key were encoded there.

"What are you reading?" Julia asked.

Antonio waved her aside. "Not now."

When he did tell her it was more often than not something about the early history of the Azores, a few lines from mythology, or poetry, which only caused her more concern.

"Everything okay?" she said. His whole demeanor had changed, his expression one she had never seen before.

"I'm fine," he answered, in a brusque, harsh tone, as if his voice had become rough through long disuse. He no longer sounded like himself.

Manuel finally called to Antonio, who answered testily, "What now?"

"Take the wheel," Manuel said.

"I've never sailed before," Antonio said.

"Don't worry, I only need an hour or two," Manuel said. "Just hold the wheel steady in the direction we're going." He was asleep before his head hit the rolled blanket he used for a pillow.

Antonio took the wheel. Julia stared at her brother. It was all too much; things were happening too quickly. "Here, let me take the wheel," Julia said.

"Are you sure? You know how to sail?"

"No, but neither do you. I'm sure I can at least keep to the direction we're heading." Julia took the wheel. She kept her eye on the compass and hoped her luck held.

The evening was damp and cold. Antonio wrapped a woolen blanket around himself, and returned to his father's notes. "What were you writing?" Antonio said, pointing to Julia's pad of paper.

"Just jotting down notes." She decided against asking whether he too heard the music. She only hoped what she wrote was as beautiful as what she heard. Even now there was no pause, no interruption; the sounds continued to fill her ears unabated.

It didn't occur to Antonio to query that she was composing music at such a place and time.

. . .

Damião de Góes, who was part of Dom Manuel's court from 1510 to 1521, said that, "In the Island of Corvo, or as it is sometimes called, Island of Marco, as it is used by sailors to demark any of the others when making them, there was found on the top of a hill, on the northwest side, a stone statue placed on a ledge, and consisting of a man astride the bare back of a horse, the man being dressed, and having over him a cloak but bareheaded, with one hand on the mane of the horse, and his right arm extended, the fingers of the hand folded, with the exception of the index finger, which pointed to the West. Dom Manuel ordered a drawing of this statue, which rose in a solid block from the ledge, to be forwarded to him; after seeing it he sent an ingenious man, a native of Oporto, who had traveled much in France and Italy, to the island of Corvo, in order to remove this antiquity, who, when he returned told the king that the statue had been destroyed by a storm the previous year. But the truth was that it had broken through ill-usage, bringing portions of it, consisting of the head of the man, and the right arms with the hand, also a leg and the head of the horse, all of which remained for some days in the wardrobe of the king.

"Edrisi, too, made a strange reference to the islands: 'There has been erected on each of these islands a statue hewn out of stone, and a hundred cubits high, over each statue was set a brazen image beckoning toward the west with its hand.'

"And on the Pizigano map of 1367, which depicted Breton ships battling a dragon of the air and a sea monster, at the very edge of the western limits of the sea, there appeared a giant statue, where the island of Corvo should have been marked. Perhaps the ships were a reference to the same ill-fated French expedition mentioned by Edrisi."

The Azores, Claude Dervenn, Paris

. . .

"I was the last to die," a shrill voice screeched, rousing Antonio from the farthest depths of sleep, pulling him toward a consciousness he was in no hurry to reach. He sat up and looked at Julia fast asleep, curled against the gunwale. Johan was slumped against the cabin, snoring loudly, while Manuel was back at the wheel, grim-faced, half-awake, staring straight ahead, as if in a trance. Antonio sat with his knees up, still clutching several sheets of Sebastião's notes.

"So many deaths," the voice continued. "I am lost as to the beginning and the end. Drowning, baptism by the fire of the Inquisition, rotting in a dungeon, slashed to shreds by the swords of the Moors in Arzila, fighting the Moslems in a crusade in the Holy Land, fighting the Castilians. One loses track of the thousand different faces of death."

"Julia," Antonio whispered, although it was as if he yelled. "Do you hear that?" Julia didn't answer.

"I was the scribe of a kingdom in exile." Antonio half-heard, half-felt the words resounding like the rumble of thunder, echoing from the depths of many centuries past.

"Ah, the things we wrote . . . the glories we witnessed."

Antonio rose, unable to see anything in the darkness beyond the gunwale, where the poor light of the lantern did not reach. "Who's there?" he said.

The voice didn't silence itself the way he expected. "So much has slipped away, it's a miracle I am here able to speak for all I have seen."

Antonio grabbed the boat's lantern and peered nervously, but saw nothing unusual in the flickering light, the shadows. The skull, stuck at the end of the walking stick and tied to the mast, grinned at Antonio as the voice rose and fell, from shrill whispers to a wailing screech, then a low growl.

Julia moaned, as if troubled by dreams, still in a deep sleep.

The voice continued in a fluid and impassioned Portuguese: "Ask me what drove men to sea, what lured them from the warm haven of their homes, their friends and families, to traverse the unknowns of the Sea of Darkness. Why they left safe harbors and security for the wide-open seas, the ever-present dangers, the countless perils of the deep! How many souls the ocean claimed. Men and ships swallowed up by an angry sea, sails torn, frail timbers smashed into splinters; ships sunk in the battles with the Moors or pirates; sunk by the weight of treasure loaded in excess by men unable to let one bar of gold slip away from their grasp, men who sailed the vast oceans upon worm-rotted ships, barely seaworthy."

Without thinking, Antonio crossed himself, something he hadn't done since he was a child, and mumbled a quick, emphatic prayer to Saint Catarina of Alexandria, patron saint of philosophers, protector of the mind and its ailments, and hopefully the guardian against unwanted apparitions and hallucinations.

Johan grumbled and muttered incoherently in his sleep.

"I should have buried you as all dead men should be, deep in the earth," Antonio said in a hoarse whisper, afraid that if he spoke aloud it would prove the skull really was speaking to him. "Perhaps I'll toss you into the sea, and be rid of you at last!"

263

"All truths lie buried," the voice said. "Secrets lost over the centuries—the buried mirror that guards hidden truths. I, too, heard the sad songs the sirens sang, promises whispered in the calm of night, words spoken softly in their ears, sounds alive in the echoes retained by shells, traces as faint and slippery as the comings and goings of the sea mists— the secret kisses of those wet lips, taunting: promises of love, of beauty, of peace, of eternal happiness, islands of love!

"Nymphs of the Tagus and the Mondego," the voice continued, softer now. I invoke your help, to navigate the high seas. My Nymphs, is it not enough that such miseries should encircle me?"

Antonio recognized the references from Camões's *Lusíadas*. Just because he cared nothing for the language or the literature didn't prevent Antonio from absorbing something from Sebastião's early, if frustrating attempts to give his son an appreciation of his Portuguese heritage. Sebastião had paid Antonio to read and recite Portuguese poetry. The more he read, the more he earned, which had left Antonio with an appreciation of money, if not poetry.

"Who are you?" Antonio said.

The skull murmured a verse of a song, a stanza of poetry, names and various terms in Latin, or some other ancient language, its words mingling with the wind, the cries of birds, the water slapping against the boat.

"I hear their voices!" the skull shouted. "They are near. Change course, follow the sounds, follow the singing."

"Who?" Antonio said, still dazed. "What?"

The skull whispered, then shouted: "The Oceanids, the sea nymphs, the three thousand daughters of Oceanus, the great river, the Outer Sea, Tethys, Queen of the Ocean, Neptune's bride. The Titans, the first race, the ancient ones!"

Antonio's head spun with the names of saints and islands, gods and goddesses, nymphs, sirens, harpies, and more. "You've seen her, heard her voice," the skull cried. "She calls to you. Listen to her song, we must follow!"

Slowly the skull lapsed back into silence. Refusing to answer Antonio's questions, saying nothing of Sebastião. "All will be revealed, by and by; all will be known in its own time," it whispered ominously, then was silent. Exhausted, Antonio finally lay down to rest.

CHAPTER 3

Da lua os claros raios rutilavam
Polas argênteas ondas neptuninas;
As estrelas os céus acompanhavam,
Qual campo revestido de boninas;
Os furiosos ventos repousavam
Polas covas escuras peregrinas;
Porém da armada a gente vigiava,
Como por longo o tempo costumava.

[. . .]

Com que milhor podemos, un dizia,
Este tempo passar, que é tão pesado,
Senão com algum conto de alegria,
Com que nos deixe o sono carregado?
Responde Lionardo, que trazia
Pensamentos de firme namorado:
—Que contos poderemos ter milhores,
Para passar o tempo, que de amores?

The brilliant radiance of the moon on high
Over the silver waves of Neptune shone.
And all the stars marched onward with the sky,
That seemed a field with the white daisies sown.
And quiet all the winds infuriate lie,
Yet in the fleet good watch kept every crew

As this long while had been their wont to do.

And someone said: "What better thing could be
To pass this time that weighs upon us sore
Than to narrate some pleasant history,
That sleep's dead load may trouble us no more."
Leonardo gave answer, whose thought constantly
Upon the troubles of true lovers bore:
"And to that end what better stories may
Compete with love-tales to pass time away?"[7]

—Luís Vaz de Camões, *Os Lusíadas*

. . .

Antonio glared at the skull in the hard light of day, convinced it had all been a dream, the workings of an over-excited imagination, a nightmare resulting from finding himself out on the sea in a boat that was barely seaworthy, as well as the long hours and the stress and strain of poring over Sebastião's writings.

He glared at the others, irked by their serenity. "You slept through the night?" he asked Julia.

"Yes, I slept. Though not exactly like a baby," she said. "I ache all over."

He frowned. "Humph, and how about you?" he asked Johan.

"I think so," Johan answered, groggily. He rubbed his tired face. Antonio doubted Johan had heard anything, not in his condition.

"Why do you ask," Julia said. "Did you see or hear something?"

"Just wondering," Antonio said. Julia looked at him, concerned, which annoyed him. He didn't want her asking questions he wasn't prepared to answer. Those few nights in Praia do Almoxarife had left him unsure of everything—wild dreams, sounds, though not nearly as bad as what he'd heard last night. Still, nothing he could tell Julia about. And of course, there was *her!* It was because of Teresa that he had joined Julia on this ludicrous expedition. The memory of stumbling into Maria dos Santos's yard after that terrible first night of sweat and dreams and voices, and finding her waiting as if she had known he would come, ran through his mind, disjointed, fragmented. How could she have known? How did she know that Julia was about to leave? Her smile had unnerved him. Her calm certainty left him full of doubt. And her beauty had caused him to shake like a sinner before an angel. He'd acted like a schoolboy, stumbling over himself as he tried to talk to her, find out who she was. "Teresa," she'd said, in a voice that had wounded him to the core. "Teresa," he had mouthed, wondering if he were dreaming.

He licked his lips, remembering the taste of her mouth, luscious as the sweetest plum, so alluring, irresistible, and the lingering impression her mouth had left on his. Had he really shown such passion, he who had never made a fool of himself over any woman? Her lightest touch was a rush of adrenaline. He recalled the sea in her eyes, being mesmerized by her every word, before he asked himself: "What am I doing here, how could I have left her?" They had made love, as unbelievable as that now seemed. He had lain against her dark skin, so taut, so responsive to his. He swallowed, as he tried to push the memories from his mind. It was too unreal.

267

He had never been interested in Sebastião's writing before. He'd read a couple of stories, which hadn't made much of an impression. Fiction was a waste of time. He sought facts and reality, not stories that were merely the product of someone's overactive imagination. But now everything was topsy-turvy. What was real, what was made up? He was in no position to say.

"You didn't hear anything either?" Antonio asked Manuel.

"Like what?"

"I don't know, noises, strange sounds, anything," Antonio said.

"Only the sea, the wind, and him," Manuel said, gesturing at Johan. "Noisy son-of-a-bitch snores like a pig. The sound of the water and the boat. Nothing else."

The skull was dry, lifeless, bone, and nothing more. Antonio tried to laugh off the idea of a speaking skull. Ridiculous, of course, like so many other absurdities he had heard of late. There was nothing to indicate that his state of mind, coupled with what his father had called the particular sensitivity of location—the simple fact that the islands themselves worked on one's imagination—hadn't affected Antonio's perceptions and caused him to imagine the whole thing.

The wind, he reasoned, with not nearly as much confidence as he would have liked, whistles in the stays of the boat, the cleats, the mast, and makes strange sounds.

There was still a noise, a background hum; maybe it was only a tension that continued to hang in the air, or something he felt, rather than heard, an expectancy, something about to break.

The skull's voice, the strange words, he assured himself, were merely some lingering extension of Sebastião, the ancient bone acting as some sort of receiver or transmitter feeding Antonio's over-wrought mind.

. . .

1462. The Portuguese king granted concessions to Diogo Gomes and João Vogado to search for the islands of Capraria and Lovo.

. . .

Pushing aside thoughts of Teresa and the skull, Antonio resumed sifting through the pile of notes he had set down beside him. "Many things associated with the islands became as lost as the islands themselves," Sebastião had written. "After a terrible storm on the tiny island of Corvo, a pot of ancient Phoenician coins was said to have been unearthed in a field. Where these coins are now is anyone's guess. There was a stone statue the islanders called, *O Homem de Pé*—The Standing Man—allegedly found there by the first settlers. Whether this statue's outstretched arm pointed to the west, to yet another island, or to the continent that would be called America, no one knows, because the statue is no longer there. Only a strange lava formation remains, which some people believe has been weathered down and disfigured by centuries of wind and rain, but which was once believed to be the missing statue. Cuneiform characters had also been carved at the base of the statue. Some say that Columbus took the statue as a sure sign that his path lay to the west."

Antonio followed his own sign, a faint luminescence, a glowing trail in the water that stretched ahead, pointing the way.

"What's that on the water there?" he shouted.

Manuel, Julia, and Johan looked. "Where?" they said.

"Dead ahead," Antonio said, still pointing, a vague, tantalizing image, now moving in the water, now in the air, hovering like a stray wisp of mist, then glowing like a streak of fire churning up the water. He reached out his hand to touch it, but found only empty air, though some slight presence remained, the sense that his fingers had touched something. Fumbling with the papers in his hands, he pulled out more notes from the satchel—pages about the early exploration of the islands, the history of the volcanic eruptions and earthquakes over the centuries—achingly aware of his longing to reach the vision he'd seen, to see it materialize.

There were quotes by Camões, by Cervantes, Calderón, and Gil Vicente, from Sebastião, as well, questioning reality, questioning life, questioning love. "Life is the dream we spin as we grow, constructing illusions around us, illusions which separate us from others, which tie us to still others, illusions upon which we stand, and which represent who and what we are." The sentences, fragments and phrases were a spell Antonio read and turned over in his mind. "What is reality when compared to the illusions that defy and overleap our limitations, our fears, illusions which can lift us up from the dark, the lower regions wherein we cheapen and shortchange ourselves? Anti-illusion is anti-art, a return to the base, to the superstitious, the primitive, to fear. It is, in effect anti-love—life pared down to the level of pure instinct—while love is our greatest artistic expression, as both the ultimate object and the medium.

"How desperate our need is for the delusions and fantasies by which we sustain our hopes and dreams; no matter that these fancies may not represent reality, or exist in the 'real world,' for there is a separate reality of the heart, mind, spirit and soul, which without these wisps and figments can only wither. One's life should be a search for the highest of these ideals, the unmappable regions of love, the imagination, the impossible.

"I make up a story, amend the facts I find in recollection, in order to portray an essence, a truth that can't be found and stated in any other way," Sebastião's notes continued. "What is reality stripped bare? Facts, numbers, dates, cold and dead to life, like a barren rock, a grain of sand, with no perspective of human relationship, or even of how that grain of sand relates to a beach, the sea, or an island; a life without poetry, without art. It is better to reach for the impossible, to fight against entropy and limitations; better to know we are composed of star-stuff, of the same planet we inhabit, of all life therein, that we in fact contain all the universe within ourselves. Imagination alone can make us what we may become."

• • •

Fernão Domingues de Arco. Donee of an island that was said to exist to the west of Madeira. He lived on the island of Madeira and on June 30, 1484 was given the captancy of that hypothetical island to discover. This donation, imprecise and obscure, has been taken as proof that it was known that Brazil existed, before its official discovery.

—*Grande Enciclopédia Portuguesa e Brasileira*, Lisboa, 1945

• • •

The skull leaned forward into the wind and sniffed at the air, as if it had a nose capable of detecting even the finest scent. Did its jaw move? At times Antonio could swear he saw a finger, moistened with a real mouth, with saliva, raised in the air to determine the direction of the wind.

Neither Julia, nor Johan, nor Manuel appeared to notice anything unusual. They ignored the skull, as if it weren't there, and sat apparently unmoved by the sounds that filled Antonio's ears, though Julia appeared distracted by the music she scribbled frantically in her book.

"It'll be a miracle, if we don't end up on the bottom of the sea," Antonio said, staring out at the waves, which even now seemed ever-ready, almost anxious, to engulf the small boat.

The wind rang through the stays and lines as the full moon rose in the sky. The stars slowly appeared, creating vague, mysterious designs: auguries the skull appeared to decipher, as it issued an occasional demand to change course—an esoteric numerical code, or symbolism hidden in those patterns that stretched across the light-years of space, as if the route to the Hidden Isle could be ascertained by following a particular handful of those distant lights, millions of light-years away. If only one could glean the secret of their message, a road map drawn in the heavens, illustrating a path across the ocean, to the very goal they sought. Don't scoff. Sailors have long used the Pole star, the Southern Cross, and others, as mile posts, to guide their way through treacherous seas. Vasco da Gama is credited with having discovered what is called "the sea road" to India, a route of favorable winds and currents; sailors used the very same route for 400 years; scattered points of light to some, a road map to others. Unfortunately, Antonio had never known one star from another, nor was he aware of any secrets written across the heavens. He peered at the stars and planets. Some were brighter, some fainter, nearer and farther, but nothing special, except he noted that there were far more than he had ever seen before.

He shrugged. What to one person might appear as nothing but meaningless circles or squiggly lines, might to another confer a whole book of hidden meaning. Perhaps the skull read fantastical designs, meaningful symbols in the heavens, the way Western Europeans see the man in the surface of the moon, the Chinese see a frog and a rabbit, Eastern Indians see a woman's hand prints, the Scandinavians, a boy and a girl with a pail, the Gouro of the Ivory Coast, see a drummer man, and the Polynesians a woman, Hina, the maker of the clouds. He was content to let the skull cipher out the mysteries of these patterns and symbols.

271

Antonio's fleeting visions were illuminated by the bright moon and stars, perhaps the way unicorns were said to be projections of the moon, or the work of *fadas*—fairies—if not nymphs and sirens, who caused him to see what his heart desired to see. Take desire, an aching heart, take mysterious or unknown surroundings, throw in a dose of eerie incandescence, and most anything can happen.

He pointed to his visions, though he dared not speak her name aloud, then traced the constellations, as the skull called out to them. "See there?" he said.

Julia looked where he pointed, watching his every move and nodding. "Yes, beautiful." Could Nicolau see, she wondered, at that very moment, those very same stars? Did he envision Julia as easily and as intensely as she envisioned him? For Julia now heard intermittent strains of someone, perhaps Nicolau, singing the words of *The Lusiads:*

> *Que as Ninfas do Oceano, tão fermosas,*
> *Tétis e a ilha angélica pintada,*
> *Outra cousa não é que as deleitosas*
> *Honras que a vida fazem sublimada.*

> For Tethys, the sea-nymphs with such beauty bright,
> And the painted Island of angelic kind
> Are nothing more than honors which delight,

Whereby life is exalted and refined.

The skull grinned its eternal grin as the wind sang through its remaining teeth, creating a persistent moan, and then it sang its usual litany of gods and goddesses: "Apollo, dear Muses, Neptune, Mars." Julia and Manuel, while perhaps deaf to the skull's ranting, grew agitated nonetheless. They peered around nervously, as if sensing a disturbance in the air. And Johan, Antonio noticed, groaned and muttered a word or two in his stupor, as if responding to the skull's cries.

Julia swooned to the music that filled her ears, as Antonio continued to read from Sebastião's notes. Music was the very essence of what connected her to Nicolau. If only she could tell him, I'm coming back, wait for me, I will return. She trembled, as if he inhabited the air or sea, nearby. There was an intangible quality of the sea breeze, the heavenly bodies above, the sheen of the ocean itself, as if they too were trying to point out the way. There he is, see, off in the distance, now nearer, now farther away. The wind carried his voice, the sound of his song, Camões's words, unmistakable, a sound that drew her on across the waves, across the deep:

Impossibilidades não façais,
Que quem quis, sempre pôde; e numerados
Sereis entre os Heróis esclarecidos
E nesta Ilha de Vénus recebidos.

The impossible you do not undertake.
Where will is there's a way, and you shall stand
With splendid figures of heroic kind
And in the Isle of Venus welcome find.[9]

Antonio, as one might imagine, unfamiliar with many of the names he heard, was at a loss to comprehend much of the skull's ravings. The modern poet—to say nothing of the layman today—being, for the most part, ignorant, much less intimate with the gods and goddesses of antiquity. When was the last time anyone invoked Aeolis, for example, Jupiter or even Venus? These ancient gods, once so prominent and revered, have fallen out of favor, been forgotten, discarded—perhaps there were just too many to keep track of, each with their own agenda—in favor of the convenience of monotheism; though experience has certainly shown us that the one can often be as contradictory as the many.

Then again, in *The Lusiads* Camões not only paid tribute to the gods, both benevolent and wicked, who participated in the history of Portugal, he also didn't hesitate to implore the muses to assist in the writing, to sustain the poetic fervor of his inspiration, and help him bring the poem to completion. Who is to wonder then if, hearing their names spoken after so long a silence, these gods stirred, yawning and stretching, with the skull's persistent invocations? The fact that the ancient gods are no longer regularly summoned and promised homage, nor offerings, votive or otherwise, nor even remembered in song, poetry or drama, might explain the state of the world in this time of ours. These gods no doubt sleep in forgetful repose, no longer active participants in our day-to-day affairs. If they appear somewhat groggy and confused, it is with patience and understanding that we await their coming round and impressing us with the immortal attributes for which they long ago earned their fame and glory.

Still, if there is one thing that a reading of the ancient myths teaches us, it is that the ancient gods could be—and quite often were—jealous, spiteful and petty. Not to mention treacherous. If we could, we might wish to warn our intrepid sailors, especially Julia and Antonio, who are perhaps now for the first time feeling their own ancestral past stirring within, of these facts, warning them to be on their guard.

273

Beauty is a mirror reflecting joy and sorrow, the spirit of life, love, and the   275
abyss of loss.

—Sebastião do Canto e Castro

. . .

Antonio received instructions from the skull, which appeared to navigate by memory and intuition, a bit of guesswork now and then, and a fair amount of correcting and re-correcting their course. Manuel simply chuckled to himself and headed the boat wherever he was asked. *"Loucos,"* he muttered. They sailed a somewhat erratic, even comical route, first one way, then another, forward, suddenly turning about, headed into the wind, then downwind. To anyone observing or following, theirs would seem a blind, reckless course of zigzags and roundabouts, the helm either in the hands of a drunk or a lunatic.

Antonio couldn't help but laugh at the irony and humor of their predicament: that he, a Canto e Castro, instead of being in command of a fleet of ships, a proud Admiral of the realm, or even the captain of a ship worthy of the name, like so many of his ancestors, instead resembled more a certain fabled Canto e Castro he had often heard mentioned in reference to the lunatics and eccentrics in the family when he was a boy—a man who had sailed from the island of Terceira to São Miguel, in a boat constructed entirely of newspapers.

In perusing Sebastião's notes Antonio discovered that this dubious sailor was not a Canto e Castro after all, but was one of the famed Corte-Reais of Terceira, one Francisco Moniz Barreto Corte-Real. But, as Sebastião had written, "If some time during the past two or three hundred years a Canto e Castro had married a Corte-Real, then that would be more than sufficient for us to claim him as one of our own."

In 1895, this particular gentleman, on a wager, left under cloak of darkness at three o'clock in the morning in order to escape the port authorities, making the 30-hour trip through the rough and dangerous waters between the two islands, before the 12-foot boat reached the port of Ponta Delgada. The brave navigator had survived foul weather and even a fire his lantern had accidentally ignited aboard the small craft. All he had brought with him was a jug of water, a bottle of *aguardente*, some bread, and a chart showing the route, made, not by himself, but by the man who had actually constructed the boat. Although a descendant of the great navigators, João and Miguel Corte-Real, still, as the Portuguese saying goes, *"Nem sempre o filho de peixe sabe nadar"*—the children of fish don't always know how to swim—for this Corte-Real knew nothing of the art of navigation or sailing.

Nevertheless, the people of São Miguel turned out in droves to welcome the heroic mariner as he arrived, as did the people of Terceira when he made his triumphant return some days later. The islanders were proud of this native son who had succeeded in a feat of daring, a task no one had ever attempted, let alone accomplished.

"My, how the mighty have fallen," Antonio commented, regarding the precipitous plummet of fortune which the centuries had wrought; feats by ancestors like Francisco Corte-Real did little to bolster his faith, or his confidence. He had rather fancied his relatives were all brave, daring men like Dom Fernando de Castro, sent to conquer the Canary Islands, by Prince Henry in 1424; or Pedro Annes do Canto and João da Silva do Canto, Captains of the Armadas and Generals of the Seas of the Azores, Captains of the noble city of Angra do Heroísmo, and members of the king's council. Instead, true Renaissance figures like Dom João de Castro had faded from the world's stage to be replaced by the likes of a man who sailed a boat made from newspapers, and then Sebastião's reenactment of that voyage some seventy years later. "One cannot take oneself too seriously," Sebastião had pointed out.

"Even worse," Antonio grumbled, "An idiot like me stuck on this dilapidated boat, following the directions of a skull, and sailing toward our doom."

"What was will be again," the skull murmured. "That which was lost will be found, and vindication *fait accompli,* once we reach the Enchanted Isle."

Antonio nodded, less than convinced, paying little heed to the skull's words. The more he read of Sebastião's notes, the more obvious it became that nothing was precisely what he had assumed it was, not even the family. Reality was warped, as if by the sun or the dampness, the humidity of the Mid-Atlantic. It was like finding one day that your parents aren't really your parents, that you were adopted, or that the war hero you always believed your father to be, and were told he was, is shown by an article in a faded old newspaper to have been a coward, or a traitor instead. And once one fact is called into question and disproved, who's to say that the rest of the foundation of your reality isn't rotted through and through, and that it won't come crashing down on you like a gigantic house of cards?

277

· · ·

In 1486 King João II issued a patent to one Fernão Dulmo of Terceira "to seek and find a great island or islands or mainland by its coast, which is presumed to be the Isle of the Seven Cities." Dulmo was Flemish, and had come to the Azores with the primary purpose of exploring the Western Atlantic.

Dulmo established himself at the bay of Quatro Ribeiras, on the north of Terceira. He began to act as captain of this part of the island. His name became linked with that of João Afonso de Estreito and a proposed voyage to the west.

We know of these projects because of two letters by King Dom João II, one written to Estreito and Fernão Dulmo with the date of July 24, 1486, and the other to Estreito, dated August 4th, 1486. Because of these letters we know that they were to mount an expedition which would lead to "an island or islands, or a coastline, which they assumed would be the Island of Seven cities"; that the expedition would consist of two caravels, taking six months' worth of supplies, and that they should start out by the month of March 1487. It is unknown whether this expedition ever took place.

—*Grande Enciclopédia Portuguesa e Brasileira,* Lisboa, 1945

. . .

The skies grew dark and increasingly menacing. Smoke, ash and storm clouds filled the air. Antonio was now at the wheel. "Perhaps, we should return to Faial," Julia said, increasingly apprehensive. "We should've seen the island by now. We seem to be going in circles. We've sailed far longer than it should have taken." The skull tormented Antonio with dire prophecies: "It's death to go back. We've gone too far. We must push on. There is no escaping Fate."

"Just a little farther," Antonio said. "We've come too far to give up now."

"What are you plotting behind my back?" Johan said, waving his bottle as if it were a weapon. He voiced his accusations with greater intensity, staring wide-eyed as they sailed farther out to sea. "They're coming for us," he shouted. "We'll be fighting before the day is through. We'd do well to prepare for battle." He pointed and jabbed as if his finger were a sword.

"We should get rid of him," Manuel said. "He's nothing but trouble, that one. Why the hell did you let him aboard?"

Julia agreed. "We can't trust him."

"I know," Antonio said. "But it's too late now. We just need to keep an eye on him."

Manuel grumbled something about foreigners, and people who couldn't hold their liquor.

"Ahead we will find the island," the skull said. "Listen to the voice that calls, to the music of your past." The mere mention of a word or a name— *Lusitânia, The Island of Brasil, Sete Cidades, Colum, Bartolomeu Dias, Vasco da Gama*—spoken by the skull, or by Antonio as he read aloud his father's notes, and carried across the sea by the wind, invoked or at least accompanied visible changes, as the light danced upon the water to strange effect, the winds and the waves rose and fell, and the fogs and mists, swarmed and quickly enveloped the boat, completely blinding those aboard. And through it all, other sounds became mingled one with the other, as Julia wrote sheet after sheet of the plaintive, haunting music.

There were times when Johan perked up, his head cocked to one side, as the skull called out. Johan would answer back, as if roused by either the words or voice of the skull. Since his replies were incomprehensible, Antonio shrugged them off as coincidence.

Antonio drank from the bottle of *aguardente* that Johan offered, and shivered beneath a wool blanket in the stern of the boat. Julia was surprised to see him drinking, something Antonio never did. He, too, gazed repeatedly at the sea as if he saw something troubling in the water.

In a low, rough voice, the skull sang ancient songs, poem fragments, melodies penned by roving troubadours in the twelfth or thirteenth centuries. There was a strange blending of sounds as the next moment Johan shouted in his sleep, "Save the treasure, don't forget the water," and then Manuel, if he was awake, might sing a few lines of a shanty sung by sailors on the high sea, songs which the natives of Africa, North and South America, which the peoples of India and Malaysia must have heard when the Portuguese brazenly sailed upon their shores. They must have wondered, were these gods or devils, these light-skinned creatures who arrived aboard strange monsters which evidently floated down from the sky with painted wings; creatures who spoke strange languages and who wore even stranger garments, not to mention their weapons and paraphernalia. Such strange sights and sounds struck terror in the hearts of the natives when the Portuguese fired their cannons or when the natives heard the sailors play their bagpipes, and assumed these instruments were fearsome creatures, whose deafening howls sent the natives scurrying back into the brush, to escape the demons that attacked their shores.

Antonio chewed on the stale rolls, washing them down with liquor that warmed his stomach, and studied the sea for any sign of mysterious islands, the sails of a boat, for any sirens or other beings and creatures, repeatedly invoked by the skull. Anything, he thought, is preferable to this nothingness, the remoteness and puniness of being set against the surrounding sea and skies. Perhaps that's why sailors conjured fantastic visions—to break the monotony.

Julia asked herself, "What have I left behind? Am I moving geographically, treading water, pushed along by the wind? Or are oceanic currents drawing me along specific sea routes toward a determined spot?" She grew anxious when the mists momentarily parted and she saw in the distance a dark and foreboding bulk, mysterious, menacing, as though it were ready to bear down upon the small craft like a raging storm. Could it possibly be what it appeared to be? Although remote and faint it loomed threateningly. She could almost make out torn, ragged sails, an overall sense of decay about the ship, which looked very much like a sailing vessel of old, a carrack or galleon, following in the wake of Manuel's boat, before it vanished once again into the fog, the mists that rolled and played upon the surface of the sea.

Throughout the long day she perceived shadows everywhere. Tricks of sunlight, clouds, and waves. Here a creature rose from the depths, there a ship appeared on the horizon, and elsewhere, a stretch of land materialized before again being swallowed by the mists. And not merely shadows, but refrains, too, heard again and again, echoes, murmurings, whispers.

Antonio sighed and dreamt of Teresa as the skull sang a song about a forbidden love, of a woman more beautiful than any mortal could compare, nor the gods endure, yet a woman so good that not even the worst of misfortunes could succeed in turning her heart: *"Linda Senhora, muito fiel, cheia de graça"*—Beautiful woman, so faithful, full of grace.

Julia wished Nicolau were there beside her. Perhaps, if he had returned to Praia do Almoxarife, he could see her in the garden of Maria dos Santos, where the pool of water might have calmed once more, now smooth as a mirror, revealing the boat, which strangely seemed to cast a reflection, no longer of a small boat, but of a ship, an ancient galley or galleon, sailing through the Sea of Darkness.

. . .

This rock is ours. Give it a name, call it by this holy word, offering breath and sound, the word itself, the spoken word. Let the singers sing and the poets recite poems. Let those with desires and longing wrench their hearts and shed tears of supplication, of hope, the words of our prayers resounding over the passing centuries, growing, summoning the earth to rise from the depths of the sea. Give us pearls, give us heaven, magic, the words igniting the fires of passion, to give substance to the vision their hearts call forth, creating something out of nothingness, as the word enlivens the soul which lives it—so, too, the poem gives that which it seeks, life.

—Sebastião do Canto e Castro

. . .

The boat glided, drawn by a particularly strong current, or perhaps pulled by spirits, nymphs, dolphins, or sea creatures like *ramoras* or suckerfish. It was once believed that if enough of these attached themselves to the bottom of the hull they could change the course of a ship; and toward what new disaster or strange unknown lands would they draw the men held captive in their craft? To the very ends of the earth where the seas boiled, to where the ocean plummeted off the edge, hurtling all to fiery pits below? Or to the Sargasso Sea, that region, first noted by the Portuguese, who called it *O Mar de Baga*—the Baga Sea, *baga* being the Portuguese word for a small grape-like fruit. Later it became known as *sargaço* or sargasso, which has many small grape-like berries, which explains why the Portuguese at one time called sargasso the sea grape. There the seaweed was so thick the boat would become stuck, unable to sail, trapped until the men ran out of fresh water and food, and slowly died, or driven to madness, dived overboard to drown in that forest of kelp. It was also said that weed could drag a ship down to the bottom of the ocean. Then there were the horse latitudes, where the ship would end up becalmed, adrift but going nowhere, for in this desert there is not a breath of wind.

281

Julia observed the goings-on around her: A fish broke the surface of the water and set her nerves on edge; Johan stared at the water, as if he might jump overboard, and a moment later glared and snarled at his companions as if he might attack them, then grinned and laughed maniacally, rolling cigarettes and passing his bottle round, as though they were all the best of friends.

"We should tie him up," Antonio said, "before he does something."

"I have rope here," Manuel said, pointing to a coil of heavy rope."

"Maybe you're right," Julia said. Later, when Johan was asleep they tied him securely, as insurance against any sudden outburst of violence.

"There," Antonio said. "Now at least I can close my eyes without thinking I'll be strangled in my sleep."

Julia sought the safety of the familiar, the terra firma of her father's notes: ". . . the search for love and meaning, for justice, the search for beauty," Sebastião had written. "Do I possess the strength, the faith, to rise to the challenge? Can I traverse the boundaries, overcome the barriers, which separate me from the goal? Fernão Dulmo, Afonso do Estreito, Diogo de Teive, Fernão Teles, and others failed to reach the

Enchanted Island, and yet it lured them on time and time again. A vision, a hope, a dream, how little we need for us to follow some illusory plan of action with no regard for consequences or thought of practicality. How can we know the influences that play a part in what we do, where these influences originate, if they are passed down from others? We may not decide anything alone."

"Yes," Julia said. That one's actions, decisions and choices could be inherited was troubling. How could people avoid succumbing to the foolishness of the past, if that were the case? Did she follow the same perilous path her father had journeyed, as if it were some terrible family curse, payback for centuries of crimes and misdeeds? Would she find death, as Maria dos Santos had hinted at their first meeting? She glanced at Antonio. He would insist that coming to the islands was a mistake, an error in judgment, an act of self-destruction. Could Mateus have been right, was some force attempting to eliminate the family once and for all? Or was that as outlandish as it sounded? Julia sensed that this was where she had been headed all her life, here to this place, at this time, the hand of destiny, her fate, written long ago. And Antonio? If something happened to the two of them, it would be the end of Sebastião's lineage. Or was it only coincidence that her father had disappeared at the same time a new island was rising from the depths, that she had met Nicolau and that she was now here? The family had suffered the very same fate as Portugal—perhaps the fall of one signaled the fall of the other. Weren't the two inextricably linked?

Even as she heard strange voices speaking stranger words, Julia felt an odd lack of apprehension or surprise, as if resigned to her fate, and the events taking place around her.

"Come Proteus, thou old man of the sea, shepherd of Neptune's sea creatures. What shape will you assume, what prophecies foretell of our fate?" The skull implored the love and indulgence of Venus and Mars, two gods who had always taken upon themselves to favor the Portuguese. "Zetes and Calais, you winged warriors, sons of the nymph and the North wind, come fight as you fought with the Argonauts of old!"

It is the mythic quality of beauty, that Holiest of Holy Grails, for which I search. When an object so deeply loved is lost, any new object of beauty that even remotely resembles the original becomes enhanced and increased by its haunting promise of substitution, coupled with its melancholy remembrance, the reminder of the original loss, and the impossibility of its true replacement. What once was can never be again. It becomes instead a matter of perpetual reaching for, of attempting to hold onto these phantoms, for the mind tinged with memory wants so desperately to believe that the impossible is true, fooling itself time and time again, seizing hold only to find it has grasped empty air. The mirage has vanished.

—Sebastião do Canto e Castro

• • •

Antonio took fleeting catnaps in the daylight, trading off at the helm with Manuel and Julia, one moment lulled by sweet dreams of Teresa, the next rudely jarred to consciousness by Johan's cries and sobbings, followed abruptly by loud and angry outbursts, or the skull's insistent pronouncements, calling men to arms, ordering all hands on deck, shouting for sails to be unfurled, or giving some other indication that he was referring to another place, another time.

Julia, Antonio and Manuel did their best to ignore Johan, who struggled repeatedly against the ropes that held him when he was awake, and sputtered, "Murderers! Thieves, villains!" pleading wheedlingly one moment, threatening the next. "Please, untie me. I'll be good."

To drown out some of the unwanted sounds that hummed and pulsed through the air, disturbances that were felt more than heard, Julia recited a poem of Pessoa's, breaking open her weathered copy of *Mensagem*, or *The Lusiads*, by Camões, or another poem of one of Portugal's heroes, and for the moment the skull and even Johan would quiet down.

Julia didn't peer too closely at anything other than the distant stretch of sea, her father's notes, and the music she jotted down in her notation book, while the boat changed. The feel of it was different as it rode upon the waves, the sounds and smells, too, stranger, more varied: shouts, curses, a number of voices, the sound of ropes and sails and creaking timbers.

"Are we getting close?" Antonio asked. "Are we nearly there?"

"Yes," a voice, cavernous like the peal of thunder, answered. "Yes, listen."

And he heard in the distance, faintly, a beautiful voice singing a sad song, a plaintive cry to a far-off love. Or, he'd see a light shining dim and pale as the moon, on the horizon, just above the water, a thin wisp glowing in the night. And the voice would say. "There she is. There is our siren, the nymph, the muse!"

If Julia felt a momentary panic, a sense of the impossibility of what was happening, of what she was doing, she thought of Nicolau, who instantly buoyed and steadied her spirits. Though she couldn't gauge how he felt about her, he had kissed her, after all. She thought long and hard on that kiss. It had been their first, but was it their last, too? As things go, one kiss often follows another, and from there, if there is one possibility, one potential outcome, there are at least ten, a hundred—at least one of which we might look back upon and say was inevitable; choices made perhaps without too much thought or reflection, because for some of us our roles in life are clearly drawn and difficult to veer from—as in the case of climbing aboard a boat and sailing off—others more carefully weighed and pondered.

Had it only been a kiss and nothing more, even then Julia would likely have relished it and relived that moment again and again, but there was more than merely that, for the kiss was accompanied by the remembrances of a touch, a caress, an embrace, a look. Imagination being what it is, it wasn't long before the irresistible image of what might naturally have followed filled her once again with that by now familiar *saudade*.

"If only we practiced love the way the faithful practice their religion," Julia read among her father's notes. "Imagine. So many willingly make sacrifices for religion, why not love, which naturally entails the greatest of sacrifices. There were the unhappy sacrifices for love made by Camões which impassioned his poetry; there was the sacrifice made by Inês de Castro and Dom Pedro; or my grandfather Raimundo who sacrificed his inheritance for the love of his wife, Etelvina; those who married secretly, those who lost everything for their love, those who waited, who were left behind; a thousand examples, as many as there are types of loves: Will the other reciprocate? Will the other die first? Will it be a lasting, happy love? Will it be an intensely passionate love, or a calm, quiet one? And so on. To have loved once, will love appear again? Or will it come to pass that after a lifetime one will look back and say it was all an illusion? Far better then to die happy, fully convinced and absorbed by the illusion, believing with heart and soul. The projection or the illusion of oneself meeting and falling in love with the illusions and projections that represent the woman he loves, two illusions entwined, sustaining one and the other.

285

"That leap of faith, that suspension of disbelief as necessary for the belief in God, as it is necessary for the successful creation of anything of genius—the sculptor must see the statue that lies within the stone—is also as essential for love and life," Sebastião wrote. To go off sailing for paradise, to believe in magic, the miracle of love, as it was necessary for the mariners to believe in the Fountain of Youth, the Island of Gold, or the Island of Seven Cities, as for myself to believe in a new island, the Enchanted Island, and the resplendent glories of the past resurrected by taking hold of the myths and legends and charting the unknown in search of the future."

Half-dozing, half-dreaming, Julia returned again and again to the moment of their kiss, their farewell, as if only in remembering Nicolau could she escape the impossible; the touch of his lips against hers; their embrace; the depths of his eyes—eyes in which burned an intensity, a passion equal to her own. Their music. That was the deep well that sustained her.

Perhaps Nicolau was as perplexed, as surprised and pleasantly jarred out of his normal routine as was Julia. After all, when love appears suddenly it can be quite startling, especially at such an unexpected time and place. Who would have guessed that here and now, so far from home (wherever that was), indeed when there were so many ques-

DARRELL KASTIN

tions without ready answers, that this would be the moment when she would fall in love?

• • •

Excerpt from the writings of Sebastião do Canto e Castro:

I awoke to the mournful lament of bells ringing. These weren't the bells of Quebrado calling the faithful to mass. It was the middle of the night, and these bells were ringing in the old village of Quebrado do Caminho.

I turned over, tried to escape the sound, but the lugubrious tolling persisted. A moment later, I heard children singing, quietly, but insistently. I quickly dressed and made my way down the dirt road to the old town. When I'd nearly reached the church I suddenly found myself accompanied by a small ragtag band of children, who more or less led me into the building. A number of people of all ages were gathered there. José Manuel was seated in their midst.

"Welcome, welcome," he said, motioning me to sit down in a chair beside him.

"What's going on here, José?" I looked around in disbelief. "Who are all these people?"

"They are friends. They live here."

"But who, why?"

"Little Mariazinha here has told me that something terrible will happen soon." He nodded at a little wisp of a girl, sickly thin, with haunted eyes. "She is blessed with the abilities to foresee the future."

The girl looked up at me with a ghostly smile. I reached down and patted her head.

"Where are they from?" I asked.

"Most are from Quebrado, some from the other villages, like Santa Luzía, Santo António, São Roque, even as far as Prainha. They are the forgotten ones," he said proudly. "They are the special ones, each of them. Look."

José pointed to one of the adults. An old man with one leg and white hair, seated at the edge of the group, was working with some pieces of wood. I saw that he was assembling a bird. He handed it to a boy who sat nearby. The boy leaped to his feet, petting the bird, holding it carefully in his hands, as if it were real.

"Jorge has made Carlos a new toy," José said. The boy ran around the room with his bird, laughing for joy. There were others, too: one held a

wooden flute, another a puppet.

"These children live here?"

José nodded.

"They roam around singing and ringing bells and playing in the streets of old Quebrado do Caminho? Don't they have homes, go to school; what about parents, families?"

"This is their home," José said. "We are their family. Don't worry, there are several of us here who take care of them. Jorge here not only makes toys for them, but beds and crutches and anything else they need." José nodded at the other adults who were busy with the children. "Agostinho brings them food, Maria Emília brings clothes."

I sat down and in a matter of minutes felt completely at home. The church was filled with warmth, not only from a fire that burned in a wood stove, but the people themselves, who chatted, played and cared for one another. Many of the children were quite serious and grown-up in their manners. After settling in, I noticed things I hadn't seen at first: not only did Agostinho have only one leg, but some of the children had a distant, unfocused gaze in their eyes; one girl carried a strange wooden box around clutched tightly to her chest, and didn't speak; Jorge, the old toy-maker, had a way of working pieces of wood and paper, bits of string and cloth into clever toys: foolish-looking pirates and witches, charming birds and delicate boats, which seemed to have a life of their own, with moving limbs and mouths, eyes that blinked.

"In the days before the earthquake that destroyed Quebrado," José said. "When you rode or walked down the streets you saw one of the children out there waving his arms or standing at attention, or a little girl in rags talking to no one. When the earthquake struck there was panic everywhere. People screamed, ran, crying in all directions. Nobody knew what to do, or where to go. But these children, they knew. They took control when most of the villagers had lost their wits, simply wandering aimlessly in the cold and the rain, many bleeding, hurt.

"People who were injured were brought from their homes. A hospital was set up, roads were cleared, food and water gathered, animals tended to. If it weren't for these children here, there would have been many more deaths."

As José spoke I had a recollection of reading somewhere that often during catastrophes mental patients reacted perfectly rationally and orderly to the situation, without the typical panic and hysteria those people who would be considered normal might exhibit.

"Many of these people have nobody, no family, and no one to take care of them. They have each other, and Agostinho, Maria Emília, myself, and a few others who help out now and then. Not everyone in Quebrado has forgotten what these children have done. They have the animals, and old Quebrado do Caminho. No one else comes here."

The children gathered closely around, and looked at me as if gauging me, looking for some special quality or capacity. I smiled and they smiled back. I was glad they didn't seem to fear me. As far as I could see they were without fear of any kind.

After a few moments some drinks were passed around, tea and juice, as well as fresh rolls and cheese. José said that each of the children had their own story, the old folks, too. "Everyone here has a special story of their own."

I was entranced by this hidden world. Quebrado de Caminho was the poorest village on Pico, if not all the islands. The houses didn't have the luxuries of piped water or electricity, and many of the children went without shoes. Poor women took the boat to Faial, loaded down with baskets of potatoes or whatever else they had managed to grow. They walked the streets barefoot, shouting their wares with all their passion, as if offering earnest entreaties to God, in a plaintive wail so reminiscent of the Middle East. These women returned to Quebrado at the end of the day with their baskets loaded with dirt because Quebrado was so poor they didn't even have the soil in which to grow fruit and vegetables.

I was brought some blankets and set up a place to sleep. Everyone made himself comfortable. Children everywhere in the room settled in for the night, Agostinho and Maria Emília were busy tucking the smaller ones in, and José tended the fire. Then, without warning, the entire room brightened, as if the moon had entered the building. I leaped to my feet.

"Teresa," I said, too loudly. "You, too?" She blushed, smiling, as though pleased by my obvious surprise.

"Yes," José said. "Teresa spends much of her time here, too. She is a favorite among our little ones, though of course the older among us feel the same." It was as though spring had just entered the room. I'd encountered yet another surprise, another mystery of the Azores, as I readied myself to hear the stories in the night of old Quebrado, which, José said, was still referred to by those who knew about it as the Village of Idiots.

. . .

Antonio's eyes gleamed with an unnatural light. However, it wasn't the sunlight reflecting off the surface of the sea that caused the strange effect, as Julia surmised, but finding Teresa's name in his father's notes. There was no mistaking the person his father had described. Nor could Julia see that all the hairs on the back of his neck had risen, and that he breathed over and over the sound of her name: *"Teresa."*

Antonio peered through the crude navigational instruments, as the skull instructed him in their usage. They were unfamiliar, primitive devices, awkward to handle. Though fully functional, they belonged in a museum. As to where they had come from, how they had found their way onto the boat, these questions might have concerned him had he not been more curious about their use, and had he not had other questions on his mind.

Leaning over the prow of the boat, he couldn't explain how and why he saw a figurehead at the bow. He stared at the carved face that turned toward him, a look of melancholy and tenderness, the flowing hair, the ample breasts. Who was she? Did she represent someone—a wife or lover, perhaps, of the man who had carved her image? She seemed so alive, so real. Did her hair blow in the wind? Did she raise an arm that gestured to Antonio, then pointed out to sea?

As if the madness of others were contagious, and spreading—Sebastião's disappearance, Johan's drunken ravings, the skull, and Antonio's odd behavior, now her own—Julia also heard *and* saw things. First the music, then her father's notes, the stories, the new island, Nicolau, strange voices. Delusions. She laughed. Instead of creating something new externally, changing others, indeed changing the world through her music, she had, in effect, changed herself.

She wrote sporadically, in fits and starts, music unlike anything she had ever heard before, orchestral, classical in the beginning, then changing with the introduction of a guitar, an accordion, harmonica, a bagpipe, flutes and drums. A modulation, led by an oboe or clarinet, here, by violins or cellos there, expressing longing, searching, love and loss, and then the notes finding some back route, another change of key, suddenly sounding inevitable, as if that were where the music had been headed all along, since the very first notes.

Antonio felt fainter, as if he were fading. Looking at his surroundings, he wondered how he could be any less real than everything around him? The skull became more life-like, more substantial, its weathered face more defined, as if they were trading places.

He reached out and touched the wood of the mast thick as a tree, and two more, one tall, one shorter, farther aft. The little fishing boat was no more. He was aboard a ship.

He glanced up. Men climbed the rigging, unfurling large sails, the cross of the Order of Christ emblazoned across in red.

A deep, vibrant voice rang out, calling to the sirens, the sea nymphs, to the daughters of the Ocean, and Venus to show the way: "Daughter of the sea foam, mother of Eros, wife of the Vulcan god, guide us to your fair island."

Antonio heard the goddess sing her reply. It wasn't a sound that could be ignored or stopped, not even by Ulysses who plugged his men's ears with wax and lashed himself to the mast to avoid yielding to the spell of the sirens. Even that would have proven useless.

Antonio, the *americano,* the city boy, the young and inexperienced Canto e Castro, who had lived his life ignoring his family's past, and denying his own Portuguese legacy, rose up the rigging, every muscle, every fiber straining for the woman who sang, be she devil or witch, temptress or mermaid, seductress or avenging goddess.

Like the statue said to be carved upon the cliffs on the island of Corvo, of a man on a horse, pointing to the west, Antonio now pointed to the Enchanted Island, the Island of Lovers, to the woman whose song drew him across the sea.

· · ·

Somewhere near-by the local legend of the mermaids is said to have originated. They are supposed to come on moonlit nights, when they lie and sing on the beaches of Santa Maria. Fishermen used to lie in wait for them, and when they sprang out suddenly the mermaids dived instantly into the water. A baby mermaid was left behind, and one of the men adopted her. He "cut off her gills to make breathing possible" and entrusted her to his wife, who brought up this weird being like one of her own children. After a while the scale-covered tail split apart into legs of human shape. She grew up into a fair-haired girl with blue eyes, who was so lovely that a local lad married her, and they had several daughters. Their descendants can still be detected, it is said, by the traces of scales which cling to their wrists.

—*The Azores*, Claude Dervenn, Paris

291

Excerpt from the writings of Sebastião do Canto e Castro:

In a voice that exceeded even the most famous feiticeiras of old in its ability to cast a spell, Maria Teresa spoke in soft, low tones. This young woman possessed a quality long-sought after by alchemists the world over. Had they but known that what was needed to transmute, to alter substances, turning one thing into something else, resided in her voice, if not her heart and soul, they would have flocked to the islands from near and far, each attempting to capture that inexplicable, ethereal magic. For to hear her voice in all its wondrous inflections, its light yet moving timbre, as if each word was a kiss or caress, was to change immeasurably. The sound of her laughter, to hear her recite a poem, or a story, was to be transformed; here was song and poetry, the embers and flames of love, resplendent, as if she were the personification of these elements, or one of the muses.

I gazed at Maria Teresa in the half-light, entranced by the striking, startling beauty of this young woman, who almost made me forget I was an old man. I was barely aware of the actual words she spoke. It was the tone and musicality of her voice that held me. Also, I had a strange feeling of déjà-vu; listening to Maria Teresa's story was so reminiscent, as if I had known the story once long ago. With my eyes closed, I sat hypnotized by her voice and the words she spoke, as they wove their magic:

"Luísa de Fraga removed the dead flowers from the vase and tossed them out. She looked out her window. It was a gloomy day, cloudy, but no rain. 'It would be better, I think, if it did rain,' she said, closing the door behind her as she left her home. She pulled her shawl around her shoulders. It was cold, too, but not too cold. 'No matter.' She walked down the cobbled street to the

Residencial Melo, where she worked, cleaning the rooms after the guests had left, or looking after Senhora de Melo's large number of children, who flowed through and around the building as if they were water-spirits summoned by a surging spring that bubbled without end. Luísa didn't mind the children or their infectious joy and laughter.

"Passing the quay Luísa saw Vasco working on his boat. 'Always working, that one.' He waved and she waved back. 'He is a good man, that Vasco.' Lonely, she thought, alone with his boat, only the sea for company. No wife to come home to.

"Luísa glanced at him again. He was tall and sea-burnt, a handsome man. He was kind and didn't drink like many of the other men. He was married, she thought, not to any woman of flesh and blood, but instead to a dream of distant ports, lured by the seductive waves splashing against the sides of his boat, the secret murmurings of the mysterious ocean, those deep currents through which he expertly navigated his fishing boat. She laughed. Look at me, she thought, romanticizing a man who, after all, was rugged, plain and simple.

"At the residencial *Luísa performed her duties but could only think of the wind and sea, of poor lonely Vasco out there in his boat for many long days at a time; how he could use the touch of a woman; she saw him gathering the nets, hauling in the fish, working on the boat, fighting storms—a solitude as large as the ocean itself.*

"At night, in the most vivid of dreams, she sometimes sailed with him, slept at his side, next to the wheel of his boat, or watched the curling smoke rise from the cigarette in his mouth, his eyes squinting as he read the unfathomable language of the sea.

"That same morning, Vasco stood on the dock waiting to see Luísa walk by, as she did every morning, so he could wave and see her return the gesture. The boat was ready to go and soon he would go to sea to fish. He wouldn't see Luísa for many days.

"He wondered about her. What kind of life did she have? Was she happy? He didn't know how anybody could be happy, alone, stuck here in a tiny village on a tiny island, without a family of her own.

"Vasco dreamed of sailing off to other shores, Luísa at his side—lands where there was more than the familiar taste of sadness and poverty, an empty house, an empty life.

"As Luísa left her home and walked to work, Vasco lifted his arm and

waved, and as she had done hundreds of times, Luísa waved back at him.

"She's a nice girl, he thought, smiling. Vasco wondered why no one around had snatched her up and taken her for a wife. Fools! Too blind to see what was right in front of them.

"Vasco sailed later that day while Luísa worked and the island and the sea seemed even more lonely and forsaken for the fact that neither would see the other.

"For a week and more this separation and its accompanying heaviness lasted. Then Vasco returned to the island, the hull of his boat filled with a fine catch. He thought about how good it would be to spend time in the village.

"He looked forward to waking in the morning, waiting for Luísa to pass by on her way to work. Perhaps he would try to speak to her when she walked back home at the end of the day, to return to that house where she lived all alone since her ailing aunt had died.

"Luísa's aunt had known Vasco's family. She had liked him and consid- ered him a suitable match for her niece, but unfortunately she had died before she could bring the two of them together, while Luísa had spent most of her youth taking care of the old woman.

"Luísa hung the laundry at the residencial, *thinking she could see Vasco's boat in the distance returning from sea.*

"She had missed Vasco, seeing him only from distances that eyes alone could not encompass. She reprimanded herself for allowing such thoughts to distract her from her work. But when she rubbed her eyes and looked again, the boat was still there and getting closer. She wasn't imagining, after all.

"An hour later Vasco's boat lay moored along the quay. His heart raced. He made up his mind finally to walk past Luísa's house. He would conquer his shyness the way he had conquered his loneliness at sea. There were a hun- dred reasons why he might have to go past her house. She might be outside, where maybe she would see him and they could talk. He didn't know what he would say to her, but hoped that he would think of something suitable when the moment arrived.

"He walked down from the dock and looked ahead, toward Luísa's house, as if he might see her there, half-expecting with each quickened beat of his heart that she would appear before his eyes.

"Vasco cut across the shoreline instead of walking inland to the road, hop- ing this way to avoid any curious eyes that might take notice of him. The least little sign would start the old women of the village off with their gossip,

295

and the last thing he wanted was to drag Luísa through that sort of talk.

"The waves burst upon the black rocks, and for a moment Vasco turned his gaze back toward the ocean, for to this man of the sea the roar of the waves were always speaking to him. Its voice spoke of many things: warning of storms, and of treacherous rocks or reefs lying just beneath the waves, telling him where fish were plentiful; old, sad songs of loss and heartbreak, or the joyous chatter of dolphins swimming alongside his boat to keep him company.

"But never before had the waves spoken of what he now saw: a small bright patch of white on one of the rocks where something had apparently washed up. He walked over to investigate.

"Vasco stared at the child in disbelief. Who was she? Where had she come from? Was she alive? She lay curled up on the rock, dressed only in a white dress—no, not a dress, but a plain shift. Her long wet hair hung over her face. He brushed the hair away. She was no more than six or seven years old. And Vasco was sure he had never seen her before.

"He touched the girl to make sure she was still breathing. She was cold, but alive. How could she have survived? She lay asleep, obviously exhausted from her ordeal. Vasco took off his coat and wrapped it around the child. He picked her up and started back toward his boat. He would take her to Doctor Pacheco. Realizing however that Luísa's house was closer, he decided instead to take her there, while he went to locate the doctor.

"He carried the girl across the field. Though drenched, she was light in his arms. Luísa went home for her lunch each day. She would know better than he how best to tend to the child until the doctor arrived.

"Vasco tapped the door with his boot. He could feel the child's soft breathing against his chest. He breathed a sigh of relief when Luísa opened the door.

"'Luísa,' Vasco said. 'Please, where can I put her?'

"Luísa gasped, surprised to see Vasco standing before her, and of course, even more surprised to see a young child in his arms. For a moment she couldn't find her voice.

"'I found her down by the rocks, in the water, half-drowned. She must have just washed up.'

"'Here,' Luísa said, moving out of the doorway to let Vasco inside. 'Who is she?'

"'I don't know. She's not from here. Perhaps she fell from a passing boat. I will leave her with you while I go find Doctor Pacheco.' Vasco set the child

down on the couch.

"Luísa reached down and stroked the girl's forehead. 'She's freezing, Vasco. Go, quickly. I'll take off these wet clothes before she catches her death.'

"Vasco nodded. 'Thank you,' he said awkwardly.

"'Don't thank me,' she said. 'Just hurry.'

"Vasco ran out and went to search for the doctor.

"Luísa pulled off the girl's shift and fetched a dry blanket to put round her. 'Who are you, little one?' she asked. The girl still hadn't awakened. Luísa put her ear to the child's chest. She got up, relieved to hear a heartbeat. She brushed away strands of the girl's hair. 'You poor dear.'

"She went and heated some milk to give to the girl. She hoped Vasco wouldn't be long. She hadn't realized until now, but her own heart was beating very fast.

"While she waited, she gazed upon the child. The girl's mother and father must be worried sick. How it must be to have a child of your own, she thought. After some time the little girl stirred, and opened her eyes. They were dark, nearly black, and quite large. The child slowly sat up and stared at Luísa.

"'Don't be frightened,' Luísa said.

"The child said nothing.

"'What's your name?'

"The little girl looked around the room and again stared silently at Luísa, as though waiting for something or someone.

"'Poor thing, you must be hungry. I'll get you something to eat.'

"Vasco returned in a rush with the doctor, who looked the girl over and pronounced that she was miraculously in satisfactory condition. 'I don't know how she survived,' Doctor Pacheco said before leaving. 'She must swim like a fish.' He laughed, patting the girl's hair.

"Doctor Pacheco promised to return the next day to check up on her. In the meantime they were to keep her warm and well-fed.

"After some time, the child rose out of bed, as if she had merely been resting. Luísa fixed some soup and bread and put out a bowl for Vasco, as well, who watched the child the way any worried father might. 'Can you speak, child?' Luísa asked, after they had eaten.

"The girl did not answer, but seemed revived and perfectly normal in every other way—happy even, as though nothing unusual had happened. She didn't seem sad, or frightened. Neither did she appear anxious to leave, *to go home, wherever home was.*

"'How did you end up in the water?' Vasco asked. 'Did you slip, fall off a boat?'"

"The child looked at them as they spoke and seemed to hear, but made no reply, no gesture to answer their questions. 'Poor baby!' Luísa cried. 'She cannot even speak.'

"Luísa and Vasco sat and quietly looked at one another with an awkward realization that, after dreaming for so long of such a moment, they were alone together for the first time. And they now had this mysterious girl, this gift of the sea, between them, as silent as they each were.

"Vasco finally got up to leave, and said good night.

"'Good night, Vasco,' Luísa said. 'I'll take good care of her.'

"'I know you will,' Vasco said. 'I will stop by tomorrow, if that's all right.'

"'Yes, of course. Until tomorrow.'

"He walked back to his boat, feeling a new sense of belonging. Luísa, too, felt different as she fixed up a place for the girl to sleep beside her own bed. And that night she and Vasco unknowingly shared the same dreams: the three of them happy, together, one family.

"Word quickly went round about the girl. The police on São Miguel and Santa Maria, Terceira, Pico, Faial, São Jorge and Graciosa, Flores and Corvo—indeed all of the islands—were notified, but no one had any report of a missing child.

"The girl became a favorite topic in the cafés and market; how Vasco had found her in his nets, and that she had gills as well as lungs; that she couldn't speak because she spoke only the mysterious language of fish; Senhor Lourenço swore that when she was first found she'd had a tail, that she was nothing less than a mermaid and that he had also seen Vasco cut off the girl's gills in order for her to breathe out of the water and so she wouldn't try to return to the water. The women of the village claimed that her presence was a miracle confirmed by the fact that not only had she survived, but that she had finally brought together Vasco and Luísa, as well as the fact that the girl couldn't talk. 'It's a sign,' they declared, gravely.

"Luísa cared for the child, who stayed with her, for a boat was no place for a little girl. Vasco remained alone on his boat, though he visited every day. He brought the girl gifts from the stores, and sometimes something for Luísa as well, the two of them blushing over the active little girl who sparkled and danced between them. They called her Mariazinha and found that she was

special indeed. She always knew when Vasco was about to leave and when he would return, and when Luísa couldn't find something, Mariazinha would always know where to find it.

"Luísa refused ever to let the girl go near the water, saying that she still carried the secrets of the sea with her, and that at any time the sea might reclaim her, for whenever Luísa kissed her she tasted the ocean. But Mariazinha was not afraid of the sea, and in fact feared nothing at all.

"Still, they never did learn where she had come from. 'Who are you?' Luísa sometimes asked, but the child couldn't answer except to smile, as if such things were unimportant, or beyond explanation.

"Once more Vasco sailed his boat out toward the open sea, waving farewell to little Mariazinha and Luísa, who waved back, until the distance made it impossible to see them any longer.

"He thought about Luísa even more now than before, and she too dreamt of him. After a year, Vasco finally got up the nerve to ask Luísa to marry him. 'It's only right that the girl should have a real family,' he said. Luísa didn't require him to say more than that. 'Yes,' she said. The world around them, though it had never witnessed the tremendous unspoken love these two possessed for one another, yet whispered, 'At long last.' For the love that was never spoken was yet as palpable as the rain or the wind, and evident in the outpouring of love the two showered upon the child.

"The days were more lonely than ever before, and his return that much more joyful, knowing that not only Luísa, but the strange and silent little girl, whose only sound came when she opened her mouth to laugh and Vasco clearly recognized the laughter of waves breaking, were there waiting for Vasco's return.

"And it is said even to this very day that a child is occasionally born in the village who bears the remains of gills and traces of scales upon their wrists, an obvious descendant of the child of the sea."

299

BOOK THREE

Calma

Que costa é que as ondas contam
E se não pode encontrar
Por mais naus que haja no mar?
O que é que as ondas encontram
E nunca se vê surgindo?
Este som de o mar praiar
Onde é que está existindo?

Ilha próxima e remota,
Que nos ouvidos persiste,
Para a vista não existe.
Que nau, que armada, que frota
Pode encontrar o caminho
À praia onde o mar insiste,
Se à vista o mar é sozinho?

Haverá rasgões no espaço
Que dêem para outro lado,
E que, um deles encontrado,
Aqui, onde há só sargaço,
Surja uma ilha velada,
O país afortunado
Que guarda o Rei desterrado
Em sua vida encantada?

Calm

Of what coast do the waves speak
That cannot be found
No matter how many ships set out to sea?
What do the waves encounter
That never appears in sight?
This sound of waves crashing
Where can it be?

Island near and remote
That we hear persistently
But to sight does not exist.
What ship, what armada, what fleet,
Can find the route
To the beach of an insistent sea,
If there's only sea within sight?

Will there be tears in space
That open to another side,
And that finding one of these
Here, where there is only seaweed,
A hidden isle rises,
Blessed country
That protects the exiled King
In his enchanted life?[10]

—Fernando Pessoa

CHAPTER I

God gave the Portuguese a small country as cradle but all the world as
their grave.

—Padre António Vieira

. . .

Anyone especially observant might have noticed a stranger lurking
about the island of Faial. This man has spent several days roaming, first
in Horta, then in Praia do Almoxarife, taking the boat to Pico, stopping
by the police station, the cafés, the waterfront, watching the *residencial,*
shadowing the places where until recently Julia and Antonio could be
seen. As so often happens in these matters, while he is obviously observing or inquiring into someone else's activities—perhaps in the role of
detective, or police inspector—at the same time he is unaware of just
how much suspicion he himself is arousing. Then again, as heroes and
defenders so often come to resemble those whom they fight, perhaps
he is some underworld figure, a criminal who, because of the thin and
blurred line that separates good and evil, only appears to be a policeman—so those who observe him think.

A handful of the curious islanders watch the man's comings and
goings with keen interest.

"Look at him, will you? Like a cat stalking its prey."

"He'll soon have his mouse, don't you think?"

"Or rat. I'd sure hate to be in that person's shoes."

He soon identifies himself as a detective, sure enough, showing off his badge with a well-practiced ease, a casual disdain. And just who might this detective be, this stranger who has stepped onto the stage so late in the action? Someone hired by Julia's family? Mateus, perhaps, who uses his paltry savings, or a representative of the mainland authorities alarmed by the lack of progress of the island police. Or is he the author who, like Alfred Hitchcock, has decided to make a cameo appearance in his own book? Of course I wouldn't venture to say, but perhaps offer a wink of complicity, although our detective might very well take offense at finding himself so ill-used. Either he thinks he moves unnoticed, unaware that he is watched and commented on by those observing him, or he is unconcerned, perhaps somehow using the attention to his own advantage. He goes about his business, a thoroughly modern professional, making inquiries, mentally taking notes of potentially useful information. Like a shadow, he reveals nothing, keeping everything—his thoughts, opinions—close to the vest.

He is tall, six-foot-one, give or take an inch or two, though it's his thin build, more than anything, his thick-soled shoes, his road-weary gaunt face, and an undernourished look, that gives him the appearance of a clothed telephone pole more than a man of flesh and blood.

He stations himself at a number of locations on Faial and Pico, and speaks to a variety of people, witnesses: "What did you see?" "When did you last see Senhor Antonio do Canto e Castro? Or his sister, Julia?" "What did you notice—anything strange or unusual?" "What did he say?" "What do you know regarding Senhor Sebastião do Canto e Castro?"

Much to the consternation of those he speaks to, he doesn't use a tape recorder or even take notes of what is said, for the one thing these people do not know about our mysterious detective is that he has an uncanny memory for remembering everything: who said what, when, where and how. The slightest detail—the make of a car, a gun, the fine particulars of clothing—nothing escapes his observant eye.

However, it should be pointed out that the detective spends much of his time sitting alone in the cafés, drinking cup after cup of undiluted coffee.

"He is thinking, pondering the facts of the case," some say.

"He is stumped," say others. "He hasn't got a clue."

"He's waiting, look at him, like a hawk, watching."

"Waiting for what?"

"How should I know? I'm no detective."

Of course, the inspector—Leonardo Brum, we should tell you, is the name he goes by—chain-smoking cigarettes and looking frightfully unfit, likely suffering either indigestion or a stomach ulcer, questions Maria Josefa and João Correia at the *residencial*. There, he finds himself in the position of being asked ten questions for his every one by Maria, who volunteers that Antonio is a good young man, quiet and well-mannered; Julia Canto e Castro, younger still, is reckless, troubled by her father's disappearance. At the same time she wants to know, "Has Antonio done something?" "Is Julia all right?" "Do you know where they've gone to?" "Are you going to arrest them?" "Is Antonio suspected of a crime?" "Where is Sebastião?"

Oddly, it is João Correia who first suggests the new island as Julia's possible purpose in sailing off into *O Mar Tenebroso*—The Sea of Darkness.

"What do you mean?" Leonardo Brum says.

"Only that there are times when circumstances may drive someone to do something she might never have thought possible," João says, warming up to the subject, gesturing with his hands, his voice rising in pitch and volume.

Leonardo Brum nods, distractedly. *"She?"* he says.

João, too, nods. "Just think how during a fierce battle sometimes a soldier, never noted for his bravery, will suddenly display superhuman daring and make a hero of himself."

"Yes, yes, of course. So what?" Senhor Brum says. "What has any of this to do with Julia or Antonio do Canto e Castro? They haven't gone to fight a battle."

"No, no, of course not. At least, I don't think so. But now, with her father's disappearance under mysterious circumstances, and Julia's return to these islands, the earthquakes and the new island, with all this, and reading about their ancestors, the history—isn't it just possible that as a result of everything, Julia felt or heard something she couldn't ignore?"

"Don't you mean, Antonio?" Leonardo Brum said.

"No, if they've gone to sea, it was Julia, not Antonio, who decided to go."

"But a woman?" Brum says. "A young woman. Would she have—"

"You don't know Julia," João said.

"I don't see how—"

"Think of it," João Correia blurts out, unable to contain his excitement, though he continues to speak in his slow thoughtful manner. "The startling experience of finding one's true self, suddenly discovering she is a daughter of the islands, of all the Castros and Cantos who preceded her, that the person she was in America cannot be the same person here on the Azores."

Leonardo Brum's only reaction is to raise a single querying eyebrow. Brum later speaks with José Manuel, who is uncharacteristically reticent. He only tells Leonardo Brum the facts of Julia's arrival on the islands, her visits to the building on José's property, and her abrupt departure. Brum peers into the room used by Sebastião. He takes everything in with a glance, touches a stack of papers and books here and there, and quickly closes the door behind him.

Senhor Brum then speaks with Maria dos Santos. She showers him with glowing words. "She's a remarkable girl," Maria says. "Beautiful and strong, sympathetic—a jewel. And such a voice!" Leonardo cannot altogether hide his growing interest in this woman who has recently and recklessly departed from the island, in the company of two unsavory characters, it seems, and a brother outfitted like some criminal.

"She is certainly in danger, but may yet find her way safely through." Maria dos Santos says.

"What makes you so certain she is in danger?"

Maria dos Santos tisk-tisks the detective. "We are, each of us, in danger," she says, as though speaking to a small child, "no matter what we do. Even if we do nothing."

Leonardo Brum nods, scratching his head. He finds this woman's gaze quite unnerving, to say nothing of her voice, which comes off like honey, but has the effect of an intoxicant. He prides himself on his ability to read people, but Maria dos Santos is nebulous, all wet paint, swirling every which way, impossible to pin down. He takes her statement about doing nothing personally.

"Especially when we go searching for the past in uncharted territory," Maria adds cryptically. "Besides, she's out there on a boat, who knows what may happen? Do they have boats in California?"

"Yes, yes, of course," Senhor Brum replies, frowning, disconcerted by Maria's rather idiotic question.

"You may find yourself in danger, too, though not from a threat you would expect to be faced with," Maria dos Santos says. Again, he prickles with her words. But before he can ask what she means by that, she adds, "Did I tell you that Julia first came here because she heard voices? She liked my garden. These flowers and birds are the best judge of a person."

"Thank you, senhora. I assure you we shall do our best." Leonardo doesn't bother to ask her what she meant by voices, or why she had mentioned her garden.

Leonardo Brum speaks much longer, and we might add more successfully, with Nicolau dos Santos. Maria dos Santos, Brum decides, is not an altogether reliable witness. He determines she is an eccentric, old windbag quite capable of confusing what she imagined with what has occurred, a daydream with reality, her over solicitousness lending an air of exaggeration to her words. While most people are guarded and say too little, she says too much, clouding the issue with superfluous information and nonsense.

Nicolau, on the other hand, he notes, is responsive and clear-headed; he answers a question with simple statement, facts, not embellishments. Nicolau tells Leonardo Brum all he wants to know about Julia. Brum appears to have forgotten about Antonio. He carries photographs of both, but it is the picture of Julia he gazes at repeatedly, holding it in his sweaty hands. He responds to talk of Julia with a quickness of step and speech, a sort of clipped movement to his gestures. He suffers from an ungovernable nervousness in relation to attractive women, which unfortunately also causes him to sweat profusely.

Leonardo is a clandestine poet in his off hours. He reads voraciously and dabbles at his art, sometimes with pleasure, more often with a wistful regret, a common enough condition among those who wish they had more talent or less of a desire to pursue that talent.

He feels what he calls "a poetic response" to nature, to beauty, to life and love, to their intensity and their appalling intransigence, and often feels compelled to write as a result. "So why is it I am not a great poet?" he asks, time after time, convinced that it will be the first question he will ask if he makes it to heaven. If it were only so simple that an appreciation and attraction for a scene of pristine nature or a beautiful young woman could produce a brilliant poem!

He observes Nicolau's concern for Julia's safety. "Aren't you going to search for her?" Nicolau asks.

Senhor Brum responds in a vague, non-committal manner. "We will

309

do what we can. What did Julia Canto e Castro discuss with you?"

Nicolau recounts his conversations and activities with Julia. He tells Senhor Brum that Julia had told him relatively little concerning her father. "She spent much of her time reading," he says.

"Did she ever say anything to you about any conjectures she might have made as to what happened to her father?" Leonardo asks.

"No. Mostly we discussed other things," Nicolau says. Senhor Brum again raises his eyebrow, which effectively dispenses with the need for speech. "We discussed music, songs and poetry," Nicolau says, before the detective can imply anything.

"Poetry?" Leonardo says eagerly, leaning closer. His eyes sparkle and his smile grows wider.

"Yes, Camões, Quental, Pessoa, mostly," Nicolau says, noting the inspector's sudden increased interest with more than a little surprise.

"Ah, yes, our greatest poets," Leonardo says, shaking his head and becoming more animated with the mere mention of poetry. He savors the surprise his reaction engenders. He is used to people assuming a detective would be interested in reading nothing beyond police manuals and the like. Brum asks himself if perhaps Julia and Nicolau are lovers. Aside from being a detective and a lover of poetry, he is, is oddly enough, a romantic at heart, not that he would admit to such. It is merely that he perceives evidence of romance when it lingers the way a sensitive person can detect the scent of a perfume long after the person wearing it has left the room.

Julia, Brum thinks, is an attractive young woman, intelligent besides, and this Nicolau, being good-looking and sensitive might have won her with his charm; there is always something alluring about the foreigner. Or perhaps with some particular artistic gifts he might possess: poetry? On the other hand, one could hardly blame him for being seduced by the charms of Julia. She possesses a strong heart, he surmises, a thirst for life and strength of spirit. He imagines an air of quiet sensuality, some-thing nebulous, like the mists that cling to certain places on the islands, a touch of mystery. Gazing into her eyes, one would see fires banked and capable of erupting into a conflagration. Ah, *Paixão*, he mutters to himself. He can only wonder what her voice is like, what else he could learn if only he could hear her sing.

Leonardo pushes these thoughts aside. There'll be time enough for further inquiries later.

. . .

Nothing is created in a vacuum. Ideas find their own creators. Great books, like great discoveries or inventions or great truths, await the moment they are uncovered, revealed to the awaiting world. No new idea, no dream, is thought or dreamt alone. No story is created from nothing, but is born of a coupling with many others. Several inventors often within days, weeks or months complete the same invention irrespective of one another; all discoveries are the same, never wholly independent. It is no less true for lives that touch and are built anew, yet connected by and to others. Two people on opposite sides of the world can simultaneously strive for the very same point, the same goal, ignorant of one another and thus attain some strange sort of union, much in the same way that two people from different times can also aim for the same thing, the same moment and place.

—Sebastião do Canto e Castro

. . .

"I return to the beginning, the past, to the source, to remember what I have so long since disremembered." The moonless night was too dark for Antonio to see who spoke, whether it was the skull or the man he had seen earlier, or rather the beginnings of a man, who had taken the skull's place; still, he stared deeply into the darkness from where the voice emanated.

"I cannot be responsible for what others forced me to do. Yet, I saw her, I, who never paid any heed to any of the human lives the fates toyed with, something about *her* made me feel different. For the first time, I wanted to help her, wanted to save her from their planned ghastly fate. I questioned their choices, hinted that they were indeed jealous, that her beauty and the love she and her lover shared made them envious, made them hate her."

This talk of a beautiful woman led Antonio to envision Teresa, as the ship plowed through the waves and the bright pinpoints of light above, from one world to another.

Julia, who stood nearby, felt a presence, an interested intelligence in everything around her: the boat in which she sailed had become imbued with life, as if it were a sea creature that carried her purposefully toward some obscure destination. The ocean, too, as it watched, gesturing, as if to say, I make an unspoken agreement with all who travel across my vastness; those who fail to live up to their end of the bargain, I claim, others I allow to reach a safe harbor. The sky, the moon, with its pale, mournful eye, the stars in their remote station, and the blazing sun, all gazed down like spectators awaiting the outcome of a quest or challenge, as the gods peering down from Mount Olympus had watched Odysseus through his many trials and tribulations.

The air changed, altered by a wind that blew from the east, a blast of air off the Saharan deserts. Sand and the dust from the bones of count-less dead Moors and Portuguese soldiers, carried hundreds of miles by the winds to seed the sea and the islands. Perhaps, too, there was a shift in the currents, for the ship changed course, and the water also changed, from a deep, dark blue, to an emerald-green, to gray, and now as clear as spring water. Time itself changed, performed invisible, yet perceptible aberrations, and contortions slipping into a new shape and design.

With these unknown influences and unseen forces at work, Julia gazed up to see the stars and planets. No longer merely distant dots illu-minating the firmament above, but three-dimensional participants, the apex of a triangle of which she too was a part, a new geometry. It was as if everything that occurred in the external world had its counterpart in her body and mind. She didn't stop to ask how the boat was no longer a boat, but a *Galeão, or Nau*—a sailing ship, from centuries past—or how she felt comfortable on the vessel, as if she had spent her life aboard ship, or how she knew the winds, and the seas, through which they sailed— all this was inexplicable.

Looking to where in his dreams he'd spoken to a skull, Antonio saw a sailor, older, taller, more sea-worn and life-weary than he could have expected to see. He was relieved to find that neither the sea nor the rising moon was visible through the man—disconcerted that he half-expected to see such things. How all this had transpired, or whether this was how everything really and truly was, and what had been before was merely a passing apparition, he wasn't able to say. He simply gazed at the masts and sails, cannons and decks, anchors and coils of rope, and felt oddly reassured by what he saw.

"Who are these ghosts?" he asked the old mariner, solid, flesh and blood, who stood beside him. The crew moved noisily as they performed their tasks, climbing the rigging, hauling in the sails, readying the cannons and scanning the horizon.

"They are men who seek far-off places," the old man replied. "They will take us to the Enchanted Isle. They are our only hope."

"I'm prepared for whatever comes," Antonio said, aware of a sudden newness, a *nowness* in which he existed with the sea, the air around him, the island pulling him closer to its shore.

It was difficult to distinguish the old sailor's murmurings from the cries and screams of the wind, the sound of the waves, the ship, and the crew, the sounds of numerous other voices, some near, others more remote.

Antonio read Sebastião's notes, then passed them to Julia who studied them, as she shut out what was taking place around her. "Let the Church explain away the religious figurines which Frei Álvaro de Castro, the grandson of Álvaro Pires de Castro, had made," she read, "each of them bearing the same woman's face, so melancholy, like the one in *Penha Garcia,* wearing the crown of Portugal upon her head, and at her breast a small child; the church may call this sculpture *Nossa Senhora do Leite*—Our Lady of Milk—when in fact she represents Inês de Castro with her son, Dom João, the rightful heir to the Portuguese throne."

The sea in front of the boat churned and bubbled violently. Stray wisps of mist spiraled, rising from the sea like the plumes blown from the blowholes of a thousand whales. A gigantic, bellowing monstrosity rose suddenly from the waves, while Antonio stared, frozen in fear, unable to speak or shout. Adamastor, the creature Camões depicted in *Os Lusíadas,* guardian of the watery sea, the towering personification of *O Cabo Das Tormentas*—The Cape of Storms—one of the giant sons of Earth, brother of Enceladus and Briareus, who prophesied hostile winds, raging tempests, and agonizing deaths to those who dared to follow Vasco da Gama in sailing around the Cape, towered above the floundering ship.

Adamastor was fierce and hideous in appearance: a drenched, scraggly beard mingled with seaweed, lengthy strands of sea-soaked hair flowing in the breeze, eyes sunk deep in that horrid face. Its expression was all malignancy: yellow teeth, larger than the masts of the ship; a mouth as deep and black as the deepest pits of Hell itself. It stirred the waters around the boat, sent waves crashing every which way.

The monster raised a powerful arm that dwarfed the ship. Antonio watched in horror, as the giant's hand, clenched in an enormous fist,

313

was about to smash the boat to splinters. All was lost. Its massive arm rose slowly into the air, but though the hand was poised to strike it did not fall. Instead, it pointed with one finger away into the distance, its mouth opened wide in a terrifying black yawn, if not to speak, perhaps to swallow the boat and all aboard. Then, from its mouth there came an ear-shattering roar, like a thousand waves crashing at once.

The man at Antonio's side continued to speak—oblivious to the monstrosity—calling upon the nine muses: "Calliope, Erato, Euterpe, Melpomene, Thalia, Clio, Urania, Polyhymnia, Terpsichore. Come, daughters of Zeus, one Muse for each island."

There were no yells or cries from the crew. Antonio glanced at his sister, who bent over her music and Sebastião's writings as if she hadn't seen the monster.

"We seek the tenth island, the Island of the Fates," the man shouted, as if he caught glimpses of the muses' shy visages peering out from the splash of waves, the sea form, as if at any moment they might rise up and reveal themselves. "Help us reach the Enchanted Isle!"

Adamastor, now mute, slowly sank back below the surface of the ocean, its arm still pointing as it disappeared beneath the sea.

· · ·

By 1500, and as early as 1498, Gaspar Corte-Real had sailed from the Azores to the New World, landing on the coast of Newfoundland. Gaspar returned to the New World with several ships but was never heard from again. Gaspar's brother, Miguel, married to Isabel de Castro, disappeared in 1501, after going off to search for his brother. Vasco Corte-Real was the surviving brother. King Manuel refused to allow Vasco to search for his brothers, unwilling to lose yet another member of their illustrious family.

This same year, Pedro Álvares Cabral, married to yet another Isabel de Castro, became the official discoverer of Brazil. Isabel was the daughter of Constança de Albuquerque, the sister of Afonso de Albuquerque. Both Afonso and Constança were the grandchildren of Guiomar de Castro, who was, in turn, the granddaughter of Álvaro de Castro, Inês's brother.

It was this persistent idyll—evoked by the names of ships lost upon the seas down through the ages, and enlivened by tales of remote islands and strange, unknown continents—the thought not that the grass might be greener, but might well be strands of spun gold. It was of such stuff that men's dreams were woven, and heaven forbid someone they knew should be enjoying favors from which they were themselves excluded. It was this that led men to seek—creatures of the deep, storms, boiling seas and other dangers be damned.

—Sebastião do Canto e Castro

. . .

Leonardo Brum ponders the dates of both Julia's and Antonio's arrival on the islands. He again questions Maria Josefa. "Why does a young woman like Julia Castro leave her family and come to the island alone?"

"Because she is too much like her father, Senhor Canto e Castro," Maria Josefa says, as if the answer if obvious.

He nods. Impetuous, he jots down mentally. "She knows her own mind," he mutters. "But why didn't her brother come with her? Or another member of the family?"

Maria Josefa shrugs. "She's always been an independent girl. She always does what she wants to do, that girl. *Teimosa*—stubborn," she adds, shaking her head in disapproval.

Our intrepid detective studies the facts before him, examining them from one angle, then another. What is missing? What is inferred? How do the pieces of the puzzle fit together, and where does the trail of possibilities lead? Solution, he knows, is quite often a matter of perspective, the right approach, of not blinding oneself to the possibilities. The trail of familial history, of a vanished father, missing villagers and boats, and now a missing daughter and son. Could they have all gone mad? And interspersed throughout: earthquakes and volcanoes, a new island rising from the ocean, strange supernatural occurrences, a ghost ship, a siren, as if all of nature were somehow involved in the plot.

Various people in the cafés and elsewhere are quick to tell him about Antonio's strange appearance and behavior, of Julia's recklessness, not to mention their suspicions of Johan who they say likely murdered the others. Many recount Sebastião's idiosyncrasies, accompanied by the inevitable: *Tal pai, tal filho*—Like father, like son. Still, these accounts are somewhat tempered by Nicolau's insistence that he saw nothing at all strange or unusual in Julia's behavior. However, Senhor Brum muses, if he does indeed love her, would he not be blind to these idiosyncrasies? What others see as odd, he may see as nothing less than charming and endearing.

"What next?" Brum asks. He attempts to put himself in Julia's place. What would I do, where would I go if I were in her shoes? Would a woman in love leave behind Nicolau dos Santos, the object of her love, he wonders. But, then perhaps Julia had guessed, put two and two together and arrived at a logical place in which to find Sebastião do Canto e Castro.

It is this possibility that disturbs Leonardo Brum. For, if Julia had simply gone to one of the other islands, why take a small boat? Why not merely take a plane or one of the *lanchas,* which would have taken her with much less difficulty, expense and discomfort?

Unless, of course, the place where Julia thought she might find her father was the new island that was causing so much trouble. Leonardo Brum lights another cigarette and scratches his head.

"A young woman who takes command of a boat and sails into the unknown," he mutters. *"Mystifying."* Yes, that was all he needed, for these fool *americanos* to go and get themselves killed—perhaps, father, son and daughter. What a mess that would be.

The new island, after all, would be susceptible to volcanic eruptions, or sinking back beneath the sea. A catastrophe!

Perhaps, yet another visit with Nicolau dos Santos would be in order.

Many a tourist has had the tranquillity of his quiet stroll down the Avenida da Liberdade in Lisbon disturbed by viewing the mosaic memorial to "The Discoverer of America" commemorating not Columbus, but the voyage of João Vaz Corte-Real, twenty years earlier. Many an American has been surprised to learn that the first European settlement in North America was not that of the English in North Carolina or Virginia, not even that of the Spanish in Florida, but that of the Portuguese at Ingonish in Nova Scotia. Many a Canadian has been amazed to hear that the laconic and disappointed Portuguese expression 'ca nada' ('there is nothing here') gave form to the name of his nation.

The Secret Discovery of Australia, Kenneth Gordon McIntyre
Medindie, South Australia, 1977

. . .

At times, the sailor—tanned by the sea, bearded, scarred, tattooed, pierced, and clothed as befitted a sailor—although still evoking the skull with his ringing voice, kept Antonio entranced by reciting tales culled from the vaults of its ancient memories, as if this sea voyage had awakened him from a long stupor; even Julia would stop reading or composing, her head tilted to one side, as if to hear better what was easily lost amid the wind and waves, the shouts and curses of the men, the creaking of the ship:

"In a kingdom far far away, many years ago, there was a scribe who wrote at the whim of the three princesses whom he served. They lived on an island, which is no more; an island where it was always spring, and where grew a prodigious quantity and variety of foods. An enchanted isle, for the spell was never broken; its tranquility unmarred by boredom, or the cruel passage of time.

"Here the three sisters, goddesses who reigned over the island, *as moiras*—the Fates, wove, spun, and clipped the lengths of threads and cloth wherein they depicted the fate of men's lives: who should live, who should die, who should find wealth, and who should toil and struggle without success. And in order to record what they had decided, they had their scribe write out the stories they wove. How was he to know that the game they played was deadly serious? He was merely a lowly chronicler who did as he was told and nothing more, who wished only to faithfully document the stories he heard.

"He no longer remembered how he had come to the island, for those who remained drank from a spring like the River Lethe and thus forgot their past, the lives they had left behind. The sisters never told the scribe how they came up with their tales of wars, intrigues, murders, love affairs, adventures, countless heroes and villains. Perhaps they dreamt them. What was clear was that one sister decided to favor this person or that, even as another sister became angry with these people in this land and wished to punish them, And in this way they competed with one another, for it is only natural that one finds jealousy among sisters—even goddesses.

"Like all storytellers they had their favorite characters, and those whom they disliked. They created stories that inevitably befell each of these unknowing souls. Their plots meant nothing to the scribe. What did it matter to him the fate of people so far away, of countries so remote, as to seem from another time altogether, which they were? For on their island, there was no time. What would these people's lives mean to him, he who served the Fates, even if these sisters saw fit now and then to bring one of these foreigners to their shore?

"Let them have their adorers: What goddess could do without subjects to admire them, those who serve as a mirror, fawning over their matchless beauty, bathing them in ceaseless adulation?

"Perhaps a ship drifted by chance upon the island, saving the men from a watery grave. It's possible the sisters had no part in bringing men there. But I don't think it likely. They were, after all, maidens without men to call husbands, and what maiden does not like to hear now and then that she is the most desirable among all women—even if their flatterers are mere mortals? Then again, who better than mortals to play and toy with?"

· · ·

There are particular points that contain their own time, where time and events converge, where the normal laws of nature that govern our world no longer apply—or, if they still apply do so in a modified manner, one we would find ourselves unable to explain.

Such a spot would appear to lie among the Azores islands between the islands of São Miguel, and Terceira, at least with the advent of the uprising of the bank of Dom João de Castro, which, breaking through the surface of the waters, has created new problems for modern physicists as pertains to the laws of time and space; for at this one particular spot on the map, past, present and future become a brief, flickering instant which unaccountably repeats like a skip in time.

319

· · ·

The ancient charts and maps Julia studied depicted a different world. They showed the New World as yet indistinct, the northernmost part of North America named after Azorean sailors, Labrador, named after the Azorean explorer, João Fernandes Lavrador, Terra Corte-Real, named for the Corte-Reals, or Terra Portugalense, and the seas between Europe and the American continents full of strange islands.

She scanned the seas ahead, as if one of the islands shown on the maps might materialize, and in the ever-changing mists, coming out of a sudden squall, or light drizzle, strange shapes did appear. Now and again she saw fins, a tail, or arms, even what must have been flowing hair, sometimes red, sometimes blond, or darker, tricks the light and water played on her eyes.

In the warm, liquefied night, a murmur, wail or cry. Now and then the specter of an island rose from the depths, first here, then vanished, then again, there—elusive, always just beyond reach, on the borders of sight, the ship always following in pursuit.

Julia stared long and hard at the sea, at the sky, and asked, "Who am I, where have I come from, what strange destiny am I fulfilling?"

As if picking up on her musings, Antonio questioned the man who stood beside him: "Tell me again, where are we going?"

"We sail to find your destiny." As if to convince Antonio that all was right and no treacheries were afoot, the man spoke again. "The island is not far, and there a goddess, one of the Fates, a woman like no other—as they say, a place of dreams."

. . .

Senhor Brum again calls on Nicolau dos Santos. He is moved vicariously through Nicolau's descriptions of his outings with Julia, their conversations, and moments together. He sighs frequently, convinced that Julia is the type of woman one doesn't often meet. No, he thinks, life is instead too often a matter of the commonplace, of settling for second best.

Leonardo Brum questions Nicolau about Julia's intentions, suggesting she might have let slip a word or two concerning why she had arranged to take a boat, where she had intended to sail to, etc.

"No, Julia never said anything to me about sailing anywhere," Nicolau says.

Does he feel slighted or hurt, Brum wonders. "And nothing about a boat?"

Nicolau shakes his head.

"What about the new island?"

"Oh, she mentioned it. That it was strange how there may be a tenth Azorean island, how it had risen before, long ago, she said."

Senhor Brum shifts gears. He tries an indirect tactic, a subtle maneuver to discover the true nature of the relationship between Julia and Nicolau. Even before he can get the words out, he begins to blush. "I assure you," he says, "I have only the welfare of this young woman in mind. I don't wish to pry, of course, into matters which may or may not be pertinent, but you see in my position how am I to know what is and what isn't important in the case. Perhaps there are things you may not wish to divulge . . ."

And the beet-faced man, asking the question, or rather making these statements, looks up to see Nicolau too is blushing. He doesn't need to inquire further, some declarations being loudest and clearest without the use of words. In order to diffuse the various shades of embarrassment, he again steers the conversation elsewhere: "Did you exchange anything, books, papers?"

"Only some poems," Nicolau says. "Pessoa."

"Which poems?"

"Those in *A Mensagem—The Message.*"

"Ah, yes. 'The Portuguese Sea,' 'The Last Ship,' 'The Symbols.'"
Nicolau nods, smiling.

"Do you think Julia or her father believed in them?"

"In what?"

"The legends? This Hidden One? The Fifth Empire?"

"I don't know," Nicolau says. "Is that what people are saying?"

"Yes, a madness, that the daughter followed in the father's footsteps."

"She did tell me once, when the island first surfaced, that she would like to see it for herself," Nicolau said. "But after that she never mentioned going there."

"Ah, so perhaps she had to choose, the new island, or the Enchanted Isle."

The island is a metaphor. We are each of us no less than an island in a sea of   *323*
humanity—at the same time an island that contains its own internal sea—
upon an island adrift in the great uncharted cosmos.

—Sebastião do Canto e Castro

. . .

The three sisters, *As Moiras*—the Fates, in whose hands lay human destiny, lived on the Enchanted Island. Clotho, the youngest, spun the thread of life; her sister, Atropos, wound the thread and determined the length of life; and, Laquesis, the eldest, cut the thread, thus providing an end to each life. These are the names the Greeks gave them. Few, if any, know their true names, and to utter those names aloud is to possess more knowledge than is safe for any mortal to possess, some particular knowledge often being more dangerous than ignorance.

The Fates were the daughters of Zeus and Hera, or Jupiter and Juno, as the Romans called them. They were known as the daughters of Night, of Darkness, the first divine generation, which belonged to the elemental forces of the universe. Maybe they were the daughters of Erebus and Nyx, instead, who like Jupiter and Juno, were not only brother and sister, but husband and wife as well, for with so many gods, as it frequently happens with humans, sometimes we can't be sure of the parentage. Like King Fernando and his sister Beatriz, the daughter of Inês de Castro, they may have simply found one another impossible to resist, and perhaps the fraternal connection mattered little. King Fernando of

Portugal, called *O Formoso*—The Handsome—was noted, aside from his good looks, for his amorous adventures and his fondness for waging war against his neighbor, Castile. Perhaps he was driven by a desire to emulate Jupiter, for being king of a country—and a wealthy one at that, for the peaceful reign of King Pedro, his father, had filled the coffers of the country—perhaps he could not but aspire to the next highest achievement, namely that of a god. It may have been only the loud protests, the outrage of the court and the clergy, and his inability to obtain a papal dispensation allowing him to marry his half-sister that finally convinced Fernando to temper his passion for Beatriz and marry her off instead to the Count of Albuquerque, Don Sancho, brother of King Enrique II of Castile.

The Fates cared nothing for who was related to whom, who was a beautiful princess, who was a lowly servant. Given their playful, mischievous nature, this only made their tasks more enjoyable and interesting. Thus they ever outdid their own complicated machinations.

They wove their magic charms, sang, danced and played in their garden, which comprised the entire island, not merely its pristine beaches, and its rolling hills and meadows, but its forests and mountains, too. The few mortals who now and again chanced to find themselves delivered from imminent peril and certain death, who awoke from their troubles on the shores of this hidden island, went about as if in a dream from which they did not wish to awaken, and the rest of the world, the world of poverty and pestilence, of war and death, of pain and suffering was so far removed as to no longer exist, lost in the realm of another lifetime, another world.

It was said that those who drank from the Fountain of the Muses, whose waters poured forth from the very heart of the island, received eternal life, for no one ever died here; they received as well a curtain of forgetfulness that blotted out the past. Although considering what occurred next this may be merely myth.

The island was said to drift, though it rarely came into view of any other land, and then only for a glimpse so fleeting that it left those few souls wondering if indeed they had seen anything. The Fates enjoyed revealing the island to a ship desperate for sight of any land, before the mists closed in and shrouded the island from view.

The three sisters were far more beautiful, alluring and enchanting than any mortal women. Men gazed upon them as if they were the sun or the distant stars, which while lovely to behold, could be possessed by no man.

However, one day a man came to the island aboard a ship that had drifted, lost for many weeks. Most of the crew had died, and those who hadn't were quickly revived, elated to waken from their terrible nightmare in such a wondrous place, though most were certain they had indeed died and been cast upon the shores of the Garden of the Hesperides, or some equally pleasant paradise that was said to exist somewhere in the uncharted Sea of Darkness.

The captain of this ship was a proud, arrogant man. He observed all that his men did, and shared in the prodigious bounty—fruits, nuts, fish and delicacies, all in abundance and unlike any they had ever known; they bathed and drank in the life-bestowing properties of the water, and gazed upon the incomparable beauty of the three goddesses.

Their captain did all this, yet at the same time, at the back of his mind he began to hatch a terrible plan, a plan he shared with no one, roaming instead over the entire island, speaking with all who lived there, including a number of his own countrymen whom he found there. They told him they had been brought there in the loving arms of sirens, or that they had clung to a log or a plank from a wrecked ship and washed up on the shores of the isle—perhaps they spoke truthfully, or they said what they thought he wished to hear. They claimed they had not aged. Some professed to have lived there many years. They also informed him that no one ever died or suffered any illness. He merely listened and worked stealthily to put his plan into action, until the day when he finally proclaimed himself king and absolute ruler of the island.

It was then that everyone learned the awful truth, how in order to rule over the island as king, he saw fit to take a queen for himself, and none other than Clotho, who for all intents and purposes we could just as easily name Cordelia or Ophelia, or simply, Maria, for Clotho of course was not what she would have called herself. He seduced the youngest of the sisters, perhaps because it was she who spun the very threads of life, but also, you might assume, because she was said to be the prettiest. Don't think such things cease to matter just because one is a goddess. These three women were the fiercest of competitors.

The terrified islanders learned that not only had the spell been broken by this impetuous man, whereby the Fates could no longer guide

325

mankind's destiny, but that the island itself would now sink to the bottom of the sea, where it would remain for eternity, rising to the surface only once every year, and then for only one day.

The captain, who had proclaimed himself king and defiled the goddess, saw in a flash how everything on the island was changing, how quickly their paradise was withering; he sought to take the sister he had chosen as queen and escape.

The Fates, however, either to avenge the abduction of their sister or perhaps because the other two were jealous that he had chosen Clotho, or Maria of the Fates, and not them, it matters little, prevented this from happening. Instead, they left him chained to a bald outcropping of rock, where he lay cursing and shouting even as the island began to sink beneath the waves.

One man, it is known, did escape, though how and why no one can say with any certainty, for some strange power was known to prevent anyone from ever leaving the island, perhaps as a safeguard against bringing others, since it could hardly remain a paradise if everyone and their brother were to show up. Once word got round they would come in droves, from all corners of the known world, and overnight there would not just be overcrowding to deal with, but pollution, deforestation, development. How many times have we seen it happen? Rivalries for one thing and another would naturally follow: I chose that tree, that's my cave, my strip of beach, my lover. Before you know it, what was once a beautiful paradise is transformed into a sprawling, filthy, crime-ridden chaos, filled with the very same problems they had longed to escape. Perhaps there wasn't anything that kept people from leaving but only the fact that it was so thoroughly and completely a paradise that no one ever wished to leave, not in a thousand years—not even to tell those they had left behind in distant ports, some people being unwilling to share their good fortune with others, even their own flesh and blood, or their dearest friends.

Some believed that the man who escaped the island was a sailor aboard the captain's ship, that he wrote beautiful verses and that it was he whom Clotho really and truly loved. Others insist it was the captain and no other, and that the younger Fate helped him to escape.

The man, though he could not die, was condemned to row everlastingly upon the sea, unable to find his way back to Portugal from whence he came, or any other land, carrying with him the knowledge of what was lost, and yet, once a year—or so it is said by some—he comes upon the island as it rises for one day from the depths of the ocean, and there he sees the sister whom he loves more than life itself. Clotho herself could not leave the island, and though to her a year is but a moment, a mere breath, she suffers for the man she loves, for whom a year of waiting to hold her in his arms and then for only a few hours is an agony that only his love has allowed him to endure, only to be torn from her arms at the end of that day as the island once again returns to its watery undying grave.

There are as many versions of this story as there are to any event, legend or myth, handed down through the ages. How many names and histories of God are there among nations and peoples, each with its unique version of the story of creation? Such variations and misrepresentations that God wouldn't likely recognize the portrayal of Himself were He to come face to face with His own image. Much the way a notorious criminal often has crimes ascribed to him that he could not possibly have committed because he was out of the region or otherwise engaged; it being impossible to be in two places at the same time, or so we are told. So, too, God has to deal with all manner of events that others claim He is responsible for, often of a contradictory nature: killing off vast numbers of people while miraculously saving one or two, always for some special purpose.

We frequently accept as true a scrap of information, simply because it fills a void, even though it is exaggerated out of all proportion, or skewed, distorted by dint of our prejudices and biases, something—indeed anything—being preferable to nothing.

This writer claims that King João I of Portugal was courageous and heroic. Another states that like his descendant, João of Bragança, who took the Portuguese throne back from Philip of Spain and became King João IV, he took the crown unwillingly, pushed into it, a man forced by overwhelming circumstances to become greater than he wished. By the same token, so too can King João II be seen as a far-seeing leader, a visionary, a man who bravely faced his enemies at home and abroad, or as a tyrant and murderer, a cruel or just monomaniac.

Some say there is and was only one island where the Fates lived. Some say that the man who escaped eventually returned and sank with the island, or that he never left to begin with, or that he left and never found it again. Take your pick; we tend to believe that which serves our own purpose. Then again, perhaps we are on the wrong island altogether, and these aren't the Fates, but the Furies: Erinys, Eumenides, Semnae, Dirae, those avenging spirits, Alecto, the Unresting, Megaera, the Jealous, Tisiphone, the Avenger—she's the one you really have to look out for. No wonder all hell has broken loose, no wonder the world's a disaster. Furies instead of Fates.

Maybe that explains all that rough water and nasty weather up ahead.

. . .

Julia read Sebastião's account of how, during a recent trip to Portugal, he had retraced the steps taken by the funeral procession for Inês de Castro, from Coimbra to Alcobaça, mile by mile. And just as Sebastião explained his need to step into the cordoned-off area where Inês de Castro's tomb sat, to touch the carved stone and feel its surface like a man reading Braille, even placing his ear to it in a sort of communion with the bones of his ancestor, so too had Julia, when she had gone to see the Casa dos Remédios in Angra, touched the stones in the chapel where her ancestors had been interred. Not going quite so far as King Sebastião, who had opened his ancestor's tombs to commune with them, yet not so different, really, in the spirit of the action.

Her father had sought out a message, something retained in the stones, whether Pedro's and Inês's tombs, or the old palace at Serra d'el Rei, where Pedro and Inês had spent much of their time together, or other ruins across the countryside where various Castros had built their palaces. When living people are no more we can sense their presence in the stones which house their remains or in the buildings they inhabited. But when there is no grave, no tomb, where then can we go? How many over the centuries have looked to the sea for such a purpose, knowing that somewhere out there the loved ones lie buried beneath the waves?

Julia watched Antonio with growing pride and admiration. He appeared to be filled with a steely sense of purpose, determination and drive, a new-found spirit, as a true descendant of Dom João de Castro, kin to Afonso de Albuquerque and the brave Corte-Real brothers, a grandson of Dom Fernando de Castro, and countless others, who sailed across treacherous seas, to fight and die in the deserts and jungles of Africa, in India, in the Spice Islands, or in Brazil. There was a point when life became sharpest as one fought for what one believed.

What she saw as Antonio's look of determination was, in reality, his mounting anger and disgust over what he read: "If only fate hadn't intervened," Sebastião wrote, "then Inês de Castro's son, the Infante, or Prince, Dom João would have become King of Portugal and the family would have ruled the country instead of João de Avis, one of Pedro's bastards.

"Why was it that Inês's children weren't killed? Why were they spared, if King Afonso's advisors feared they might try to seize the throne for themselves? All the more reason, then, to make sure none of the Castro children was left alive."

There were pages of various coats-of-arms, along with descriptions and explanations for what the symbols meant. *"Perestrelo,"* Antonio read, "came from *Pallasteli,* meaning, blanket of stars. *Esmeraldo,* from emerald." Their own name, Canto, meant corner, or song; Castro, a hilltop fort. Did they perhaps signify something else, something archaic, lost to the ages? Strange names, esoteric wordings and phrases, hinting at alchemy, astronomy. "Zarco was derived from Hebrew, later changed to Câmara, obscuring the fact that the name Gonçalo Estevez Arco could become Gonçalo Zarco. Obscuring a Jewish ancestry. The Zarcos, the Câmaras, and the Meneses, were connected with the Jews, and/or New Christians, and connected with the Azores and Madeira, to Columbus and the Castros, as well.

Antonio studied the Canto e Castro coat-of-arms, deciphering the meaning of the symbols: on one side, that of the Castros, a silver shield with six red circles, topped by a silver lion rising in attack. Six red circles. What meaning and significance did they conceal? Inês's and Álvaro's half-brother and sister, Fernando and Joana, had thirteen circles on their coat-of-arms. Some claimed the six were due to Inês and Álvaro being illegitimate, but others claimed they represented six vanquished Moorish kings. On the Canto side, a red shield with an angle pointing upright, a rampart in silver atop the apex on which was the Greek symbol of Venus, representing the female sex. "John of Chandos," he read, "incorporated the symbol onto his coat-of-arms as a result of winning a challenge with another knight in a matter concerning a woman, in the name of chivalry.

"Perhaps an unforeseen advantage to Spain's annexation of Portugal in 1580 was their erasure of all evidence of having been duped by Por-

329

tugal's King João II when he sent them Columbus to lead the Spaniards on a wild goose chase to the west, knowing full well what they would find, or rather what they wouldn't find—namely, India. How many Portuguese documents, books and treasures found their way to Spain during the sixty-year occupation? History as the art of lying, of selective omission. Keep the flock ignorant and busy with superstition, enough to miss what's really going on; keep them believing that Jews or Muslims or Christians were the cause of plague or drought or famine, or witches, or devil-worshippers. Knowledge is dangerous; however, thinkers, men and books can be burned, knowledge suppressed. A new history written."

Julia now held the ship's wheel piloting them to the island they sought, as if she had made this journey a thousand times. She heard the cry of a *cagarra* following close behind the ship, and looked back over her shoulder. The ghost ship which had pursued them had merged with their vessel, had become one.

"The sea is a silent witness," the old sailor said, as if sharing Julia's somber mood. "The countless lost names of those who sailed these waters, searching. Secret voyages, unrecorded voyages, voyages lost to time."

Julia adjusted their course slightly, two degrees to port, and held the wheel steady, honing in on their destination.

· · ·

On the island the madman attempts what no one has ever attempted. The two older sisters languish, contented, drowsy with the lack of stimulation, of activity, intoxicated by their beauty, the sound of their voices, and the ceaseless praise and adulation of their subjects. They swoon as if drugged, and perhaps someone has slipped them a substance to which they are unaccustomed. The goddesses are content to live eternally as objects of desire, worshipped by all the people on the island, men, women and children, to be admired and served. Not that they are not worthy of all this attention, for they are truly beautiful to behold as they bathe in the waters, or lie in hammocks, tended by a retinue of eager devotees.

The madman, however, has his eyes on the youngest, coaxing her with promises of things that not even a god could procure. He whispers in her ear, sings to her, songs, words she swears she has heard before, long ago, for how does one measure time when one is immortal? They say there are no new stories, but that the same stories are told and retold again and again, and if this is so, might not the same lives be lived over and over as well, the same chance encounters?

They are sweet songs the madman whispers, poems of love-everlasting, the undying truth of beauty, the flames of passion, in which one is consumed in the very conflagration of one's desires. Needless to say, she is bewitched. He may not be all that good-looking, nor rich and powerful, no Ulysses, surely, but the man can certainly spin words. She is enraptured, spellbound, and thus promises him anything in return.

"Spin," he says, "spin the dreams I will share with you."

And though it has been long, and an uncertainty has crept into her actions through disuse, she scrambles to oblige, finding fibers, hairs, bits of cloth or spider webs, anything she can possibly weave. And he tells her his dreams as he had had the scribe write them out, what seemed a lifetime ago. The thing he doesn't realize is that the woman spinning has her own dreams, and weaving the words he speaks, with the spells that are hers to give, she moistens the strands and threads with her saliva, and weaves her tapestry, little realizing that she is weaving her own dreams into his.

"In the beginning," he says . . .

331

In 1630, the cone, which in the valley of the Furnas had remained quiescent ever since 1563, again burst out, and entirely desiccated the lake at its foot. This lake, before the eruption, covered a space of three miles in circumference, having a depth of about 100 feet. It is now filled up with cinders, pumice-stone and scoriae, and is known as the Lagoa Secca, or the dry lake. This eruption was chiefly remarkable for the volumes of ashes it sent forth, enveloping the island in an Egyptian darkness, greatly terrifying the inhabitants. The impalpable dust covered the land in many places to a depth of from 5 to 17 feet, destroying all vegetation for the time being, but adding fertility to the soil itself.

In Terceira the fall of ashes was so continuous and alarming that the inhabitants record the year in their annals as *"O anno da cinza,"* or, the ash year.

The Azores: or Western Islands
Walter Fredrick Walker, London, 1886

. . .

Antonio lay slumped in the ship's prow, leaning against a large coil of thick rope. The ship, creaking and groaning, sailed through the dark, churning water. He was neither seasick nor cold, neither famished nor tired. He had no fear of the ship sinking, no fear of the waves. The adventurer, the sailor keeps his sights on the goal, not the possible dangers that lie en route.

He knew his mission. He had his duty to fulfill, his fate. He was prepared for what lay ahead.

Julia stood at the helm of the ship. Sebastião was right, she thought, at least in part. Conjurings, transformations, words, invocations. Hadn't it been words that had brought her here? Words that had led her to this transformation, to love, to adventure, as much as it was music, too. Sounds and words brought together, everything converging as if according to some fantastic design, some intricate plan.

She'd always thought of her father as an actor long immersed in a role, lost to himself. But had the role been written for him, and was he playing it, believing each and every word, identifying completely with the role that was constructed by someone else? What strange magic had those words, uttered so thoughtlessly, brought about? What permutations had they unsuspectingly wrought?

Her dreams awoke in her a sense of dread and foreboding, shadows lurking, running. Shadows of what? Perhaps there was a code in Sebastião's writings, the stories, poems, names; certain cryptic messages hidden therein. If only the code could be broken. What secrets from the past, she wondered, had been preserved, carefully hidden away?

Antonio looked around at the ship. A sword hung at his side, and the air was heavy with the smell of gunpowder. Cannons. He was a new or an old self, someone remade, searching for an island, following a siren or goddess across the sea, and prepared to do battle. Against whom? For whom? He heard a voice: "You fight the unfinished battles of your ancestors." A familiar voice. His father's? He looked round. Nothing. Only a voice in his head.

Perhaps Sebastião had had a confrontation with a modern-day Coelho, or Gonçalves or Pacheco, a descendant of one of Inês's assassins. Had they picked a quarrel? Sebastião's notes revealed that the descendants of Diogo Lopes Pacheco still gathered once a year to celebrate their ancestor's narrow escape by dressing as a beggar and fleeing to France.

"I'm aboard ship, a ship armed for battle, sailing to a distant island," Antonio mumbled. And why not? He was a descendant of his ancestors, so why wouldn't the descendants of his ancestors' enemies be alive, too, waiting perhaps, for just such an encounter at long last? Perhaps the heirs of others who had conspired against Dona Inês de Castro, against her brothers, Dom Fernando and Dom Álvaro Pires de Castro, and her sons, the Princes Dom João and Dom Dinis, against Dom Álvaro's son Dom Pedro, who fled to Castile, and his grandson, Dom Álvaro, whose enemies whispered in the king's ear, suggesting that he was having an affair with the queen, Dona Leonor?

Enemies in all the battles against Spain, against the Moors, the Turks, in Asia, Africa and South America. The battles and battlers of antiquity, their fights unfinished, suspending their many hopes and dreams, expectations and desires, constant in the heart and soul of each of these men and women. Not merely their battles, but their loves, cut short, unconsummated, undeclared, thwarted by chance and circumstance. Who could say that our love won't be rekindled and recommence when your grandchild or great-grandchild meets mine? Could the seeds of such a love be carried forth through the generations?

We'll meet again in five hundred years' time. And the conclusion. . . ?

· · ·

The orchids arranged for Inez were of a beautiful and rare variety then known only to orchid-growing Portugal. The flower was named for her afterwards, and in Brazil today is known as the Inez de Castro orchid.

Queen After Death
Harman Black, Real Book Co., NY, 1933

· · ·

Words, ideas, spoken aloud, fumbling in the darkness . . . attempting to create, to spark, an alternate history: "Inês did not die, but escaped . . . fled. Or, Afonso, her first child, instead of dying in childhood, went off, to live far away. And his family continued to proliferate, in secret."

The old man, the scribe, forced to write, to rewrite what had already been written. Plucked from his boat, on which he had wandered for as long as he could remember, wandered over the oceans of the world, seeing every shore, every island, every continent, from one end of the earth to the other, but never landing, never touching ground. What he wouldn't do to touch once again the land of that one place, the island.

Cursed instead to wander an eternity, hoping against hope, feeling that if not now then someday he would again see the goddesses. Until then, rowing toward that goal ever out of reach. It was his only hope, his eternal hope, that he could regain his rightful place.

Until a lunatic seized him, demanded that he write, as he had written so long ago, for the Fates, yes, the very Fates, on the Enchanted Island, writing as they dictated to him; for not all that they proposed was acted upon, not all their stories were written down in his book, the chronicle of life and death. Held prisoner by a madman, who desired nothing but a rewriting of history, to claim for himself what he claimed were his entitlements, his birthright!

· · ·

Senhor Leonardo Brum takes frequent trips to Pico, Terceira, and São Miguel, then back to Faial. Those islanders who make it their business to keep a sharp eye on the affairs of others keep busy guessing where he is, when he will return, whether or not he is making any progress in his investigations.

"Look, he goes again to Madalena," someone in a small group says, as they watch Senhor Brum board the early morning boat to Pico.

"Maybe he'll disappear, too, like Senhor Canto e Castro and his children?"

"Perhaps," says another. "That is if he doesn't give up and go back home first."

"He's a busy fellow, that one—always coming and going."

"It's always those who make the most noise and fuss that get the least done."

The others nod, smiling, confident the man they observe is going in circles.

Perhaps Senhor Brum keeps moving in order to resist succumbing to the *mornaça* of the islands, that languorous, peaceful, come-what-may attitude, which one can readily slip into without noticing. The islanders have witnessed countless strangers arriving with big plans for building a fancy hotel or resort to cater to their own kind, only to succumb to the *mornaça* they were sure could never affect them, their plans laid aside like so many dreams beyond reach. *Amanhã*—tomorrow, they say. Or maybe he has fallen under the spell of Maria dos Santos, whose garden, each time he stops to visit, leaves him disoriented. Perhaps it's his infatuation for Julia, and his attempt to avoid what she has awakened in him, a feeling that keeps him on tenterhooks, which keeps his mind adrift, unable to focus, without her suddenly looming like a rock or a reef in a wide expanse of ocean.

. . .

She weaves, spins her thread, following the spirit if not the letter of his whispers, his dreams and desires, transcribed and illustrated by her deft fingers—and with each kiss between them, each caress, as he surrenders more and more to love, she finds ways of transmuting, of incorporating, like the thinnest of filaments, what is necessary. The threads become life itself. She captures his poetry and spittle, the liquid strands of their lovemaking, the beating of his heart, weaves breath into the patterns—even the elusive essence of love itself.

The madman watches and holds his breath as the cloth unfolds before his eyes, the scenes beautifully depicted, transporting the two of them back in time, or toward the future, if not some other universe altogether.

The music begins soft, sweet, stirring. Eros and Aphrodite have been busy working overtime; for in these dark times of ceaseless war, of death and fear, when human life is cheap and all too expendable, true love is a rare event, no matter how much the troubadours sing of it. Too often people quickly tire of each other—a woman gives her affections to another, a husband leaves his wife in order to possess someone else. People make deals with the devil for even the slightest perceived advantage.

The siren casts her spells, creates magic, assisted in her task by her feelings for the man who lies beside her, who encourages her, pouring warm sand from his hand onto her naked feet, allowing his finger now and then to brush against her skin, so supple and smooth. Thus her feelings, unlike anything she has ever experienced herself, imbue her song with a quality that is extraordinary.

But then, in the case of Dona Inês and Dom Pedro, nothing is ordinary. When together, their hearts beat quickly, like birds, as if love itself quickens the pulse of life. Inês is striking, and for Pedro nothing else matters, not his father's gruff and stern demands and warnings, not the jealousy of the nobles, not even the disapproval or the discontent of *o*

337

povo—the people—who he will someday come to rule; not the Church with its hypocrisy and selfish motives, nor those false friends, spies in the service of unnamed others, plotters and conspirators, who lurk in corners and shadows.

Pedro's love for Inês has transformed him from a shy, doubting young prince who stuttered and stammered and who felt more at home among his beloved animals, or even his peasants, rather than the clergy and noblemen of the court, to the very picture of a king, strong and confident. His time with Inês is full of tender, loving moments, a complete contrast to the time he spends hunting wild boar with friends, or fighting the bulls in Atouguia da Baleia. If only this time could last, if only their togetherness could be prolonged.

The scene ends with Inês's aria, a song of such passion, a promise of enduring love, that by necessity, the gods (we shan't name them—they know who they are) seethe with envy, for there isn't a god on earth or in heaven who enjoys being shown up by a mortal.

Needless to say, some of these malicious gods and goddesses begin plotting some evil, as do those envious persons around Inês and Pedro who would see them come to harm, as if too great a love, the best in any of us, brings out the worst in others.

But let us concentrate instead on Inês's song, the joy with which she sings of her lover, and their children, the jewels in her golden crown of love.

In 1638, an eruption occurred just offshore of the island of Terceira near Ponta do Queimado. An island approximately one league in length formed. The island slowly disappeared.

. . . almost on the very spot where, just 100 years before, an eruption had broken out, and three miles off the western coast, flames shot up, accompanied by quantities of broken lava and cinders, forming an islet which, at the expiration of twenty days, when the eruption ceased, fell in and disappeared.

The Azores: or Western Islands
Walter Frederick Walker, London, 1886

• • •

"Words are not enough," Sebastião wrote. "Though they are a large part of it, something more is needed. What other elements—fire, water, earth, air? Which of these, and of what kind? Not merely any old earth, for example, would do, but the right one. Azorean and Portuguese captains always carried a bit of their home soil with them as they sailed in their great ships across the vast oceans. If they died in some strange land at least they would be buried with the dirt of their homeland.

"The alchemist can take the words written on the page, speak them aloud, and with a combination of select elements forge a new truth. *Como os tesouros dos duendes*—Like the fairy treasures.

"Men at sea are easily frightened, superstitious. Many things can portend bad luck, an evil omen: a comet, the shape of a cloud, a strange light, a shadow. They desire something whole, something solid they can hold onto; they mistrust water, mistrust words, Love—all that can slip through one's hands. They must be appeased repeatedly, soothed and assured: We will find gold, mountains of it, and silver, jewels, so many riches, and a fountain, so they say, a fountain of pure water which will cure any ills and sustain life.

"Perhaps a rock as opposed to soil; a rock cannot grow anything, it is true, but then a rock has lasting significance, special properties, a solidity of earth, of meaning, of words; like the menhirs dotting the landscape of Portugal which the Celts saw fit to erect, stone edifices standing mutely from time immemorial, pre-Christian, pre-Moslem, pre-Roman. The edifices of one god used to serve another. Or, like the *padrões,* those stone pillars, erected by Diogo Cão where he made land on Africa, to mark the Portuguese presence, during his two voyages. The *padrões* still survive, either whole or in fragments, the pieces of one preserved as fetishes by the local natives."

· · ·

What can we say but that a conspiracy of the gods is afoot? Alecto— she who sleeps not—one of the furies, in league with none other than Anteros, the brother of Eros, and his opposite, god of unhappy love, and the fire-breathing Typhon, father of the Sphinx, the Chimera and a host of other monsters, begetters of ill winds; and last but not least, Scylla, a once-fair sea-nymph who loved Glaucus, but who was changed by a jealous Circe into a monster.

Hated and despised outcasts, like lepers, these unhappy gods and creatures hatch their plans of destruction, vengeance, spite, working the elemental forces and human nature to perform their will. As much as mortals and divine beings both enjoy seeing others who are worse off, in order to feel superior to them, those who are among the dregs, who are the lowest of the low, also enjoy having company in their misery.

· · ·

The madman watches, thoroughly impressed, while the goddess works her magic. He remembers seeing women in Portugal making lace, such fine, delicate work; or, Fátima Madruga, from Pico, who made scrimshaw a fine art, etching reverse images of men and women, of ships, the sea, and whales, utterly exquisite, utterly beautiful, rubbing them with ink, to bring out the proper portrait. Now this incomparably fairest of the Fates weaves, or rather, reweaves the past, with a similar equanimity. He marvels at how expertly she introduces a strand of color here and there, as she spins the stuff of dreams, each strand a strand of life.

"How long can you make one life?" he asks.

"As long as you wish," she says, spinning without interruption.

"Say, then, that Inês de Castro lived to become Queen of all Portugal, not merely Queen after death. Imagine Dom Pedro living well on to old age, with his beloved Inês at his side. Instead of dying in his forties, he might have lived into his eighties. They would have had more children, naturally."

She smiles at this. "Of course."

"And though Dom Fernando was the heir he was a weak and sickly man. Perhaps he still would have been king, but then perhaps not, for he probably would have died during King Pedro's long life, during which time the country wouldn't have gone to war with Castile the three times King Fernando waged war against them. Perhaps war with Castile would have been unnecessary, for Dom Pedro might have had the Castros help him defeat his nephew, King Pedro of Castile, and Pedro and Inês might have ruled both countries together."

"Would that have been enough?" she asks.

"Yes, love, of course. Their son, João would have become king, and Pedro's bastard, João de Avis, would never have been born, or at least would have never been king. With Dom João de Castro as king, perhaps he still would have married Maria Teles de Meneses, but he wouldn't have killed her, because his mother wouldn't have died in such a brutal, horrible way before his eyes, and he wouldn't have had that wretched whore, Queen Leonor, insinuating that her sister, Maria, had been cheating on him, suggesting that if she were eliminated, then Prince João could marry her daughter, Princess Beatriz, and become king of Portugal.

"No, with Prince João now king, and his wife, Maria, queen, Maria's evil sister, Leonor, would remain married to her first husband, who if he had any sense at all would have killed her with his own hands, in the manner by which she coaxed Prince João to murder his wife; for all she

341

succeeded in doing was destroying her sister's life, Prince João's life, and nearly destroying Portugal itself, causing King Juan of Castile to invade, claiming the throne for himself."

He paused and watched as she passed the red thread between her lips. She had first moistened her lips with the tip of her tongue. His body trembled. "I know full well, love, that it's superfluous to speak of your beauty, how incapable words are to convey, and yet, it is my torment to try."

She smiled. "Are you done, darling?" she asked.

"No, not at all." He is puzzled, confused. Something inside him speaks: I don't deserve a love such as this! He shakes his head, attempts to distract himself from such thoughts. What human could possibly deserve a love like her? She is a goddess, after all, beautiful beyond comprehension, a heart that knows only to give without condition, and take as if taking were a holy act. She is immortal besides. Who in all the world deserves such a prize? Now, since he drank from the lips of the youngest Fate, his muse, he too would know immortality.

But with such rewards, is there not a price to pay? His own words come back just then to haunt him: there is always a price to pay. No, this is not the place or time for cynicism. Instead of becoming used to her beauty, she grows more beautiful with each passing day, and though he thinks he can't possibly love her more than he already does his love for her also keeps growing.

"Do you think our love is like theirs?" he asks.

"Our love is like theirs when they were happy, together, alone, yes," she answers. "Of course, they wouldn't have become the tragic love story of the ages then."

"No," he says. "We cherish our tragedies. But they would be remembered instead for loving like no other king and queen had loved, greater than King Arthur and Queen Guinevere. Their love would have been no less remarkable, and thus the poets would have still found inspiration in their story."

"But Guinevere ran off with Sir Lancelot, after betraying King Arthur."

"That's why I said a love *greater* than Guinevere and Lancelot."

"Do people really need their tragedies, the way they need their heroes?"

"What are the lives of the saints, but tragedies, bathed in blood?"

"We can appreciate the love Inês and Pedro had, the fact that she stayed regardless of the dangers, instead of remaining safely in Castile, without her gruesome murder and coronation, and the executions of her killers."

"Indeed."

"But then wasn't your Álvaro de Castro appointed Count of Arraiolos, and then made Constable and Governor, mainly because he was the brother of Inês? If she lives might he not lose the sympathy vote?"

"Yes, but if she lives he won't have to rely on that, for Pedro and Inês will gladly bestow on him all he deserves and so much more. And once Prince João de Castro is king, if Álvaro is still alive, he won't have to face that awful decision of going against his nephew, Prince João, when he invades Portugal from Castile, where he fled after the murder of Maria Teles. If João is king, Álvaro would gladly serve him faithfully."

"Can I tell you a secret?"

"You can tell me anything."

"My sister, the one they call Laquesis, was very jealous of her."

"Jealous of whom, love?"

"Not only Prince Dom João's wife, Maria Teles, but especially Inês. Oh, she never said so, but the look in her eyes whenever her name was mentioned, I believe someone even dared to say that Inês's beauty compared with Laquesis's, who couldn't bear that a human woman could even remotely resemble her."

"Her beauty, such as it is," he says, "pales beside yours. Maybe it was you she was jealous of."

"Perhaps, since my affection was towards Inês and her sister, Joana."

"And Maria Teles?"

The young Fate nodded, and shed tears. "How could such a tender and sweet love, and two lives entwined, as theirs were, become so horribly ruined, their love so disfigured? They who were so beloved, so admired by everyone, noble or commoner."

"Everyone except your sister," he says. "One act of barbarity begets another."

"The sins of the father—?"

"Or the mother. Perhaps that is our true legacy."

"What are you saying?"

"Unhappy love, love doomed from its inception, disastrous romances, heartbreak, like ripples in a pond, reappearing through the generations."

"But aren't you happy?"

"With you, yes, but ours is different."

343

"The benefit of falling in love with a goddess, you mean?"

"Of course, and not just any goddess," he says, as she smiles and demurs. "What do your sisters have against the Portuguese? One would think they'd tire of their vitriol, that it would burn itself out. To rob Dona Violante de Castro's chance of love, thwarting her marriage to the much-loved, young Dom Fernando, having him captured by the Moors to rot and die in a Moroccan prison, causing his brother, Prince Henry, the so-called Navigator, indeed the entire royal family and all of Portugal such grief and sadness."

The Fate nods, wiping away a tear. "There was a poet once who came and loved Laquesis. He write poems for her only a true goddess could have inspired, and before that another, a captain, I think, an explorer, and while she let them escape, she has sent many a ship to the ocean floor, urging Neptune to destroy them with the very sea they sought to explore. And Atropos."

"The ugly?"

"Don't call her that. She wasn't always that way."

"I'm sorry, but you know she'd turn me into a toad if given half the chance."

"Her dislike goes back even farther, and runs deeper, for she fell in love with one long ago, when your people only just started out on their first steps into the sea, but when the captain saw her, he grew fearful, and when she was unable to draw him closer, to seduce him with her beauty, or her voice, when none of the charms she employed worked, she grew furious, and swore eternal revenge."

"I'm glad you are so different from them."

"Kiss me," she says. It was one of the many things for which he adored her, a simple, child-like request, kiss me, or her smile, which could melt even Lachesis's frozen heart, or the way she loved him with her eyes, eyes as green as the fields through which they ran and played.

"What will our children be like, yours and mine?" he asks.

"Our children will be the legends of tomorrow. Os Desejados—The Desired Ones."

CHAPTER 6

Inez (de Castro) was buried at Alcobaça with extraordinary magnifi-
cence, in a tomb of white marble, surmounted by her carved statue; and
near her sepulcher Pedro caused his own to be placed. The monument,
after repeatedly resisting the violence of curiosity, was broken into in
1810 by the French soldiery; the statue was mutilated, and the yellow
hair was cut from the broken skeleton, to be preserved in reliquaries and
blown by the wind.

The Encyclopaedia Britannica
Eleventh Edition, Vol. V
New York, 1910

. . .

Looking out his hotel window at an inspiring view of Pico, Leonardo Brum attempts to formulate a summation and surmise the possible
results and conclusions of his investigation. Like many Portuguese, he
struggles against allowing his feelings to interject, his love of the language to color his opposing tendency toward a more concise prose.

He sees in the disappearance of Julia, Antonio and Sebastião something of the tragic, the poetic, resonant with the fate of so many Portuguese, and indeed the country as a whole. He might have worded it
as "you can take the man off the island, but you cannot take the island
out of the man." He muses whether it is a matter of pride, a need to
suffer perhaps, or a result of some other failing. Furthermore, he finds
it impossible to desist from interjecting his own feelings for Julia upon

Nicolau and Julia both, the plight of a woman in love braving the ocean in order to save her father. He'd be damned if he were going to see this as merely an unfortunate mishap. There was something subtle, if not philosophical, entwined in the whole affair. He was sure of it. If only he could tease the hidden meaning out of it.

Is this what happened when man dared to dream? Did these two dreamers, like Icarus, fly too high? Did fate conspire to rob Julia and Sebastião of the largesse it so carelessly bestowed on others, many of whom are far less deserving? Is there some message or warning to the Portuguese, especially those inflamed by the words of poets like Camões and Pessoa? Or did it have something to do with her famous ancestor, Dona Inês de Castro?

Perhaps a hidden meaning, a warning to himself. Is he too in danger of being swept up by the dramatic events that have caused people and boats to become lost? He remembers Maria dos Santos's words, and chuckles to himself, confident his ratiocinative abilities are ammunition enough against such eventualities.

· · ·

The weather worsened. It began to rain, the wind intensified and the waves grew rough, lashing the sails and rigging of the ship. "If a past wrong is righted," Sebastião had written. "What changes are wrought by amending these wrongs?" Julia tried to keep to the task at hand, juggling the notes she shared with Antonio. She ceased writing down the music that filled her ears, and assisted Antonio in taking their bearings, utilizing the nautical instruments she found close at hand, determined to follow the music that guided their route just as the stars had guided her Portuguese forebears in their travels. She again took over the wheel and steered the ship as though she were headed home.

"We must be close, now," she said, though no one responded. "The island must be near."

Antonio heard a sound, similar to that of the wind roaring down the flanks of Pico, a rumbling, like thunder or an earthquake. "The wind," he said, shivering, only to hear a voice a moment later, a song carried by the winds, haunting and aching, leading him as if a line pulled him in tow.

He glanced over at a sailor who scowled and grumbled under his breath. The man was drunk. Antonio hoped there wouldn't be a mutiny. The man waved his bottle at Antonio. An offering? Are you with us? Antonio took the bottle, sipped the brandy, and banished such thoughts.

. . .

Some families are marked out for adventure and romance by the high gods. . . . The Fates would seem to brand these creatures with extraordinary character, extraordinary beauty, or a sweet, perilous kind of folly, by which they can never be forgotten or mislaid.

"This one," we may imagine them to say, "has a soul of wind and laughter. He shall dance for us when he grows up, in our theatre of Europe. And this woman's beauty and charm will certainly afford us excellent entertainment by-and-by. So we will pitch her where she can set some man alight. The conflagration should prove amusing."

Such folk, perhaps, were the daughters of Don Pedro de Castro, Juana and Inez.

Peter The Cruel, Edward Storer, London, 1911

347

. . .

Physicists and astronomers speak of wormholes in space, Black Holes, Quarks, Dark Matter, elements that exhibit "charm," and the bending of time and space. The region where Antonio and Julia found themselves was far stranger and more unpredictable.

There is an Indonesian term, *Djam Karet,* which in translation means, "the hour that stretches." Who's to say that they hadn't stumbled into some strange region of time and place similar to this, just as there are special places where things roll uphill, and one's perspective is thrown off kilter by inexplicable forces?

. . .

Nicolau walks out to the shore of Praia do Almoxarife and peers into the waves. He prays for Julia's safety. He whispers words that no one listening would understand, words he learned from his grandfather long ago, words which might be a spell or incantation, or perhaps the names of gods and goddesses, the elements or forces that might aid the woman for whose safety he is so concerned. And the way the waves respond, the murmurs they produce, might lead one to deduce that his words are understood.

At this very moment, on the island of Pico, Leonardo Brum meets with Nicolau's sister, Teresa, for the first time, and wonders, what is God up to, and if not God, then the Fates, or the gods, the one or the many? For while he has allowed himself to be charmed by Julia, a woman he has yet to meet, he now has before his disbelieving eyes, a vision, a beauty, to be sure, but one so different that to him it seems impossible: Can two such women exist at one and the same time in his life? It seems more than a heart can bear.

Julia possesses an attractiveness that is apparent to anyone with eyes, he thinks. It is easy to appreciate her looks as well as her intellect, her spirit, her artistic talents, though he hadn't heard these firsthand. Teresa, on the other hand, is as indefinable as a sudden squall, as gorgeous and heart-rending as the most spectacular sunset.

Teresa's hair falls in a cascade of dark waves like the deepest ocean swells; her eyes flash with an intensity that wrings his heart, and her mouth—he pushes that thought away, for he is no young man, no lover of someone as beautiful or young as Teresa, only an old man who can admire, or cherish from afar. Still, he muses, a mouth as delectable, as tantalizing as the ripest strawberry or mango, and as unobtainable as the distant stars!

We must forgive Senhor Brum his extravagances of description. "I am Portuguese," he would simply say, by which he would lay claim to a soul both poetic and sentimental. This, he shares with Sebastião, who had written that the Portuguese were never afraid of emotion; that writing, like music, stripped bare of sentiment and emotion was vapid, lifeless. So let our Senhor Brum experience his effusion of words and physical sensations in peace.

He speaks to Teresa, asks questions, to which he receives nothing but the fire of her eyes, and the tone and timbre of her voice, which he would gladly remain and listen to until the islands were over-swept by the sea, which like death must eventually claim all things.

"Is there nothing you can tell me, to help me determine where Julia and Antonio are?"

She is vocal, yet reticent, as though speech were not her natural form of communication. "No, nothing," she says. He smiles unintentionally and repeats the word, "Nothing," but the sound of the word is the dull thud of a stone on the ground, while hers is a sweet musical tone.

My God, he thinks, she speaks like I don't know what. Trying to talk to her is like speaking to a mermaid. She is an elemental being, if anything. I would venture to wager that she isn't composed of flesh and blood but of seawater and stardust, of music and desire.

"You understand that it is important to find them, especially before they come to harm?"

"I understand they will find what they seek and learn what they will know."

Jesus Cristo, Leonardo thinks, steadying himself. She is surely Maria dos Santos's granddaughter. He prolongs his visit as long as he can but knows he must take his leave. He makes the understandable mistake of shaking hands, and returns to his room convinced his hand will never be the same. "Why do I feel like a schoolboy?" he asks himself. But he knows full well. He remembers more than once in his life being unable to choose between two women, both of whom appealed to him for different reasons and in far different ways. That was nothing compared with the predicament in which he now finds himself. After going years without experiencing, without feeling, without seeing, it's a miracle to be suddenly struck dumb. "It's like asking someone to chose between the sun and the moon," he says, in a voice that breaks with emotion, though it's only a game, this choosing, a crazy impossible mission on which his heart sends him. "What eddies are caused by the proximity of two such beauties? Perhaps a poem to each would be in order."

He wishes he had at his disposal all the numerous genealogical books and charts that fill the shelves of his study. "What goes on with these two families?" he asks himself.

. . .

The children of Inez [de Castro] shared her habit of misfortune. From her brother, however, Álvaro Perez de Castro, the reigning house of Portugal directly descends.

The Encyclopaedia Britannica
Eleventh Edition, Vol. V, New York, 1910

. . .

Antonio remained on deck, studying the stars and planets, while he strained to hear the song of a woman whose voice he would have followed to the ends of the earth. Several large, black birds, which might have been hawks, or perhaps only crows followed close behind the ship, as if keeping vigil. He listened as well to the murmurings of the sea and the wind, while the old sailor beside him probed the fathomless depths of memory for all he had forgotten—a fragment of a love poem or a song written by King Dinis, a lyric composed by Dom Pedro for Dona Inês de Castro.

One moment he heard the laudatory words of Portugal's greatest playwright, Gil Vicente, singing the praises of Dona Inês de Castro, pointing veiled jibes at the Castilians who found out too late that they had been tricked by King João II, that Columbus was *Colom,* the pseudonym of a Portuguese spy. The next moment, a sonnet composed by Camões, paying tribute to the beautiful and graceful Dona Isabel de Castro:

> *Quem viu uma confiança tão segura,*
> *tão singular esmalte da beleza,*
> *que não padeça mais . . .*

> Who's seen such assured self-confidence,
> such singular radiant beauty,
> should suffer no more . . .

Then a song for Dom João de Castro, son of Dona Inês de Castro and Dom Pedro, a lament for a boy whose mother was slaughtered by order of the boy's grandfather; a young man who inherited his mother's beauty and secretly married the woman he loved, only to have his mind poisoned by the Queen, his wife's jealous sister, who convinced him to murder his wife; a lament for the country he had to flee, when the queen accused him of assassinating her sister, a lament for his hot-headedness which caused him to invade Portugal from Castile, and thus lose his kingdom; a lament that echoed through the hallways of his castle in Valencia de Don Juan, his town, which bore the coat-of-arms of this rightful king of Portugal. And his brother Dom Dinis, who refused to kiss the hand of the treacherous queen, Dona Leonor, and thus was also banished to Castile; and when his brother Dom João died, also invaded Portugal, claiming the throne for himself.

A lament of remorse.

CHAPTER 7

1720 — "In December, an offshore eruption occurred between São   *353*
Miguel and Terceira. An island formed, having an area of 17 sq. km.
The island, about the size of Corvo, existed until 1723, when it sub-
sided beneath the ocean surface. This region is identified on marine
charts as the banks of Dom João de Castro."

History of the Azores, James Guill
Golden Shield Publications, Tulare, CA, 1993

• • •

Julia woke to find the ship enshrouded in a thick fog. Mist obscured
the sky and the ocean, even the masts and sails of the ship. It clung
to the shrouds and gunwales. She heard murmurings from the men,
unnerved by the eerie calm. She walked the decks of the ship, urging
them to press on, to muster their nerve.

"We must forge on," she said, with a quiet determination.

The sails and rigging stirred. The wood planks of the ship creaked,
but it seemed, too, as if the ship no longer moved, but was stuck fast
in the fog. She leaned over the gunwale and listened to the waves keeping time, slapping against the planks of the ship. Voices called, blood-
to-blood, sea-to-sea—she heard it both internally and externally at one
and the same time.

Ghost-men bustled constantly around her, performing their tasks, as
if she weren't there.

Darkness fell and as the mists lifted momentarily the old man who
captained the ship peered out over the sea. "We're getting closer. It's

there. I can smell it."

All eyes scanned the sea ahead.

"Look, there," a voice in the rigging called out, pointing.

The brilliant streak of a comet was seen directly above the ship, its tail lit up against the dark backdrop of space, perfectly visible. She remembered the man she had left behind, and hoped he peered up to the heavens at that moment.

Meanwhile, far away in a place near Praia do Almoxarife, some know as Água Zangada, an old woman named Maria dos Santos and her grandson, Nicolau, peer into a pool of still, quiet water, at shadows reflected in the dark surface.

"You must go, Nicolau," the old woman says. "Now is the time."

• • •

"What are we searching for?" Sebastião wrote. *"Love? A bit of dream figment, a ghost-phantom, or flesh and blood? A missing part of ourselves, a completeness, or an end to ourselves, an undoing? Are we born with this aching, shadow piece, this* saudade *seeking wholeness?*

"There are passions that are irresistible and all-consuming, which most people will never know or comprehend, seeing it only as a myth. But which can alter who and what a person is, and, once tasted, can never be forgotten or substituted. Do we stop to ask ourselves what love is? What is its essence? A relinquishment or an attainment? A sacrifice or reaching out for something beyond reach: eternity, infinity, God?"

• • •

"Our children," the madman said, softly. "When so many were prevented from joining together and leaving their children to the world. Is it really so easy to amend the past?"

"Here, with you, anything is possible, silly." She purses her lips, and he kisses her.

"But there are so many if onlys, so many what ifs," he says, when they pause. "Our past is a long line of regrets. Slavery, the Inquisition, the murder of Jews, Moslems, wars, colonization, senseless slaughter, corruption . . ."

"One thing at a time. We have to start somewhere, and follow where that leads."

"Of course, *minha moirinha*—my dear little Fate. Right you are. We can say that if Fernando de Castro and Álvaro de Castro hadn't decided to wage a war against King Pedro of Spain, siding with João Afonso of Albuquerque, who just happened to be the son of King Afonso IV's most bitter enemy, his half brother Afonso Sanches, then King Afonso, really would have had no reason to kill Inês de Castro. Fernando de Castro, Álvaro de Castro, and João Afonso wouldn't have been whispering in Pedro's ear to seize his nephew's crown and become King of both Castile and Portugal. If those nobles hadn't fought to protect their power, their feudal rights—?"

"Yes," Maria of the Fates said. "King Afonso had no love for those nobles, and the idea of Portugal being swallowed up by Castile was more than he would stand by and allow."

"A lack of foresight, and a habit of being on the wrong side is the Castro affliction."

"But we're making amends for all that. Here, we are setting all things right."

"Finally."

"You are my impatient one." Her smile melts away his doubts and anxieties.

$$\cdot \quad \cdot \quad \cdot$$

There is no reason to doubt that the stories which the Phoenicians allowed to leak out to other interested seamen were deliberately designed to scare away potential competitors. The same thing has happened throughout the whole history of maritime discovery. In the 15th century, when the Portuguese were uncovering the hitherto unknown shores of West Africa, they encouraged the belief among other nations that the world came to an end not far south of the Canary Islands. Long after the Portuguese had been active on these shores, trading in gold and slaves, other European seamen heard only of a sun so hot that it boiled the pitch out of your ships so that they sank. They heard of the unending Stream of Ocean which poured away over the world's end, and of the winds that blew your ship steadily to the south until you were sucked away over the edge of the world. When few other European nations began tentatively to investigate this mysterious coast, the rumour was spread about that only the specially-designed caravels of the Portuguese could sail safely in these waters. Like the Phoenicians of the *Odyssey*, the 15th-century Portuguese were credited with magic ships, and with mysterious navigational abilities known to no others.

Ulysses Found, Ernie Bradford, London, 1964

. . .

The siren's voice grew stronger and clearer. She sang of the loss of love and fortune, the loss of home. Antonio gripped the bulwarks of the ship, peered into the expanse of sea, swept up by the stirrings within: to take arms, to conquer, to rule, to love. For, it spoke to the ancient blood that flowed through his veins, to whispered dreams. A restorative or tonic that awoke passions, like a thousand different springs, combined and commingling, the sounds of Inês's children, Dom João and Dom Dinis, and their children, and their children's children, down through the centuries.

He heard the song of Dom Fernando de Castro, Count of Trastámara, brother of Dona Inês and Don Álvaro de Castro, who led the army of Dom Pedro I, the king of Castile, against his half-brother Enrique. King Pedro was usurped, then murdered by Enrique, who took the crown for himself. Dom Fernando lost everything, his lands, his castles, his country. He went to England to urge King Edward III's son, John of Gaunt, to invade and dethrone King Enrique, only to die in Gascony, buried in the Bayonne Cathedral, forever bereft of his homeland.

Julia heard the plaintive song of Dom Fernando's sister, Joana de Castro, who gained a crown when she married King Pedro I of Castile, but lost both the next day, when Pedro abandoned her and returned to his lover. She heard the rending cries of Joana when King Enrique imprisoned Don Juan, the son she bore Pedro. While Antonio read and heard of yet another heir robbed of his throne, Julia heard tales of lovers separated, of love denied, and lovers betrayed.

Joana withdrew to the solace of her castle at Dueñas, which Pedro gave her as a parting gift, where she continued to live as the Queen of Castile. She was buried in the Cathedral of Compostela, her sepulcher bearing the coat of arms of Castile and León and the Castros—her story forgotten, overshadowed by her beautiful sister's more tragic and gruesome legend.

. . .

It was the singular destiny of women of the Castro family to inspire love in regal bosoms. Pedro I of Castile had let himself become hopelessly ensnared by the charms of Dona Joana de Castro, and their scandalous affair had deeply shocked the Spanish court. Later, Dona Inês de Castro was to inspire in another Pedro, the first Portuguese monarch of that name, one of the greatest passions in history. When she was struck down by a dagger thrust, inspired by those who feared her baleful influence upon the dynasty, her royal lover went mad, tore out the hearts of her assassins with his own hands, drank their warm blood with a savage snarl, and stunned his courtiers and the world, and gave vent to his own hatred and despair, by having his mistress, even as she lay there cold in death, crowned queen of Portugal.

Every Inch a King, Sergio Correa da Costa
Charles Frank Publications, Inc., New York, 1950

. . .

The ship came alongside the tiny boat that lay more submerged than afloat upon the water. It was plain to see that it was only the result of a miracle that the boat held together at all, for its timbers were clearly not only ancient, but rotted completely through and through.

However, it wasn't upon the boat that the men from the ship fixed their attention, but upon the old man who clung to the oars, as if he would use them to protect himself against the men from the ship. Those aboard ship glanced at one another silently, with knowing looks. The man was touched by lunacy. His eyes could barely be seen, furrowed as they were, overshadowed by tremendous white eyebrows above, and a bushy beard that covered his entire face below. His hair was long and stringy, and just as yellowed as his beard, his limbs excessively thin and wiry, coupled with an overall appearance that was exceedingly old, as to suggest biblical origins.

The men aboard ship approached him cautiously, though no one got up the nerve to come near enough to touch the boat, which was on the verge of falling apart and sinking into the depths below.

"Come, friend, let me help you, before you sink," said the man from the ship, stretching out his hand to assist the old man.

"No, no," the other shouted, waving the oars with a surprising agility and a wild look flashing in his eyes.

"You will drown."

The man on the ship held the thick-bound book in his hands. It was certainly old, but how old? Pages were torn and stained. There was no title page, no author listed. What appeared to be the word *Crónica*— Chronicle—could be barely deciphered.

• • •

Maria of the Fates spins gossomer thread, letting the imagination of her lover be her guide, regardless of contradictions or complications. "What do you see?" she asks.

"Dom Pedro living happily," he says.

"Not insane?"

"What man would have acted differently, given the circumstances? People speak of Dom Pedro's excesses, but don't mention that Dom João I burned a servant for having an affair. No, I see a long peaceful reign, a dynasty of Castros, an empire of poetry, music, and discovery, not tied to a corrupt State, or a corrupt Church, the bloody Inquistion, but bound to a higher law, a higher aspiration. I see, not a legacy of death and depravity, not a place of dreams denied, but at long last come to fruition, the only limitation being the extravagances of desire. The true Enchanted Isle—that is the future I see, the future our children will inherit."

And without losing a beat she threads new life with his every word.

CHAPTER 8

Dispatch sent by Leonardo Brum:

Horta, Faial

I have attempted to piece together the facts, what little I have managed to glean from those who knew or who had seen or heard Julia and Antonio do Canto e Castro and their father, Sebastião, all of whom are still missing.

I have examined the evidence from every angle, and while it is possible that this family was involved in some unknown practice or activity, criminal or otherwise, there is no evidence to support any such conclusion; they are merely some of the rumors that abound in this case.

I think it is far more likely that they were affected by the same particular madness, a possible genetic factor. They seem to have believed that the new island rising from the sea is the same enchanted island mentioned in the legends of the islands. Pure fantasies!

They seem to have both been affected by talk of sirens and ghost ships. Both have taken boats and, I'm convinced, gone to find this supposed island, where they have likely come to harm.

· · ·

Antonio struggled to sort through the remaining sheaves of paper as mounting winds and waves lashed against the battered ship. He fought to steady himself, and in the dying light read what was written. In some combination of the weather, his father's notes, the ship and the men around him, Antonio felt he was instrumental; he was the courier, like Mercury, sent by Jupiter on high Olympus to the gods of the seas down below, his message of welcome to the Portuguese on their historic voyage round Africa to reach India, to inform them that he was on their side. Antonio felt that he too must reach the island, play his part in reconciling the fates to his family's past, their new, long-fought-for kingdom. That he must help make it real.

While her brother concentrated on fulfilling his noble past, and righting wrongs, Julia bent her will to reaching the island to find her father, and though it was yet nebulous as regards her conscious mind, to bring to fruition a love long-denied by Fate.

She stood at the ship's wheel like some avenging spirit, ready to sweep aside all who would stand in her way.

360

· · ·

The Portuguese entered India with the sword in one hand and the Crucifix in the other; finding much gold they laid aside the Crucifix to fill their pockets.

Dom João de Castro, 1548

· · ·

Nicolau dos Santos convinces a hesitant Senhor Brum to contact the Navy to ask the rescue forces to immediately search for Julia.

"How can I ask them to search? I don't even know where she went. Where would I tell them to look?"

Nicolau insists. "Find the new island. I'm sure she is there."

"And what makes you so sure of this? You told me that she never said anything about sailing a boat, or where she might have gone."

"I know what I said, and I told you the truth. I'm certain that is where Julia is, and that she is in serious trouble. Please, senhor, before it is too late!"

Nicolau is extremely persuasive, and Senhor Brum, while he doesn't admit that he is susceptible to seasickness, feels his reluctance melt away. "Well, I will contact the proper authorities and see what we can do."

"I must go with you," Nicolau says.

Senhor Brum begins to object, but Nicolau informs him that he will otherwise find someone to take him if he should refuse. "All right, all right," he says. "We shall go together to find Julia and the others."

It's only after boarding ship that Senhor Brum realizes with a storm of conflicted emotions that Teresa has joined them.

. . .

In November of 1576 a comet was seen streaking across the heavens, striking fear into the hearts of many who saw the comet as a sign of impending evil.

An astrologer prophesied that it meant that the king would die in Africa and that his army would be destroyed, a prediction that filled the population with terror.

361

. . .

The siren sang of Dom Sebastião, The Desired One, the long hoped-for male heir to the throne and the last king of Portugal of the Avis dynasty, who saw himself as Christ's Captain against the Infidels. A weak, strange, fanatically religious boy of fourteen when he ascended the throne, he suffered from various maladies and was believed to be impotent. He spent much of his time in prayer, locked in his sparsely furnished bedroom, refusing to consult with his great-uncle, the Cardinal Henrique, who would later rule Portugal after Sebastião's death, or his grandmother, who had ruled before him. With a recurrence of the plague in 1569, Dom Sebastião left Lisbon for Sintra and Alcobaça, where he ordered the stone tombs of his ancestors opened; he upbraided Pedro I for spending all his time with Inês and other ladies of the court rather than in enhancing Portugal's greatness by conquering the Moors.

"Sire, you must marry," his advisors said. "You must enlarge the royal council, cease your ascetic way." But King Sebastião put off his advisors. First he would fulfill his dream of leading the Portuguese army in Northern Africa, fighting the Moors, emulating his famed ancestors. The only woman in whom he showed any interest in marrying, Dona

Joana de Castro, would surely wait until his moment of glory.

In June 1578 35,000 soldiers, mostly Portuguese, but including a band of some 2,800 soldiers from Germany and the Netherlands, some English adventurers and ships, 1,000 Andalusians and another 2,000 adventurers raised in Lisbon, Estremadura, the Alentejo and the Algarve, sailed Sebastião's fleet of 500 ships to Tangier and Arzila.

One of the ships weighing anchor in the Tagus at the beginning of the journey pulled up the body of a dead man, a sure sign of bad luck.

At the end of July, after having camped out in unprotected tents at Arzila, Sebastião and his men decided to march by foot to take Larache. 15,000 on foot and 1,500 on horse, around 1,000 carts, several thousand followers including servants, priests, even poets, musicians, as well as a number of wives, lovers and prostitutes were part of the entourage. They reached Alcácer Quibir on August 3rd, tired, short on food and water, and suffering beneath the heat of the blazing desert sun.

The following day, facing a far greater Moroccan army, Sebastião and eight thousand of his soldiers fell.

· · ·

On that fatal day there fell eight thousand of the king's men. Fifteen thousand more were carried off to the slave markets of Morocco. Of the entire army, only some fifty men escaped to bear the tale of the tragedy to Lisbon, arriving there on August 10, six days after the disastrous defeat.

On the battlefield were found ten thousand Portuguese guitars!

Luís de Camoens and the Epic of The Lusiads
Henry H. Hart, University of Oklahoma Press, 1962

· · ·

As the ship neared its destination, a rising tension swept through those aboard, an expectation that confrontation lay in wait ahead, some unseen danger that might prevent them from reaching the island. Antonio felt for his sword, gripping the handle, testing his strength, as the moment for battle approached. Like his heroic ancestors, he too would face his enemies with vigor and resolve.

Some of the men grumbled, trembling with fear. Antonio would lead by example; their fate was in others' hands. Destiny had seen fit to bring them to this place, at this moment.

"This is what they deserve," he heard the old man say, "for placing a usurper on the throne."

Julia leaned against the gunwale of the ship. "We must not fail them." She spoke with such force of conviction the others could only nod in mute acceptance of her words, like the lashing of the winds. "All hope rests with us."

CHAPTER 9

D. Sebastião, Rei de Portugal

Louco, sim, louco, porque quis grandeza
Qual a Sorte a não dá.
Não coube em mim minha certeza;
Por isso onde o areal está
Ficou meu ser que houve, não o que há.
Minha loucura, outros que me tomem
Com o que nela ia.
Sem a loucura que é o homem
Mais que a besta sadia,
Cadáver adiado que procria?

Dom Sebastian, King of Portugal

Mad, yes, mad, because I wanted that glory
Which Fate gives nobody
Self-certitude was uncontainable in me.
That's why there lies on sandy shores
The being that I was, not what I am.

My madness—let others take from me
And what goes with it.
What is a man without madness
But some healthy beast,
A corpse postponed that breeds?[11]

—Fernando Pessoa

· · ·

The waves rose like towering mountains, the troughs between them stretching like impossibly deep, black caverns. Peering up at the sky was like gazing into a long unlit tunnel. But there was no time for such idle gazing at the heavens, for all around the ship the crest of one wave and another threatened at each and every moment to come crashing down upon the ship, engulfing it and sending it to the ocean floor.

To make matters worse, the winds howled fearfully, raging, terrifying shrieks, tremendous gusts that pummeled the ship from all directions. The pounding rain, the long flashing streaks of lightning and the deafening thunder that followed were no less terrifying.

· · ·

And so I come to the end of life, and all will see that I loved my native land so well that I was content to die not only in it, but with it.

—Luís Vaz de Camões

· · ·

The siren sang of Dom João de Castro, grandson and namesake of the Viceroy to India, who sailed with Dom Sebastião's ill-fated army. He survived the battle of Alcácer-Quibir and capture by the Moors, finally released in 1579, after being ransomed. Refusing to acknowledge the Castilian, King Philip as Portugal's new king, he fled to France and England, following Dom António, the Prior do Crato, pretender to the Portuguese throne, for even an illegitimate grandson of a Portuguese king is better than rule by a Spanish king. However, Dom João soon tired of the rivalries and problems besetting the king in exile and, discouraged, left in 1587 to settle in Paris, where he devoted himself to the study of astrology. He became convinced that Sebastião had survived the massacre, that he represented the salvation of Portugal from the hands of the Spaniards. The Jewish writer, Isaac Abravanel, in 1503 had foretold the coming of the messiah. The Inquisition, in 1541, interrogated a cobbler from Trancoso, Gonçalo Anes Bandarra, because of similar prophecies and the strange portents revealed in his *Trovas*, the Portuguese popular songs of the time. Dom João de Castro studied the prophecies of Gonçalo Anes Bandarra, and began writing works that identified Sebastião with the Hidden One, or Messiah.

367

Since the disaster at Alcácer Quibir, rumors had circulated that King Sebastião had "escaped death on the desert sands." The bones that years later were returned to Portugal were generally not believed to be those of the missing king. Some said he "lives on the Isles of the Blessed. One foggy morning he will return to rule again, freeing Portugal from its oppressors and usher in a new age, the Fifth Empire, a new age of revival."

This fervent wish, this undying belief, developed into a faith all its own, called *Sebastianismo*. Dom João de Castro was the first apostle of the religion of Sebastianism, which spread, not only across mainland Portugal but as far as Madeira and the Azores, India and Brazil. For many years there were rumors of Sebastião's reappearance. On occasion someone claiming to be King Sebastião appeared in Portugal, but was exposed and punished; one was admirably, if not successfully, defended by Dom João de Castro. These 'false' Sebastiãos were quickly beheaded, or drawn and quartered.

Many years later, in 1666, the Inquisition punished the daughter of a guitar player in Lisbon who claimed to have visited the Hidden Isle and spoken to Sebastião and seen King Arthur, Enoch, Elijah and Saint John.

In the myth of *Sebastianismo,* the king was referred to as The Hidden One. Sebastianism proved instrumental in rallying the people to revolt against the Spanish in 1640, led by the Duke of Bragança, who became King João IV; the myth was revived again during the French invasions, and again in 1910 with the revolution that ended the monarchy and brought about the Republic.

· · ·

The island was a place, not of lost dreams or abandoned fate—at least not in any perceivable sense. It was desolate. A land where one might find oneself stranded, alone, with nothing but sand and rock, where a person could find no hope, but only go mad, and the best that could happen was a mercifully quick death.

It was only a stark, harsh, utterly lifeless outcropping. What hopes or dreams could one cling to in this bleak and barren landscape? Could they look around and imagine a lush beautiful island, where semi-goddesses ran free, eager to shower unrestrained love and affection on the shipwrecked sailor who washed upon that shore? Perhaps they would gaze out over the water that is now newly obstructed by this islet of rock, and there in the distance see the isle their hearts had sought, that other place.

Could they resist its call, remain where they were, or would they succumb, and swim out from the rock to reach that other shore, so near, so dear?

· · ·

Este sonho que eu sonhei,
É verdade muito certa;
Que lá da ilha encoberta
Há-de chegar este Rei.

This dream that I dreamed,
Is most certainly true;
That there from the hidden island
This king will arrive.

—Gonçalo Anes Bandarra

· · ·

Bearing was lost, steering impossible, sails torn into streaming shreds before they could be safely lowered. The wind lashed at everything, and the rain fell in blinding torrents.

The ship was on the verge of sinking, or being torn apart by the forces assailing it from all sides.

The crew shouted, as they tried to save the ship, one or two pointing to what appeared to be an island in the distance. They struggled to maneuver the ship to the island, hoping to sail round the island's lee side and find shelter from the wind and waves.

CHAPTER 10

Dom João, Infante de Portugal 371

Porque é do português, pai de amplos mares,
Querer, poder só isto:
O inteiro mar, ou a orla vã desfeita—
O todo, ou o seu nada.

John, Prince of Portugal

Because it's like the Portuguese, lords of oceans,
To want, and capable only of this:
Either all oceans or washed up drift of shores
Everything, or the nothingness of it all.[12]

—Fernando Pessoa

• • •

Where is everything? Sebastião wrote. The lands, the houses, the cattle and horses, all gone. Everything stripped bare. The house, standing
like an empty tomb, echoes with the voices of the ghosts who wander its
halls looking for their descendants, finding only strangers there. Where
is the furniture, the carriages, where are the crystal glasses, the silver
plates and platters, the paintings and tapestries that hung on the walls?
All sold off to pay the bills, while the vultures swarmed round to grab
at the spoils, to pick the carcass clean, to take home a piece of the once-

mighty Canto e Castros. The fine linens, the curtains, the beveled mirrors, into which Violante do Canto herself peered before meeting the almost King, Dom António, the Prior do Crato. And the majestic bed upon which she had lain—all gone.

In whose cabinets do the weapons of the family now hang, the medals of The Order of Christ, the armor, swords, and shields emblazoned with the coat-of-arms? Not so much as a trinket, no gold or silver broach, no library full of books, to remind the lonely ghosts of what was forever lost.

For the Canto e Castros there existed an irreistible urge to recreate, to take the ordinary, the commonplace, and ammend it by lifting it up until it attainsed proportions of the mythic. For the alternative was nothingness. Thus, the family played a game of pretending, displaying of attitude buoyed by insurmountable pride. We will not let them see us as we really are. We will not admit defeat. A family and a country; both clung desperately to the sacred image of what was, not daring to look at the hows and whys—that would necessitate admitting what could never be admitted—until both could be summed up by a single phrase: "We had it all, we lost it all."

In 1918, the last feeble attempt to reclaim the past was achieved when Rear-Admiral José do Canto e Castro was elected President of Portugal, after two Azoreans had already held the position, but it was an empty, futile gesture. The republic proved to be unstable and short-lived. After only six or seven months, the Admiral was voted out, followed by even more instability, which ultimately led to the dictatorial rule of Salazar, as the Portuguese government and families split into various factions all at odds with one another: Monarchists, Socialists and Communists, Fascists, the military—Castros in each group opposing one another.

In retrospect the reasons are always clear, the results, unavoidable. Antero de Quental, greatest of Azorean poets, outlined the reasons in "Causas da Decadência dos Povos Peninsulares" ("Causes of the Decadence of the Peninsular Peoples"), a pamphlet published before he shot himself in a square in Ponta Delgada, on São Miguel, in 1891: The expulsion of the Jews, which robbed the country of its best scientists, doctors, artisans and thinkers; the establishment of the Inquisition; and the disaster at Alcácer Quibir, in 1578. Portugal might have survived any one of these calamitous events, but taken together, they forced the country down a road from which there was no turning back. The Lisbon earthquake of 1755 was simply the coup-de-grace, destroying the building that housed the archives of the explorations, the logbooks, maps and charts, leaving Portugal bereft of much of its past.

Quental was part of the group of writers that included Eça de Queiroz and other greats of the age, who referred to themselves as the *Vencidos da Vida*—Life's Vanquished. Like many Portuguese writers, Quental's was an unhappy life. Given his name, Antero, after, Anteros, brother (and opposite) of Eros, son of Venus and Mars, and god of unhappy love, the avenger of unrequited affection, one might say he never stood a chance; for Anteros is one of those gods, who, while his brother gets all the fame, all the renown, it is he who—take a look around—holds sway in the world.

Anteros is also one of those gods on whom you don't want to turn your back.

*   *   *

There was a moment when everything froze, as the ship was swept up upon the very crest of an enormous wave. Julia peered down from the edge of the precipice, the abyss, and thought how odd it was to suffer a hallucination at that moment, when they were about to be engulfed. For gazing down into all that bottomless sea, she saw a vision of a beautiful island, a paradise of plenty, warm and ideal. And there, in the split second before it all disappeared, she thought she saw several faces . . . but, no, impossible, it was madness to think.

*   *   *

E pera isso queria que, feridas
As filhas de Nereu no ponto fundo,
De amor dos Lusitanos incendidas
Que vêm de descobrir o nono mundo,
Todas nũa ilha juntas e subidas,
Ilha que nas entranhas do porfundo,
Oceano terei aparelhada,
De dões de Flora e Zéfiro adornada;

Assi Vénus propôs; e o filho inico,
Pera lhe obedecer, já se apercebe

My request is this, that the daughters
Of Nereus, in their watery depths,
Should burn with love for the Portuguese
Who came to discover the new world,
And should assemble and await them
On an island I am preparing
In the midst of the ocean—one supplied
With all Zephyr and Flora can provide.

So Venus proposed, and mischievous
Cupid prepared at once to obey her[13]

—Luís Vaz de Camões, *Os Lusíadas*

. . .

On the Azores the rains fell; storms one after the other deluged the islands. Cyclones inundated the towns and villages with a torrential downpour day after day, swelling streams and creek beds, turning streets and roads into raging rivers. Rain, wind and waves, unlike anything anyone had ever seen before. Mountainous waves slammed against seawalls and ports, destroying more than several breakwaters with their terrific force.

Fishing boats had to be rescued and search parties were sent out into the dangerous waters. A Portuguese destroyer was sent to assist. Still the rain continued to fall.

People sat in their homes, peered out their windows at the flood, wondering if they'd all be swept out to sea. Already the sea and the skies were one, all water, all sea.

. . .

Vi tantas águas, vi tanta verdura,
As aves todas cantavam d'amores.

I saw such waters, such greenery,
All the birds were singing of love.

—Sá de Miranda

. . .

The island lay like a crown. From a high point in the middle smoke bellowed into the air. A volcano, and an island, new and raw, untouched by life.

Antonio peered at the spectacle before him and heard a familiar voice whisper, "The Enchanted Island. Do you see?"

"There it is, at last," someone else said.

"Yes, look there," said another. "We've found it."

Antonio stared, ready to behold all the lost treasures of the world. He'd imagined an island much grander, much more magnificent than any other, lush and forested in a canopy of green, of gentle breezes and beaches of fine glistening sands. But instead, he saw only brown, gray and black, cooling lava, bare, lifeless rock.

The ship fought the waves to reach the island, but as the vessel came about Antonio saw Julia pointing to where another island, not on the larboard side, as the first island, but to starboard, like a projection, a ghost-image, of another ship, the one superimposed upon the other, all reflection and refraction, a convergence of space and time, a small boat and a carrack or galley, a ghost ship, which rode the winds and the waves. It was like a confluence of several raging rivers running together. Here and now, there and then. The sky and the sea, a new island as well as a very old island; a modern boat with a modern man, an ancient ship with an old crew; a siren who sings a love song of the islands, while several black birds circled overhead.

This island was a glimmering jewel, radiant in the green sea—an island of dreams.

"There's the Hidden Island," Antonio shouted, trying to get the others to look, to see what he saw, but they ignored him, pushed him aside. Instead, they lowered the boat, eager to reach the island they saw. The first island.

"At long last," said the old sailor at Antonio's side. "I am here at last!" He dove into the water and swam toward the island, not where the men lowering the boat were headed but toward the Enchanted Island.

375

Antonio unsheathed his sword but it was too late. The others were gone. Julia sprang to life, grabbing hold of the ship's wheel, and steering the ship away from the island, toward the Enchanted Isle, just as the dory was being rowed away from the ship.

Julia steered as the sounds of the tempest and the music built to a crescendo. Antonio stood on the prow at the ready for what was to come, the song of the siren filling his ears.

．．．

Many names were used to express the idea of an earthly paradise hidden somewhere in the western seas. It was the Atlantis of which Plato had written; Bimini, wherein rose the fountain of perpetual youth; the Isle of Seven Cities, founded by the seven Portuguese Bishops who had fled thither from the fury of the Moors; Avalon, where King Arthur slept; the Fortunate Isles, the Isles of St. Brendan, of Antília or of Brazil . . . Portuguese and Breton fishermen still hear the sirens singing; and it was not until 1721 that the last expedition set sail from the Canaries in search of St. Brendan's Isle. Even in 1759 the abode of the saint was sighted, but the crass materialism of the age explained it as an effect of mirage.

Vasco da Gama and his Successors
K.G Jayne, London, 1911

．．．

The end came suddenly. Perhaps the sisters of Clotho found that she and her lover had planned to make the island remain above the surface of the ocean, or feared they would try to leave, but clearly they did not manage this on their own. Vulcan and the Cyclopes, likely Neptune, too, involved themselves with preventing what they saw as one calamity by causing a catastrophe of their own. Or it may have simply been rot, the boat's planks too long in the water, worm-eaten, rat-gnawed, or a submerged reef or rock that caused the boat to begin breaking apart and sinking into the sea.

Rain fell in a deluge, unlike anything Julia had ever seen. Lightning flashed and waves tossed the boat about as if it were a stick. Julia strained to see, to breathe. But as the ocean roared up into the air, and the rain drove itself down on the surface of the sea, she felt she was already drowning. There was only water, both above and below, and she was swimming—swimming aboard a boat, swimming through the sea-soaked air, gasping as she struggled to reach Antonio.

With the sea swirling all around her, Julia couldn't tell where she was, or what lay closer to her, the island, the ship, or her brother. It was all she could do to keep her head above water. Odd that it was at this moment she remembered Sebastião taking her to Praia do Almoxarife when she was a child, her swimming at the beach there, and a boy a few years older taunting her beyond the waves: "Swim farther," he said, diving in and out of the water like a creature born of the sea, smiling at her and swimming toward deeper water. "Come with me."

She was certain the boy was Nicolau.

377

Antonio clung to whatever he could grab hold of—the stays, the now frail, tiny mast, shrunk to the ordinary; everything churned round and round like a whirlpool, the sea, the boat, the winds. He had never been a very good swimmer. His time had come—the cold depths awaited him, if sharks didn't get to him first. Either way, mere moments were all he had.

He held on to Sebastião's writings, fragments, a sentence, a word, unable to let go of the precious packets of notes, like those captains who refused to leave their ships, filled with the treasures of India, even as those ships sank from their excess weight. Or like Camões who gripped the manuscript of *The Lusiads,* even as he was swept by a wave off the ship he sailed from Macao to Goa, during a typhoon. Antonio clutched what he assumed would be the last notes he would ever see before the ocean swallowed him at last. Perhaps during those few seconds that stretched and distorted completely out of shape and seemed the longest minutes he had ever experienced, he didn't really read, but only imagined or dreamt he read, or lived what he thought he had in fact only dreamed.

"Julia," he shouted, looking to see where she had gone. "Julia."

From the roiling waters of the sea, out of the wind-whipped skies, whirling with dark clouds and rain, clutching at the mast and prepared to die, Antonio heard a voice that rose like the wail of a banshee.

He looked to see the ship, but it was gone. A gust of wind blew open his satchel and swept Sebastião's remaining papers into the water. Antonio let go of the mast and grabbed at the papers, but at that moment a wave swept him away. He thought not of saving himself at that moment, as if that were an impossibility or unimportant, but of saving all the pages he could.

He clawed at the sea, thrashing in the water, hoping to save something, anything that had been washed overboard.

. . .

Over the years some people have claimed that the Azores have been the scene of a number of inexplicable occurrences. In 1871, for instance, the brig *Mary Celeste* was found under sail by another ship in the vicinity of the island of Santa Maria.

The *Mary Celeste* was boarded by men from the other ship, but no one was found aboard. How or why the ten people on board had completely vanished remains a mystery to this day.

More recently, several sailboats also have been found among the Azores with no one aboard, no evidence of foul play and no explanation of what had occurred.

. . .

Antonio fought against the pull of the deep, moving through the currents, the depths of the ocean, the layers of the past, the centuries of history, the various and numerous voices calling to him, claiming him after eons and eons, their prodigal, bastard child.

It was impossible to tell up from down. All was a twisting spiral of blinding, numbing cold. There was no light, only shadows, and shadows of still more shadows. He wondered if it would ever end, or if this was death, eternal. There were terrible, horrifying sounds. Antonio wondered what demon or monster could possibly make such a noise: If it were, perhaps, the feared Adamastor, returning?

Have I been tricked, he wondered, grasping at mirages?

Seawater filled his lungs. He felt something brush up against him. Were there strands of hair? Something (someone?) grabbing hold of him? Was there a boat, perhaps the ship's dory? He reached out, tried to grab hold.

Antonio stopped fighting. He belonged to the waves now, his numbed body slipping into shock.

There was only death.

But before he sank, he saw one final vision, not the Enchanted

Island—no, that was gone, faded as it sank back beneath the surface. No, he saw the sea filled with ships, giant ships, monstrously dark, and heard that strange churning sound which filled the air.

Then nothingness.

It is on the Azores . . . and particularly on São Miguel, that traditionalists locate Poseidonis, the capital of Atlantis.

This is also the opinion of our friend José da Silva Fraga, who told us, in excellent French, the legends of the double lake of the Sete Cidades.

"The Azores," said José da Silva Fraga, "were once called the Enchanted Isles. They appeared and disappeared like mirages, and they have given rise to the legend of São Brandan Island.

"Traditions—which necessarily came from Europe, since the islands were uninhabited when Cabral discovered them in 1432—say that a submerged continent surrounds the nine islands. It can only be Atlantis, of course . . .

"From the promontory named the Vista de Rey (King's Vista) on São Miguel, there is one of the most beautiful views in the world. You look out over a vast, green basin studded with Hydrangeas and Azaleas. At the bottom of it are two lakes whose harmonious curves are intertwined to form the symbol of infinity. One lake has blue water, the other has emerald-green water, and seven legends explain the difference.

"One of them tells the story of the kingdom of Atlantis and its sovereigns, King White-Gray and Queen White-Pink. For a long time they were in despair at not having any children. Finally they had a beautiful little daughter, but a powerful and rather disagreeable fairy forbade them to see her until she was twenty years old.

"On São Miguel, below the Vista de Rey, the king built seven cities of happiness for the little princess to live in. No one, not even the sovereigns, was allowed to enter them. Then, as in all legends, the king broke the prohibition; but just as he was about to enter a city and see his beloved daughter at last, the ground trembled, volcanoes spat infernal fire, and water rose to engulf the seven cities.

"At the bottom of the green lake are the princess's little green slippers; at the bottom of the blue one is her blue hat."

This is only a legend, of course, but it is the only one that explicitly gives the location of the capital of Atlantis.

Mysteries of Forgotten Worlds, Charles Berlitz, New York, 1972

. . .

Julia found herself in a sea churning with beasts and monsters so often depicted in the ancient maps and charts. There were loud roars and turbulent waves, and she knew she had but seconds, as the boat sank. Many thoughts rushed at her in no particular order: her father, Antonio, Nicolau, her music. That she would die without ever truly experiencing the fruition of love, without achieving any of the things she had hoped to achieve with her art, just when she was on the verge of finding what had been missing for so long; that which she had had and known when she was still a child.

Consciousness is a strange, slippery thing. In that shadowy uncharted realm, a moment can flower and bloom, last for what seems like hours, crammed with a multitude of experience and sensation, just as days and weeks can flash by in the space of one breath, an entire lifetime pass by in an instant, and maybe under the proper conditions, not one lifetime but many.

. . .

As he drowned, Antonio heard the siren, as if through many miles of seawater. Was she trying to save him, or take him down to the Enchanted Isle, to that domain Sebastião had seized for his kingdom? Sebastião and Clotho, or Maria of the Fates, would welcome him, "Yes, Antonio, our fortunes may have failed, our family fallen up there, where disaster and disappointment lurked behind every corner, but here the dream lives on; here, we have everything; this is truly our kingdom, and if I figure it out someday, this island will rise up and stay there, and I will be Dom

Sebastião who has returned."

These were some of his fragmented, disjointed thoughts as he sank, the island dragging him down to its hidden realm in the depths. But then a flicker of consciousness, a spark of recognition, a sound, a voice calling, summoning, repeating his name over and over. And he began flailing his arms to reach her.

As the noise grew closer, and rose in volume, Antonio felt himself being raised, while the sea (and the siren?) pulled him back down—a moment of monumental struggle. Which would prevail, in this tug of war for Antonio's body? Or was it for his soul? The water lapped at him, an infinitesimal number of droplets of salt water, the sea of Portuguese tears, each drop seeking to drag him down, to claim him as their rightful legacy, heir presumptive of the ocean's graveyard.

In his delirium, Antonio didn't realize that the screaming monster drawing him up with its tentacles, in the deathtrap of its swirling pincers was nothing more than a rescue helicopter; that the person who tried to cling to him was in fact Teresa who forced breath back into his lungs. The sea fell away, as he was lifted into the air. Below, in the churning sea, were the ships—not the *naus*, or carracks, but several belonging to the Portuguese navy, even a destroyer among them, sent out to search for him and the others.

· · ·

Julia couldn't move for the longest time, could barely breathe. When she did, a fragrance in the air helped clear the fog, easing her mind, and leaving her light-headed.

There were times when she struggled against the sheets and blankets as if she were still in the water and a sea of liquid fire burned her. She called out. Then a cool hand on her forehead soothed her, and a whisper urged her back to sleep, to rest, to peacefulness, to the present.

She heard voices now and then as if from a great distance, and wondered who they were. Had she been plucked from the sea by the siren, or one of the Fates of the Enchanted Island, was it they, perhaps, who tended and cared for her?

Someone spoke her name, and in her dreams she heard him sing to her softly in the night. It may have only been hours or even minutes, but it seemed like days and weeks before she was sure, before she knew she wasn't dreaming him, that he was real and she found his name on her tongue: Nicolau.

· · ·

It was several days before Julia fully came to. She spent that time recuperating in the hospital. During much of her stay Nicolau was at her side. Sometimes she awoke, opened her eyes and saw him looking at her. A smile, a whisper, *"Amo-te*—I love you." Or, she would hear his words reaching across the incredible gulf, the painful distances and irregular terrain she had traversed. Or felt his hand resting on hers, the touch of his flesh itself a calling, "We are here, together, now; this is our time, our place, not where you have been. Stay."

"Antonio's fine," Nicolau said, as soon as Julia was awake. "Like you, he's suffering from exposure. He nearly drowned, but he's awake and struggling with the nurses."

Julia managed to smile. "Manuel and Johan?" she said.

"They were picked up before you were found. Johan was drunk, talking of pirates, mermaids, and treasure. Manuel and Johan said they got into the dory to get to the island, but that Antonio and you stayed aboard and turned the boat away. Johan never stopped shouting and almost jumped overboard to get back to the boat."

"Really?"

He nodded. "Manuel thought he'd gone crazy, and hit him with an oar. Later Johan said you and Antonio were trying to keep him from something."

"How is he now?"

"He's better. They kept him locked up for a few days to sober up. Now I hear he's quiet. No more drinking or crazy talk. Perhaps he doesn't remember."

Nicolau told Julia about the earthquakes that occurred when she was still lost on the boat. "They were terrible, Julia. Nothing like the other tremors. There were many casualties on Terceira. Many buildings fell and a number of people were killed, not only there, but on the other islands, too."

"My God, I'm glad you're okay. How's Maria dos Santos and José,

Maria Josefa and João?"

"They're all fine."

"And Quebrado? The village of—the children and everyone? Teresa?"

"Fine, all of them. But many others weren't so fortunate. Doctors have flown in from the mainland and the United States. They've set up make-shift hospitals. Hundreds of people are displaced. Many have lost their homes, and refuse to go near or inside any buildings."

"What about the island?" she asked. "The new island?"

He paused before answering. "It disappeared with the last earthquake," he said.

· · ·

In a repeat of history the island of Dom João de Castro sank back below the surface of the ocean after several days of spewing hot steam, ash and smoke. There was a series of severe earthquakes in quick succession, and several large waves caused damage on some of the low-lying towns of the neighboring islands.

Streams of lava rolled out upon the surface of the sea, which hissed and boiled, sending vast numbers of dead fish in all directions. Then it quickly calmed down again and everything returned to normal: The island was gone, the sea between Terceira and São Miguel barren of anything except a lingering memory, a faint image of what might have been, along with a feeling or suspicion that perhaps it too was a mirage, a dream. Farther south, from Santa Maria, too, there was nothing to be seen, only the sea.

Perhaps God was playing tricks, amusing Himself, confounding the human race, putting up something, taking it away a moment later—now you see it, now you don't. Or it could be that He simply changed His mind, trying for aesthetics, something to break the unchanging monotony of the sea; let's stick another island here, only to find He didn't much like the view.

The islands quickly settled back into the here and now, the present, where things were quiet and still; no more earthquakes or new islands rising from the depths; no more mysteries or miracles; no more drowned men or ghost ships or sirens singing in the night. The islands healed their wounds, just as Julia and Antonio slowly recovered.

. . .

Antonio struggled hard to remember. Fragments, bits and pieces were all he had, all he'd been left with. What had happened to the skull? Hadn't it been there with him aboard ship, or on the tiny boat from the island? But which island? Where was Julia? He tried to recollect but could remember only a confused array of images, nothing that made sense: a figure who had jumped overboard as they approached the island, a vision of Teresa dos Santos, clinging to him.

He heard words, strains of poetry, a melody now and then. Or was it only the wind and the sea that even now filled his ears?

. . .

As soon as Julia was coherent, Leonardo Brum came to speak with her. It was strictly routine, a matter of tying up some loose ends, getting Julia's point of view, since he had already spoken with Manuel, Johan, Nicolau, and the doctors who monitored Julia's and Antonio's progress.

As Leonardo Brum expected, Julia shed no real light on what had occurred. She could remember little of what happened. Poet and unrepentant romantic that he was, Senhor Brum was still a man who operated with facts, not dreams and hallucinations.

He interviewed Antonio but was forced to conclude that Antonio had no more knowledge of what had happened than he, Senhor Brum, had. "I saw the island, and Sebastião there, but I think it sank before we reached it." He mentioned some nonsense about a skull, then an old man who swam to the island. Something about the Fates. And Teresa dos Santos, which caused Senhor Brum to shiver uncontrollably.

"Is she?" Antonio asked. "Was she the one—?"

"Yes," Brum said, his mouth suddenly very dry. "She leapt in to save you. How, no one can say. But there you have it. It's a miracle you both weren't killed. Apparently, she is much stronger, and a far better swimming than anyone might guess." He shook his head. "Clearly, an elemental," he added.

"What?"

"Nothing," Brum said. "Nothing important."

Antonio nodded. "I wish I could remember more."

"You are very lucky," Brum said.

Antonio shook his head. "I know." How was he to know Senhor Brum wasn't referring to the fact that Antonio had survived his ordeal, but that he couldn't rid his mind of the image of Teresa breathing life into the young man's body?

"Well, I have all I need," Brum said, leaving Antonio to his own musings.

"End of story," Brum mumbled, as he left the hospital. When all was said and done, he was happy to see Julia and Nicolau together. There was something vaguely satisfying about the other man getting the woman. Nicolau gets Julia, Brum mused, and I'll write a poem. He was, after all, enough of a realist to expect nothing more and nothing less.

Senhor Brum was ready to return home. He would make his full report and be done with it. He weighed whether he should see Teresa one last time, before leaving. He already had the idea in mind of sitting down to write an epic poem, "The Enchanted Island and the Luminescent Woman," a modern man's search for ideal love.

. . .

"You've changed," Julia said. "For that matter, I hardly recognize myself."

"You have no idea," Antonio said. Their first meeting since being rescued was slightly awkward. Nicolau had left them alone so they could sort things out between them.

Julia knew that something had happened beyond the little she remembered, and that nothing would be the same.

"I don't know what to think about Sebastião," she said. In a way it was as if he had died, and yet, it was impossible for Julia to see it that way, to feel that this prosaic end was what had occurred. Something kept her from accepting the obvious.

"I know what I saw," Antonio said. "It may be impossible. But it's all I have. He was there, the island was there, and now they're both gone."

Julia nodded. She hadn't known what to expect regarding the new island. She'd hoped it would rise even higher, towering like Pico above the sea, the tenth Azorean isle, which even she had come to think of as somehow, if not exactly belonging to the Canto e Castros, then at least a part of the family, spiritually if not materially.

The next day Julia and Antonio were released from the hospital on São Miguel. Accompanied by Nicolau they flew directly to Horta.

Maria Josefa and João fussed over the two shipwreck victims. Maria Josefa especially doted on Antonio, much to his dismay, insisting he build his strength by eating plenty of soup, sautéed beefsteak and eggs with enough garlic and onion to destroy any malady.

João said how proud Sebastião would be, of both of them, but especially Julia. He handed them a newspaper clipping. "I'm afraid it's more bad news," he said. The article stated that the Casa dos Remédios, on Terceira, the manor house where their grandfather and countless Canto e Castros over the centuries were born, and which still bore the family crest, had been completely destroyed by the earthquake.

Antonio drew out a long low whistle, as if the news made words insufficient.

"The island's gone," Julia said, "father's gone, and now the Casa, too?"

Nicolau reached out his hand and touched Julia. She squeezed his.

"It's just an old building, anyway," she said. "Some castle." She tried to laugh, but was too weak to make the effort. It still hurt to laugh, or cough, or move. "Damn. I feel like I've been kicked and beaten."

"You have, haven't you?" Nicolau said. "It's amazing, what you've been through."

"My God," she said, "when Mateus finds out. It'll break his heart."

Of course it wasn't just an old building. It was a monument, a symbol, redolent of past greatness, the history of Portugal, and the family.

• • •

Nicolau brought Julia some papers. She looked them over in disbelief. It was more of Sebastião's notes, to be sure, but also the music Julia had written. Sheet after sheet of music.

"Where did you find these?" she asked.

"In your clothes," Nicolau said, somewhat embarrassed. "They were in your pockets."

Some of the notes were unreadable, blurred by the water. Others she could make out what was written, faintly, jotted down in haste.

. . .

Fragment from the notes of Sebastião do Canto e Castro:

Is it better to love the unattainable, the ideal? To spend one's life reaching for what one can never have? Perhaps better isn't the proper term. Some can be content with the here and now, with reality, just as they are able to perform in the world in which they exist, able to do as others do, never asking, "At what price?" To join in the rules and restrictions of what we would term the 'normal life,' so admirable in our eyes to see our sons and daughters get in line like good soldiers and play according to the set rules, down the road to affluence.

But for some this is impossible. Their eyes and ears are ever on something more remote, attuned to a sight or sound as real as this pen I hold in my hand and yet which others cannot hear or see.

It is the lone dreamer, the rogue heart, the iconoclast, who blazes a new trail, who makes the future and keeps the real treasures from crumbling to dust.

389

CHAPTER 12

As filhas do Mondego a morte escura
Longo tempo chorando memoraram,
E, por memória eterna, em fonte pura
As lágrimas choradas transformaram.
O nome lhe puseram, que inda dura,
Dos amores de Inês, que ali passaram.
Vede que fresca fonte rega as flores,
Que lágrimas são a água e o nome Amores.

The nymphs of Mondego long remembered
That dark death with mourning,
And their tears were transformed
To a fountain in eternal memory;
Its name "the Loves of Inês,"
Who wandered there, still endures.
Fortunate the flowers that bloom above
Such waters, such tears, telling of Love![14]

Luís Vaz de Camões, *Os Lusíadas*

. . .

Julia felt her way through the changes that had taken place. Antonio and her spoke hesitantly, as if both were afraid to speak of what had happened. She viewed her islands, nine in number, back to normalcy, bereft of mad dreams; her father's room smaller, dingier. Just an ordinary cluttered room.

Antonio felt the change in the islands, too; strangely enough, he missed the skull. He wondered if he'd really seen the man fall or jump overboard and swim to the island, or if the extremes of weather, coupled with the bizarre circumstances in which he'd found himself had caused him to imagine the ridiculous? Something kept him from saying aloud the name he longed to hear, the face he most desired to see.

"What will you do now?" Julia asked.

Antonio shrugged. "Go home, I guess," he said. "I'll have a mess to attend to when I get back." He swallowed. "And you?"

"I don't know," she said. This is not the way it's supposed to end, she thought. How many endings can a life have? She stared out at the future, one just as uncertain, as dark as before. Nothing was clearer, only more complicated. Where would she go? What would she do? She knew what had been lost. But what had she gained?

Julia didn't need to hear official word about her father's fate to know that nothing would come of that; like the drowned man, the ghost ship, and the siren, some things would never be explained or known for certain. Many things remained locked away from knowledge, burned in the conflagrations of the Inquisition, the fires of the volcanic eruption, the earthquake, tidal wave and fires that destroyed Lisbon, buried from sight beneath the waves, like Atlantis.

Julia spent days deciding her next move. She had to return to the United States—that much was clear. Things had to be arranged, put in order. At the same time she was certain that she wouldn't stay, that her return would be a short one, and she would then have to start all over.

Antonio made plans to return to the States in a few days. "Are you coming with me?" he asked.

"Yes."

"Good." He smiled, relieved that he wouldn't have to return home empty-handed.

. . .

—A vós, meu canto,
Canto de indignação
A vós, os povos do universo, o envio.
Ergo-me a delatar tamanho crime,

E eterna a voz me gelará nos lábios.
Lira da minha pátria, onde hei cantado
O lusitano—envilecido—nome,
. . . este só brado
Alevanta final e derradeiro:
Nem o humilde lugar onde repoisam
As cinzas de Camões, conhece o Luso.

To you, O peoples of the universe,
I send my song of indignation...
I rise up and denounce so great a crime
and my voice will freeze eternally on my lips
Lyre of my fatherland, on which I have sung
the Portuguese name, now humbled . . .
raise this single last and final shout:
The Portuguese do not even
know the humble place
where the ashes of Camoëns rest![15]

—Almeida Garrett, "Camões"

• • •

As Julia and Antonio prepared to leave, they received one more unexpected blow—notification in the form of a telegram that Mateus do Canto e Castro had died peacefully in his sleep in Rio. Julia couldn't help but reflect on the irony that fate had timed her grandfather's death to coincide with the earthquake, the sinking of the island, and the destruction of the Casa dos Remédios. At least Mateus had been spared the news about Sebastião and the Casa.

"What now?" she asked. Her mind spun with the latest news, the sense of loss. "What now?" What remained? Her music, and, of course, Nicolau.

"I'm sorry," Nicolau said.

"We only met Mateus once," Antonio said. "We really knew about him only by reputation."

"When I was ten years old Mateus came and visited the family in California," Julia said. "He stayed a couple of weeks. Our only visit."

"What was he like?"

"Mateus was tall, thin and solemn," Antonio said, with a laugh. "Dignified."

"Not solemn, really," Julia said. "He carried himself with stern pride. He spoke no English. But he had a twinkle in his eye and a good sense of humor."

"Although he sighed frequently," Antonio said. "Aware of the importance of the name he possessed, and of the fact that it was all he had—he believed he'd been robbed of a kingdom."

Mateus had been extremely poor in Julia's mind. She had searched the great empty depths of her grandfather's eyes only to find a vast, desolate landscape.

"Looking into Mateus's eyes was like peering across the remains of an ancient ruin," she said. Even his body reflected this state of existence; he appeared emaciated, the bones of his hands and his joints stuck up through his skin, wherein were carved the countless disappointments, the failures—far too numerous for one lifetime. "Even still, Mateus had a quick wit." While fate had taken from him everything it so generously lavished upon his ancestors, nothing could rob him of his name or his family history, which were the most precious things he possessed.

Her grandfather, Julia explained, was quick with a joke, recited poems and had fiercely-held opinions about a wide range of topics; his eyes flickered and sparkled anew, reveling as he retold stories of the majesty of the past, the names and lives he had long consigned to memory and loved to recount: the titles, the awards, the medals, the positions held—they were his rosary, uttered to preserve their splendor, to prevent them from fading completely into oblivion.

"I wish I could have met him," Nicolau said.

"Sebastião was the only one who defended Mateus," Antonio said. "He said that though his father had dreamed of vague conquests, of fine sagas and noble deeds, the kind of fame for which the family was renowned, clearly he was too old to do anything. He had spent his whole life, instead, trying to recapture some of that lost eminence in his art—in painting, poetry, music."

Mateus had lived in a tiny apartment in Rio and owned very little in the way of possessions—the family crest, a few volumes of poetry and essays he had written, some paintings, several books on the family—and was able to come to America only because the rest of the family pooled their money to purchase a ticket. Of course, compared with the millions in Brazil who had far less, he was hardly poor, but in Julia's mind no one had suffered such great losses as Mateus had experienced. The steep decline from such grandiose heights seemed to magnify the thousand-and-one indignities that those losses brought.

"We once owned castles," Mateus would tell any unwary listener. "Half the island of Terceira was ours, ships, armies of servants. Now, the lands and homes are lost, all the tapestries, and belongings embossed with the Canto e Castro coat-of-arms are scattered, lost. Like the treasures Spain carried out of Portugal when they left in 1640, like the town of Olivença, which they stole in 1820."

"The saddest thing," Julia said, "the one shock he never got over, was when he was a young boy and went alone to the barber for a haircut, the man with the scissors began to speak of the family, recounting stories about Dona Violante do Canto who stood so boldly, so bravely, as she defied the Spanish invaders, and the great lineage, and the castle the family had possessed for four centuries, and how proud Mateus should be, Mateus turned to the man with a face as blank and unknowing as a complete stranger's.

"'What is the matter, boy?' the barber shouted. 'Don't you know who you are?' Mateus shook his head, no. 'Your family is famous,' the barber said. Mateus went to the library and looked up information on the family. There it was: the *Casa e Capella de Nossa Senhora dos Remédios*— The House and Chapel of Our Lady of Remedies, built in the sixteenth century, by Pedro Anes do Canto, an enormous manor house, a splendid monument to the family history, the coat-of-arms proudly displayed above the huge doors. Mateus had occasionally passed by the manor when he went out with his family.

"Gone. It was now an orphanage. His family lived in a rented home, very small, very ordinary.

"He read about others: members of the Order of Christ, proud captains of the Azorean fleets, constables over vast armies; his uncle, Admiral José do Canto e Castro, President of Portugal in 1918; Dom João de Castro, Viceroy to India; Dona Inês de Castro, whose tragic story every school child knew; all the people his father never mentioned. Why had he been silent?"

His brothers and he, Mateus discovered, were the last born in what he would always refer to as "the family castle." In the complicated entanglement of last will and testament, the property and wealth of the Canto e Castro family was divided up in the generation preceding Raimundo's. While Mateus's father had inherited the family estate, his aunts had inherited all the income property and money. It was understood that they would in turn leave what they had to Raimundo; that was the way things were done. Raimundo had been raised as the son of nobility, which every generation preceding him had so far enjoyed.

When Raimundo married Etelvina da Silva, a mere nobody without land or money or even a name that rang of nobility, his aunts, appalled at his choice of a poor commoner, were persuaded by the advice of various affiliates of the Church that they should leave the land and money to a thankful God and a worthy Church, rather than a disobedient nephew.

As a result, Raimundo took possession of an estate with no means to provide upkeep; being schooled in the aristocracy, he knew nothing about earning a living. He decided to sell the estate, take his family and move to Lisbon, where he would learn a profession, a trade, with which to support his wife and children and close the door on the family forever.

In 1908 Raimundo sold the house to the *Irmandade de Nossa Senhora do Livramento*—The Fraternity of Our Lady of Deliverance, which founded the Orphanage of João Baptista Machado. Mateus was only five years old at the time, thus unable to realize the significance of all the upheaval in their lives.

Raimundo, left with little money, due to the lack of interested buyers of used manors, coupled with heavy taxes and debts, took up the trade of milliner in Lisbon. He returned to Angra several years later, just in time to see sweeping changes in fashion usher the demise of one more popular item, as the bottom fell out of the hat market.

Mateus grew up unable to rid his eyes of the ever-present visions of what might have been, what should have been. He never forgave his father for selling the house, his aunts for condemning him to a lost past, the Church for taking what wasn't theirs, Fate for robbing him of his destiny. He savored the bittersweet utterance of naming those personages he claimed for his own: Saint Isabel, King Dom Dinis, John of Kent, Dom Pedro, Dona Inês de Castro, Dona Violante do Canto, Dom João de Castro, King Sancho IV of Castile.

In his dreams he heard the sound of voices ringing down the stone hallways of the great family manor, echoes from the ages: music the musicians played, religious services in the chapel, everything larger, grander, richer than the impoverished life in which he now moved.

He didn't have to say any of this. It was conveyed by his expressions, his manner of speaking, by his frequent sighs, and his every gesture. His eyes, though blind, were permanently fixed upon the accumulation of those losses, thousands of miles away, accrued through the centuries. They were clearly visible, itemized, chronicled. All one had to do was gaze into his eyes: *This is the true measure of my loss.*

"What an incredible story," Nicolau said.

"It would have destroyed Mateus to learn of Sebastião and the Casa dos Remédios," Antonio said. "Perhaps it's best this way."

Julia nodded. Though she was loathe to admit it, Antonio was right.

• • •

Days passed, and things slowly returned to normal. Antonio busied himself elsewhere, while Julia spent time with Nicolau, regaining her strength.

"Where will you go?" Nicolau asked. "What will you do?"

Julia shook her head. "I don't know," she said. "What about you?"

"Me?"

That wasn't what she meant. What she meant was, "What about us?" But she couldn't seem to articulate her thoughts and feelings. She went through the motions, acted automatically, still stunned and just trying to get by. It wasn't that easy. Nothing was the same. Not the islands, not her family; certainly she wasn't the same. She took the boat to Pico, to José Manuel's Village of Idiots, another place that had obviously meant a lot to Sebastião.

"I'm sorry about everything, Julia," José said. "It's a shame about your father and Mateus."

"Thank you, José." Julia felt sorry, too, especially for not having gone to see Mateus, though she still found it difficult to think of Sebastião as dead, perhaps numbed by so many disasters one after another. "How's everyone here?"

"Everyone's fine, nothing serious," José said. "We were very lucky. But we have a lot of work to do, rebuilding and helping out others.

Luckily, we are stocked with more than enough supplies, much of which Sebastião provided."

Julia's thoughts drifted. "I wonder if the island will come up again?"

José shrugged. "Perhaps. It might fifty or a hundred years from now."

Julia didn't bother telling José she wasn't referring to that island.

"What will you do now?" José asked.

"I'm not sure. I have to go back to California, see my family. After that? I don't know. I might go to the mainland. See some sights, write some music. Who knows, maybe make a pilgrimage to Alcobaça and the Quinta das Lágrimas, in Coimbra. Something makes me want to see the places Sebastião visited, from Álvaro de Castro's tomb in Lisbon, to the *Paço* in Serra d'El-Rei, where Inês and Pedro stayed. And Santiago de Compostela, where Inês de Castro's sister Joana is buried."

"It sounds like a good trip for you," José said." There was a long pause.

"I hate to leave," Julia said. "A part of me would love to stay."

José nodded. "Nicolau?" There, he said what had hung in the air unspoken.

"I'm not sure," Julia said.

"Well, I hope you come back soon," José said. They hugged.

Julia took the boat back to Horta. Antonio was there when she arrived. They said their goodbyes to Maria Josefa and João at the *residencial*. Maria Josefa was tearful in her eulogy of Sebastião.

"It won't be the same without your father here," she said. "I can't believe what they say." Antonio shook his head, unable to speak. "I keep expecting him to walk in here at any moment," Maria Josefa said.

"I know, it doesn't seem possible that he's really gone," Julia said.

João nodded, silently, his eyes welling with tears.

Julia kissed Maria Josefa and João, realizing with a shock just how fragile the two of them now appeared. As if they too had been altered by the recent events.

"Don't forget you have a place to stay anytime you are here," Maria Josefa said. "Both of you. Our home is your home. Come back soon."

Antonio thanked Maria Josefa and João, then accompanied Julia to Praia do Almoxarife.

When they reached Maria dos Santos's place, once again Julia was struck at how everything had changed. There were no strange sudden flights of exotic birds or plants behaving oddly. She didn't notice the calm surface of the spring.

"So, you are leaving our paradise," Maria dos Santos said, as Julia approached.

Julia smiled. "I have to return home, at least for a short time," she said. "And then, I'm not sure. We'll see."

"Yes, of course," Maria said. Antonio said goodbye to Maria dos Santos, shook hands with Nicolau, then wandered off alone. Nicolau stood quietly by Julia's side. Once again there was awkwardness between them. They were as shy as in their initial meeting. They sat down together on the bench in the garden, and again Maria dos Santos left them alone. There was so much Julia wanted to say, and yet, how to start, how to put in words what she wanted Nicolau to understand?

"Thanks for rescuing me, for helping me," she said. "If it wasn't for you—"

He touched her arm. "I'll miss you," he said. For the first time Julia fully realized that the next day she would no longer be on the islands, that she was in fact leaving Nicolau behind.

"I'll miss you, too," she said. "Very much. I'll write, I promise."

She stopped speaking, and for the first time since returning from the sea they resumed that long-anticipated, unfinished kiss. They held each other, and as her lips parted to meet his, many questions, she found, were finally answered, so many doubts swept away, for he had waited just as long as she had.

"I'll write, too," he said.

"Often?" she said. He nodded.

They sat for some time, without any need for words. She called out to Antonio, but it was some time before he appeared, looking guilty. "Sorry," he said. He didn't look sorry, but Julia was too preoccupied to notice.

A moment later, silent as a shadow, Teresa stood beside them. Nicolau introduced them.

"Finally, I get to meet you," Julia said. *"É um grande prazer."*

"O prazer é todo meu," Teresa said. "The pleasure is all mine." The two women embraced. Julia couldn't take her eyes off Teresa, who glanced now at her brother, now at Antonio, then at Julia, furtive and silent a creature plucked from the depths of the sea.

"I'm so glad to know you," Julia said. She looked at her brother. "Are you all right Tónio?" He still looked shell-shocked.

Antonio said nothing. "I guess it's time to go," Julia said. Antonio leaned and kissed Teresa's cheek. Nicolau and Julia embraced once more before parting.

Julia and Antonio returned to Horta, then took the boat to Terceira. The boat trip was uneventful. After they had embarked Julia spoke to her brother. "Teresa is certainly beautiful." He grunted. "Don't you think so?"

"Yeah."

Julia sat and watched the islands fade in the distance. Antonio kept to himself, pensive, absorbed in thought, trying to calm the pounding of his heart.

He relived certain moments over and over: his insides crumbling when he had grabbed Teresa's hand and looked for the vestiges of scales on her wrists. *"Sereia,"* he whispered.

Julia wished she could have taken Nicolau with her. She dreamed that they would go off together, that they would write music together, that she would sing their songs. She wondered if José or Maria dos Santos, who both seemed to know everything, knew that she had vowed to return in a year's time, to be back on the islands, to see if Sebastião's island would rise from the sea for one day, and perhaps there Sebastião and Clotho would stand side by side on the shore, as ridiculous as that still sounded.

And if not, then what?

Of course, as if Nicolau were in on it all along—not merely Maria dos Santos and José—as if he had known everything, he had sat calmly, listening to Julia, and avoiding everything that he should have said, with the trace of a smile on his lips.

On reaching Terceira Julia and Antonio didn't stop to see the ruins of the Casa dos Remédios. "I can't deal with that," Julia said, which was fine with Antonio. Instead, they went straight to the airport to catch the plane back home. An eerie feeling accompanied Julia, as if she were returning, not only from a long and distant voyage, but from a different time as well.

Back in Praia do Almoxarife, Maria dos Santos called to her grandson. "Nicolau come look," she said, pointing down at the still pool of water. "What did I tell you?"

"I don't have to see, *vovó.* I know. I see her returning, too."

"Yes, yes," Maria said. "It is as clear as day. She will come back. She is not leaving, not really."

Nicolau smiled, nodding. "I know, *avó.*"

Teresa's voice sang quietly, yet longingly, carried by the breeze from the beach where she stood, as if to someone far away. And though perhaps the words were indistinguishable, there was no mistaking their meaning.

Reversals of fortune, lives swept by the changing tides of government, luck, fate. When, where and how does the tale begin? Better yet, how can we know how the story ends when we don't know where we've been, what lies in the remote past, when, where and how our story originated?

If only we could look at our past, our antecedents, as if looking at countless reflections caught between a series of mirrors, an infinity of selves, showing a progression, clear and distinct, that reveals the inevitability of the present. Julia, Antonio and Sebastião had each grappled with this. Julia and Antonio were blinded to the fact that they would sail the ocean in search of their father as a direct result of who and what Sebastião was, his writings about the islands and the family history, his early stories of their common past, his unconscious elaboration of their family history, of believing what he wished to believe; just as Sebastião was who he was as a result of Isabel's stubborn determination and Mateus's fierce longings. He'd never forgotten the family legacy, never wavered in his belief of past and present wrongs, and irrevocable rights. Mateus treated his noble past in the same way as a family who continues to set a place for a family member who has died, who leaves their room untouched and continues to act as if that person is still alive and well; he regarded himself as unchanged and in no way diminished, in the same light as his ancestors. And before Mateus, of course, was Raimundo, who knew the family was doomed, but defied fate and his aunts by marrying the woman he loved.

The loss of the family estate neatly coincided with the assassination of King Carlos and his son, Prince Luís Filipe (who were shot in Lisbon in 1908), and the subsequent overthrow of the monarchy in 1910, in a revolution which marked the birth of the republic, further eroding the wealth and power of the aristocrats, the old nobility.

And one could trace it back across the generations, before Mateus and Raimundo, through the centuries: to Domitila do Canto e Castro who found history repeating itself when she met Dom Pedro, heir to the Portuguese throne and the soon-to-be emperor of Brazil. How they must have felt an overpowering sense of déjà-vu when looking into one another's eyes. Their love affair produced several children, a title for herself—the Marquesa dos Santos—and an unparalleled scandal, which, like the all-too similar scandal of Dom Pedro and Inês de Castro five centuries earlier, caused her to become anathema in court circles, and finally prevented her from marrying Dom Pedro and becoming Empress of Brazil. A deep shudder ran through all those in whose veins the blood of the Canto e Castros flowed. To come so close yet again.

However, the truth that leads us to ourselves is typically found more in fragments, lapses here and there in the historical record. One may be nothing like a father but resemble a grandfather or a great-grandfather, or physically resemble one side of the family, while mentally and emotionally resembling the other.

How can the answer be adequately or easily given when in fact we come from disparate directions at one and the same time, and indeed are like a thousand rays of light shining from a thousand directions united in one focal point, one beam of light? When we know a great-grandfather's history, but of the woman he married we know next to nothing outside of a name and a place of birth? Who was she? What was she like? Was she intelligent, artistically inclined, strong or weak in character, petty or generous, warm and loving, or cold and distant? At the same time, much like a story which comes from different places, different sources, as opposed to simply from one writer's mind, a story indeed comes of this tale and that, many various books, first-, second- and third-hand, and so on; it comes of places and people seen and heard; it comes of generations, of many ideas layered and intertwined. As do we.

Perhaps the story is a retelling of another older story that preceded it, and that in turn was one retold from yet another earlier tale, and so on and so forth, traced back through the eons to a time which preceded the written word. An ancient story superimposed upon a modern one.

Thus our misfortunes may be passed down to our descendants, who will look at their circumstances, all too ready to blame those around them, never knowing the true origins of their sorrows. Still, what made Sebastião different from Mateus is that he could see not only what was lost but what remained: "Portugal, the Azores," he was quick to say, "are steeped in our own rich history, music, literature, archeology, the beauty of the land—these things should be treasured, not forgotten. Our people shouldn't look elsewhere, but should value what we ourselves possess; instead of looking at what we've lost, look at what we have."

The same, Julia thought, could be said of the family. I will look forward, create new music that is here and now, though informed by the past. Songs of the Azores, of Portugal.

405

. . .

Sepultura Romântica

Ali, onde o mar quebra, num cachão
Rugidor e monótono, e os ventos
Erguem pelo areal os seus lamentos,
Ali se há-de enterrar meu coração.

Queimem-no os sóis da adusta solidão
Na fornalha do Estio, em dias lentos;
Depois, no inverno, os sopros violentos
Lhe revolvam em torno o árido chão

Até que se desfaça e, já tornado
Em impalpável pó, seja levado
Nos turbilhões que o vento levantar

Com suas lutas, seu cansado anseio,
Seu louco amor, dissolva-se no seio
Desse infecundo, desse amargo mar!

Romantic Burial

There where the sea breaks in a roaring

And monotonous boil and where winds
Rear their lamentations along the beach,
There it will be that they bury my heart.

Let it be scorched on slow days by parched
Lonely suns in Summer's forge;
Then, in Winter, let violent gusts
   . . . Spit-turn the arid ground over it.

Until the heart disintegrates and, turned
To impalpable dust, is carried off
   . . . In eddies whipped up by the winds.

Its battles, its tired agonies,
Its mad loves, all dissolve in the womb
Of that barren sea, that bitter sea.[16]

—Antero de Quental

THE END

Epilogue

Where one story ends a hundred or more new stories are just beginning. Julia did, indeed, return to the Azores, finding that she could no longer leave the islands behind. Nor the man who had managed to become as much a part of her as the music they now shared. Julia and Nicolau spent many days in Praia do Almoxarife, in Horta, and on Pico, composing music and performing. They traveled to the mainland where they performed and in time recorded their music. But they preferred the islands and returned frequently, continuing to work on songs of the islands and a lengthy piece of music titled: *Inês de Castro, Queen after Death*.

Antonio returned to the States, unsure of everything, but that he could not go back to the life he had lived. He assumed charge of Sebastião's writings. That which had never interested him, which he had always thought of as unimportant, now became all-important. Of course, he knew it was unthinkable to remove his father's works from the Azores, and so of necessity he made numerous trips back to Faial and Pico, spending as much time in the company of Teresa dos Santos as with Sebastião's writings, neglecting his business ventures, much to Clara's deep regret and consternation. Instead, he assisted Teresa in helping the children of old Quebrado do Caminho.

Leonardo Brum faced the realization that he was unsuited for his profession. He did write an epic poem, "The Enchanted Island and the Luminous Woman," which was only a thinly disguised ode in devotion to Teresa dos Santos; and was soon publishing mysteries under an assumed name with a modicum of success. Once a year he returned to the islands, though he couldn't say why. Some vague yet persistent *idée fixe* tugged at his memory, like someone with an appointment but unable to remember with whom or precisely where it was to take place.

It was Senhor Brum who, pursuing his own genealogical research, discovered that Nicolau and Teresa dos Santos were direct descendants of Dom Pedro, the Just or Cruel, by the child of Inês and Pedro, Dom João, whose son, Dom Fernando, the Inconsolable, fathered some forty-two children. Their grandfather, Teodoro, he learned, too, was the only son of a mysterious foundling whom people said had come from the sea. Though, "This tale," Senhor Brum wrote, "is likely apocryphal." He did find it somehow satisfying and natural that Julia and Antonio, descendants of the Castros, should unite with Teresa and Nicolau, descendants of Dom Pedro, fulfilling a destiny that had awaited six centuries to come to fruition.

"Let the doubters and naysayers scoff," Brum wrote. "The world is filled with incredible coincidences and miracles for those with eyes open enough to see. The skeptics would do well to remember the Portuguese saying, that everyone in Portugal is a cousin, and everyone a descendant of King Dinis."

Maria Josefa and João Correia continued to run the *residencial*, of which Brum became a regular guest. Maria insisted that someday Sebastião do Canto e Castro would return, and that when he did, she would have his room ready for him and give him a piece of her mind for his irresponsibility.

Maria dos Santos and José Manuel worked their magic in Praia do Almoxarife and in Quebrado do Caminho, taking the *Lancha do Pico* back and forth, often accompanied by Teresa and Antonio.

The Azores was quiet and peaceful once again. It was still rumored now and then that Sebastião had been seen in various places, and the islanders continued to create a number of stories concerning his mysterious fate.

Some said that he now captained the ghost ship and that the ship had sailed into the Indian Ocean, or elsewhere, doomed to wander the seven seas. Others voiced the opinion that he had escaped and made his way to an island in the South Pacific, or possibly Australia, where he assumed a new life. Someone even went so far as to suggest that they had all been fooled and that Leonardo Brum, the detective, was none other than Sebastião in disguise.

In time, almost everything was forgotten, although with each storm or earthquake, people said it was nothing like what they had seen during "the Year of Miracles."

Notes

[1] Fernando Pessoa, "The Fortunate Islands," trans. Edwin Honig and Susan M. Brown, *Poems of Fernando Pessoa* (New York: The Ecco Press, 1986).

[2] Fernando Pessoa, "A Última Nau," trans. Edwin Honig and Susan M. Brown, *Poems of Fernando Pessoa* (New York: The Ecco Press, 1986).

[3] Fernando Pessoa, "António Vieira," trans. Edwin Honig and Susan M. Brown, *Poems of Fernando Pessoa* (New York: The Ecco Press, 1986).

[4] Fernando Pessoa, "António Vieira," trans. by Darrell Kastin.

[5] Amália Rodrigues, "Tears," trans. Darrell Kastin.

[6] Fernando Pessoa, "Horizon," trans. Edwin Honig and Susan M. Brown, *Poems of Fernando Pessoa* (New York: The Ecco Press, 1986).

[7] Luís Vaz de Camões, *The Lusiads,* trans. Leonard Bacon (New York: Hispanic Society of America, 1950).

[8] Luís Vaz de Camões, *The Lusiads,* trans. Leonard Bacon (New York: Hispanic Society of America, 1950).

[9] Luís Vaz de Camões, *The Lusiads,* trans. Leonard Bacon (New York: Hispanic Society of America, 1950).

[10] Fernando Pessoa, "Calma," trans. Darrell Kastin.

[11] Fernando Pessoa, "Sebastian," trans. Edwin Honig and Susan M. Brown, *Poems of Fernando Pessoa* (New York: The Ecco Press, 1986). The translation was modified by Darrell Kastin.

[12] Fernando Pessoa, "D. João, Infante de Portugal," trans. Edwin Honig and Susan M. Brown, *Poems of Fernando Pessoa* (New York: The Ecco Press, 1986).

[13] Luís Vaz de Camões, *The Lusiads,* trans. Landeg White (Oxford: Oxford University Press, 1997).

[14] Luís Vaz de Camões, *The Lusiads,* trans. Landeg White (Oxford: Oxford University Press, 1997).

[15] Almeida Garrett, "Camões," trans. Edgar C. Knowlton, Jr., *Boletim do Instituto de Luís de Camões* [Macau] 6.1-2 (1972) quoted in Ronald W. Sousa, *The Rediscoverers* (University Park: Pennsylvania State University Press, 1981).

[16] Antero de Quental, "Romantic Burial," trans. Leonard S. Downes, *Portuguese Poems and Translations* (Lisbon: n.p., 1947).